the World

•Ironpass

•Northwarden

•Highcastle

THE BLACKWOOD

•Dolth   Rodez•

Euper•   Ran•

•Romney   •Tiburn

Bas-Tyra   •Sadara

•Silden   Cheam•

Cross   Rillanon•

•Timons

Vale

THE KINGDOM SEA

THE
KINGDOM
OF
ROLDEM

EN REACHES

Deep Taunton•

Mallow Haven•

OF GREAT KESH   The Peaks of Tranquillity

Pointer's Head•

Krondor
Tear
of the Gods

RAYMOND E. FEIST

Krondor
Tear of the Gods

An Imprint of HarperCollins*Publishers*

This work is based on the game "Return to Krondor" published by Pyrotechnix, Inc.

A hardcover edition of this book was published in Great Britain by
Voyager, an imprint of HarperCollins Publishers.

EOS
An Imprint of HarperCollins*Publishers*
10 East 53rd Street
New York, New York 10022-5299

Library of Congress Cataloging in Publication Data:
Feist, Raymond E.
Krondor, tear of the gods / Raymond E. Feist.—1st ed.
p. cm. — (Book three of the Riftwar legacy)
"Based upon the game Return to Krondor, produced by Pyrotechnix, Inc."—T.p. verso.
ISBN 0-380-97800-8   I. Title: Tear of the gods. II. Title.
PS3556.E446 K745 2001   813'.54—dc21   00-048460

First Eos hardcover printing: March 2001

First Eos International Printing: May 2001

Eos Trademark Reg. U.S. Pat. Off. and in Other Countries,
Marca Registrada, Hecho en U.S.A.
HarperCollins® is a trademark of HarperCollins Publishers, Inc.

Printed in the U.S.A.

FIRST EDITION

10 9 8 7 6 5 4 3 2 1

www.eosbooks.com

ACKNOWLEDGMENTS

As with other projects, I am in debt to many people, but more so with this than almost any other work I've undertaken. That was due in significant part to the evolution of the game, "Return to Krondor," the core story of which also serves as the core of this novel. I would be lax in my crediting those responsible for that project, upon which this rests, if I did not point to the work of many people, some who will go uncredited upon the game itself, for dealing with dozens of potentially terminal problems, distractions, and delays.

Literally hundreds of hands touched "Return to Krondor" in its evolution, too many to single out here. Knowing this list is incomplete, I would like to thank:

Andy Ashcraft, Craig Boland, Chuck Mitchell, Susan Deneker, Leanne Moen, and Michael Lynch who at various times had to listen to my opinion when they probably would rather have been working.

Scott Page, who found himself unexpectedly dealing with other people's messes, but who stayed the course.

Bob Ezrin, who was the Father of Us All during very trying times at 7th Level, who had to clean up an impossible mess made by other people who betrayed his trust, and who held my hand and kept the company alive when he rather would have been in the studio making music.

St. John Bain, who inherited a mess, and who with good humor and determination made someone else's vision his own;

Raymond E. Feist

indefatigable is the only word that describes his commitment to Krondor.

Steve Abrams, old friend and partner-in-crime, whose contributions to my work over the years have often gone uncredited, but never unappreciated.

Jonathan Matson, my agent, for all the usual reasons, and in this case, for all the unusual reasons.

My daughter, Jessica, and my son, James, for making every day spent with them better.

Jennifer Brehl and Jane Johnson, my editors in New York and London, for so much more than the job description requires.

On a personal note: This book was produced during a very difficult time for me personally, the end of my twelve-year marriage, and there are people out there who helped me through that period, people who did not have anything directly to do with the production of this novel, but who, by keeping me relatively sane during that period, helped me finish the project.

So, special thanks to Steve Abrams, Andy Abramson, Jim Curl, Jonathan Matson, Rich Spahl, and Janny Wurts for keeping me together early on, and being there for the long haul. There have been others, but the aforementioned went above and beyond the call. Words cannot express my gratitude. I am blessed beyond belief by friends of special quality.

And to the "gang" at Flemming's in La Jolla, the best steak house and wine bar in California, for giving me a place to hang.

Raymond E. Feist
San Diego, CA
August 30, 2000

For Bob Ezrin,
who else?

CONTENTS

PROLOGUE

Attack

T he weather worsened.

Dark clouds roiled overhead as angry lightning flashed, piercing the night's blackness on all quarters. The lookout atop the highest mast of the ship *Ishap's Dawn* thought he saw a flicker of movement in the distance and squinted against the murk. He tried to use his hand to shield his eyes as the salt spray and biting cold wind filled them with tears. He blinked them away and whatever movement he thought he had seen was gone.

Night and the threat of storms had forced the lookout to spend a miserable watch aloft, against the unlikely chance the captain had drifted off course. It was hardly possible, considered the lookout, as the captain was a knowledgeable seaman, chosen for his skill at avoiding danger as much as any other quality. And he knew as well as any man how hazardous this passage was. The Temple held the cargo's value second to none, and rumors of possible raiders along the Quegan coast had dictated a hazardous tack near Widow's Point, a rocky area best avoided if possible. But *Ishap's Dawn* was crewed by experienced sailors, who were now closely attentive to the captain's orders, and each was quick to respond, for every man

I

aloft knew that, once upon the rocks at Widow's Point, no ship survived. Each man feared for his own life – that was only natural – but these men were chosen not only for their seamanship, but also for fealty to the Temple. And they all knew how precious their cargo was to the Temple.

In the hold below, eight monks of the Temple of Ishap in Krondor stood around a most holy artifact, the Tear of the Gods. A jewel of astonishing size, easily as long as a large man's arm and twice as thick, it was illuminated from within by a mystic light. Once every ten years a new Tear was formed in a hidden monastery in a tiny secret valley in the Grey Tower Mountains. When it was ready and most holy rites completed, a heavily armed caravan transported it to the nearest port in the Free Cities of Natal. There it was placed upon a ship and carried to Krondor. From there, the Tear and an escort of warrior monks, priests, and servants would continue on, eventually reaching Salador to then be taken by ship and transported to the mother Temple in Rillanon where it replaced the previous Tear, as its power waned.

The true nature and purpose of the sacred gem was known only to the highest ranking among those serving within the Temple, and the sailor high atop the main mast asked no questions. He trusted in the power of the gods and knew that he served a greater good. And he was being handsomely paid not to ask questions as much as to stand his watch.

But after two weeks of battling contrary winds and difficult seas, even the most pious man found the blue-white light which shone every night from below, and the monks' incessant chanting, nerve-wracking. The duration of the unseasonable winds and unexpected storms had some of the crew muttering about sorcery and dark magic. The lookout offered a silent prayer of thanks to Killian, Goddess of Nature and Sailors (and then added a short one to Eortis, who some said was the true God of the Sea) that come dawn they would reach their destination: Krondor. The Tear and its escort would quickly leave the city for the east, but the sailor would remain in Krondor, with his family. What he was being paid would allow him a long visit home.

The sailor above thought of his wife and two children, and he smiled briefly. His daughter was now old enough to help her mother around the kitchen and with her baby brother, and a third child was due soon. As he had a hundred times before, the sailor vowed he'd find other work near home, so he could spend more time with his family.

He was pulled from his reverie by another flicker of movement toward shore. Light from the ship painted the storm-tossed combers and he could sense the rhythm of the sea. Something had just broken the rhythm. He peered through the murk, trying to pierce the gloom by strength of will, to see if they might be drifting too close to the rocks.

Knute said, "The blue light coming from that ship gives me a bad feeling, Captain."

The man Knute addressed towered over him as he looked down. At six foot eight inches tall he dwarfed those around him. His massive shoulders and arms lay exposed by the black leather cuirass he favored, though he had added a pair of shoulder pads studded with steel spikes – a prize taken off the corpse of one of Queg's more renowned gladiators. The exposed skin displayed dozens of reminders of battles fought, traces of old wounds intersecting one another. A scar that ran from forehead to jawbone through his right eye, which was milky white, marked his face. But his left seemed to glow with an evil red light from within and Knute knew that eye missed little.

Save for the spikes on his shoulders, his armor was plain and serviceable, well oiled and cared for, but displaying patches and repairs. An amulet hung around his neck, bronze but darkened by more than time and neglect, stained by ancient and black arts. The red gem set in its middle pulsed with a faint inner light of its own as Bear said, "Worry about keeping us off the rocks, pilot. It's the only reason I keep you alive." Turning to the rear of the ship, he spoke softly, but his voice carried to the stern. "Now!"

A sailor at the rear spoke down to those in the hold below, "Forward!" and the hortator raised one hand, and then brought its heel down on the drum between his knees.

At the sound of the first beat, the slaves chained to their seats raised their oars and on the second beat they lowered them and pulled as one. The word had been passed, but the Master of Slaves who walked between the banks of oars repeated it. "Silently, my darlings! I'll kill the first of you who makes a sound above a whisper!"

The ship, a Quegan patrol galley seized in a raid the year before, inched forward, picking up speed. At the prow, Knute crouched, intently scanning the water before him. He had positioned the ship so it would come straight at the target, but there was one turn that still needed to be made to port – not difficult if one reckoned the timing correctly, but dangerous nevertheless. Suddenly Knute turned and said, "Now, hard to port!"

Bear turned and relayed the order and the helmsman turned the ship. A moment later Knute ordered the rudder amidships, and the galley began to cut through the water.

Knute's gaze lingered on Bear for a moment, and then he returned his attention to the ship they were about to take. Knute had never been so frightened in his life. He was a born pirate, a dock-rat from Port Natal who had worked his way up from being an ordinary seaman to being one of the best pilots in the Bitter Sea. He knew every rock, shoal, reef, and tide pool between Ylith and Krondor, and westward to the Straits of Darkness, and along the coast of the Free Cities. And it was that knowledge that had kept him alive more than forty years while braver, stronger, and more intelligent men had died.

Knute felt Bear standing behind him. He had worked for the enormous pirate before, once taking Quegan prize ships as they returned from raids along the Keshian coast. Another time he had served with Bear as a privateer, under marque from the Governor of Durbin, plundering Kingdom ships.

For the last four years Knute had run his own gang, scavengers picking over wrecks drawn upon the rocks by false lights here at Widow's Point. It had been the knowledge of the rocks and how to negotiate them that had brought him back into Bear's service. The odd trader named Sidi, who came to the Widow's Point area every year or so, had asked him to find a ruthless man, one who would not shirk from a dangerous mission and who had no aversion to killing. Knute had spent a year tracking down Bear and had sent him word that there was a job of great risk and greater reward waiting. Bear had answered and had come to meet with Sidi. Knute had figured he'd either take a fee for putting the two men in touch, or he might work a split with Bear in exchange for use of his men and his ship. But from that point where Knute had brought Bear to meet with Sidi, on the beach at Widow's Point, everything had changed. Instead of working for himself, Knute was now again working as Bear's galley-pilot and first mate – Knute's own ship, a nimble little coaster, had been sunk to drive home Bear's terms: riches to Knute and his men if they joined him. If they refused, the alternative was simple: death.

Knute glanced at the strange blue light dancing upon the water as they drew down upon the Ishapian ship. The little man's heart beat with enough force to make him fear it would somehow break loose from within. He gripped the wooden rail tightly as he called for a meaningless course correction; the need to shout diverted into a sharp command.

Knute knew he was likely to die tonight. Since Bear had expropriated Knute's crew, it had simply been a matter of time. The man Knute had known along the Keshian coast had been bad enough, but something had changed Bear, made him far blacker a soul than before. He had always been a man of few scruples, but there had been an economy in his business, a reluctance to waste time with needless killing and destruction, even if he was otherwise unfazed by it. Now Bear seemed to relish it. Two men in Knute's crew had died lingering, painful deaths for minor transgressions. Bear had watched until they had died. The gem in his amulet had shone brightly then, and Bear's one good eye seemed alight with the same fire.

Bear had made one thing clear above all else: this mission's goal was to take a holy relic from the Ishapians and any man who interfered with that mission would die. But he had also promised that the crew could keep all the rest of the Ishapian treasure for themselves.

When he heard that, Knute had begun to make a plan.

Knute had insisted upon several practice sorties, claiming that the tides and rocks here were treacherous enough in the daylight – at night a thousand calamities could befall the unprepared. Bear had grudgingly acquiesced to the plea. What Knute had hoped would happen did: the crew learned to take orders from him once Bear gave over command of the ship. Bear's crew was made up of thugs, bullies, and murderers, including one cannibal, but they weren't terribly intelligent.

Knute's was a daring plan, and dangerous, and he needed more than a little luck. He glanced back and saw Bear's eyes fixed on the blue light of the Ishapian ship as they bore down on it. One quick glance from face to face of his own six men was all Knute could afford, and then he turned back to the Ishapian ship.

He gauged his distance and the motion, then turned and shouted past Bear, "One point to port! Ramming speed!"

Bear echoed the command, "Ramming speed!" Then he shouted, "Catapults! Ready!"

Flames appeared as torches were quickly lit, and then those torches were put to large bundles of skins full of Quegan Fire oil. They burst into flame and the catapult officer shouted, "Ready, Captain!"

Bear's deep voice rumbled as he gave the order: "Fire!"

The lookout squinted against the wind-driven salt spray. He was certain he saw something shoreward. Suddenly a flame appeared. Then a second. For a moment size and distance were difficult to judge, but the sailor quickly realized with a surge of fear that two large balls of fire sped toward the ship.

Angry orange-red flames sizzled and cracked as the first missile arced overhead, missing the lookout by mere yards. As the fireball shot past, he could feel the searing heat.

"Attack!" he shouted at the top of his lungs. He knew

7

full well the entire night watch had seen the fiery missiles; nonetheless it was his task to alert the crew.

The second fireball struck mid-decks, hitting the companionway that ran from below to the foredeck, and an unfortunate priest of Ishap was consumed in the sticky flames. He screamed in agony and confusion as he died.

The sailor knew that if they were being boarded, staying aloft was not a good idea. He swung from the crow's nest and slid down a stay sheet to the deck below as another ball of flame appeared in the sky, arcing down to strike the foredeck.

As his bare feet touched the wooden planks, another sailor who shouted, "Quegan raiders!" handed him a sword and buckler shield.

The thudding of a hortator's drum echoed across the waves. Suddenly the night came alive with noise and cries.

From out of the gloom a ship reared, lifted high by a huge swell, and the two sailors could see the massive serrated iron ram extending from the galley's prow. Once it slammed into its victim's hull, its teeth would hold the rammed ship close, until the signal was given for the galley slaves to reverse their stroke. By backing water, the galley would tear a massive hole in *Ishap's Dawn*'s side, quickly sending her to the bottom.

For an instant the lookout feared he would never see his children or wife again, and hastily uttered a prayer to whatever gods listened that his family be cared for. Then he resolved to fight, for if the sailors could hold the raiders at the gunwale until the priests emerged from below, their magic might drive off the attackers.

The ship heaved and the sound of tearing wood and shrieking men filled the night as the raider crashed into the Ishapian ship. The lookout and his companions were thrown to the deck.

As the lookout rolled away from the spreading fire, he saw two hands gripping the ship's gunwale. The lookout gained his feet as a dark-skinned pirate cleared the side of the ship, and boarded with a leap to the deck, others following.

The first pirate carried a huge sword, curved and weighted, and he grinned like a man possessed. The lookout hurried toward him, his sword and shield at the ready. The pirate's hair hung in oiled locks that glistened in the light from the flames. His wide eyes reflected the orange firelight, which gave him a demonic cast. Then he smiled and the lookout faltered, as the filed pointed teeth revealed the man to be a cannibal from the Shaskahan Islands.

Then the lookout's eyes widened as he saw another figure rear up behind the first.

It was the last thing the lookout saw, as the first pirate swung his sword and impaled the hapless man, who stood rooted in terror at the sight before him. With his dying breath, he gasped, "Bear."

Bear glanced around the deck. Massive hands flexed in anticipation as he spoke. His voice seemed to rumble from deep within as he said, "You know what I'm after; everything else is yours for the taking!"

Knute leaped from the raider's craft to stand at Bear's side. "We hit 'em hard, so you don't have much time!" he shouted to the crew. As Knute had hoped, Bear's men rushed to kill the Ishapian sailors, while Knute signaled to the handful from his old crew, who headed toward the hatches and the cargo nets.

An Ishapian monk, climbing up the aft companionway to

answer the alarm, saw the pirates spreading out in a half-circle around him. His brothers followed after. For a moment, both sides stood motionless, as they measured one another.

Bear stepped forward and in a voice like grinding stones said to the first monk, "You there! Bring me the Tear and I'll kill you quickly."

The monk's hands came up and moved rapidly in a mystic pattern while enchanting a prayer to summon magic. The other monks took up fighting stances behind him.

A bolt of white energy flashed at Bear, but vanished harmlessly just inches before him as the ship heeled over and started to dip at the bow. With a scornful laugh, Bear said, "Your magic means nothing to me!"

With surprising speed for a man his size, Bear lashed out with his sword. The monk, still recovering from the shock of his magic's impotence, stood helpless as Bear ran him through as if cutting a melon with a kitchen knife. The pirates let loose a roar of triumph and fell upon the other monks.

The monks, though empty-handed and outnumbered, were all trained in the art of open-handed fighting. In the end they could not stand up to pole weapons and swords, knives and crossbows, but they delayed the pirates long enough that the forecastle was already underwater before Bear could reach the companionway leading below decks.

Like a rat through a sewer grating, Knute was past Bear and down the companionway. Bear came second, the others behind.

"We've got no time!" shouted Knute, looking around the aft crew quarters; from the abundant religious items in view, he judged this area had been given over to the monks for their personal use. Knute could hear water rushing into the hole below the forecastle. Knute knew ships; eventually a bulkhead between the forecastle and the main cargo hold would give way and then the ship would go down like a rock.

A small wooden chest sitting in the corner caught his eye and he made straight for it, while Bear moved to a large door that led back to the captain's cabin. Movement was becoming more difficult as the deck was now tilting, and walking up its slick surface was tricky. More than one pirate fell, landing hard upon the wooden planks.

Knute opened the small chest, revealing enough gems to keep him in luxury for the rest of his life. Like moths to a flame, several raiders turned toward the booty. Knute motioned to two other pirates close by and said, "If you want a copper for all this slaughter, get up on deck, help open the hatch, and lower the cargo net!"

Both men hesitated, then looked to where Bear struggled to open the door. They glanced at one another, then did as Knute instructed. Knute knew they would find two of his men already at the hatch and would fall in to help. If Knute's plan were to work, everyone would have to do his part without realizing that the order of things on the ship had changed.

Knute unlatched a trapdoor in the middle of the deck, and let it swing open, revealing the companionway leading down into the cargo hold. As he stepped through the opening toward the treasure below, the ship started to take on water, and he knew she was fated to go down quickly by the bow. He and his men would have to move fast.

Bear was smashing himself uphill against a door that obviously had some sort of mystic lock upon it, for it hardly moved under his tremendous bulk. Knute cast a quick glance backward and saw the wood near the hinges splintering. As he lowered himself into the hold, Knute looked down. He knew that there was enough treasure below to make every man aboard a king, for the odd man named Sidi who had told Bear about this ship had said that ten years' worth of Temple wealth from the Far Coast and Free Cities would accompany the magic item Bear was to bring him.

Knute regretted having met Sidi; when he had first met him, he had no idea the so-called trader trafficked in the magic arts. Once he had discovered the truth, it was too late. And Knute was certain there was far more to Sidi than was obvious; Sidi had given Bear his magic amulet, the one that he refused to remove, day or night. Knute had always stayed away from magic, temple, wizard, or witch. He had a nose for it and it made him fearful, and no man in his experience reeked of it like Sidi, and there was nothing tender about that reek.

The cargo hatch above moved, and a voice shouted downward, "Knute?"

"Lower away!" commanded the little thief.

The cargo net descended and Knute quickly released it. "Get down here!" he shouted as he spread the large net across the center of the deck. "We're taking on water fast!"

Four sailors slid down ropes and started moving the heavy cargo chests to the center of the net. "Get the small one first!" instructed Knute. "They'll be gems. Worth more than gold, pound for pound."

The sailors were driven by two goals: greed and fear of Bear. The massive captain was smashing through the door above with inhuman strength, and everyone in the crew knew as well as Knute that Bear was becoming more violent by the day. Even his own crew now feared to be noticed by Bear.

One of the men paused to listen to the fiendish shout as

Bear finally smashed through the door. A half-dozen pirates, finished with butchering the ship's crew, descended the ropes from the deck above and looked questioningly at the pilot. Knute said, "The captain said everything else was ours for the taking if he got that damn stone the priests were guarding. You going to let all this sink?"

They shook their heads and set to, working in pairs to move the larger chests and sacks into the nets, although Knute could see the doubt on their faces. But they hurried and got most of the booty in the net and tied it off.

"Haul away!" Knute shouted to the men above.

Pirates grabbed small chests and sacks and attempted to get back to the forward ladder. The ship was now heading down by the bow, picking up speed and rocking slightly from side to side. "Tell them to back water!" shouted Knute, as he negotiated the ladder to the upper deck, clutching the small wooden chest as a mother would a baby. He saw a brilliant light coming through the captain's cabin door and his eyes widened. Bear stood outlined against the glare, obviously struggling through the water as if engaged with a foe of some kind. "Get out!" shouted Knute. "You're going to drown!" Not that Knute would shed a tear if that happened, but if Bear somehow came to his senses and made good his escape, Knute wanted to appear convincing in his role as loyal and concerned pilot.

Knute hurried to the gunwale and nimbly leaped atop it. Glancing at those behind him who were sliding across the deck, trying for the boat below, he called, "Hurry!" The galley was backing away, and water rushed quickly into the hull of the Ishapian ship. Knute knew that, had he not given the order to back the galley, the weight of the dying ship might have pulled its bow under the waves.

A longboat bobbed on the water a few yards below and he muttered, "By the gods, I've gotta get out of this business."

He glanced upward and saw the cargo boom with the net loaded with treasure being lowered to the deck of the galley. With a quick prayer to every god he could remember, Knute leaped from the sinking ship, hitting the water while he clutched the small chest with all his might. Weight pulled him downward and he struggled, and finally his head broke the surface as voices echoed across the water. With his free arm he struck out for the longboat, reaching it quickly. Strong hands reached over the side and pulled him aboard.

"The ship sinks!" men yelled as they leaped from the deck into the foam.

"Leave the rest!" shouted a man holding what appeared to be a large sack of gold coins. He hit the water, and after a minute his head broke the surface. He struggled mightily to get the sack aboard Knute's boat.

"No! Noooo!" came Bear's anguished cry from the bowels of the sinking ship as Knute helped the pirate aboard the boat.

"Sounds like the boss is having a problem," said the drenched pirate.

"Row," instructed Knute. The sailor complied and Knute looked over his shoulder. "Whatever the boss's problems, they're no longer ours."

"You going to leave him?" said one of Knute's men.

"Let's see if that cursed amulet keeps him alive on the bottom of the sea."

One of the pirates grinned. Like the rest of his brethren he had been obedient out of fear as much as any loyalty to Bear. "If it does, he's going to kill you, Knute."

"He's got to find me first," said the wily pilot. "I've sailed with that murdering lunatic three times, which is two too many. You've been his slaves long enough. Now it's our turn to live the high life!"

The pirates rowed. One of Bear's crew said, "If he does make it out alive, he'll find others to follow him, you know that? Why shouldn't I cut your throat now and gain his favor?"

"Because you're greedy, like me. If you cut my throat, you'll never get that galley safely out of these rocks. Besides, even if Bear lives, it'll be too late," said Knute. "We'll all be safely gone."

They reached the galley and quickly climbed aboard, other longboats and a few swimmers reaching the ship at the same time. The ship creaked as the longboats were hoisted aboard. Men scrambled up ropes while others lowered nets to haul the riches taken from the Ishapian ship. The crew moved with an efficiency rarely seen, spurred on by equal shares of avarice and the fear that Bear would suddenly appear. Finally they lashed the cargo to the center deck and Knute said, "Get underway!"

"Where are we going?" asked one of the pirates who had rowed Knute to the galley.

"To a rendezvous down the coast. I've got some men waiting for us who will offload this cargo, then we row this galley out to sea and sink it."

"Why?" asked another man as the crew gathered around Knute.

"Why?" echoed Knute. "I'll tell you why, fool. That ship we took was the property of the Temple of Ishap. In a few days the entire world is going to be looking for the men who sank it. Bear's got that ward against priests, but we don't. We'll divide up our shares and go our separate ways, tonight!"

"Sounds good," said one of the sailors.

"Then get to the oars! The slaves are half dead and I want us split up and every man on his own by sunrise!" shouted Knute.

Just then, Bear's voice cut through the storm. "It's mine!! I had it in my hands!"

All eyes turned to the sinking ship, and against a lightning flash they could see Bear standing at the rail. Slowly, he climbed atop it, shook his fist as the retreating galley, and leaped into the water.

Like a spur to a horse, the sight of Bear plunging into the water as if to swim after them caused the sailors to spring to action. Below, the hortator's drum began to sound as slaves were unchained and pushed aside by frantic pirates. Knute paused a moment to look where Bear had stood outlined against the lightning flashes. For an instant Knute could have sworn Bear's eye had been glowing red.

Knute shuddered and turned his mind away from Bear. The man was terrible in his anger and his strength was unmatched, but even Bear wouldn't be able to storm into the Prince's city and find Knute.

Knute smiled. The men waiting for him were expecting a ship full of riches and a dead crew. Poisoned wine and ale waited below, and Knute would pass it out minutes before reaching the rendezvous. By the time the cargo was offloaded and aboard the wagons, every pirate and slave below would be a corpse. His own men would also be departed, but that was an unfortunate circumstance he couldn't avoid. Besides, it meant more for him and those driving the wagons.

All his life he had waited for an opportunity like this and he was going to be ruthless in taking advantage of it. None of these men would lift a finger to help Knute, he knew, if his life was at risk, so what did he owe them? Honor among thieves might exist with the Mockers, where the Upright Man's bashers ensured honorable behavior, but on a ship like Bear's, the rule was strictly survival by strength, or by wits.

Knute shouted orders and the ship heeled over as it turned against the waves, striking for a safer course away from the rocks of Widow's Point. Soon the ship was clear of the last of the underwater rocks, and the rowers struck a steady pace. The little pilot moved to the stern of the galley and looked over the fantail. In a brief flash, for an instant, he thought he saw something in the water. It was a swimmer, following after the ship with a powerful stroke.

Knute's eyes strained as he peered through the darkness, but nothing more was glimpsed of the swimmer. He rubbed his eyes. It must be the excitement, he thought, the chance to at last be rich and out from under the heel of men like Bear.

Turning his mind to the future, he again grinned. He had made deals before. He would pay off the wagoners, have them killed if necessary, and by the time he reached Krondor, every silver coin, every golden chain, every sparkling gem would be his.

"Where are we going?" asked a pirate.

"*Captain*," said Knute.

"What?"

"Where are we going, *Captain*," Knute repeated, coolly.

The pirate shrugged, as if it didn't matter, and said, "Where are we going, Captain? How far down the coast are your men?"

Knute grinned, knowing that this man – like every other man in the crew – would happily let him play at command up to the minute they'd cut his throat if they thought he would make them rich. He played along. "We're meeting a gang at the beach north of Fishtown, outside of Krondor."

"Fishtown it is!" said the man, quickly adding, "Captain!"

Throughout the night the crew rowed, and when dawn was less than two hours away, Knute called one of his most trusted crewmen over. "How are things?"

"Bear's men are nervous, but they're not smart enough to plan anything if they think they might lose out on what we've taken. But they're still jumpy. You don't cross someone like Bear and sleep soundly."

Knute nodded, then said, "If everything's secure, there's some wine and ale below. Break it out."

"Aye, Captain," said the man, his grin widening. "A celebration, eh? That will take the edge off."

Knute returned the grin, but said nothing.

Within minutes the noise of celebration emanated from below. For hours all Knute had heard was an ominous silence punctuated by the sound of rhythmic rowing, oars groaning in their oarlocks, wood creaking as the hull flexed, and the rattle of tackle and blocks in the rigging. Now the murmur of voices arose, some joking, others surprised, as men made the rounds of the rowing benches with casks and cups.

One of the pirates looked at Knute across the deck and Knute shouted, "See that those aloft go below for a quick drink! I'll take the helm!"

The pirate nodded, then shouted aloft as Knute made his way to the stern of the ship. He said to the helmsman, "Go get something to drink. I'll take her in."

"Going to beach her, Captain?"

Knute nodded. "We're coming in a bit after low tide. She's heavy as a pregnant sow with all this booty. Once we offload, when high tide comes in, she'll lift right off the beach and we can back her out."

The man nodded. He was familiar with the area near Fishtown; the beaches were gentle and Knute's plan made sense.

Knute had chosen a slow-acting poison. As he took the helm, he calculated that he'd be coming into the beach by the time the first men began to pass out. With luck, those still alive would assume their companions were insensible from drink. With even more luck, the wagoners he had hired out of Krondor wouldn't have to cut any throats. They were teamsters working for a flat fee, not bully boys.

Knute had piled one lie atop another. The wagoners thought he was working for the Upright Man of Krondor, the leader of the Guild of Thieves. Knute knew that without that lie he would never control them once they saw the wealth he was bringing into the city. If the teamsters didn't believe a dread power stood behind Knute, he'd be as dead as the rest of the crew come morning.

The sound of the water changed, and in the distance Knute could hear breakers rolling into the beach. He hardly needed to look to know where he was.

One of the pirates came staggering up the companionway from below and spoke. His speech was slurred. "Captain, what's in this ale? The boys are passin' . . ." Knute smiled at the seaman, a young thug of perhaps eighteen years. The lad pitched forward. A few voices from below shouted up to the deck, but their words were muffled, and quiet soon descended.

The oars had fallen silent and now came the most dangerous part of Knute's plan. He lashed down his tiller, sprang to the ratlines and climbed aloft. Alone he lowered one small sail, shimmied down a sheet, and tied off. That little sail was all he had to keep him from turning broad to the waves and being smashed upon the beach.

As he reached the tiller, a hand descended upon Knute's shoulder, spinning him around. He was confronted by a leering grin of sharpened teeth as dark eyes studied him. "Shaskahan don't drink ale, little man."

Knute froze. He let his hand slip to a dagger in his belt but waited to see what the cannibal would do next. The man was motionless. "Don't drink ale," he repeated.

"I'll give you half the gold," Knute whispered.

"I take all of it," said the cannibal, as he drew out his large belt knife. "And then I eat you."

Knute leaped backward and drew his own knife. He knew that he was no match for the veteran killer, but he was fighting for his life and the biggest trove of riches he would ever see. He waited, praying for a few more moments.

The cannibal said again, "Shaskahan don't drink ale." Knute saw the man's legs begin to shake as he took a step forward. Suddenly the man was on his knees, his eyes going blank. Then he fell face forward. Knute cautiously knelt next to the man and examined him. He sheathed his knife as he leaned close to the cannibal's face, sniffed once, then stood.

"You don't drink ale, you murdering whore's son, but you *do* drink brandy."

With a laugh Knute unlashed the tiller as the ship swept forward into breakers. He pointed it like an arrow at a long, flat run of beach and as the ship plowed prow first into the sand, he saw the three large wagons sitting atop the bluffs. Six men who'd been sitting on the shore leapt to their feet as the ship ground to a halt in the sand. Knute had ordered the wagons not be brought down to the cove, for once loaded they'd be sunk to their hubs in sand. The teamsters would have to cart all the gold up the small bluff to the wagons. It would be hard, sweaty work.

No sooner had the ship stopped moving than Knute was shouting orders. The six wagoners hurried forward, while Knute pulled his knife. He was going to ensure no one below recovered from too little poison, then he was going to get that treasure to Krondor.

There was one man in the world he knew he could trust and that man would help him hide all these riches. Then Knute would celebrate, get drunk, pick a fight, and get himself thrown into jail. Let Bear come for him, thought Knute, if by some miracle he had survived. Let the crazed animal of a pirate try to reach him in the bowels of the city's stoutest jail, surrounded by the city watch. That would never happen – at the very least Bear would be captured by the city guards; more likely he'd be killed. Once Knute knew for certain Bear's fate, he could bargain for his own life. For he was the only man who knew where the Ishapian ship had gone down. He could lead the Prince's men and a representative of the Wreckers' Guild to the site, where the Wreckers' Guild's mage could raise the ship and they could offload whatever trinket it was that Bear had been after. Then he'd be a free man while Bear rotted in the Prince's dungeon or hung from the gibbet or rested at the bottom of the sea. And let everyone think the rest of the treasure went down with the pirate ship in the deep water trench just a mile offshore.

Knute congratulated himself on his masterful plan, and set about his grisly work, as the wagoners from Krondor climbed aboard to offload "the Upright Man's treasure."

Miles away as the dawn broke, a solitary figured emerged from the breakers. His massive frame hung with clothing tattered and soaked from hours in the brine. He had tossed aside his weapons to lighten himself for a long swim. One good eye surveyed the rocks and he calculated where he had come ashore. With dry sand under his now bare feet, the huge pirate let out a scream of primal rage.

"Knute!" he shouted at the sky. "By the dark god I'll hunt you down and have your liver on a stick. But first you'll tell me where the Tear of the Gods is!"

Knowing that he had to find weapons and a new pair of boots, Bear turned northward, toward the secret temple at Widow's Peak and the village of Haldon's Head. There he would find some men to serve him and with their help they would track down Knute and the others. Every member of his crew who had betrayed him would die a slow, agonizing death. Again Bear let out a bellow of rage. As the echoes died against the windswept rocks, he squared his shoulders and began walking.

ONE

Arrival

James hurried through the night.

As he moved purposefully across the courtyard of the Prince's palace in Krondor, he still felt the odd ache and twinge, reminders of his recent beating at the hands of the Nighthawks while he had been their captive. For the most part he was nearly back to his usual state of fitness. Despite that, he still felt the need for more sleep than usual, so of course, he had only just settled into a deep slumber when a page came knocking upon his door and informed James that the overdue caravan from Kesh had been sighted approaching the city. James had gotten up and dressed despite every fiber of his being demanding that he roll over in his warm bed and return to slumber.

Silently cursing the need to meet the arriving magician, he reached the outer gate where two guards stood their stations.

"Evening, gentlemen. All's well?"

The senior of the two guards, an old veteran named Crewson, saluted. "Quiet as the grave, Squire. Where're you bound at this ungodly hour?" He motioned for the other guard to open the gate so that James could leave the precinct of the palace.

Stifling a yawn, James said, "The Prince's new mage has

arrived from Stardock, and I've the dubious honor of meeting her at the North Gate."

The younger guard smiled in mock sympathy. "Ah, you've all the luck, Squire." He swung the gate wide to allow James to depart.

With a wry smile, James passed through the opening. "I'd rather have a good night's sleep, but duty calls. Fare you well, gentlemen."

James picked up his pace, as he knew the caravan would disband quickly upon arrival. He wasn't worried about the magician's safety, as the city guard would be augmented by caravan guards coming off duty, but he was concerned over the possible lapse in protocol should he not be there to greet her. While she might be only a distant relative of the Ambassador from Great Kesh to the Western Court, she was still a noble by rank, and relations between the Kingdom of the Isles and Great Kesh had never been what one might call tranquil. A good year was one in which there were three or fewer border skirmishes.

James decided to take a shortcut from the palace district to the North Gate, one that would require he pass through a warehouse district behind the Merchants' Quarter. He knew the city as well as any living man, and had no concerns about getting lost, but when two figures detached themselves from the shadows as he rounded a corner, he cursed himself for a fool. The out-of-the-way route was unlikely to be host to many citizens abroad on lawful business at this time of night. And these two looked nothing like lawful citizens.

One carried a large billy club and had a long belt knife, while the other rested his hand easily upon a sword. The first wore a red leather vest while his companion wore a simple tunic and trousers. Both had sturdy boots on, and James instantly recognized them for what they were: common street thugs. They were almost certainly freebooters, men not associated with the Mockers, the Guild of Thieves.

James pushed aside his self-recriminations for taking this shortcut, for the matter was now beyond changing.

The first man said, "Ah, what's the city coming to?"

The second nodded, moving to flank James should he try to run. "It's a sad state of affairs. Gentlemen of means, wanderin' the streets after midnight. What can they be thinking?"

Red-vest pointed his billy club at James and said, "He must be thinkin' his purse is just too heavy and be hopin' for a helpful pair like us to relieve him of it."

James let out a slow breath and calmly said, "Actually, I was thinking about the foolishness of men who don't recognize a dangerous mark when they see one." He drew his rapier slowly and moved the point to halfway between the two men, so that he would be able to parry an attack from either man.

"The only danger here is tryin' to cross us," said the second thug, drawing his sword and lashing out at James.

"I really don't have time for this," James said. He parried the blow easily and riposted. The swordsman barely pulled back in time to avoid being skewered like a holiday pig.

Red-vest pulled out his belt knife and swung his billy club, but James ducked aside and kicked out with his right leg, propelling the man into his companion. "You still have time to run away, my friends."

Red-vest grunted, recovered his balance, and rushed James, threatening with the billy club while holding his knife in position to do the real damage. James recognized the man's outrage – this was no longer a simple mugging; these two men now meant to kill him. He ignored the billy club, dodging toward it rather than away, and sliced at the man's left wrist. The knife fell to the stones with a clatter.

While Red-vest howled in pain and fell back, his companion came rushing in, his sword cocked back over his shoulder. James danced backward for two steps, and as the man let fly with his wide swing – designed to decapitate the young squire – James leaned forward in a move he had learned from the Prince, his left hand touching the stones to aid his balance and his right hand extending out. The attacker's sword passed harmlessly over James's head and he ran onto the point of James's rapier. The man's eyes widened in shock and he came to an abrupt halt, looked down in disbelief, then collapsed to his knees. James pulled his sword point free and the man toppled over.

The other brigand caught James by surprise coming over the shoulder of his collapsing friend, and James barely ducked away from a thrust that would have certainly split his head. He took a glancing blow on his left shoulder, still sore from the beating he had taken at the hands of the Nighthawks, and gasped at the unexpected pain. The hilt of the knife had struck, so there was no blood – his tunic wasn't even ripped – but damn it, he thought, it hurt!

James's training and battle-honed reflexes took over, and he turned with the attacker, his sword lashing out again as the man went by, and stood behind him as he too went down to his knees, then toppled over. James didn't even have to look to know his sword had cut Red-vest's throat in a single motion.

James wiped his sword off on the shirt of the first man he had killed and returned it to its sheath. Rubbing his sore left shoulder, he shook his head and muttered, "Idiots," quietly under his breath. Resuming his journey he marveled, not for the first time, at humanity's capacity for stupidity. For every gifted, brilliant man like Prince Arutha, there seemed to be a hundred – no, make that a thousand – stupid men.

Better than most men in the Prince's court, James understood the petty motives and narrow appetites of most citizens. As he turned his back on the two dead men, he acknowledged to himself that most of the population were decent people, people who were tainted by only a little larceny, a small lie about taxes owed, a little shorting of a measure, but in the main they were good.

But he had seen the worst and best of the rest, and had gone from a fraternity of men bent on trivial gain by any means, including murder, to a fellowship of men who would sacrifice even their own lives for the greater good.

His ambition was to be like them, to be noble by strength of purpose and clarity of vision rather than by accident of birth. He wanted one day to be remembered as a great defender of the Kingdom.

Ironically, he considered how unlikely it was that that would ever happen, given his current circumstance. He was now commissioned to create a company of spies, intelligence men who were to act on behalf of the Crown. He doubted Prince Arutha would appreciate him telling the ladies and gentleman of the court about it.

Still, he reminded himself as he turned another corner – glancing automatically into the shadows to see if anyone lurked there – the deed was the thing, not the praise.

Absently rubbing his right shoulder with his left hand, he noted how it had been overstrained by the swordplay. The little exercise with the two brigands was reminding him he wasn't fully healed from his recent ordeal in the desert at the hands of the Nighthawks – a band of fanatic assassins. He had been up and around within days of returning to Krondor, but he was still feeling not quite right after three weeks. And two sore shoulders would continue to remind him of it all for a couple of days, at least.

Sighing aloud, James muttered to himself: "Not as spry as I once was, I fear."

He cut through another alley that brought him around the corner to the street leading to the North Gate. He found himself passing the door of a new orphanage, recently opened by the Order of Dala, the goddess known as "Shield to the Weak." The sign above the door featured a yellow shield with the Order's mark upon it. Princess Anita had been instrumental in helping to secure the title to the building and funding it for the Order. James wondered absently how different his life might have been had he found his way to such a place when his mother had died, rather than ending up in the Guild of Thieves.

In the distance he could see two guardsmen speaking with a solitary young woman. He left off his musings and quickened his pace.

As he approached, he studied the young woman. Several facts were immediately manifest. He had expected a noblewoman of Kesh, bedecked in fine silks and jewelry, with a complement of servants and guards at her disposal. Instead he beheld a solitary figure, wearing clothing far more appropriate for rigorous travel than for court ceremony. She was dark-skinned, not as dark as those who lived farther south in Great Kesh, but darker than was common in Krondor, and in the gloom of night, her dark hair, tied back in a single braid, reflected the flickering torchlight with a gleam like a raven's wing. Her eyes, when they turned upon James, were also dark, almost black in the faint light.

Her bearing and the set of her eyes communicated an intensity that James often admired in others, if it was leavened with intelligence. There could be no doubt of intelligence, else Pug would never have recommended her for the post as Arutha's magical advisor.

She carried a heavy staff of either oak or yew, shod at both ends in iron. It was a weapon of choice among many travelers, especially those who by inclination or lack of time couldn't train in blades and bows. James knew from experience it was not a weapon to be taken lightly; against any but the most heavily-armored foe a staff could break bones, disarm or render an opponent unconscious. And this woman appeared to have the muscle to wield it effectively. Unlike the ladies of Arutha's court, her bare arms showed the effects of strenuous labor or hours spent in the weapons yard.

As he neared, James summed up his first impression of the new court magician: a striking woman, not pretty but very attractive in an unusual way. Now James understood his friend William's distress at the news of her appointment to the Prince's court. If she had been his first lover, as James suspected, William would not easily put her behind him, not for many years. Given his young friend's recent infatuation with Talia, the daughter of a local innkeeper, James chuckled to himself as he surmised that William's personal life was about to get very interesting. James didn't envy him the discomfort, but knew it would no doubt prove entertaining to witness. He smiled to himself as he closed upon the group.

One of the two guards conversing with the young woman

noticed James and greeted him. "Well met, Squire. We've been expectin' you."

James nodded and replied, "Gentlemen. My thanks for keeping an eye on our guest."

The second guard chimed in. "We felt bad, I mean, her bein' a noble and all, and havin' to wait so long, but we didn't have enough men to send with her to the palace." He indicated the other pair at the far end of the gate.

James appreciated their dilemma. If any of them had left his post, for whatever reason, without permission, the guard captain would have had their ears. "Not to worry. You've done your duty."

Turning to the young woman, James bowed and said, "Your pardon, milady, for making you wait. I am Squire James of Krondor."

The young magician smiled and suddenly James reevaluated his appraisal. She was very pretty, if in an unusual fashion for the women of the Western Kingdom. She said, "It is I who should apologize for arriving at this unseemly hour, but our caravan was delayed. I am Jazhara, most recently of Stardock."

Glancing around, James said, "A pleasure to meet you, Jazhara. Where is your entourage?"

"At my father's estates on the edge of the Jal-Pur desert. I had no servants at Stardock and requested none to travel here. I find that the use of servants tends to weaken the will. Since I began studying the mystic arts, I have always traveled alone."

James found the availability of servants one of the key attractions of the Prince's court; always having someone around to send on errands or fetch things was very useful. He was also now embarrassed to discover he should have ordered a squad of soldiers to escort Jazhara and himself back to the palace; her rank required such, but he had assumed she'd have her own bodyguards in place. Still, if she didn't bring it up, neither would he. He merely said, "I quite understand. If you are willing, however, we can leave your baggage under the watch of the guards, and I will arrange to have it brought to the palace in the morning."

"That will be fine. Shall we go?"

He decided to avoid shortcuts and keep to the broader thoroughfares. It would take a bit longer to reach the palace, but would afford them safer travel. He suspected that in addition to knowing how to use that staff to good effect, Jazhara probably had several nasty magician's tricks at her disposal, but the risk of an international incident to save a few minutes' walk wasn't worth it.

Deciding that being direct was his best course, James asked, "What does your great-uncle think of this appointment?"

Jazhara smiled. "I do not know, but I suspect he is less than happy. Since he was already unhappy that I chose to study at Stardock – over my father's objections – rather than marry a 'suitable young lord,' I fear I've likely put him in a dark mood."

James smiled. "Having met your great-uncle on a few occasions, I should think you'd want to stay on his good side."

With a slight twist of her lips, Jazhara said, "To the world he is the mighty Lord Hazara-Khan, a man to be dreaded by those who put their own interests ahead of the Empire's. To me he is Uncle Rachman – 'Raka' I called him because I couldn't manage his name when I was little – and he can deny me little. He wanted to marry me off to a minor prince of the

Imperial House, a distant cousin to the Empress, but when I threatened to run away if he sent me south, he relented."

James chuckled. They rounded a corner and headed down a large boulevard that would eventually lead them back to the palace.

After only a few minutes, James found himself enjoying the company of this young woman from Kesh. She was quick, observant, keen-eyed, and witty. Her banter was clever and entertaining without the acerbic, nasty edge one found so often among the nobles of the Prince's court.

Unfortunately, she was too entertaining: James suddenly realized he had turned a corner a few streets back without thinking and now they were in the area he had planned on avoiding.

"What is it?" Jazhara asked.

James turned and grinned at her, a grin that could barely be seen in the faint glow of a distant lantern hanging outside an inn. "You're very perceptive, milady."

"It's part of the trade, sir," she replied, her voice a mix of playfulness and caution. "Is something wrong?"

"I just got caught up in our discourse and without thought turned us into a part of the city it might be best to avoid at this hour."

James noticed a very slight shift in the way she held her staff, but her voice remained calm. "Are we in danger?"

"Most probably not, but one never knows in Krondor. Best to be alert. We shall be at the palace in a few minutes."

Without comment, they both picked up the pace slightly, and hurried along, each watching the side of the street for possible assailants in the gloom, James taking the left, Jazhara the right.

They had rounded the corner that put them in sight of the palace district when a sound echoed off to James's left. He turned and as he did so he recognized the trap: a pebble being tossed from the right.

As he turned back toward Jazhara, a small figure darted from the shadows. Jazhara had also spun to look in the same direction as James and was slow to recover.

The assailant darted close, a blade flashed, and suddenly a child was running down the street clutching Jazhara's purse.

James had been prepared for an attack, so it took an instant for him to realize that a street urchin had robbed Jazhara. "Hey! Stop! Come back here!" he shouted after the fleeing child.

"We have to stop him," said Jazhara. "Besides a few coins, my purse has items which could prove fatal to a child."

James didn't hesitate.

He knew the city as well as any man, and after a moment's pursuit, he slowed. "What is it?" asked Jazhara.

"If memory serves, he just ducked into a dead end."

They turned into the alley after the cutpurse and saw no sign of him.

"He's gone!" Jazhara exclaimed.

James laughed. "Not quite."

He moved to what looked to be some heavy crates, and reached around behind them, pulling away a piece of cloth tacked to the back. With a quick motion, in case the young thief was inclined to use the blade to defend himself, James snatched a thin arm.

"Let me go!" shouted a young girl who looked no older than

ten, dressed in rags. She dropped her blade and Jazhara's purse on the cobbles.

James knew it was a ruse to get him to release her arm and pick up the purse, so he held firm. "If you're going to be a thief, you must learn who to mark and who to leave be."

He turned to block her path if she tried to run and held her arm loosely. Kneeling so that he was at eye level with her, he asked, "What's your name, sweetheart?"

Quickly sensing that this man and woman weren't trying to harm her, the girl relaxed slightly. "Nita," she said with a tiny hint of defiance. "Mommy called me that after Prince 'Rutha's wife, 'Nita."

James couldn't help but smile. He knew Princess Anita would be flattered to hear of that tiny honor. "I'm Squire James, and this is Jazhara, the court mage."

The girl seemed less than reassured at being confronted by two members of the court. "Are you going to take me to jail?"

"James," said Jazhara, "you're not going to put this child in jail, are you?"

With mock seriousness, James said, "By rights I should. A dangerous criminal like this preying on innocent people at night!"

The child's eyes widened slightly, but she stood unafraid and didn't flinch. James softened his tone. "No, child. We'll not put you in jail. There's a place we could take you, if you like. It's called the Sign of the Yellow Shield. They take care of children like you."

The reaction was instantaneous. "No! No! You're just like the other men. You're just like the bad men!" She struck at James's face with her free hand, and tried to pull away.

James hung on. "Hold on! Hold it! Stop hitting me for a minute."

The girl ceased hitting him, but still kept tugging. James slowly let go of her arm and held up his hands, palms out, showing that he was not going to grab her again. "Look, Nita, if you want to stay here that's fine. We're not going to hurt you," he said softly.

Jazhara asked, "Who were you talking about, Nita? Who were the bad men?"

The girl looked up at the mage and said, "They say they're like the Yellow Shield, and all good children go with them, but they hurt me!" Her eyes started to fill with tears, but her voice was firm.

James asked, "How did they hurt you?"

Nita looked at the former boy-thief and said, "They took me to the big house, and they locked me in a cage, like all the other children. Then they told me to dye cloth for Yusuf, or else they'd beat me, and some of the other children, the bad children, they took and they never came back and there were rats and squirmy things in our food and – "

"This is horrible," said Jazhara. "We *must* act on this 'Yusuf,' but first we must care for Nita."

"Well, I suppose we could take her to the palace," began James, turning to look at Jazhara.

It was the chance the girl had waited for. As soon as James looked away from her, she was off, sprinting down the alley toward the street.

James stood and watched her turn the corner, knowing that he could probably chase her down, but deciding not to. Jazhara stared at James with an unspoken question in her eyes. James said, "I told her she could stay with us if she wanted to."

Jazhara nodded. "Then you will do something about this?"

James leaned down to pick up Jazhara's purse. He dusted it off and as he handed it to her he said, "Of course I will. I grew up on these streets. This isn't about duty; it's personal."

Jazhara turned away from the palace and started walking back the way they had come.

"Hey!" said James, hurrying to catch up. "Where are you going?"

"Unless this Yusuf lives in the palace, we need to go deeper into this poor section of the city, I am guessing."

"Good guess," said James. "There's a dyer named Yusuf up in what's called 'Stink Town,' to the north – it's where all the tanners, slaughterhouses, and other aromatic businesses are housed. But now?"

Looking at James with a resolute expression, Jazhara said, "We can't start any sooner, can we?"

"Apparently not," replied James. Then he grinned.

James kept his eyes moving, peering into every shadow, while Jazhara gazed resolutely forward, as if fixed upon a goal. As they walked purposefully through the Poor Quarter of Krondor, Jazhara said, "Do you expect trouble?"

"Constantly," answered James, glancing down a side-street they were passing.

The rising stench in the air told them they were close to their destination, the area of the Poor Quarter given over to those businesses best kept downwind. "Where do you think this Yusuf resides?"

James said, "The cloth-makers are all located at the end of this street, and along two others nearby." Turning to look at

Jazhara, he said, "You realize, of course, that the place will almost certainly be closed for the night?"

Jazhara smiled. "Which will give us an opportunity to look around unnoticed, correct?"

James smiled back. "I like the way you think, Jazhara."

Several times along the way they passed individuals hurrying by; the city was never truly asleep. Those who passed cast appraising glances at the pair, either as potential threats – or as possible victims.

They reached an intersection and glanced in both directions. Off to the left, all was quiet, but to James's surprise down the street to the right a few places were still obviously open for business. "The dyers' trade must be very profitable for these establishments to be conducting business all night."

"Or they're paying nothing for their labor," said Jazhara as they passed one such open establishment. The door was ajar and a quick glance inside indicated there was nothing suspicious taking place; a dyer and others – obviously members of his family – were busy preparing a large shipment of cloth. Most likely it was to be delivered at dawn to tailors who had ordered the material.

They moved along the dimly-lit street until they reached a large, two-story building, before which stood a large man with a sword at his belt. He watched with a neutral expression as James and Jazhara approached.

James asked, "What is this place?"

The guard answered, "This is the shop of the honorable Yusuf ben Ali, the illustrious cloth merchant."

Jazhara asked, "Is he in?"

"No. Now, if that's all, you'll excuse me." Since the guard

showed no sign of leaving, it was clear that he expected James and Jazhara to move along.

James said, "I find it odd to believe your master is out at this late hour, and you are merely standing here guarding a workshop in which no one is working." He moved to stand before the man. "I am Prince Arutha's squire."

Jazhara added, "And I his newly-appointed court mage."

At this the guard's eyes flickered over to her for an instant, then he said, "My master is indeed within. He is working late on a shipment that must leave tomorrow on a caravan and wishes not to be disturbed by any but the most important guest. I will see if he considers you to be important enough." He turned his back on them, saying, "Follow me to my master's office, but touch nothing."

They entered the building and discovered a brightly-lit display area, showing finely-woven cloth dyed in the most marvelous colors. A bolt of crimson silk was allowed to spill from a rack, the best to show off its scintillating color. Surrounding them was indigo and bright yellow linen, cotton of every hue, all waiting for potential buyers. A door to the rear of the showroom was closed, and a narrow stairway ran up along the left wall to a single door. A large chandelier ablaze with a dozen candles hung from the ceiling.

Beyond the viewing area, huge vats of dye stood, while large drying racks held freshly dyed cloth. James saw two children, no older than ten years, moving a rack aside to make way for another being pushed by another pair of children. The youngsters were dirty, and a few appeared to shiver beneath their thin ragged clothing. Jazhara noticed one little girl, who looked to be about seven years old, yawn, struggling to keep her eyes open as she pushed the heavy drying rack. Two guards stood watching the children.

The guard who had accompanied them inside said, "Wait here. I will fetch my master."

James asked, "Isn't it late for the children to be working?"

The man said, "They are lazy. This order must be ready by noon tomorrow. Had they finished at dusk, they would be asleep in their beds now. They know this. Do not talk to them; it will only slow them down. I will return with my master."

The man hurried across the large room and disappeared through the rear door. A few minutes later, he and another man returned. The newcomer was obviously a merchant, yet he carried a curved desert sword – a scimitar. He wore Kingdom tunic and trousers, but elected a traditional desert man's head cover, a black cloth wound as a turban, its length allowed to drape below the chin, from right to left, the end thrown across the left shoulder. He had a dark beard and the swarthy looks of Jazhara's countrymen, a fact confirmed as he reached them and said, "Peace be upon you," the traditional greeting of the people of the Jal-Pur.

Jazhara replied, "And upon you be peace."

"Welcome to my workhouse, my friends. My name is Yusuf ben Ali. How may I serve?"

James glanced back at the laboring children. "We've heard how you work around here. This place is being shut down."

If the man was surprised at this pronouncement, he didn't show it. He merely smiled. "Oh, you've heard, have you? And what exactly did you hear?"

Jazhara said, "We've heard about your working conditions and how you treat children."

Raymond E. Feist

Yusuf nodded. "And let me guess, you heard it from a young girl, perhaps less than a decade in age? Or was it a young boy this time?"

"What do you mean?" James asked.

"My dear sir, it was all a lie. My competitors have taken to paying children to accost guardsmen and other worthy citizens. They ply them with stories of the 'horrors of Yusuf's shop.' And then they vanish. My shop is then closed down for a few days while the Prince's magistrate investigates, and my competitors flourish."

Jazhara said, "But we've seen the working conditions inside."

Ben Ali glanced over at the ragged youngsters and shook his head slightly. "My dear countrywoman, I may be unable to provide for the children as I would like, but even I have a heart. They have a roof over their heads, and hot meals, and clothes. It may not be the extravagance that you would be used to, but, as the wise men taught us, poverty is food to a righteous man, while luxury can be a slow poison." He inclined his head toward the children. "We work late tonight. This is not unusual in my trade, but I assure you most nights these children would be safely asleep. When this shipment is done, I shall send them to their beds and they will be free tomorrow to sleep; then, when they awake they shall have a day of rest and play. What would else you have me do? Put them back on the streets?"

Children working to support their families were nothing new in the Kingdom. But this smacked of something close to slavery and James wasn't convinced this man Yusef was what he seemed. "What about up there?" he asked, pointing at the stairs.

"Ah, the second floor is under construction – we make

40

KRONDOR: TEAR OF THE GODS

improvements. It is not safe at present to see, but when it is done it will expand our capacities, and will include better quarters for the children."

James was about to speak, when Jazhara said, "James, may I have a moment alone with this gentleman?"

James was surprised. "Why?"

"Please."

James glanced from Jazhara to Yusuf, then said, "I'll be outside."

When he was gone from the building, Jazhara lowered her voice and said, "You work for my great-uncle?"

Yusuf bowed slightly. "Yes, kin of Hazara-Khan, I do. And I wished to speak to you alone. You did well sending our young friend away. A Kingdom nobleman is a complication. Does he know your great-uncle's position?"

Jazhara smiled. "As Governor of the Jal-Pur, or as head of Keshian Intelligence in the north?"

"The latter, of course."

"He may suspect, but what he knows is not the issue. This place is what matters. Is what the young girl said true?"

"The Imperial treasury hardly provides enough support for this operation," said Yusuf. "I must supplement my means; this shop is very successful, primarily because the labor is almost free." He looked at her disapproving expression and said, "I'm surprised at you. I expected a great-niece of Hazara-Khan to value practicality over misguided morality. Deceit, after all, is the first tool of our trade. What I do here aids me in my work."

"Then what the girl said was true. Does my great-uncle know about this?"

"I have never bothered to inform him of the details of my

operation, no. But he appreciates my results. And now that you are here, they will be greater than ever!"

"What do you mean?"

"It is well known of your falling out with your family and your choice to study magic at Stardock. Only your great-uncle's power has shielded you from those in the Imperial Court who think you a potential risk. It is time for you to grow up and face your responsibilities. You are a child of the Empire, a citizen of Great Kesh. Your loyalties must lie with them."

"My loyalties also lie with this court, and the Prince. I am the court mage, the first to be appointed to this position."

Yusuf studied the young woman's face. "Sometimes the ties of blood must be held above the ties of hollow words."

"I am not a spy!"

"But you could be," insisted ben Ali. "Work for me; grant me secrets from the lips of Krondor's courtiers and make your family proud!" His expression darkened. "Or disgrace your country, your family, and continue as you are. Your great-uncle can provide only limited protection if you swear that oath to Arutha." He paused, then added, "These are harsh choices, Jazhara. But you are now an adult, and the choice, as ever, must be yours. But know that from this point forward, whatever choice you make will change you forever."

Jazhara was silent for a long moment, as if considering the merchant's words. Finally she said, "Your words are harsh, Yusuf, but your actions have shown me where my loyalties lie."

"Then you will help me?"

"Yes. I will honor his teachings and the ideals of my nation."

"Excellent! You'd best leave now, before your friend becomes suspicious. Return again when you're settled into the prince's court and we shall begin."

She nodded and walked toward the door. She passed the still-laboring children, one of who looked up at her with eyes dulled from lack of sleep. In those eyes, Jazhara noted a flicker of fear. When she reached the door, she glanced over her shoulder at the smiling spy and the three guards who stood nearby.

James waited at the end of the alleyway. "Well?" he asked as she approached.

"Yusuf is a spy for my great-uncle."

James could barely conceal his surprise. "I don't know which I find more astonishing; that he is what you say, or that you've told me."

"When I left my father's court and trained at Stardock, I set aside my loyalty to Great Kesh. What my great-uncle does, he does for the betterment of the Empire." With a nod of her head to the entrance to Yusuf's shop, she added with a steely edge to her voice, "But this one seeks to line his pockets with gold from the suffering of children, and his service to the Empire is of secondary concern, I am certain. Even were I in service to Kesh, I would not long abide his continued existence." She gripped her staff and James saw her knuckles go white. Although he'd known the court mage for but a few hours, he had no doubt she was not making an idle threat; no matter where Jazhara's loyalties might lie, she would see Yusef pay for his crimes against the children.

"What do you propose?" he asked.

"There are but three guards. You are, I assume, a competent swordsman?"

"I am – " began James.

"As I am a competent magician," interrupted Jazhara. "Let's go."

As they strode back toward the dyer's shop, James felt the hair on his arms stand up, a sure sign magic was being gathered. He had never liked the feeling, even when he knew someone on his side was employing it. Jazhara said, "I will distract them. Try to take Yusuf alive."

James pulled out his rapier and muttered, "Four to one and you want me to try to keep one of them alive? Wonderful."

Jazhara entered the shop ahead of James, and Yusuf turned as she did so. "What – ?" he began.

Jazhara's pointed her staff at him and a loud keening sound filled the air as a ball of blue energy exploded off the tip of the staff. It struck the merchant, doubling him over in pain.

James rushed past the magician, quickly scanning the room for a sign of the children. They were gone. The three armed guards hesitated for a moment, then sprang into action. James was about to strike the guard on his right when the energy ball caromed off Yusuf and struck the guard to James's right. James quickly switched his attack to the center assailant.

James had fought multiple opponents before, and knew there were certain advantages. The most important thing he had found was that if his opponents hadn't practiced as a unit they tended to get in one another's way.

He lunged and took the center assailant under his guard, running him through. As he withdrew his blade, he leapt to his right and as he had hoped, the man on James's left stumbled into the dying man in the middle.

Yusuf's sword suddenly slashed the air near James's head. He had recovered from the magic Jazhara had thrown at him and was now on James's right, his scimitar expertly slicing the air.

"Great," James muttered. "The spy has to be a master swordsman."

The two remaining thugs had regained their feet and were a danger, but Yusuf was the true threat. "Jazhara! Keep those two off me, if you please."

Jazhara advanced and another burst of energy shot across the room, this time a red blast of lightning that caused the air to crackle as it struck the floor between James and the two guards. They quickly retreated as smoke began to rise from the wooden floor.

James didn't have time to appreciate the display, for Yusuf was proving a formidable opponent. It looked as if there would be almost no chance of keeping the Keshian spy alive, unless he got lucky. And given a choice, he'd rather keep himself alive than spare Yusuf and die in the process.

James used every trick he knew, a lethal inventory of combinations and feints. Twice he came close to cutting the Keshian, but twice in turn Yusuf came close to ending the struggle, too.

James circled and the turn brought Jazhara and the other two thugs into view. One had left the magician and was coming to help his master finish off James, while the other approached the magician warily, as Jazhara stood ready with her iron-shod staff before her.

James didn't hesitate. He feigned a blow to Yusuf's right hand, and as the Keshian moved to block, James spun to his own right, taking him away from the Keshian spy. Before Yusuf could recover, James was standing at his exposed left side, and all the merchant could manage was to fall away, avoiding a killing blow. This brought James right into the reach of the approaching guard, who lashed out high with his sword, a blow designed to decapitate the squire.

James ducked and thrust, running the man through. He then leapt to his right, knowing full well that Yusuf would be coming hard on his blind side. James hit the floor and rolled, feeling the scimitar slice the air above him. As he had hoped, Yusuf was momentarily slowed as he tried to avoid tripping over the falling corpse of his guard, and that afforded James enough time to regain his feet.

Off to one side, James could make out Jazhara and the other guard locked in combat. She wheeled the staff like an expert, taking his sword blows on hardened oak and lashing back with the iron tips. One good crack to the skull and the fight would be over, and both James and Jazhara's opponent knew that.

Yusuf came in with his sword point low, circling to his right. James glimpsed bales of cloth and display racks to his own right and moved to counter Yusuf. The spy wanted James's back to possible obstructions, so he might cause the squire to trip.

James knew it was now just a matter of who made the first mistake. He had been in struggles like this before, and knew fear and fatigue were the enemies most to be avoided. Yusuf's face was a study in concentration: he was probably thinking the same thoughts.

James paused as if weighing which way to move, inviting Yusuf into committing himself to an attack. Yusuf declined. He waited. Both men were breathing heavily.

James resisted the urge to glance to where Jazhara struggled to finish off her opponent, knowing that to do so would invite an attack. The two men stood poised, each ready for an opening, each waiting for the other to commit.

Then James had an inspiration. He intentionally glanced to the left, at Jazhara, seeing her block a blow from the guard; she took the tip of the staff inside the man's guard, and James saw her deliver a punching blow with the iron end of the staff to the man's middle. He heard the man's breath explode out of his lungs, but didn't see it, for at that precise moment, James spun blindly away to his left.

As he had expected, Yusuf had acted the moment James's eyes wandered, and as he had also suspected, the attack came off a combination of blade movements. A feint to the heart, which should have caused James's sword to lash up and out, to block the scimitar, followed by a looping drop of the tip of the scimitar to a low, inside stab, designed to impale James in the lower belly.

But James wasn't there. Rather than parry, he had spun to the left, and again found himself on Yusuf's right hand. And rather than dance away, James closed. Yusuf hesitated for an instant, recognizing he was over-extended and needed to come back into a defensive posture. That was all James needed.

His rapier struck out and the point took Yusuf in the right side of his neck. With a sickening gurgling sound, the spy stiffened. Then his eyes rolled up and his knees gave way and he fell to the floor.

James pulled out his sword and turned to see Jazhara break the skull of the last guard.

The man went down and Jazhara retreated, glancing around to see if any threats remained. Seeing only James standing upright, she rested on her staff as she tried to catch her breath.

James walked to her and said, "You all right?"

She nodded. "I'm fine."

James then looked around the room. Bolts of cloth were overturned and had been sent every which way, and many were now stained with crimson.

Letting out a long breath, James said, "What a mess."

TWO

Schemes

J ames sheathed his sword.

"Where did the children go?"

Jazhara looked around, then glanced up the stairs. "I'll look up there. You see if they are hiding in that office," she instructed, and pointed to the door at the rear of the shop.

James nodded, with a half-smile. No point in making an issue out of who was in charge, he thought, turning to comply with her instructions. She was, after all, a princess by birth. Then as he reached the door he wondered, *does* a court magician outrank a squire?

He opened the door, sword at the ready, in case someone else lurked within. He entered a small office at the center of which stood a writing table. Two burning lamps lighted the room, and a large chest stood against the far wall. The chest was apparently unlocked, its hasp hanging open, but James had received too many harsh lessons about trusting appearances, and so he approached the chest with caution. He glanced first at the papers spread across the writing table and saw several in a Keshian script he recognized. Most of these were orders for dyed cloth. Other letters in the King's Tongue were also business-related. Then he spied two documents in a script he did not know.

He was examining the chest for traps when Jazhara appeared in the doorway. Through clenched teeth she said, "The dog had the children caged."

James turned and looked through the door and saw a dozen frightened children, ranging in age from five to ten, standing mute behind the magician. They were dressed in filthy rags, their faces streaked with grime. James let out a slow sigh. Poor children in Krondor were nothing unusual; he had been an "urchin" himself before becoming a thief. But systematic abuse of children was not part of normal Kingdom practices. "What do we do with them?"

"What was that place you spoke of earlier?"

"The Sign of the Yellow Shield. It's an orphanage established by the Princess and the Order of Dala."

One of the children drew back at mention of the place, and James remembered Nita's reaction. James called into the main room, "You, boy, why does that frighten you?"

The lad just shook his head, fear written across his face.

Jazhara put a reassuring hand on his shoulder. "It's all right. No one will hurt you. Why are you frightened?"

A girl behind the boy said, "These men said they were from the Yellow Shield and if we came here they'd feed us."

James rose, left the office, pushed past Jazhara to where the nearest thug lay in a pool of blood. To an older boy he said, "Run outside and find a city watchman. You should find one two streets over by the Inn of the Five Stars. Tell him Squire James requires two men here as soon as possible. Can you remember that?"

The boy nodded and ran off, leaving the street door open behind him. James glanced after him and said, "Well, if he doesn't head straight for a hideout somewhere, help should be here in a few minutes."

49

Jazhara watched as James turned the dead Keshian over and looted his purse. "What are you looking for?" she asked.

James held up a ring. "This." He rose and handed it to her to examine.

She turned the ring over in her hand. It was a simple iron ring with a small painted yellow iron shield fastened to it. "Those who serve the Order of Dala wear a ring similar to this. I suspect these men showed this to the children to lure them here, claiming they were taking them to the orphanage."

Jazhara glanced toward the children, several of whom nodded. "That would explain why Nita was so adamant about not going there," she said.

James returned to the office and looked again at the closed chest. He hesitated, then opened it. Inside were more documents. He removed a few and asked, "Jazhara, can you read these? They appear to be in a form of Keshian I don't understand."

Jazhara took the proffered documents and glanced at the topmost. "I can read them, but it's a desert script, from the area around Durbin, and not from the interior of Kesh."

James nodded. He could only read formal court Keshian. Jazhara's eyes widened. "Filthy traitor! Yusuf has been using my great-uncle and his resources, setting Kesh against your Prince, and your Prince against Kesh!"

James looked perplexed. Finding out that Yusuf was a Keshian agent was hardly a shock. Discovering he was also betraying his master was. "Why?"

Jazhara held out a single page. "To serve someone named 'the Crawler.'"

James rolled his eyes heavenward, but stayed silent. The Crawler had been a thorn in the side of both the Prince and the Mockers for months now and James was no closer to establishing his identity than he had been the day he had first heard his name. Hoping for some clue, he asked, "What else does it say?"

Jazhara finished reading the document, then looked at the next. "This Crawler is someone of note, someone who rewarded Yusuf handsomely for his betrayal. There are references to payments already made of large amounts of gold and other considerations."

She hurried through several other documents, then came to one that caused her to stop and go pale. "This cannot be . . ." she whispered.

"What?" asked James.

"It is a warrant for my death should I choose not to serve Yusuf. It bears my great-uncle's signature and seal."

She held it out with a shaking hand and James took it. He examined the paper closely then said, "It isn't."

"Isn't?" she asked softly.

"You said it cannot be and I'm saying you're right. It isn't real. It's a forgery."

"How can you be certain?" she asked. "I've seen my great-uncle's script and seal many times and this appears to be from his hand and ring."

James grinned. "It's too flawless. I doubt that even your great-uncle could order the death of his favorite niece without some noticeable trembling in his hand. The letters are too prefect. I can't read the words, but I can see the handwriting and it's a clever forgery. Besides, even if the handwriting displayed that slight agitation I'd expect, there are two other reasons."

"Which are?" she asked as the sound of approaching footsteps reached them.

"Your great-uncle would never be stupid enough to sign his own name to a death warrant on any Keshian noble, especially one in his own family. More to the point, we've seen a fair number of documents bearing his seal in the palace over the years and there's a tiny imperfection in his signet." James pointed. "Look here. Where the long point of the star touches the bottom of the seal there should be a fine crack, as if the ring has a tiny fracture. This seal doesn't have it. The ring wasn't his."

"Then why?" asked Jazhara. As she spoke, a small company of the city watch appeared outside the door.

"Because," said James, striding toward the door, "if the new court mage in Krondor dies and someone in the Imperial Court starts casting around for someone to blame, who better than the head of the Keshian Intelligence Corps? Someone in the Empress's Palace might wish to see him removed and replaced with his own man."

"The Crawler?" asked Jazhara.

James turned and nodded.

"Then he is someone of importance," she said. "To threaten my great-uncle is to risk much. Only a man with his own power base within Kesh would dare this."

At the door, a guard of the watch said, "One of these children came to us and we hurried here as quickly as we could, Squire. What can we do to help?"

James replied, "There are some bodies inside that need to be removed, but otherwise everything's under control." He glanced at the children who hovered around them in a circle, as if ready to bolt should the alarm go up. "You'd better take charge of this lot before they scatter."

"Where shall we take them?"

James said, "To the Shield of Dala Orphanage the Princess helped found, over by the Sea Gate. Last I heard they had plenty of beds and hot food."

Several children started to inch away, as if getting ready to flee. Jazhara crouched and reached out as if to gather the fearful children to her. She said, "They are not like the men who have hurt you. There you will truly find food and warm beds."

Confronted otherwise with the prospect of a cold night with only stones to sleep upon and an empty belly, the children remained. The guard looked around. "Well, then, if you're all right getting back to the palace without a guard, Squire, we'll get this bunch moving. Come along, children," he said, trying not to sound too gruff.

The children left with two of the guards while the remaining pair peered into the building. "We'll have these bodies gone by morning. What about the building?" one of them asked.

James replied, "It'll be looted five minutes after you leave, so I'm going to poke around a little more and take anything important to the prince. Once we're gone, get rid of the bodies and let whoever wanders by take what he wants. If the previous owner has any heirs, I would welcome them coming to the palace to complain."

The watchman saluted and James and Jazhara reentered the dyer's shop. Jazhara thoroughly examined every paper in the chest and James inspected every likely spot that might harbor a secret hiding place. After an hour, James announced, "I don't think there's anything else."

Jazhara had been carefully reading the papers found in Yusuf's office. "There's enough here to warrant a full investigation from my great-uncle's end," she said. "This attempt to have my death placed at his feet in order to discredit him . . . it would have created a virtual civil war in the north of the Empire, for the desert tribes would know it to be a false accusation."

"But the Empress and her council in the City of Kesh might believe it."

Jazhara nodded. "Whoever this Crawler is, he seeks to benefit from confrontation between our peoples, James. Who would gain from such chaos?"

James said, "It's a long list. I'll tell you sometime. Right now, we should get to the palace. You have barely enough time to take a short nap, change into clean clothing, eat, then be presented to Prince Arutha."

Jazhara took a final long look around the room, as if searching for something or trying to impress details on her memory, then without comment she lifted her staff and moved purposefully toward the door.

James hesitated for a half-step, then overtook her. "You'll send word to your great-uncle?" he asked when he caught up with her.

"Certainly. This Crawler may be Keshian and what occurs here in Krondor may be but a part of a larger scheme, but it's clear that my great-uncle is at risk."

James said, "Well, there's the matter of the Prince."

"Oh." Jazhara stared at James. "Do you think he would begrudge my great-uncle a warning?"

James touched her shoulder lightly. "It's not that. It's only . . ."

"Matters of politics," she finished.

"Something like that," James said. They turned a corner. "It may be there's no problem in communicating this discovery to your great-uncle, but Arutha may request you leave out certain facts, such as how you got the information."

Jazhara smiled slightly. "As in not revealing we know Yusuf was ostensibly an agent working on behalf of Great Kesh?"

James grinned. "Something like that," he repeated.

As they continued to walk, she added after a while, "Perhaps we could simply say that while dealing with an illegal slavery ring, we discovered a plot to murder me and pin the blame upon my great-uncle, to the purpose of having him removed from his position as Governor of the Jal-Pur."

"My thinking exactly."

Jazhara laughed. "Do not worry, my friend. Politics are second nature to Keshian nobles not born of the True Blood."

James frowned. "I've heard that term once or twice before, but must confess I'm vague as to what it means."

Jazhara turned a corner, putting them on a direct path back to the palace. "Then you must visit the City of Kesh and visit the Empress's court. There are things I can tell you about Kesh that will not make sense until you have seen them with your own eyes. The True Blood Keshians, those whose ancestors first hunted lions on the grasslands around the Overn Deep, are such. Words would not do them justice."

A hint of irony – or bitterness – tinged her words, and James couldn't tell which, but James decided not to pursue the matter. They crossed out of the Merchants' Quarter and entered the palace district.

As they approached the palace gates, Jazhara glanced over to the large building opposite and noticed the solitary guardsman there. "An Ishapian enclave?"

James studied the sturdy man who stood impassively at his post, a lethal-looking warhammer at his belt. "Yes, though I have no idea of its purpose."

Jazhara looked at James with a wry smile and a twinkling eye and said, "There's something occurring in Krondor about which you're ignorant?"

James returned her smile. "What I should have said is that I have no idea what its purpose is – *yet.*"

The guards came to attention as James and Jazhara reached the gates and the senior guard said, "Welcome back, Squire. You've found her, then?"

James nodded. "Gentlemen, may I present Jazhara, court mage of Krondor."

At this, one of the other guards began to stare at Jazhara. "By the gods!" he exclaimed suddenly.

"You've something to say?" James inquired.

The guard flushed. "Beggin' your pardon, Squire, but a Keshian? So close to our Prince?"

Jazhara looked from one to the other, then said, "Set your minds at rest, gentlemen. I have taken oath and I will swear fealty to Arutha. Your prince is my lord, and like you, I shall defend him unto death."

The senior guard threw a look at the outspoken soldier that clearly communicated they would be talking about his outburst later. Then he said, "Your pardon, milady. We are honored to have you in Krondor."

"My thanks to you, sir," replied Jazhara as the gates were opened.

James followed, and as the gates were closed behind them he said, "You'll have to excuse them. They're naturally wary of strangers."

"You mean, wary of Keshians. Think nothing of it. We would be equally suspicious of a Kingdom magician in the court of the Empress, She Who Is Kesh. When Master Pug entrusted me to this position, he was very clear that my appointment is *not* to be political."

James grinned. Nothing in the court was not political, but he appreciated the sentiment. He regarded the young woman again. The more he knew her, the better he liked her. Mustering up his best courtier's tone, he said, "A woman of your beauty and intelligence should have no trouble with that. I myself am already feeling a great sense of trust."

She laughed. Fixing him with a skeptical expression, she said, "Your compliment is appreciated, Squire, but do not presume too much, too quickly. I'm sure your Prince would be upset were I forced to turn you into a toad."

James returned the laugh. "Not half as upset as I'd be. Forgive my impertinence, Jazhara, and welcome to Krondor."

They paused at the main entrance to the palace, where a page waited. "This boy will escort you to your quarters and see to whatever you need." Glancing at the sky, James added, "We have two hours until dawn, and I will attend the Prince an hour after he breaks fast with his family. I'll have someone come fetch you to court for the presentation."

"Thank you, Squire," said Jazhara. She turned and mounted the steps to the palace doors. James watched her go, appreciating just how nice her retreating figure looked in her travel clothes. As he took off in the direction of his own quarters, he muttered to himself, "William's got good taste in women, that's for sure. Between Talia and this one, he's got his hands full."

By the time he reached a small gate near the palace wall, on the path leading to the rear servant's entrance, his mind had already turned from exotic beauties from distant lands and was wrestling with mysteries more deadly, such as who this Crawler was and why was he trying so hard to plunge the Kingdom into war.

Arutha, Prince of Krondor and the Western Realm, second most powerful man in the Kingdom of the Isles, looked at his squire and said, "Well, what do you think of her?"

"Even if Duke Pug hadn't vouched for her, I'd be inclined to trust her, to take her oath of fealty as heartfelt and genuine."

Arutha sat back in his chair, behind the desk he used when conducting the more mundane daily routines of ruling the Western Realm. It was his habit to take a few minutes there to ready himself for morning court, before the conduct of his office was taken out of his hands by de Lacy, his Master of Ceremonies.

After a moment of reflection, Arutha said, "You must be tired. If loyalty were even a remote issue, Jazhara would not be here. I mean, what do you think of her as a person?"

James sighed. "We had . . . an adventure, last night."

Arutha pointed to the documents upon his desk. "Something to do with a dead cloth-dyer of Keshian ancestry who appears to be working for Lord Hazara-Khan, no doubt."

James nodded. "Yes, sire. She's . . . remarkable. As much as I've been around magic in the last ten years, I still know little about it. But she seems . . . I don't know if powerful is the correct word . . . adept, perhaps. She acted without hesitation when the need arose and she seems capable of doing considerable damage should that be required."

"What else?"

James thought. "I think she's able to be very analytical 'at a full gallop' as they say. I can't imagine her being rash or foolhardy."

Arutha nodded for James to continue.

"We can deduce she's educated. Despite the accent, her command of the King's Tongue is flawless. She reads more languages than I do, apparently, and being court-born will know all the protocols, ceremonies, and matters of rank."

"Nothing you've said is at variance with Pug's message to me concerning this choice." Arutha indicated another piece of parchment on his desk. "You have a nose for smelling out things even a magician of Pug's puissance might not recognize."

"In that, Highness, she's what you require in an advisor on things magical, I would wager."

"Good." Arutha rose and said, "Let us go and meet her, then."

James hurried to reach the door and open it for his prince. While no longer Senior Squire of the Court of Krondor, he was still Arutha's personal squire and usually attended him when he wasn't off on some mission or another for Arutha. James opened the door.

On the other side, Brion, the newly-appointed Senior Squire, awaited Arutha's appearance. Brion was the son of the Baron of Hawk's Hallow in the eastern mountains of the Duchy of Yabon. A tall, rangy, blond-headed lad, he was a hard-working, no-nonsense sort, the perfect choice for the tedious work of Senior Squire, work James had to admit he had never fully embraced with enthusiasm. Master of Ceremonies de Lacy and his assistant, Housecarl Jerome, were thrilled with the change in assignments, as they had both been forced to compensate for James's absences when he was out and about on Arutha's behalf. James glanced at Brion as he followed Arutha, leaving James with the other squires awaiting the duties of the day. When Arutha was seated, Brion nodded to Jerome, who moved to the large doors that would admit today's court to the Prince's presence. With a dignity James still found impressive, the old Master of Ceremonies moved to the middle of the entrance, so that as Jerome and a page opened the doors, those outside would first see de Lacy.

With a voice still powerful, the Master of Ceremonies said, "Come forth and attend! The Prince of Krondor is upon his throne and will hear his subjects!"

He turned and walked toward the dais, while pages led members of the court to their assigned places. Most of those in attendance were regular members of Arutha's court and knew exactly where they should stand, but a few newcomers always needed a boy nearby to instruct them quietly in matters of court protocol. And Brian de Lacy was a stickler for protocol.

James saw several officers and nobles of Arutha's staff enter and take their customary positions while petitioners who had convinced someone on the palace staff they needed to speak personally with the Prince followed. Jazhara was first among those, since she would soon make the transition from newcomer to member of the court.

James was impressed. Gone was the dusty, efficient travel garb, and now she wore the traditional formal raiment of her people. From head to foot she was dressed in a deep indigo silk, and James had to acknowledge that the color suited her. She wore far less jewelry than was customary for a woman of her rank; but the pieces she did wear – a brooch which held her veil pinned to her shoulder, which in her homeland would be worn across her lower face in the presence of strangers; and a single large bracelet of gold embedded with emeralds – were of the highest quality. The former thief suppressed a smile as he considered what they'd fetch if sold to some of the less reputable gem dealers in Krondor.

Master de Lacy intoned, "Highness, the court is assembled."

With a slight inclination of his head, Arutha signaled for court to commence.

James glanced around to see if William was present. As a junior officer of the Prince's guard he had no particular reason to be here, but given his history with Jazhara, James thought it possible he might put in an appearance.

De Lacy spoke: "Highness, we have the honor to present to you Jazhara, newly come to Krondor from Stardock, recommended to your favor by Duke Pug."

Arutha nodded for her to come close and Jazhara approached with the calm, effortless poise of one born to the court. James had seen more than one previously confident petitioner stumble while under the Prince's gaze, but Jazhara reached the appropriate spot and bowed, a low, sweeping gesture, which she executed gracefully.

"Welcome to Krondor, Jazhara," said Arutha. "Duke Pug commends you to our service. Are you willing to undertake such?"

"With my heart and mind, Highness," answered the young desert woman.

De Lacy came to stand halfway between Jazhara and the Prince and began the oath of service. It was short and to the point, to James's relief; there were far more tedious rites that he'd been forced to endure in his years of service to the crown.

Jazhara finished with, "And to this I pledge my life and honor, Highness."

Father Belson, a priest of the Order of Prandur, and Arutha's current advisor on issues concerning the various temples in the Kingdom, approached and intoned, "Prandur, Cleanser by Fire, Lord of the Flame, sanctifies this oath. As it is given, in fealty and service, so shall it be bound, in protection and succor. Let all know that this woman, Jazhara of the House of Hazara-Khan, is now Prince Arutha's good and loyal servant."

Belson conducted Jazhara to her appointed place in the court, next to his own, where both would be available should Arutha need their opinion on some issue concerning magic or faith. James glanced at the remaining company and realized court would be blessedly short this morning. There were only two petitioners and most of the regular court staff appeared anxious to be elsewhere. Arutha was a ruler who, to everyone's relief except perhaps de Lacy's, preferred efficiency to pomp. He left grand ceremony, such as the monthly galas and other festive occasions, to be overseen by his wife.

Jazhara caught James's eye and gave him a slight smile, which he returned. Not for the first time, James wondered if there might be something more in this than merely a collegial gesture, and then he mentally kicked himself. James's view of women was quite outside the norm for men his age in the Kingdom: he liked them and wasn't afraid of them, though he had been from time to time confused by them. Still, while he enjoyed intimacy with a woman as much as the next man, he avoided complicating liaisons. And a relationship with one of the Prince's advisors was only slightly less complicating than one with a member of his family; so he shunted aside such thoughts. With a slightly regretful inward sigh he told himself, *it's just that she's exotic.*

When court was over and the company dismissed, Arutha

rose from his throne and turned to Jazhara. "Are you settled in?"

"Yes, Highness," she answered. "My baggage was delivered to the palace this morning and all is well."

"Are your quarters adequate?"

She smiled. "Very, Highness. Master Kulgan told me what to expect, and I believe he was having some fun with me, as they are far more commodious than I had expected."

Arutha smiled slightly. "Kulgan always possessed a dry sense of humor." Motioning for James, he said, "Squire James will conduct your tour of Krondor today, and should you need anything, he will ensure you get it."

"Thank you, Highness." With a grin, James said, "As you know, we had a bit of a tour last night, Highness."

Arutha said, "I saw the documents this morning." To Jazhara and James he said, "But first, you two, in my office, please."

Brion hurried to open the door and Arutha led Jazhara and James into his private office. As he was about to step through, Arutha said, "Squire Brion, see what Master de Lacy has for the squires this morning."

"Sire." Brion bowed and departed.

Arutha sat. "Jazhara, allow me to begin by saying that had I a moment's concern regarding your loyalty to our court, you would not be standing here."

Jazhara inclined her head and said, "Understood, Highness."

"James, as soon as possible, please familiarize our young magician with everything we know so far about the Crawler. That will require, I suspect, a fair amount of personal history, since his confrontation with the Mockers is significant in understanding his motives. Be frank. I have the impression this young lady doesn't shock easily."

Jazhara smiled.

Arutha fixed a solemn gaze on both of them. "This Crawler has had his hand in no small amount of mischief over the last year or so. He was indirectly involved in one of the more threatening attacks on our sovereignty and created a situation that put a great strain on our relationships with a neighboring nation to the east. The more difficult he is to find, the more I worry about him." Addressing James he said, "Be thorough. You needn't return to the palace, unless I send for you, until you feel Jazhara has seen all she needs to see."

James bowed. "I will be thorough, Highness."

Jazhara bowed as well and followed James out of the Prince's office into a side corridor, where James asked, "Where to first, my lady?"

Jazhara said, "My quarters. I'm not traipsing around Krondor in this gown. And I feel only partially dressed if I don't have my staff in my hand."

James smiled. "Your quarters it is."

As they walked through the palace, Jazhara said, "I haven't seen William yet. Is he avoiding me?"

James looked at her. Frank, indeed, he thought. He said, "Probably not. While he's a royal cousin, he's also a junior officer and has many duties. If we don't run into him during our travels, I know where we'll be able to find him this evening."

Jazhara said, "Good. We need to talk, and I'd rather that occurred sooner than later."

James noticed she was no longer smiling.

THREE

Vow

T he watchman saluted.

James returned the acknowledgment, while Jazhara took in the sights of Krondor. She was wearing her travel garb once more. She carried her iron-shod staff, and her hair was tied back. She looked . . . businesslike. James found it interesting to contrast how she looked now, and how she had appeared at court earlier that morning. Two very different women . . .

They had begun early in the day, visiting the shops and markets of what people commonly referred to as the "Rich Quarter" of the city, a place in which shops displayed items of great beauty and price to buyers of means. Jazhara had lingered at several shops, much to James's chagrin, for he had never enjoyed the pastime of looking at goods he had no interest in buying. He had several times been assigned to the Princess's shopping expeditions, mostly to keep Elena out from under her mother's feet as much as to guard Arutha's wife. It was perhaps the only time in his life when he hadn't particularly enjoyed the Princess's company.

James had then taken Jazhara through the so-called "Merchants' Quarter," where the traders and captains of commerce had their places of business. The center of this district was dominated by a coffeehouse. They had paused to enjoy a cup of the Keshian brew, which Jazhara pronounced as fine as any she had tasted at home. This had brought a smile from their server, a young man named Timothy Barret, the youngest son of the owner. Businessmen flocked to Barret's to conduct business, mainly the underwriting of cargo ships and caravans.

After leaving the Merchants' Quarter, they had visited one working-class district after another. It was now past sundown and the evening watch was making its rounds. "Perhaps we should return to the palace?" James suggested.

"There's still a great deal of the city to be seen, yes?"

James nodded. "But I'm not certain you'd care to spend time there after dark."

"The Poor Quarter?"

"Yes, and the docks and Fishtown. They can be pretty rough even during the day."

"I think I have shown I am capable of taking care of myself, James."

"Agreed, but I find it best to keep the opportunity for trouble to a minimum; it has a habit of finding me anyway."

She laughed. "Perhaps more tomorrow, then. But what about William? You said he would likely be off-duty this evening."

James pointed to a side street. "Let's cut down there. William is almost certainly at the Rainbow Parrot."

"A soldiers' tavern?"

James shrugged. "Not particularly, though many of Lucas's patrons are old friends who served with him in the Riftwar. No, it's just the place William prefers to frequent."

Jazhara glanced sidelong at James. "A girl?"

66

James felt himself flush and decided a simple, direct answer was appropriate. "Yes. William has been seeing Talia, Lucas's daughter, for several weeks now."

"Good," said Jazhara. "I feared he was still . . ."

As she paused, James supplied, "In love with you?"

Without looking at James she said, "Infatuated, I think, is a better word. I made a mistake and . . ."

"Look, it's none of my business," James said. "So if you don't want to talk about it, fine."

"No, I want you to know something." She stopped and he turned to look at her. "Because you're his friend, I think."

"I am," said James. James had been something of a mentor to William since he had arrived at Krondor.

"And I would like for us to be friends, as well."

James nodded. "I would like that too."

"So, you know, then, that William was a boy who followed me around for years once he was old enough to become interested in women. I was a few years older and to me he seemed an eager puppy, nothing more." She paused and stared down at the street, as if recalling something difficult to recount. James, too, stood still. "I became involved with an older man, one of my teachers. It was not a wise thing to do. He was Keshian, as I was, and he shared many of the beliefs I do on magic and its uses. We drifted into a relationship without too much effort.

"Our affair became . . . awkward, for my family would not have approved of any such liaison, and rather than dictate to me, my great-uncle got word to my lover that he was to cease his involvement with me." She began to walk slowly again, as if it helped her form her thoughts. James accompanied her. "He rejected me, and left Stardock, returning to the Empire."

"And to a small reward, I'm sure."

"At the least. Perhaps it was nothing more than wanting to spare me a confrontation with my own father or perhaps he was afraid – my great-uncle's reach can be very long, even into a place such as Stardock."

"And?" James prompted.

"William was there. I was hurt and frightened and alone and William was there." She looked at James. "He's a lovely young man, honorable and kind, strong and passionate, and I felt abandoned. He helped me." Her voice trailed off.

James shrugged. "But what?"

"But after a while I realized it was as wrong for me to be his lover as it had been for my teacher to be mine. William was the son of the duke, and had another destiny before him and I was . . . using him."

James suppressed the quip that almost sprang to his lips about it not being a bad way to be used, and said instead, "Well, he wanted . . . I mean . . ."

"Yes, but I was older and should have seen the problems to come. So I broke off our affair. I fear I may have tipped the balance in his decision to leave Stardock and come to Krondor."

They turned into a street and headed toward an inn displaying a large parrot with rainbow-colored feathers on a sign over the door. "Well, I've known Will for a bit now, and I think you can put aside that concern," James said at last. "He was set on becoming a soldier, one way or another, all his life, from what he's told me."

Jazhara was about to reply, but before she knew it, James was drawing his sword and saying, "Guard yourself!"

She brought her staff to the ready and hurried after him. She saw that the door to the inn was partially open and that there was a dead soldier lying before it; and now she could hear the sound of fighting coming from within.

James kicked the door wide and leapt through, Jazhara behind him, staff at the ready. A scene of carnage greeted them. Two armed men lay dead on the ground, mercenaries judging by their dress. Several bar patrons also lay dead amidst the broken furniture. A young woman lay near the fireplace, blood pooling about her head.

In the corner William conDoin, cousin by adoption to the Royal House of Krondor and Lieutenant in the Prince's Household Guard, stood ready with his large sword held two-handed before him. Three men advanced on him.

William, seeing the newcomers, "James! Jazhara! Help me! Talia's been hurt!"

One of the men turned to engage the squire. The other two attacked William, who barely had room to deflect both strikes with his larger sword. A devastating weapon in the field, the hand-and-a-half or "bastard" sword was a liability at close quarters.

Jazhara lifted her hand and a nimbus of crimson light erupted around it. She cast it at the closest of William's opponents and watched as the light harmlessly struck the ground near his feet. "Damn," she muttered. She hefted her staff and stepped forward, leveling a jab with the iron base at the side of the man's head.

The intruder sensed or saw with his peripheral vision the attack and ducked aside. Whirling to face his new foe, he made a wicked slashing attack at Jazhara, causing her to fall back.

But she had freed William to concentrate on one foe only, and he quickly killed his man. James also dispatched his opponent, then used his sword hilt to strike Jazhara's attacker at the base of the skull. Rather than stun the man, it served only to distract him, and he turned as Jazhara lashed out again with her staff. The sound of breaking bones was unmistakable as the iron heel of the staff crushed the back of the man's head.

James looked around the room and said, "What black murder is this?"

William had thrown down his sword and was kneeling beside Talia, cradling her head in his lap. The girl's face was pale and her life flowed out by the second. "Oh, William . . ." she whispered, "Help me."

William looked down despairingly. He glanced at James, who shook his head slightly, regret clearly showing in his expression. William then looked at Jazhara and entreated, "You were one of my father's finest students. Can you perform a healing?"

Jazhara knelt beside the young soldier and whispered, "I'm sorry, William. Her wounds are too severe. Even if we were to send for a priest . . . it would be too late."

James knelt on the other side of the girl. "Talia, who did this?"

Talia looked up at James. "They were after Father. I don't know who they were. The leader was a huge bear of a man." She coughed and blood trickled from her mouth, staining her lips. "He hurt me, William. He really hurt me."

Tears streamed down William's cheeks. "Oh, Talia, I'm sorry . . ."

Suddenly the girl's distress seemed to ease. James had seen this before in those on the verge of death. For a moment their eyes brightened, as if the pain had vanished, as if the dying stood upon the threshold of entering Lims-Kragma's

Hall. At this moment, they saw clearly in both worlds. Talia whispered, "Don't worry, William. I swear by Kahooli, I will have my vengeance!"

Then her head lolled to one side.

"No . . . Talia!" William sobbed. For a moment he held her, and then slowly he placed her on the floor, and gently closed her eyes. At last, he rose and declared, "They must pay for this, James. I'm going after them."

James looked toward the doorway of the inn. If the intruders had been seeking Talia's father Lucas, that was the way the old man would have bolted. He said, "Wait, William. The Prince will have my head if I let you go off alone. You'll have your revenge and we'll be there beside you. Now, tell us what happened."

William hesitated a moment then said, "Right. Martin and I had just ended our shift. We headed over here for a drink, just like always, and that's when we saw them run out of the building. Half a dozen of them, with that big bastard leading them. Martin tried to halt them, and they attacked us without so much as a word. If you hadn't come along, I'd no doubt be lying alongside Martin." He gestured toward the dead soldier.

James inspected the carnage. In addition to Talia, they had slaughtered everyone else in the inn. The other barmaid, Susan de Bennet, lay sprawled on the floor in the corner, her head severed completely from her body with what looked to have been a single blow. Her red tresses fanned out around her head, which lay a foot away from her body, her blue eyes still wide in shocked amazement. The other patrons were likewise hacked to pieces.

"Why?" asked James. "Why charge in and kill everyone in

sight?" He looked at William. "Did the big man go after Lucas?"

"No. Some other men went out through the back. Once those five murderers backed me inside the inn, the big bastard and some others fled down the street."

"Do you have any idea where they were heading?" asked James.

Before William could answer, the building seemed to rock as the night was torn by the sound of a thunderous explosion. James was first out the door, with William and Jazhara close behind him. To the west, a fountain of green flames rose into the night as rocks shot up into the air. As the sound of the explosion diminished, the rocks began to rain down. James and his companions ducked beneath the overhanging roof eaves, and waited.

When it was clear that the last of the rocks had fallen, William said, "Listen!"

In the distance they could hear the clash of arms and the shouts of men. They hurried toward the noise, and turned the corner that led to the city jail. As they ran toward the jail, another explosion ripped through the night and they were thrown to the ground. A tower of green fire again reached into the darkness, and James shouted, "Get under cover!"

Again they hugged the walls of a building as more stones rained down upon them. William shouted, "What is that? Quegan Fire?"

James shook his head, "No Quegan Fire I've ever seen was green."

Jazhara said, "I think I know what it was."

"Care to share that intelligence with us?" asked James.

"No," she answered. "Not yet."

As the clatter of falling stones quieted, James leapt up and they continued running toward the jail. They reached a junction with two other streets, and sprinted left. A short distance further on they came to another intersection, and it was there they saw what was left of the jail. A gaping hole in the wall stood where the wooden door had once been, a few flames could be seen inside, and smoke rose from the maw. Nearby, an overturned wagon served as cover for two guardsmen and Captain Garruth, commander of the city watch. James, William, and Jazhara approached the wagon in a running crouch, keeping the wagon between them and the opening, for crossbow bolts and arrows were flying from the hole at those behind the wagon.

Glancing back, Captain Garruth motioned for them to stay low. When James came alongside, the captain said, "Astalon rot their black hearts." He nodded to the two young men he knew and said, "William. Squire James." Without waiting for an introduction to Jazhara, the guard captain continued. "As you can see, we've a bit of a problem."

"What happened?" asked James.

"Bloody brigands! They've blown out the back of the jail, and cut down half my squad."

"Who are they?" asked William.

"Your guess is as good as mine, lad. The leader's a giant of a man, bald, with a thick beard. He was wearing some sort of bone amulet, and he swung a mean sword."

William said, "That's the one, James."

"Which one, boy?" asked the captain as another arrow slammed into the underside of the wagon.

James glanced at William. "The one that killed Talia, the barmaid at the Rainbow Parrot."

Garruth let out a slow breath then said heavily, "Lucas's girl.

She is . . . was . . . such a sweet thing." He glanced at William. "My sympathies, Will."

With cold anger, William replied, "I'll have his heart, Captain. I swear I will."

Garruth said, "Well, now's your chance, lad. They've got us pinned down, but maybe the two of you can creep back down the way you came and circle behind the jail."

"Where's the sheriff?" asked James.

Garruth inclined his head toward the jail. "In there, I expect. I was due to meet with him when everything went to hell."

James shook his head. He had little affection for Sheriff Wilfred Means, but he was a good and loyal servant of the Prince and his son Jonathan was one of James's agents. He would discover if the younger Means was still alive later, he supposed.

"If the sheriff and his men were inside when the bastards blew up the jail, we won't see help here from the palace for another ten or fifteen minutes," said James.

Garruth said, "Aye, and that gives them time for whatever bloody work they've got in mind. Never seen anyone try to break *into* a jail before, so there must be something in there they want."

James said, "No, there's some*one* they want."

William said, "You think Lucas went to the jail?"

"Maybe," said James. "But we won't know until we get inside."

Garruth said, "You'd best leave the woman here until the palace guards arrive."

Jazhara said, in a dry tone, "I appreciate your concern, but I can handle myself."

The captain shrugged. "As you will."

They crouched low and returned the way they had come, until they reached the big intersection, safely out of firing range of the jail. All three stood and began to run.

They quickly reached the rear wall of the jail, in which another gaping hole could be seen. "The second explosion?" asked William.

"The first," said Jazhara. "They blew this one out to catch men eating and sleeping there" – she pointed through the hole to a table and overturned bunks – "then when those in the front of the jail ran back to aid their comrades, they set off the explosion on the other side, through which they almost certainly attacked, catching whoever was inside from the rear."

James said, "We'll not find the answer out here."

He ducked low and ran toward the hole leading into the guardroom, expecting a volley of arrows at any moment. Instead he found only two men looting the corpses on the ground. One died before he could draw his sword and the other turned on James, only to be struck from behind by William. James held up his hand for silence.

From the entrance come the sound of arrows and quarrels being fired, but all was still in the guardroom. James motioned for William to take the left side of the door into the front room, and for Jazhara to stand a few feet behind James. Then he moved to the partially opened door. He glanced through. A half-dozen men, four with bows and two with crossbows, were spread in flank formation, patiently shooting at anything that moved outside the hole in the wall. It was clear they were merely holding Garruth and his men at bay so someone inside could accomplish his mission.

James glanced at William and Jazhara, and then toward an

opening in the floor with stone stairs leading down to the underground cells. He knew there was a staircase in the front room leading to offices and the sheriff's apartment above. Which way had the big man gone? Up or down? James decided that either way they'd need Garruth and his half-dozen guardsmen to deal with the big man and his crew. So the six bowmen ahead must first be neutralized.

James held up three fingers, and Jazhara shook her head emphatically. She tapped her chest, indicating that she wished to make the first move. James glanced at William, who shrugged, so he looked back at Jazhara and nodded.

She stepped forward, raising her right hand high above her head, while grasping her staff in the left. Again the hair on James's arms stood on end as magic was gathered. A golden light enveloped the woman, accompanied by a faint sizzling sound, then the light coalesced into a sphere in the palm of her hand. She threw it as if it was a large ball and it arced into the room, landing between the center pair of bowmen. Instantly they dropped their weapons and twitched in wild spasms. The two next to them on either side were also afflicted, but held on to their weapons and managed to regain control of their movements almost immediately. The two crossbowmen – one of either side of the flank – were unaffected. Fortunately for William, the man he charged had just fired a bolt and was moving to reload his weapon.

The other man turned and fired wildly, the bolt striking the wall high above James's head. Suddenly the balance shifted. The archers dropped their bows and drew daggers, for the projectile weapons were useless at close range. James had one man wounded and down before his neighbor had freed his dagger from his belt. William's large sword was menacing enough that one of the mercenaries threw down his crossbow and attempted to leap over the desk and dash through the gaping hole in the wall.

Seeing the man attempting to flee from within, Captain Garruth and his men sprang forward and the man was down in moments. Inside, the others threw up their hands and knelt, the mercenary's universal sign of surrender.

Garruth indicated that two of his six men were to guard the prisoners. To James he said, "There are more of them than these six. I'll take my men to the basement, if you three will check upstairs."

James nodded. "Who's supposed to be up there?"

"Just the lads sleeping until their mid-watch shift, and a scribe named Dennison. The sheriff and his men sleep up there." Glancing at the hacked bodies, he said, "I doubt any of them are alive." He scratched his beard. "It was a perfect raid. They knew exactly when to hit. The company was at its lowest complement and least able to defend itself, and reinforcements were unlikely to get here quickly." He started toward the stairs leading down to the cells, and two of his men followed cautiously.

James motioned to William and Jazhara to accompany him and they made their way to the stairs leading to the upper floor of the jail. As they reached the steps, they ducked reflexively as another explosion came from above.

While smoke and stone dust poured down the steps, Captain Garruth shouted, "He's heading for the North Gate!"

James didn't hesitate. "Come on!" he bellowed, and ran through the gaping hole just a few feet away.

Looking down the crowded street leading to the North Gate, James could see the head and shoulders of a large man towering above the throng, shoving his way through the curious onlookers who had gathered to see what the commotion at the jail was. James, William, and Jazhara raced after him.

As they neared the crowd, James glanced back and saw that Garruth's men were engaged in a struggle with about a half-dozen mercenaries. To William and Jazhara, he shouted, "We're on our own!"

People who had been shoved aside by the big man found themselves being pushed aside once more, this time by James and his companions. "Out of the way! Prince's business!" he shouted.

In the din of voices he could barely be heard and finally James let William, who was stockier and stronger than James, take the lead. People jumped aside as they recognized the garb of the prince's personal household guards, when he bellowed, "Stand aside in the name of the Prince!"

Still, precious moments had been lost, and the big man was out of sight. As they neared the intersection with the road that emptied out through the North Gate, another mighty explosion could be heard, followed instantly by screams and shouts.

They reached the corner and saw a large, two-story building in flames. Smoke billowed from the lower windows as flames climbed the outside wall.

"Gods," said James. "He's fired the orphanage."

From the main door four women and a man were ushering out children, many of whom looked stunned and disoriented, coughing from the heavy smoke. James ran to the door.

The man turned, saw William's garb and shouted, "Someone's burned the orphanage! They threw a bomb through that window." He pointed with a shaking finger. "Flames erupted and we barely got out alive."

Jazhara said, "Are all the children out?"

A scream from upstairs answered her.

The man coughed and said, "I tried to go upstairs, but the fire near the stairs is too intense."

"How many are up there?" asked William.

"Three," said one of the women, who was crying. "I called the children for supper, but they were taking their time coming down . . ."

"I may be able to help," said Jazhara.

"How?" asked James.

"I have a spell which will protect you from the heat unless you touch the flame itself. But it lasts only a short time."

The man said, "Then weave it quickly, woman. Their lives are at stake."

William started to strip off his armor, but James said, "No, I'm faster than you." He also had no armor to doff. He handed his sword to William and said, "Ready."

Jazhara said, "The spell will protect you from the heat, but you must be careful not to breathe the smoke too deeply as it will kill as fast as a flame." She pulled a handkerchief from the hands of one of the nearby women and handed it to James. "Hold this over your mouth and nose."

She closed her eyes, putting her right hand on James's arm and the back of her left hand to her forehead. She made a short incantation and finally said, "There. It is done. Now hurry, for it will last but a short time"

James said, "I didn't feel anything."

"It's done," she repeated.

"I usually feel magic when it's – "

"Go!" she said, pushing him toward the door. "Time is short!"

"But – "

"Go!" she repeated with a strong push.

James tumbled head-first through the door, and ducked at the sight of flames licking the ceiling above. To his surprise, he felt no heat.

The smoke, however, caused his eyes to water and he blinked furiously to clear them. He wished he had thought to wet the cloth he held over his nose and mouth. He made for a stairway, following a serpentine route around flaming tables and burning tapestries.

He quickly reached the top of the stairs and did not have to ask if the children were still alive. Three tiny voices split the air with their screams and coughs. James shouted, "Stay where you are, children! I'm coming to get you!"

He hurried toward the shouts at the other end of the room, a barracks of sorts where the children obviously slept. Bedding was smoldering and flames climbed the walls, but he found a straight path to the children.

Two boys and a girl huddled in the corner, terrified to the point of immobility. James quickly decided that trying to guide them through the flames was pointless. The older of the two boys appeared to be about seven or eight years of age. The other boy and girl he guessed as being closer to four.

He knelt and said, "Come here."

The children stood up and he gathered the two smaller children up, one under each arm, then said to the older boy, "Climb on my back!"

The boy did, clamping his arm over James's throat. James put down the other two children, almost gagging. "Not so hard!" he said, prying the boy's arm from across his windpipe. "Here," he said, placing the boy's arms across his chest. "Like this!"

Then he scooped up the other children and hurried back to the stairs. He moved quickly down the steps and saw the flames had closed around the landing. "Damn!" he muttered.

There was nothing for it but to run. He leapt as far as he could through the flames and instantly understood Jazhara's warning. The heat itself hadn't been noticeable, but the second the flames touched him he could certainly feel it. "Oooh!" he shouted, as he landed in a relatively clear patch of wooden floor, while the planks on all sides smoldered and burned.

The roof above was making alarming sounds, creaks and groans, that told James the support timbers were weakening. Soon the upper floor would collapse on him and the children if he didn't move. The smoke was making the children cough and James's eyes were tearing to the point of being unable to see through the smoke. Taking in a lungful that caused him to cough, he shouted, "Jazhara! William!"

William's booming voice answered from slightly to his left. "This way!"

James didn't hesitate. He leapt forward, trying as well as he could to avoid the flames, but by the time he came spilling out the door with a child under each arm and one across his back, he was burned on both legs and arms. The children were crying from their burns, but they were alive. He collapsed onto the cobblestones, coughing.

Two women took charge of the burned and frightened children, while Jazhara knelt and examined James's burns. "Not serious," she judged.

James looked at her through watering eyes and said, "Easy for you to say. They hurt like the blazes!"

Jazhara took a small jar out of her belt pouch and said, "This will make them stop hurting until we can get you to a healer or priest."

She applied a salve gently to the burns and, true to her words, the pain vanished. James said, "What is that?"

"It is made from a desert plant found in the Jal-Pur. My people use this salve on burns and cuts. It will keep wounds from festering for a while, enabling them to heal."

James stood up and looked toward the gate. "He's gotten away?"

William said, "I expect so. Look." He pointed to the other side of the street where members of the city watch were moving citizens back from the fire so that a chain of men with buckets could start wetting down the nearby buildings. It was clear that the orphanage was doomed, but the rest of the quarter might be saved. William sounded defeated. "Those men are from the gate watch, so I suspect the murderer got out of the city just by walking through."

Jazhara said, "What sort of monster would set fire to an orphanage to create a diversion?"

James said, "The same sort who would break into a jail at sunset." He coughed one more time, then said, "Let's go back and see if we can find out who he was after." He started walking back toward the jail.

Soldiers from the palace had arrived to augment the surviving city guards at the jail. James had just learned that Sheriff Wilfred Means and all but six of his men had been killed. The sheriff's son, Jonathan, stood in the main room surveying the damage. James had recently recruited the young man to work secretly for him in the Prince's burgeoning intelligence network. The squire put his hand on Jonathan's shoulder and said, "I'm sorry for your loss. Your father and I were never what could be called friends, but I respected him as an honest man who was unstinting in his loyalty and duty."

Jonathan looked pale and could only nod. Finally he controlled his emotions and said, "Thank you."

James nodded. "For the time being, you and the other deputies report to Captain Garruth. Arutha will need time to name a new sheriff and you'll be undermanned for a while."

Jonathan said, "I need to go home if that's all right. I must tell my mother."

James said, "Yes, of course. Go to your mother," and sent the young man on his way. Jonathan was an able man, despite his youth, but he doubted Arutha would willingly elevate him to his father's office. Besides, having Jonathan tied to a desk wouldn't help James's plans. He put aside those thoughts and went looking for Garruth.

The captain was directing workers and soldiers as they started making repairs on the jail. "Didn't catch him?" he said when he saw James and the others.

James held up one of his burned arms and said, "Bastard set fire to the orphanage as a diversion."

Garruth shook his head. "That one is a mean piece of work." He inclined his head to the stairs leading to the cell below. "You should take a look at what he did down there. I'd not want to be on this one's bad side."

James led the others down the steps to the lock-up. The jail was a holding area for minor criminals waiting to get justice from Arutha's magistrates, or for prisoners waiting to be transferred to the palace dungeon or the prison work-gangs.

The jail comprised a large basement divided by bars and doors into eight cells – two large general holding pens, and six smaller cells used to isolate the more troublesome prisoners. At any hour of the day, drunks, petty thieves, and other troublemakers would be found locked up.

A city watchman saluted when he saw James and said, "It's not pretty, Squire. Only one man left alive here, in that far cell."

James couldn't believe his eyes. Guardsmen were carrying bodies from one of the two large cells. James instantly saw what had likely transpired. The large man had come down, perhaps with henchmen, perhaps alone, and had found two cells occupied, six empty. The small cell across the way had been ignored, while he had opened the large cell. The door lay on the floor, and James wondered what sort of man could pry it off its hinges.

Three men lay dead in the cell, and a fourth was being carried out. Three of these men had died by the blade, killed quickly from the evidence before James's eyes, but the fourth man look as if he had literally been torn limb from limb. Eyes fixed wide in pain and terror, the wizened-looking little man lay with his left arm ripped off at the shoulder, his right leg smashed and broken in several places, and his left leg severed below the knee. His blood had splattered the walls across the room.

James glanced at Jazhara and saw her looking at the corpse without flinching. William looked pale, though he had seen dead men before. The young lieutenant said, "Who could do such a thing?"

"Someone who could kill barmaids and fire orphanages," answered Jazhara.

James knelt beside the corpse and said, "I know this man. His name is Knute. Pirate working up the coast, used to come down from time to time to fence stolen property. Clever bastard, but obviously not clever enough."

"What do you mean?" asked William.

"I have an idea, but I'm keeping it to myself until I get more information," said James. With a slight smile he glanced at his companions and added, "Don't want to look too stupid if I'm wrong."

He stood and turned to the guard. Pointing at the other cell with the single living man in it, he asked, "What's his story?"

The guard shrugged. "Can't get much out of him. Local drunk, I'm guessing, Squire. Scared to madness, I'm thinking."

James motioned his companions to come with him. He crossed to stand before the drunk, who stood gripping the bars as if afraid to let go. His hair was gray and his face drawn and pale, damaged from too many nights lying drunk in the gutter. His eyes were tightly shut and he muttered, "Gods, gods, gods! Calm, calm, try to be calm. They'll be along soon. Any moment now, they've got to come soon . . ."

James said, "Scovy?"

The man opened his eyes wide, and tensed as if ready to leap away. Seeing James he said, "Jimmy! Dala bless you! You've come to save me!"

James said, "Not so fast, old man. Did you see what happened?"

Words came tumbling from Scovy's lips. "Oh, yes, yes, I saw it! Would that I had gone to Lims-Kragma's Hall before seein' what was done to that poor soul!"

"You mean Knute?"

Scovy nodded vigorously. "Knute it was. Pirate from up near Widow's Point. Smug he was, saying he wouldn't hang. Said the Prince himself would sign his pardon once he heard the secret Knute was keepin'.'"

"What secret?" James asked.

"Blast if I know, Jimmy. Knute wouldn't say. I'm thinking treasure. Knute probably had it hid . . . that's what all this fuss is about."

Jazhara said, "Tell us what happened tonight."

Scovy looked at Jimmy and said, "Get me out?"

James nodded. "If I like what I hear."

Scovy said, "Well, first this sound comes from above, like the gods' own thunder was shaking the building. Twice it rocked the building. I was sitting down, but I damned near hit my head on the ceiling I jumped so high. Scared me sober, it did. Then this man comes down the stairs. Huge fellow, with a beard and a scar through one eye, murder in the other. Knute called him 'Bear.'"

"What then?" asked William.

"Well, Knute's about to piss himself, swearing to all the gods he didn't betray Bear. The big man seems to believe him, then he reaches over and rips the door right off the cell. Calm as you please he walks in, draws a long dagger and kills those other three sods in there. The he tells Knute to follow him, and Knute takes a step forward, then Bear's grabbing him by the throat and lifts him clean off the ground.

"Knute's kicking and squealing like a pig heading for slaughter, and Bear keeps asking Knute where 'it' is. 'Where did you hide it?' he keeps asking. 'What did you do with it?'"

Jazhara said, "And then?"

"Knute just keeps screaming he hadn't done nothing . . . Bear says Knute's a liar and starts cutting into him, slicin' him apart piece by piece. He wouldn't even wait for an answer. He only stopped when he heard fighting upstairs. Then he screams like an animal and rips what's left of Knute into pieces." Lowering his voice, he said, "I'm only alive because this Bear ran out of time, I'm thinking. He was insane, Jimmy. Something about him . . . it's not right. I've seen strong men, but nothing like this one. I've seen crazy men, but this man is the craziest ever." His lips quivered as he finished his story. "Get me out?"

James nodded to the guard and said, "Release him."

The guard produced a key and opened the door. "Thanks, Jimmy. I won't forget."

"See that you don't, Scovy."

The prisoner hurried up the stairs and James turned to his companions. "Any ideas?"

Jazhara said, "This Knute betrayed Bear?"

James nodded. William said, "Whatever 'it' is, this Bear must want it very badly to risk so much mayhem and murder to recover it."

James let out a slow breath. "My thinking too." Turning toward the stairs upward, he said, "Let's see if Garruth has uncovered any more information in that mess. But one thing I know for certain."

"What?" William and Jazhara asked simultaneously.

"Arutha is not going to be happy."

FOUR

Secrets

A soldier descended the staircase.

"Captain, we found someone alive. It's Dennison," he said.

James glanced at Garruth, who nodded that the squire should investigate and James signaled to Jazhara and William to accompany him upstairs.

Up there, they found the rooms in as much disarray as the ground floor. Through a door in the far end of the hall, they could see another hole blown through the wall that was obviously the way the man called Bear had exited the jail.

Sitting on a stool with a cold wet rag pressed to his head was the jail's scribe, Dennison. The scribe looked up and said, "Thank Dala, who protects the weak and the pious. Who knows what horrors they'd have inflicted upon me had you not shown up."

William looked around the room. "What happened here?"

"I was knocked to the ground by a thunderclap, then rendered almost senseless by a second. This stool upon which I sit fell atop me, striking my head here." He rubbed at a nasty bump on his forehead. "I had blood upon my brow when they arrived, so I feigned death. They killed all the guards in the

88

KRONDOR: TEAR OF THE GODS

barracks room." He pointed to the door leading into the largest room on the top floor. "Someone with a powerful, deep voice gave the orders, but I kept my eyes closed so I can't tell you what he looks like. But I did catch a glimpse of one of his men."

"Did you recognize him?"

"I think so. I've seen him before. He's rumored to be the bosun's mate for Sullen Michael, the pirate."

James's eyes narrowed. He'd met many liars in his day, and this man was a particularly bad one. "Sullen Michael? How would a law-abiding servant of the Crown, such as yourself, know this man?"

The scribe blinked and said, "Ah, I have been known to drink ... from time to time ... and occasionally I find myself in the less savory taverns ... down by the docks." His speech became more rapid as he said, "Ah, maybe I'm wrong. Everything was happening so fast, and I only caught a glimpse before I closed my eyes again. I mean, it could have been someone else . . ." His voice trailed off as he looked around the room uncomfortably.

James glanced at Jazhara and William, and William inched over to the stairs, while Jazhara took up position between the scribe and the hole in the far wall. James said, "Given how thorough they were in killing just about everyone else, why do you think *you* were left alive?"

The color drained from the scribe's face and he stammered, "As I said, sir, I feigned death."

"Odd they didn't check more closely," Jazhara offered coolly.

James nodded to William, then the squire stepped forward and grabbed the slender scribe by the shirtfront. "It's more than passing strange that every man in this jail was killed – every man except you and the drunk downstairs."

"And the drunk only survived because he was in a different cell," William observed.

James shoved the scribe so his back was to the wall. "The raiders knew exactly when to hit this jail. Who knew the schedule?"

Going even paler, the scribe sputtered, "The sheriff! The deputies!"

"And you!" said William, pressing in close to the man. "There's a girl lies dead because of those mercenaries, a girl I loved! I think you know more than you're telling, so you'd best be out with it before I spill your blood."

The scribe was shaking with fear as he held up a placating hand and he looked beseechingly from William to James to Jazhara. "Truly, masters, I've no idea."

William whipped out his dagger and put the point against the man's throat. A thin trickle of blood snaked down Dennison's neck. "You lie! Say your prayers!"

"No, wait!" screamed the scribe. "I'll tell. I'll tell. Just don't kill me!"

James moved slightly, as if to pull William away from the scribe, and in even tones said, "Did you know this man Bear?"

Dennison nodded, looking defeated. "We did a bit of business. He used to slip me a few crowns in exchange for information regarding the jail and the guards, and on occasion I'd lighten a few sentences here and there when his men were picked up. I'd cut them loose; no one noticed. I don't know what Bear was doing with that pirate Knute, but he was mighty upset when Knute got picked up."

"What secret was the pirate keeping that would lead Bear to murder?"

The scribe let out a bitter laugh. "No one needs to *lead* Bear to murder, Squire. He finds it whenever he wants. It's why I could never say no to him all these years. He'd have killed me without even blinking that one good eye of his. I don't know why he was after Knute. I just found out that Knute had a room at Ye Bitten Dog, but I've not been able to let Bear know yet, and I wasn't about to sit up and tell his men when they were killing everyone in sight."

"Well, you're not going to tell him now," said William, as he reversed his dagger and slammed the hilt into the base of the scribe's skull.

The scribe collapsed and William said, "I'll ask the captain to get this one to the palace and keep him under close watch."

James nodded. "He speaks to no one."

William picked up the limp scribe and hoisted the dead weight over his shoulder, and carried him down the steps. Jazhara shook her head and said, "A mystery."

James said, "Whatever secret Knute hid, Bear wanted it badly enough to be named the most wanted man in the Western Realm. If I know Arutha, by tomorrow there'll be a price of at least ten thousand golden sovereigns on Bear's head. Every mercenary will give long thought as to whether they should serve Bear or turn him in."

"What do we do now?"

James glanced around and cocked his head toward the scribe's desk. "First I write a note to Arutha. Then we search every paper here, just in case our friend downstairs left something useful. And then I propose we start looking for two things."

Jazhara held up one finger. "Number one: Knute's secret."

James nodded and held up two fingers. "And number

two: Lucas. Talia's father." Thoughtfully, he said, "And I'm not going to be surprised if finding one doesn't lead us to the other."

Ye Bitten Dog was as run-down a tavern as existed in Krondor, and that was no mean feat. James shook his head. "Not my favorite drinking hole."

William indulged in a rueful chuckle. "From what I've heard, James, you used to frequent worse."

James grinned and pushed open the door. "There are no worse places. Keep your wits about you; we'll not be welcome here."

He entered, the others close behind, and instantly it was apparent what he meant. Every eye was fixed upon William, or rather upon the tabard he wore: that of the Prince's Household Guard. The blood splatters and burns didn't escape notice, either.

At the far end of a long common room a band of men huddled around a high circular table, designed so that one could drink while standing up. Their garb and bare feet identified them as sailors.

Three other men, apparently workers, stood before the fireplace, and they also stared at the newcomers.

Near the door two heavily armed men had ceased their conversation upon William's entrance.

For a long moment, silence reigned in the tavern, then slowly voices could be heard as men started speaking in low murmurs. James spied the tavern keeper and moved to the long bar.

"What the hell do you want?" was the barkeep's welcome.

James smiled. William recognized that smile. It meant trouble was coming.

"Drinks, for me and my friends."

The tavern keeper was a dark-haired man, with a thick thatch that appeared as if it hadn't been visited by a comb in a year. His chin was covered in stubble and his heavy jowls and deep circles under his eyes gave the impression of one who sampled his own ale far too regularly. He placed three full flagons on the bar and growled, "That'll be six coppers. Drink up then shove off; we've no love for stooges of the court in here."

"Charming," muttered Jazhara as she sipped at the ale. It was thin and bitter, so she placed it upon the bar and stood back to watch.

James said, "You the chap they call Lucky Pete?"

The puffy face split into a smile. "Ay, Lucky Pete, on account o' me skills with the fair sex." He winked at Jazhara and said, "Come see me later, darlin', and I'll show ya me peg leg."

He put his hand over hers. She smiled, leaned forward, and whispered, "You'll have two to show me if we don't find what we're looking for." She removed his hand.

Pete grinned and chuckled, which did nothing to improve his appearance. "Got fire, do you? I like fire in me women."

William said, "We heard a fellow named Knute lodges here."

Pete cocked his head. "Knute? Did you say Knute? I'm hard of hearin', you know, an' me memory ain't what it used to be, lad." He made a show of cupping his hand behind his ear.

James glanced around and saw others in the room were quietly watching the conversation. He had been in enough dives like Ye Bitten Dog to know that if they tried to bully Pete there would almost certainly be a brawl in short order. He reached into his belt purse, pulled out two gold coins, and placed them on the counter.

Pete's expression brightened. "Ah, yes, me hearin's improvin' by the moment!" He lowered his voice. "Yeah, I knew ol' Knute. Jes' a small-time pirate, but he did all right for himself for the most part. At least until the bloody guards caught up with him." He glanced at William. "No offense, of course."

"None taken . . . yet," William replied. "Did Knute say anything unusual over the last few days?"

Pete said nothing. After a long silence, James put another coin on the bar. More silence and James pulled out a fourth coin. Pete gathered up the gold pieces and said, "Ha! He drank so much, who could tell? I know I've never seen him so jumpy an' the funny thing of it was, when the guards nicked him, he seemed relieved; almost like he was aimin' to get nicked. Started a tussle right outside that door, he did." Pete pointed to the front door. "Most fellows like Knute, well, they jus' go to lengths to avoid jail, you know what I mean?" James nodded. "But ol' Knute just started a fuss an' then hung around 'til a watchmen comes along, then he throws a drink in the lad's face, kicks him in the shins, all manner of dotty nonsense. Knute's not a scuffler, if you know what I mean. He's a thinker, but this time he was right off his head, from what I could see."

James said, "Can we see his room?"

Pete made a display of indignation. "You must be daft! I can't be lettin' folks wander through me guest's belongin's!"

James slid two more coins across the bar. "Your guest lies dead, hacked to pieces."

Pete swept up the coins. "Well, in that case, I guess he won't be mindin'. Go along. Got the key right here." He slid it across the bar. "Left door at the top o' the stairs. You can look, but make it quick, an' don't be botherin' me other guests. An' bring the key back directly, else I'll send me friends t'see ya!"

They climbed the stairs and found themselves on a small landing, with four doors, two ahead, and one to the left and one to the right. James turned to the left door and inserted the key.

As he turned the key, James heard a sound from within. He stepped back, drew his sword in a fluid motion, and kicked the door open. Inside the room a large man was rummaging through a chest placed atop an unmade bed. He turned, pulling out a large knife as the door slammed open.

James shouted, "Drop that blade!"

The man reversed the dagger, holding it by the point, drew back his arm, and threw it at James. James shouted, "Down!" and went limp, dropping to the floor. The blade flew through the door inches above James's twisting body.

James heard the sound of glass shattering as the man hurled himself through the small window overlooking the rear courtyard of the inn. William leapt over James and was at the window before James could rise.

"Damn," said William as he looked through the opening.

James came up behind him and said, "What?"

William pointed and James looked out. The man lay sprawled upon the cobbles below, his neck obviously broken from the angle at which his head was twisted.

James said to William, "Look around and see what's here, while Jazhara and I examine our friend below."

James and Jazhara hurried downstairs and past Lucky Pete, who asked, "Where's me key?"

"William will bring it when he's done," said James. Pointing at a door next to the bar, he asked, "That the way to the rear courtyard?"

"Yes, why?"

"Because you've got a corpse back there," James replied, pushing through the door.

Pete put his elbows on the bar and said, "Happens all the time, lad."

James reached the body and knelt next to it. A small pouch was still clutched in the man's hand. He pried open the man's fingers and removed it, examining the contents. Inside was a simple key.

"What do you think it's for?" asked Jazhara.

"I'm not sure, but there's something familiar about this key."

William appeared. "Nothing up there worth stealing. Just some clothes."

"There's this," said James, holding out the key.

William examined, then said, "Come over here into the light."

They moved to the rear door of the inn, where a single lantern burned, and William took the key from James and indicated a mark on it. "See this symbol?"

James took it back from him and peered more closely. "That's Lucas's key! The one that unlocks his passage to the sewers!"

Jazhara said, "Then this must be what that villain was looking for. What does it mean?"

James tapped the key against his cheek. "Lucas has a secret entrance to the sewer, in the storage room behind the bar. He used to charge people for the use of the key, *this* key."

William, "So Knute has been using Lucas's slip-me-out to get into the sewers."

James nodded. "Yes. Probably so he could hide the treasure from his last raid, the booty he was talking about to that drunk Scovy. The one that would buy him Arutha's pardon."

"Do you think he stole the key from Lucas?" asked Jazhara.

"No, they must be in this together. Knute's murderer wanted to know where 'it' was; I wager 'it' is the treasure."

William said, "So Lucas must have escaped into the sewers when Bear attacked. But then why hasn't he contacted you or the Prince?"

Jazhara said, "Perhaps he can't."

James shook his head. "Lucas is the only man who is not a member of the Mockers who knows the sewers as well as I. He'll have several places to lie low." James's voice got lower as he thought about it. "He must know what sort of man Bear is. And he must know that if he's been involved in piracy, even just fencing stolen goods, Arutha would be unlikely to afford him significant protection. Lucas has spent his life walking a fine line between lawlessness and legitimate business, but this time he's crossed that line."

William spoke bitterly, "And his daughter paid the price."

James put his hand on William's arm. "And Lucas will have to live with that for the rest of his life."

Jazhara said, "Which will not be long if Bear finds him. Our task is clear; we must find Lucas – and quickly."

James nodded agreement. "Pray we get to him before Bear does."

"Where do we start?" asked William.

James gave his friend a wry smile and pointed downward. "The sewers."

Blood still stained the floors of the Rainbow Parrot Inn, but the bodies had been removed. A soldier stood beside the door as James, William, and Jazhara approached.

"Simon!" said William as he recognized the soldier. "How goes it?"

"Quiet, here, Lieutenant. Got the bodies out and taken to the Temple of Lims-Kragma, so's they can be properly sent on their way."

"Where are the other guards?" asked James.

"Well, Jack's at the back door, and that's it, Squire. Sergeant Tagart had the rest of the lads take the bodies to the temple. I guess the sergeant didn't think much of anyone trying to rob an inn that was already ransacked. A couple of lads will relieve us at the end of our shift, then we can go down with the others."

"Down where?" asked James.

"Why, the sewers. Ain't you heard, Squire?"

James said, "Heard what?"

"Some bloke was cut loose from the jail a few hours ago. He got someone to stand for drinks at an alehouse in exchange for telling why the jail was attacked."

James winced. "Scovy."

"Could be that's the fellow," said the soldier. "Anyway, there's been rumors aplenty. Pirate treasure in the sewers. Mountains of jewels and gold. Says a pirate named Bear hit the jail because someone there knew where the treasure was."

"So the sewers are now crawling with treasure hunters," said William.

"That's a fact, Lieutenant," said Simon. "Heard from one of the city watch who passed by a few minutes before you got here that a band of blokes came hobbling out of the big grate near Five Points, all cut up and bleeding. Word is the Mockers are trying to keep everyone else out of the sewers so they can find the treasure themselves."

James sighed. "Well, I wonder what else could happen to make finding Lucas more difficult."

"Well, someone said there's a monster down there, too, Squire."

James looked at Simon and said, "You're joking, right?"

"On my honor, Squire," said the soldier. "Seems two nights ago they found a body floating in the bay, all chewed up the way a cat does a mouse. Then they heard some fellow over at Ye Bitten Dog heard from another bloke that a band of smugglers was attacked by something that was big as a bull, with long arms and big teeth."

Jazhara asked James, "And you want to go down there?"

"No," answered the former thief, "but we have no choice. If we're going to catch Bear, we need to find Lucas before he does. I have an idea where Lucas may be lying low."

William nodded. "Even if Bear doesn't find Lucas, if Lucas was in cahoots with Knute and is sitting on that treasure, anyone else who finds it before we do will probably kill Lucas."

James said, "No more delays. Come on." To Simon he said, "When your relief shows up, tell the duty sergeant that we're in the sewers hunting the killer. I want word sent back to the palace asking the Prince to send a company down after us to help clear out these treasure hunters."

"As you say, Squire." Simon saluted.

James started to turn away, and Simon added, "One other thing, Squire."

"What is it?"

"There's a rumor surfaced a bit ago." He glanced around as if ensuring no one else was listening. "Seems a bunch of drunken lads from up Fishtown way came out of the sewers over near Five Points, dragging some fellows with them. They were pretty messed up."

"Mockers?" asked James, wondering if the fishermen might have run into the Guild of Thieves.

"No, not Mockers, Squire." He lowered his voice. "They said it was that monster I was telling you about. Went over to the Temple of Dala and had to give the priests every copper they had just to keep their friends from bleeding to death."

"The monster again?" William looked dubious. "Stop that nonsense."

Simon shrugged. "Just telling what I heard, Lieutenant. Some sort of . . . thing, bigger than a man by half. One fisherman said it just showed up in the tunnel with them and started breaking bones and biting off fingers."

"Great," said James. "Just great." Shaking his head, he led his companions into the back room and to a wall lined floor to ceiling with shelves full of dry food, extra crockery, and bottles of wine. He produced the key they had found in Knute's room and moved aside a bag of dried beans. Behind it was a keyhole large enough to accommodate Knute's key.

He inserted the key and turned it. A soft rumbling sound and a loud click followed, then James gripped the side of the shelves and pulled it to the right. It slid effortlessly to the side, revealing a half-height passage and steps leading down. "You've got to duck a bit to get down these steps," he said. "William, go fetch us a light."

William returned to the inn's common room and reappeared a moment later with a lantern. James said, "We could enter at any one of a dozen places, but picking up Lucas's trail might be easier here."

He motioned for the lantern, took it from William's outstretched hand, and led them into the darkness.

*　　*　　*

"'Ware the drop," James whispered, as he jumped three feet down from the tunnel from Lucas's inn to the sewer floor. He turned and offered his hand to Jazhara, who took it, and using her staff for balance jumped nimbly down. William leapt after her and landed on something that squished under his boot.

"What a stench!" William complained as he scraped his boot on the stones rising above the inch-deep liquid.

James turned to Jazhara and said, "I'm afraid this isn't exactly what I meant by a tour of the city. But duty calls . . ."

She asked, "Do you truly think your friend Lucas has fled down here?"

James peered around through the gloom. After a moment said, "He knows these sewers almost as well as the Mockers do." He peered at the walls and floor as if seeking a sign of where to begin. "Back at the time of the Riftwar, Lucas worked with both the Mockers and Trevor Hull's smugglers. He built up a lot of goodwill with the Mockers and so they leave him alone down here. Not many can claim that. This is where he'd go if he were in trouble."

William said, "We've a lot of ground to cover, so we'd best get started. Which way first?"

James pointed. "That way, downstream."

"Why?" asked Jazhara.

"There are some old smugglers' hide-outs that Lucas knows. Not many, even in the Mockers, know exactly where they are anymore. I'm betting Lucas is holed up in one of those secret rooms."

"You know where they are?" asked William.

James shrugged. "It's been years, but I sort of know their general location."

William let out his breath in an exasperated way. "Sort of?"

Jazhara laughed. "Better than no idea, it seems to me."

They made their way through the sewers, the sound of their passage masked by the drips, splashes, and gurgles of the water echoing off the stones. Every so often, James would raise his hand to halt them, and listen.

After nearly a half-hour of careful movement, they entered a large tunnel. The sound of rushing water came from ahead. James said, "The center of the sewer system lies up there. A half-dozen large tunnels empty into it, and it leads out to the south end of the bay. From there we will take another tunnel to the old smugglers' landing. The outflow is big enough for a boat to enter, which is why the smugglers had their landing at the opposite end, near the eastern wall of the city."

William said, "Anyone using it these days?"

"Besides Lucas? I don't know. There aren't many alive today who have been down there who aren't in the Prince's service. Maybe the Mockers have discovered those storage rooms."

They entered a larger conduit and the sound of rushing water grew louder. "Walk carefully here," warned James.

They entered a large rotunda, with six tunnels branching off, like spokes on a wheel. Above them, smaller pipes emptied out into the circular area and filthy water splashed down below them. They moved cautiously in single file on the narrow walkway along the wall, for the stones around the deep hole were encrusted with slippery filth. As they passed the second of the larger tunnels, William asked, "Where do these lead?"

"Each leads to a different portion of the city," said James. He paused and pointed to one of the tunnels on the opposite side of the gallery. "That one over there leads back toward the palace. Some prince, years ago, decided to make the sewers more efficient, I guess. There's an old cistern up there" – he pointed upward to the darkness – "and it was supposed to release water every night to help flush out the sewers. Don't know if it ever worked the way it was supposed to, but . . ." He resumed walking. "I don't know anyone who remembers it being used. Lots of merchants just dig their own tunnels to the sewer when they start up their shops. The royal engineers have maps, but most of them are outdated, useless." Almost to himself he added, "That would be something worth doing, updating those maps and requiring people to inform the Crown when they make changes."

They entered the third large tunnel and James said, "Be cautious. We're entering Mocker territory."

A short time later this tunnel emptied into a smaller circular area, with two more tunnels entering a third of the way up on either side, forming a "Y" intersection. An old man stood near the intersection, holding a long stick that he used to poke at floating debris.

William began to draw his sword slowly, but James reached back and stayed his friend's hand. "It's just an old toffsman, named Rat-Tail Jack."

"Toffsman?" whispered Jazhara.

"He scavenges for items of value. You'd be amazed at what can turn up down here."

Slowly James walked into view and said, "Good day, Jack."

The man turned. "Jimmy, as I live and breathe. Been some years."

Upon closer inspection, the man was of middle age, stoop-shouldered, and slender. His hair was matted and filthy, of indeterminate color. He had a receding chin and large eyes, and they were fixed upon James and his two companions.

"Playing lookout, I see," James said, flashing a grin.

The man stopped the pretense of poking at the sludge. "You know the trade too well, me old son."

"What's up in the wind?"

"Bloody murder and a bunch of lunatic treasure hunters. Been a handful of lads taken to the temples for healing already. Word's been passed to shut down the Thieves' Highway."

Jimmy said, "So I guess that means I'm supposed to turn around and go back."

"Even you, old son." The man pointed to the other two tunnels. "Bashers are waiting. You'd best go no further. That's Mockers territory. The big 'rats' down there will have you for supper, they will."

"Not for old time's sake?"

"Not even that, Jimmy me lad. You got the death mark lifted, I hear, but you're still not one of the Dodgy Brotherhood and when the Thieves' Highway is closed, only Mockers can pass."

William whispered, "Is there another way?"

James replied, "Too long. We'll have to try to talk our way past whoever's ahead."

"And if that doesn't work?" asked Jazhara.

James said, "We fight." He turned back to Jack. "We're looking for Lucas. Seen or heard anything from him?"

"He's hiding out, boy, somewhere down here, but I can't lead you to him."

"What about Bear?" asked William. "Any word of him?"

"There's a bad one," said Jack. "He was down here a few days ago looking for something. Killed a few of the boys. We put the death mark on him."

"He's marked by the Crown, as well," said James.

"Still don't make the Mockers and Crown friends, old son," said Jack.

James said, "Who's in charge over there?"

"Bosun Mace."

James shook his head. Bosun Mace had been a sailor in the King's Fleet who had been whipped out of service for thieving. He had joined the Mockers to put his talents to more profitable use. He was a bully, short tempered, and had never liked James when the boy had been a Mocker. He had been one of the few men who had been friends with Laughing Jack, a Basher whom James killed for making a failed attempt on the Prince's life.

"It's going to be a nasty fight," said James to his companions.

Rat-Tail Jack said, "Doesn't have to be, lad, if you use that fabled wit of yours. There's always something that can be traded for, old son."

"Such as?" asked Jazhara.

Jack said, "Go talk to Mace and when he starts to threaten you, ask him who's been chewing up his lads. That'll get his attention."

"Thanks, Jack," said James. He motioned for his companions to move forward. They took the tunnel to the left and as they did so, Jack let out a shrill whistle.

"What was that?" asked William.

"Jack's taking care of himself," said James. "If he didn't call out the alarm, the Bashers would think he was in league with us."

A short distance later they reached a widening of the tunnel and from along both sides of the wall men stepped into view, surrounding the trio. There were a half-dozen of them, all armed. A large gray-haired man in front stepped forward into the torchlight.

After a moment he smiled. It wasn't a pretty sight. Jowls covered with stubble hung from a head that seemed a size too big for anything human. His eyes looked as much like a pig's as a man's. A bulbous nose that had been broken too many times to recall was the centerpiece of his malformed visage.

"Well, Jimmy the Hand," said the large man, slapping his left hand with the long sap he held in his right. "You looking for some pain, boy?"

"Looking to talk, Mace."

"I always thought you talked too much, even when you was one of us, you little snot." With that he shouted, "Get 'em, lads!" and swung his billy club at James's head.

FIVE

Monsters

James ducked.

The billy club split the air above his head as he shouted, "Mace! Wait! We need to talk!"

Jazhara had her staff at the ready and William brandished his sword, but both held off from engaging the approaching thieves until a blow was delivered.

"I'll talk to you," answered Mace, swinging again at the elusive former thief, "with this!"

"Who's been chewing up your Bashers?" shouted James as he avoided a third swing.

The large man stopped, holding his club high above his head in preparation for another blow. "What you know about that, boy?"

James kept his distance. "I hear things."

Suddenly the man looked worried, and James knew that something grave must have occurred, for as long as he had known Mace the Bosun, the man had never shown fear or doubt. Mace lowered his billy and held up his free hand to signal the other thieves to stop their advance.

"All right, then," he said at last. "What have you heard?"

"Just that someone – or something – has been grabbing your

men and leaving them . . ." James was bluffing. He knew no details, but reckoned that what Rat-Tail Jack had referred to was in some way connected to the "monsters" Simon had described at the Rainbow Parrot. And the old toffsman's advice about bringing up this topic had proved accurate so far.

"Mangled," said one of the other thieves.

"Mangled," repeated James.

"It's fair disgustin'," said another thief. "Looks like they'd been gnawed on, like a dog does wit' a bone, you know, Squire?"

Others nodded.

"Where?" asked James.

"That's the thing," said Mace. "One place, then another — there's no rhyme or reason to it. You never know."

"How long has this been going on?" asked James.

"Fair close to a week, now," said Mace.

James said, "You let us go by, Mace, and I'll find out what's killing your men and get it dealt with."

"How you going to do that if some of my toughest men can't face this thing, whatever it is?"

Jazhara held up her hand and a globe of light sprang forth.

"Blind me eyes!" exclaimed one of the thieves. "A bloody magician!"

"The Prince's bloody magician," corrected James.

Mace waved his billy at Jazhara. "You know the Mockers have no truck with magic!" he shouted. "Prince's squire and all, you still know the Mockers' Law!"

Jazhara closed her hand and the light vanished. "Look the other way for a while."

"Or else let me call down a few squads of the Prince's

regulars," said William. "A couple of hundred armed men might flush the thing out, don't you think?"

The thought of soldiers invading the Thieves' Highway was obviously more odious than a magician, for after a moment Mace said, "All right, you can pass. But if any more of my lads gets killed, Prince's squire or no, the death mark will be back on you, boy. You have my word on that."

James bowed theatrically, and said, "Your warning is heard. Now, if we may go?"

Mace waved them by. "Tread lightly, Jimmy the Hand. There are them about who ain't members of the Guild."

"Noted. What's the password?"

"'Lanky boy'," answered Mace.

They left the Mockers and continued down the passage. When they were safely out of earshot, Jazhara said, "I understand many people fear magic, but why are the Mockers so averse to it?"

James said, "Because thieves thrive on misdirection and subterfuge. You ever hear of a thief stealing something from a magician?"

Jazhara laughed. "Only in stories."

"That's the point. If Arutha wanted to rid the city of thieves, he could for a while by having you, or someone like you, ferret them out with magic."

Jazhara peered around the tunnel. "I think they overrate our abilities. I could create some problems in a limited area for a small number of them, but once I had left, I suspect they would return, like rats."

James chuckled. "Almost certainly, but no one said a fear has to be based in reality."

Jazhara glanced at James. "Squire, I know you by reputation

to be a man of some accomplishments for one so young, but to find you to be a deep thinker is impressive."

Now it was William's turn to chuckle, leaving James to wonder if the remark was a compliment or a barb.

Twice they halted to hide as bands of armed men came by. After the second group had safely passed, James said, "That lot had been in a tussle."

William nodded as he relit the lantern. "Two of them aren't going to make it if their companions don't carry them."

"Which way do we go now?" asked Jazhara.

"Where they came from," said James.

They continued on, deeper into the sewers.

The sound of lapping water heralded the existence of another large waterway.

"This is the original river sluice," said James. "One of the early princes built it. I've been told that this was originally above ground . . . maybe designed as a small canal for barges from the river."

William knelt and inspected the stonework. "Looks ancient." He stood and glanced around. "Look there," he said, moving over to examine something on the nearby wall. "This doesn't look like the usual tunnel wall. It's more like a fortification wall." He indicated the size of the stones and the almost seamless way in which they were set.

"No foot- or handholds," James agreed.

"How did it come to be so far below the ground?" asked Jazhara.

James shrugged. "People build things. They fill in the spaces between them to make roads. At least a dozen of the sewer tunnels look like old roads that have been covered over, and that central spillway we passed earlier was almost certainly a cistern ages ago."

"Fascinating," she said. "How old do you estimate?"

"Krondor's four hundred years old," said James. "Give or take a week."

Jazhara laughed. "By Keshian standards, a young city."

James shrugged and began walking. "This way."

As they turned a corner into another passage that ran parallel to the main watercourse, something darted across their field of vision halfway down the tunnel, at the edge of the lantern light.

"What was that?" asked William, bringing his sword to the ready.

"It was big," said Jazhara. "Larger than a man by half."

James had also drawn his sword. "Cautiously, my friends."

They moved carefully down the passage until they came to the intersection where the figure had vanished. Ahead lay a long corridor leading to the right, while to the left a short passage led back to the edge of the canal. "If the thing moves through the water," said William, "that would explain why it is hard to find."

"And why it could move about from place to place quickly," observed James. "That way," he said pointing to the left.

They walked slowly, and after a dozen steps spied a faint green light wavering in the distance. Jazhara whispered, "My hair stands on end. There is magic nearby."

James said, "Thanks for the warning."

Jazhara removed something from her belt pouch. "If I give the word, fall to the ground and cover your eyes."

William said, "Understood." James nodded.

They inched toward the light, and saw a door set in the stone wall. It was open. When they reached the portal, they halted.

James attempted to make sense of what he saw. Human bones lay strewn about, along with the bones of rats and other small animals. Rags and straw had been fashioned into a large circular pallet, in which rested several large leathery objects, each as long as a man's arm. They pulsed with a sick, green inner light.

Jazhara gasped. "By the gods!" Suddenly James made sense of what they beheld. Within the leather sacks, as he thought of them, figures were visible.

"They're babies!" the magician cried, horrified. She closed her eyes and began a low incantation. At last, her eyes snapped open and she said, "This is the darkest magic. This place must be destroyed. Shield your eyes!"

Both men turned their backs to the door as Jazhara hurled the object she'd taken from her pouch. A flash of white light illuminated the area as heat washed over them.

In the sudden brilliance the far end of the corridor was revealed. There stood a misshapen, hunchbacked figure, a creature seven or more feet tall. Atop its frame sat a massive head, its visage a caricature of a human face with a protruding jaw exposing teeth the size of a man's thumb. Beady black eyes widened in shock at the burst of light. Its arms hung to the floor, and instead of hands, large callused flippers bore the creature's weight.

After a second, the monster roared and charged.

James and William stood ready as Jazhara turned.

The thing was almost upon them when James threw his dagger with his left hand, a short, deft cast, catching the creature in the chest. The monster barely hesitated, but it let out a roar of pain.

The light coming from the fire behind them revealed gaping wounds upon the creature's body. The fights with other groups in the tunnels had left the thing weakened, James hoped, and now he knew it was mortal, as blood seeped from several of the gashes.

William's sword snaked point first over James's head, and he braced to let the creature run up onto the blade. The creature slowed, and rather than impale itself, it lifted what James thought of as arms rather than forelegs. With a sudden backhand slash, the flipper-like hand sliced through the air, and James barely avoided decapitation. The flipper struck the stones with a solid crack; James knew there must be a hard callus or bone ridge along the flipper's edge that would likely cut through flesh.

Jazhara chanted a spell and held up her hand. A point of searing red light appeared upon the creature's head and suddenly it howled in pain. Both flippers came up as if to shield its head, giving William an opening.

The long hand-and-a-half sword shot forward. A short man, William was nevertheless powerful of arm and shoulder and he drove his sword home with all his weight. The blade struck deep. The creature wailed.

James shot past his companion and struck for its throat with his rapier and in seconds the thing lay upon the stones, dead.

"What is it?" asked William, panting heavily.

"Nothing natural," said Jazhara.

"Someone made it?" asked James, moving cautiously around the still corpse.

Jazhara knelt and touched a flipper, then ran her hand across the brow above the blankly staring eyes. Finally she rose, wiping away a tear. "It was a baby."

William almost gagged. "*That* was a baby?"

Jazhara turned and started walking down the tunnel. "I need to be away from here," she said, her voice choked with emotion.

James and William hurried to overtake her. "Wait!" James cried.

Reaching the intersection, Jazhara halted. Before either William or James could speak, she turned and said, "Some magic is evil beyond imagining. There is a branch of the Lesser Path, called by some 'Arcane Vitrus' in the old language. It means 'the hidden knowledge of life.' When used for good, it seeks to unravel the reason people sicken and die, or to find cures for deformity or illness. When used for evil, it can fashion creatures such as these."

"Babies?" William asked.

Jazhara nodded. "Children stolen or bought hours after birth, placed within those 'egg sacs' to be refashioned and twisted against any reasonable nature by malignant arts."

"So this monster was the first to hatch?" James asked, shaking his head.

"That poor child was no monster," said Jazhara. "Whoever created it is the monster." She looked to James. "Somewhere in Krondor is a magician who makes black mischief. Someone who wishes great turmoil in the Prince's city."

James closed his eyes. "As if Bear wasn't enough." He sighed and said, "One problem at a time. Let's find Rat-Tail Jack and Mace and then Lucas."

They turned and began retracing their steps, back the way they had come.

*   *   *

As they walked Jazhara said, "That creature can't have been down here long."

James looked thoughtful. "Mace said the trouble first started a week or so ago."

William said, "Maybe whoever created it wanted to see if the magic worked, then when it did, planned to make more."

"I think you're right," Jazhara said, "Which means the magic is very powerful, for not only does it twist the human design, it works quickly, perhaps in a few days or a week."

"So the creature really was a baby," said James. "In both senses."

"Yes, and in pain." Jazhara's voice was bitter. "This is the sort of horror that turns people against those of us who practice the mystic arts. It is why magicians are shunned and hated. I must send word to Master Pug and let him know a rogue magician of powerful arts is in Krondor."

James said, "Ah, I'd leave that to the Prince. Arutha tends to prefer a more direct approach. If he feels the need to inform Stardock, he will."

Jazhara said, "Of course. I will merely advise His Highness to send word to Master Pug."

They continued on in silence, occasionally pausing when the sound of others in the sewers reached them. Eventually they returned to the spot Mace and his gang had halted them. William said, "Are they gone?"

James kept walking. "They're nearby; trust me."

They moved to the large canal and found Rat-Tail Jack still picking over the sewage floating by. As they approached, he looked up. "You're alive? Guess that means we need to be rewarding you, Squire."

James said nothing, but looked quizzical.

"How about we don't kill you for breaking oath with the Mockers and entering the sewer without our leave? That reward enough for you, Squire?"

All James said was: "Lucas."

"Monster's really dead?"

"Yes. Now, what do you know about Lucas?"

Jack stopped poking at the floating detritus. "We was keepin' an eye on Lucas. He's an old . . . business associate from way back, but we was figurin' he was handling some business that rightly was ours. One night three boats rowed by some grim-looking lads came up the main canal from the harbor. Couldn't get close enough to see which of the old smugglers' hideaways he used, but we'd have found it sooner or later. Lucas went up to his inn.

"Then he drops right down among us yesterday and offers us his inn if we just let him pass. Well, for that nice little inn of his, we said 'pass,' and he scurries off. Knows the sewers, does old Lucas, 'cause the lad set to tail him got shaken before he reached the smugglers' landin'. Still, enough, we figure we'll get around to findin' him, 'cause the lads checkin' around up top hear rumors of pirates and gold. We figure Lucas knows where their treasure's hid. That's why he was free with his inn and all. So we figure we'll send a couple of Bashers on him but then this monster shows up and all them treasure hunters start running through the tunnels . . ."

"Where is he now?"

"We have a good idea of where he was, Squire, but you know how it goes with us Mockers. Always misplacin' things. Of course, for a price, anythin' can be found."

"We killed the monster," said William.

"And for that you get free passage, nothin' more," replied Jack.

"What's your price?" asked James.

"One favor, from you and your new friends, to be named later."

"What?" William exclaimed.

"Why?" asked James.

Jack said, "It won't be asked soon, maybe never, but we think there's trouble comin'. Big trouble. That monster was just the tiniest bit of it. And we need all the friends we can get."

"You know I can't break my oath to the Prince and do anything illegal for you," said James.

"I'm not askin' for that," said Jack. "But we need friends, don't we, Jimmy the Hand?"

James pondered the request, then said at last, "That we do, Rat-Tail Jack. You have my oath."

"We think Lucas is near the basement where old Trevor Hull hid the Princess when you were a boy. There are a couple of cellars from torn-down buildings that you can still get into, large enough to hide some treasure, and close enough to the water to get it there."

"I know the area," said James. "We'll be out of the sewers by sun-up."

"See that you are. We can't control every murderin' dog down here."

James motioned for Jazhara and William to follow him and they continued along their way, heading for the central canal.

The trio moved silently and slowly. In the distance they could hear the low murmur of men's voices.

James and his companions made their way cautiously to a point near an intersection of the main canal and another large waterway. Crouching low in the darkness, their lantern shuttered, James, Jazhara, and William waited.

Six men, all wearing black, were consulting with one another, speaking very softly. Jazhara's intake of breath behind James told him she recognized them. James and William already knew them for what they were: Izmalis. Keshian assassins. More than a dozen had turned up in the desert fortress of the Nighthawks that Prince Arutha had destroyed just months earlier.

James had no illusions: if Jazhara could strike with some magic spell that would incapacitate two or three of them for a few minutes, then he and William stood a chance. In an open fight without the advantage of surprise, it would take a miracle for the three of them to survive.

James turned and tapped Jazhara on the shoulder, pointing to the six men, and then he put his lips next to her ear. In his softest voice he asked, "What can you do?"

Jazhara whispered, "I can try to blind them. When I tell you, close your eyes tightly."

She whispered the same instructions in William's ear. Then she rose from her crouch and began an incantation, her voice soft. Something – a too-loud word, a rustle of cloth, the scrape of a boot against stone – alerted one of the assassins, who turned to peer into the gloom. Then he said something to his companions, and at one they ceased their discussion to look where he indicated.

Slowly they drew weapons. James whispered, "Do it now!"

Jazhara said, "Close your eyes!" and let loose her spell. A shaft of golden light sprang from her hand and exploded in a searing-hot, white flash. The six assassins were blinded instantly. Jazhara shouted, "Now!"

James sprang into action, with William just a step behind him. Jazhara uncovered the lantern, throwing the tunnel into stark relief. The young squire struck the first man with the hilt of his sword, knocking him into the canal. "Take one alive if you can!" he shouted.

William struck down one man, but almost got run through when he found his next opponent in a defensive posture, ready to respond to the sound of an attack. "Think I'll try to stay alive, first, James," he said, using his long sword to get over the blinded man's guard and kill him.

Jazhara came up next to William and struck another assassin across the face with the iron-clad butt of her staff. The man crumpled to the floor.

James found the next two Izmalis had regained some of their sight and were poised for attack. As James knew from experience, multiple opponents often got in one another's way, but these two looked practiced at fighting in tandem. "I could use some help," he said to Jazhara.

As soon as he spoke, both men launched a coordinated attack, and only his preternatural reflexes saved him. The first man struck out, the curved blade of his scimitar slicing at James's mid-section, while his companion struck a half-beat later, coming in where James should have been standing had he made the expected response to the initial attack.

Instead, James had blocked to the right with his blade, and instead of retreating he had pressed hard on his own weapon, forcing the first assassin to continue moving to his left. With his left hand, James gripped the Izmali's right elbow and threw his weight into the man, sending him spinning into the canal.

Suddenly the second assassin facing James was alone, with Jazhara bearing down with her staff, ready to strike, and James was now on his off-hand side.

William engaged his last opponent and called, "I've got this one cornered!"

The Izmali facing Jazhara said something in a language James didn't understand, then raised his left hand to his mouth, and toppled to the stones. William's opponent did likewise, falling into the canal with a splash.

"Damn!" shouted James, grabbing the collapsing assassin before he hit the stones. As he expected, the man was already dead.

Jazhara looked at the assassin James had knocked into the canal and said, "He floats face-down."

"What happened?" William asked.

"Nighthawks. They've taken their own lives. Fanatics." Addressing Jazhara, James inquired, "Did you understand what he said?"

"I think he ordered his companions to die, but I did not recognize the language. It is said the Izmalis have their own tongue, that no one outside their clan may learn."

William said, "We found some like these when the demon was summoned at the abandoned fortress in the desert."

"Demon?" Jazhara asked.

"I'll tell you back at the palace," said James. "But it's clear the Nighthawks numbered Keshians in their bands."

"Which makes them a threat to the Empire as well as to the Kingdom."

James regarded the young woman for a long moment, then said, "It might be wise to send some specific information to your great-uncle."

"Perhaps," said Jazhara, leaning upon her staff, "but as you've observed, that's for the Prince to decide."

James grinned. "Let's check the bodies."

They examined the four assassins who hadn't ended up in the canal and came away with nothing. The only personal items they wore were the Nighthawks amulets around their necks.

"I thought we'd seen the last of these in the desert," said William.

"We hurt them, certainly, and we destroyed one nest, but there are others." James stood up and tucked an amulet into his shirt. "I'll give this to the Prince. He won't be pleased."

"What were they doing down here?" asked Jazhara.

William said, "Searching for the treasure, I expect."

"If they're to rebuild their nasty little empire, they'll need gold," agreed James. He glanced around. "We came in time, I think." He moved to a large wall with two iron rings set into it and turned the one on the left. After a moment, a deep rumble started and the stones moved aside.

"Lucas!" he shouted. "It's James. I've come from the Prince with help!"

From deep within the darkened passage a voice called, "Jimmy! Thank the gods it's you. They've been searching for me all over, trying to kill me."

James motioned for Jazhara to bring the lantern and the three of them entered the tunnel. A dozen feet in, Lucas stood holding a crossbow, and as soon as he recognized the two young men, he laid it down, relief on his face. "The thugs of that madman, Bear, have been after me for an entire day."

"They're not the only ones," said William. "Treasure hunters and assassins and thieves as well."

"Damn," said Lucas. "Knute said his men were hand-picked,

and would keep silent, but I suspect the fool couldn't keep his own gob shut."

"What is it Bear's after?" asked James.

"Damned if I know, James," replied Lucas. The old man sat down on a water cask. "I was going to help Knute fence the booty from his last raid. I guess Knute double-crossed Bear, because Bear and some of his men showed up at my inn and started killing everyone in sight. I barely got out alive myself after telling Talia and the others to flee through the kitchen."

James and William exchanged glances. In a soft voice James said, "Talia's dead, Lucas. Bear caught her and tried to get her to tell him where you were hiding."

Lucas seemed to collapse from within. His face turned gray and his eyes welled up with tears. "Talia?" His chin fell to his chest. For a long while he sat silently, then said with a sniffle, "I lost my sons in the war, but never thought that Talia . . ." He sighed. After another long silence, he said, "This deal with Knute would have set me up. She wouldn't have had to be a barmaid anymore. She would have had a proper dowry for a proper young man." He looked up at William.

William also had tears in his eyes. "You know I cared for her, Lucas. I swear to you we'll find Bear and Talia will be avenged."

Lucas nodded sadly. "All this trouble, all this black murder, and now it's pointless. I should just return the booty to Knute."

"You haven't heard about Knute?" asked James.

"I heard the guards picked him up night before last. He's in jail."

"Not anymore," said William. "Bear broke into the jail and cut Knute to pieces."

"By the gods! He's gone mad," exclaimed Lucas.

"We'll deal with Bear," William avowed.

"Thank you, William," said Lucas, "but mind your step. Talia may be gone, but you're still with us, and I'd prefer it if you stayed that way. This Bear is dangerous, and he's got magic on his side."

Jazhara said, "What kind of magic?"

"Dark powers, milady. Knute was terrified after he saw Bear work magic. That's why he broke with him." He shook his head. "You want to see what the bastards were after?"

James nodded. "I am a bit curious."

Lucas rose and led them to a stout wooden door. He threw aside the bar on the door and pulled it open. Jazhara stepped forward with her lamp, and even James had to let out an appreciative low whistle.

The small room was filled knee-deep in treasure. Sacks of gold coins were piled atop several small chests. Solid gold statues and piles of jewelry were strewn about. Lucas stepped into the room and opened one of the chests. Inside was more gold, and a small statuette. Jazhara reached down and picked it up. "This is Ishapian," she said softly. "It is a holy icon of their church, the Symbol of Ishap."

James's eyes grew wide. "They hit an Ishapian vessel! There couldn't be a more dangerous undertaking for a pirate, by my reckoning."

Lucas said, "Most men would say foolhardy. Bear wanted something off that ship, something specific. Knute was certain that, whatever it was, it wasn't among the loot he'd stashed down here."

Jazhara asked, "How did he know that?"

"Knute told me that Bear flew into a rage when the ship

went down, despite having taken all this." He waved his hand. "It's one of the reasons Knute left Bear to drown. He was afraid Bear blamed him for the ship going down too fast."

"A reasonable fear, considering what Bear did to him," observed Jazhara.

William looked confused. "How does this help us? We still don't really know who we're chasing, and what he's searching for."

Lucas opened another chest, one that looked different from the others. It was made of dark wood, much older, and appeared never to have been cleaned. It was stained and the hinges were rusty. He pulled out a rolled-up parchment and handed it to James. Then he handed a battered, leather-bound book to Jazhara. "It's all there. These papers list every ship that Knute's crew have sunk over the years, including this last job with Bear."

James looked at the map. "This will tell us where the Ishapian vessel was hit."

"Knute was thorough, I'll say that for the little gnoll," admitted Lucas.

"It still doesn't tell us what Bear is after," observed Jazhara.

William said, "Could we bait him into coming to us if we spread a rumor that we know what he's after?"

James said, "Maybe, but first things first. I must go to the palace first and report to the Prince." He turned to Lucas. "You stay here with William. I'll send Jonathan Means and some deputies down here to take charge of all this gold."

"What will you do with it?" asked Lucas.

James smiled. "Give it back to the Ishapians. We may not know what Bear was after, but I'll wager a year's income they do."

Lucas's shoulders sank slightly, but he nodded.

Jazhara and William followed James out of the room, and they returned into the sewers. As they hurried down a corridor toward the nearest exit, they heard the secret door to the old smugglers' hideout closing behind them.

SIX

Intrigues

Arutha waited for the page to leave.

When the youngster had departed from the Prince's private office, the ruler of the Western Realm of the Kingdom of the Isles looked at James. "Well, this is a far worse mess than we had imagined, isn't it?"

James nodded. "Much more than a simple hunt for pirate loot, Highness."

Arutha graced the magician with his half-smile, and his dark eyes studied the young woman. "You've gotten quite an unusual reception in our city, haven't you, milady?"

James quipped, "Given our recent history, Highness, it may be more usual than either of us likes."

Jazhara smiled at the casual banter between the two men. "Highness, my instructions from Duke Pug were simple: Come to Krondor and help you in any fashion I might, relative to issues of magic. To those ends, I am here to serve, even if it means having to practice the more bellicose side of the art in defense of your realm."

Arutha sat back and made a tent with his fingertips, flexing them in and out a little, a nervous habit James had observed in him since the first day they met. After a moment, he said,

"We have two such topics of discussion, both of which may require, as you put it, 'the more bellicose side' of your arts."

"The creature," supplied James.

Jazhara nodded her agreement. "Highness, the presence of that monstrous child and the quality of evil magic required for such an undertaking indicate that malignant forces of great power are involved."

"Indeed," said the Prince. "Is there any reason you can imagine for someone to practice such horrific magic within the city itself? Certainly the chance of discovery was high, even in an abandoned corner of the sewers."

Jazhara said, "If the purpose was to create chaos in your city, Highness, then such a choice makes sense. For any other reason I can imagine, no; it is a choice that defies understanding.

"So, assuming the intent was to create chaos, then the potential reward would have been worth the risk of early discovery." Jazhara hesitated, then added, "The creature formed from the evil magic used upon those babies would no doubt have grown in power. The one we destroyed had killed or injured more than a dozen armed men in the course of a few days, by all reports. It was weakened when we fought it. Moreover, it was immature, still an infant by any measure. In a few more weeks, I suspect it would have been quite powerful. A host of those things loose in your city . . ."

"You draw an unattractive picture," said Arutha. "But your argument is persuasive." He leaned forward. "Since the arrival of the moredhel renegade Gorath we have been wrestling with a series of seemingly inexplicable events, but throughout those events there has been one constant: someone who seeks to plunge Krondor into chaos."

"The Crawler," said James.

Arutha nodded. "I agree."

"Who is this Crawler, sire?" asked Jazhara.

Arutha nodded to James, who said, "We don't know. If we did, he would have been hanged long since. He first appeared over a year ago, running a gang that attempted to dislodge the Mockers in Krondor. But at the same time, he appears to be working the docks, interfering with commerce. Further, we've ascertained that he had a major relationship with the Nighthawks. In other words, he's a thoroughly bad fellow."

Arutha said, "And potentially far more dangerous than we had thought initially. He seems to have had a hand in the attack on the Duke of Olasko and his family."

"The man moves in many circles," said James.

"And then there is the matter of the Ishapians," said Arutha, pointing to the statuette Jazhara had carried to the palace. "I have sent word to the High Priest of the Temple here in Krondor and I expect we'll be hearing from him soon."

"Does this have anything to do with that house across the square from the palace, Highness?" asked James.

Arutha's half-smile returned. "Not much gets past you, does it?"

James merely smiled and made a half-bow.

"Yes," said Arutha, "but I will wait upon the presence of the High Priest or his agent before sharing that intelligence with you. Go and rest, both of you, but be ready to return here at a moment's notice. I doubt the Ishapians will be long in answering my summons."

Arutha was correct. Jazhara and James were not even halfway back to their respective quarters when pages overtook them, informing them that the Prince required their immediate presence in the throne room.

They returned to find the High Priest of Ishap, along with two other priests and a warrior monk in attendance. The High Priest was an elderly man, scholarly in demeanor with closely cropped snow-white hair. Like their superior, the two priests were also bareheaded, and wore their dark hair cut short. Unlike other orders, the Ishapians tended to favor plain fashion. The priests were dressed in brown-trimmed white robes; the monk wore armor and carried a helm under his left arm. A large warhammer hung at his belt.

Prince Arutha sat on his throne, and while there were only two other officials of the court in attendance – Duke Gardan and his scribe – James realized that Arutha wanted to conduct this interview from a position of power.

The Ishapians were long thought to be the most mysterious of Midkemia's religious orders, not courting converts as the other temples did. James had encountered them before, at the old Abbey at Sarth, and knew there was a great deal more to the Ishapians than commonly believed. They held a kind of supremacy among the orders; other temples avoided conflicts with them.

The High Priest said, "Highness, your message carried a note of the imperative and I came as soon as I received it."

"Thank you," said the Prince. He motioned to Gardan and the old Duke's scribe produced the statuette, handing it to the High Priest for inspection. "Where did you get this, Highness?" the High Priest asked, traces of surprise and worry in his voice.

Arutha signaled to James, who said, "It was discovered earlier today in a cache of stolen goods. Booty from a pirate raid."

"Booty?" said the High Priest.

Arutha said, "We both know, Father, what is due to occur

this year. I need to know if that item came from the ship due into Krondor this month."

The High Priest said, "These are matters which cannot be discussed in open court, Highness."

Arutha nodded to Gardan and the duke dismissed the scribe. The High Priest looked at Jazhara and James and Arutha said, "The squire is my personal agent, and Jazhara is my advisor on all things magical. The duke has my trust beyond question. You may speak freely."

The High Priest looked as if a burden had been placed upon him, for his shoulders sagged visibly. "*Ishap's Dawn* was due in Krondor a week ago, Highness. We have sent ships out to search for her, all the way back to the Free Cities. Perhaps she is disabled or . . ." He looked at James. "A pirate raid? Is that possible?"

James said, "Apparently. A madman named Bear, aided, it seems, by dark magic, appears to have taken your ship. Guards are bringing the rest of the booty to the palace so that you may reclaim it, Father."

A glimmer of hope sprang into the High Priest's eyes. "Tell me . . . is there a large box . . ."

James interrupted. "According to his first mate, whatever it is that Bear wanted sank with the ship. It was the cause of some considerable friction between them. Bear tore the man apart with his hands trying to learn the location of the sunken ship."

The warrior monk kept an impassive face, but the High Priest and his two other companions appeared to be on the verge of fainting.

"Then all is lost," whispered the High Priest.

Arutha leaned forward. "The ship carried the Tear of the Gods?"

The High Priest said, "Yes, and all the other treasure accumulated over the past ten years by every temple from the Far Coast to the Free Cities. But all the gold and gems" – he brandished the statuette – "are meaningless without the Tear."

James caught Arutha's eye. The Prince said, "When I first came to this throne I was told something of the Tear's importance, yet you have kept its secret from the Crown. Why is this artifact of such great value?"

The High Priest said, "What I tell you, Highness, only your brother the King in Rillanon, and a very few of our order, know. I must have your vow that what I tell you here will not leave this room."

Arutha glanced at Gardan, who nodded, then to James and Jazhara, who also agreed. "We so vow," said the Prince.

"Once every ten years, a gem is formed in a secret location in the north of the Grey Tower Mountains. The origin of this gem is lost to us; even our most ancient tomes do not reveal how our order first came to know of the existence of the Tear of the Gods.

"But this we do know: all power from the gods to men comes through this artifact. Without it, we would all fall deaf to the words of the gods, the gods would not hear our prayers."

Jazhara couldn't help herself. She blurted, "You'd lose all contact with the gods!"

"More than that, we fear," said the High Priest. "We believe that all magic would fade, as well. For it is by the grace of the gods that man is allowed to practice the arts of magic, and without divine intervention, we soon would be just as other men. Soon the existing Tear in our mother temple in Rillanon will fade, its shining blue light will go dark. If the new Tear is not in place before that happens, we will lose our link with the heavens."

"Won't there be another Tear in ten years?" asked James.

"Yes, but can you imagine ten years of darkness? Ten years in which man has no commune with the gods? Ten years in which no healing can be done? Ten years without prayers being answered? Ten years without any hope?"

James nodded. "A grim picture, Father. What can we do?"

Arutha said, "We do have the location of the sunken ship."

Once again, a spark of hope appeared in the High Priest's eyes. "You do?"

"Within a fairly confined area," said James. "We have a map, and if the ship went straight down, we should be able to locate it."

"We have magic arts that can do many things, sire," said the High Priest. "But to enable a man to breathe underwater and search out the wreck is beyond our gifts. Is there another way?" He looked pointedly at Jazhara.

Arutha appreciated the gravity of the question; the temples, more than other institutions, were wary of magic they didn't control. Jazhara would be an object of suspicion at the best of times; and this was hardly the best of times. The Prince said, "Do you know another way, Jazhara?"

She shook her head. "Regretfully, Highness, I do not. I know of those in Stardock who are capable of such feats, but few of them are what you might call robust men. For such a task you'd need a strong swimmer, and a source of light."

James said, "That won't work."

Arutha raised an eyebrow. "Oh?"

James grinned. "Highness, I've lived my life near the sea. I've heard what sailors say. Once you go below a certain depth the water weighs down upon you and even with a magic spell to help you breathe, withstanding such pressures would likely prove impossible. No, there's another way."

"Tell us," said the High Priest.

"The Wreckers' Guild," said James. "It's their trade to raise sunken ships. They can bring them up long enough to be salvaged. In some cases they can repair a breach and tow a once-sunken ship safely to port for refitting. I've seen it done more than once."

"But they would have to be told of the Tear," said the High Priest. "And we cannot tell anyone of this."

James shook his head. "No, Father. All we need tell them is to raise the ship. Then someone trusted by the Crown goes into the ship, finds this artifact, and returns it here to Krondor."

The High Priest indicated the silent warrior monk to his left. "Brother Solon here should be that person. There are mystic safeguards around the Tear, so even had this creature Bear reached the Tear, he might not have been able to retrieve it. Brother Solon will be able to remove the safeguards so that the Tear can be recovered."

James looked at Arutha. "Sire, if this man Bear doesn't know the exact whereabouts of the Tear, wouldn't it be likely he'd be close by, looking for an Ishapian expedition heading for the wreck site? Logically he would wait until the artifact was recovered, then strike."

The High Priest said, "We have means of defending the Tear."

"No offense intended, Father, but from what Lucas told us of the pirate Knute's account of things, Bear has some sort of powerful protection against your magic. Otherwise how could he have taken the ship to begin with?"

The High Priest looked troubled as Jazhara said, "An amulet, I believe he said, something with the power to shield the wearer against priestly magic."

Arutha looked at James. "You advise stealth?"

"Yes, sire," said James. "We must find a way to divert Bear's attention. If we can distract him enough to keep him away from the site while we raise the ship, retrieve the artifact, then return here before he realizes he's being distracted . . ." He shrugged. "We might have a chance."

The High Priest said, "Highness, I would prefer a large armed force –"

The Prince held up his hand. "I realize the care of the Tear is the province of the Temple of Ishap, Father, but it was my jail that was destroyed, my wife's orphanage that was burned to the ground, my constables who were slaughtered; that makes it the Crown's business to ensure nothing like this occurs again.

"If, as is reported, Bear and his mercenaries are immune to your magic, it would seem force of arms may be needed to recover the Tear. How many fighting monks can you muster within a day?"

The High Priest looked defeated. "Only three, Highness. The majority of our warrior brothers were on *Ishap's Dawn*, guarding the Tear of the Gods."

James ventured, "Father, given how many were slaughtered here in Krondor, my best advice is to retrieve the Tear and get it safely on its way to Rillanon before Bear realizes it's not still at the bottom of the sea."

Arutha was silent for a moment, then said, "I will accede to James's plan." To James he said, "As for that 'distraction': order the Pathfinders out immediately, to find Bear's trail. Have William muster a full patrol of Household Guards to follow swiftly after them. From what you report, William has ample motivation to press Bear and harry him through the wilderness. Bear may be resistant to magic, but I warrant he might be troubled enough by two dozen swords to keep moving. And tell William that should he overtake Bear, the death mark is on this man and he may deal with him as he sees fit. That should be 'distraction' enough."

"And the Tear?" asked James.

"You and Jazhara go to the Wreckers' Guild and secure enough members to raise a ship. Gather them quietly at some point outside the city, leaving the city in twos and threes, then meet at one of the villages on the way to Sarth. Then ride quickly to . . ."

"Widow's Point," supplied James.

"Widow's Point," repeated Arutha, "and get on with recovering the Tear."

James bowed and said, "How many shall we take with us?"

"I want you, Jazhara, and whoever you get from the Guild, along with Brother Solon, to depart at first light tomorrow. I will send a patrol the next day, and have them go to . . ." He looked at Gardan. "What's the nearest town to Widow's Point?"

Without looking at a map, Duke Gardan said, "Haldon's Head. It lies upon the bluffs overlooking the Point. It's a refuge for scavengers who pick over the wrecks there, but for the most part is a sleepy village."

"Too close, sire," said James. "If Bear has agents near the wreck, they will almost certainly be in Haldon's Head. Our arrival alone will cause a stir, unless we depart within a day or so. It's certain the appearance of an unscheduled patrol will alert Bear's men."

"What is the next village to the south?" asked Arutha.

"Miller's Rest," said the duke.

"Then station them there. As soon as you get the Tear, James, hurry south to Miller's Rest and the patrol will escort you back to Krondor. If you encounter more than you can handle, send someone down to Miller's Rest and the patrol will ride to your relief. Is that clear?"

"Yes, sire," said James, bowing.

To the High Priest, Arutha said, "Father, go and make whatever arrangements you must and have your man meet James outside the gates two hours after first light, at the first crossroads.

"James, you take those men from the Wreckers' Guild, and leave with half of them at first light. Jazhara and the others from the Guild will leave one hour after that. You should all blend in with the normal traffic leaving the city at dawn." Looking at James, the Prince added, "Need I stress caution?"

With his almost insolent grin, James said, "Caution it is, Highness."

Arutha pointed an accusing finger. "We have seen much together, James – more than most men in a dozen lifetimes – but this task is equal to any set before you. Acquit yourself well, for the fate of us all rests in your hands."

James bowed. "I will, Highness."

To Jazhara, Arutha said, "I trust you will remind our young adventurer of the gravity of this task."

She bowed as well. "If need be, Highness."

"Then go, all of you, and may the gods smile upon your efforts."

Outside the throne room, James held Jazhara back until at

last Duke Gardan emerged from the room. "Your Grace?" James said.

The duke turned, his dark features creased like old leather, but his eyes still bright and alert. "What is it, Squire?"

"Could I prevail upon you to send word to the Officer of Stores that we'll be down to equip ourselves for this journey?"

"Some problem?" asked the duke.

James grinned sheepishly. "My credibility of late has suffered, as I have used the Prince's name a little too often – "

"Without Arutha's knowledge," finished Gardan. He returned the smile. "Very well, I'll send word at once."

James said, "When do you finally retire? I thought your departure was agreed upon."

"I was due to leave for Crydee in a month; now I do not know," he answered with an almost theatrical sigh. "When *you* stop bringing crises to the Prince, I think."

With an impish grin, James said, "I think if that's the case, you'll still be here in another ten years."

"I hope not," the duke said, "but I will most certainly be here when you return. No one is spared duty until this crisis is resolved. Now, go about your business." To Jazhara he bowed, and said, "Milady."

"Your Grace," they said in unison.

After the old duke had departed, Jazhara said, "What now?"

James said, "To the Sea Gate and the Wreckers' Guild."

At mid-morning, the Sea Gate was bustling. Cargoes being unloaded in the harbor and transported into the city spawned dozens of carts and wagons that moved slowly down the street toward the Old Market and beyond. Sailors just arrived from long journeys hurried off-ship to find inns and women. Above the docks, sea birds squawked and wheeled in flight, seeking out the debris from dropped cargo that comprised a major part of their diet.

Jazhara suppressed a yawn as they walked. "I'm so tired that watching all these people dash about makes me feel as if I'm sleepwalking."

James smiled. "You get used to it. One of the tricks I've learned in Arutha's service is to nap whenever I get the chance. My personal best is four days without sleep. Of course I had the help of a magic potion and once its effects wore off I was good for nothing for a week . . ."

Jazhara nodded. "Such things must be employed with caution."

"So we discovered on the trip home," said James, now also stifling a yawn in response to Jazhara's. "Whatever fate awaits us, I hope it involves at least one good night's sleep before we depart."

"Agreed."

They reached the Wreckers' Guild, a fairly nondescript two-story building a block shy of the Sea Gate. Several men were gathered outside, next to a large wagon. Two of them climbed atop the wagon as another pair began to walk away, lugging a large chest.

James stopped and tapped one of the men on the shoulder.

Without turning to see who stood behind him, the man snarled, "Shove off!"

Tired, and in no mood for rudeness, James said, "Prince's business."

The man threw him a quick glance. "Look, if you're here about the Guild Master, I just told everything I know to the Captain of the Watch."

James took the man firmly by the shoulder and spun him about. The mover's large fist pulled back to strike James, but before he could, the squire had his dagger at the man's throat. "Indulge me," he said with more than a whisper of menace in his voice. "Perhaps you could spare a moment and go over it once more. What exactly did you tell Captain Garruth about the Guild Master?"

Lowering his fist, the man stepped back. "It doesn't take the brains of an ox to know he was murdered."

One of the other movers, watching the exchange, shouted: "It was Kendaric what did it! He cost us all with his greed."

The first man motioned toward the Guild entrance. "If you want details, you'd best talk to Jorath, inside. He's the journeyman in charge, now."

James put away his dagger and motioned for Jazhara to accompany him. They entered the Guild Hall, where several men stood in the corner deep in discussion. A young man, barely an apprentice by the look of him, stood nearby. He was tallying various items of furniture and personal belongings and recording figures in a ledger. James approached him. "We're looking for Journeyman Jorath."

The boy didn't stop counting, but merely pointed over his shoulder with his quill at a door leading to a room in the rear.

James said, "Thanks," and moved on.

He and Jazhara entered a room occupied by a large desk and several chairs. Standing before the desk was a middle-aged man, with dark hair and a short, neatly-trimmed beard. He wore a plain blue robe, similar to what one might expect on a priest or magician. Glancing up from the document he was studying, he said, "Yes?"

"I'm from the palace," said James.

"I assume that since I've already answered questions, you're here to tell me you've made some progress." His tone dripped arrogance.

James narrowed his gaze for a moment, then let the irritation pass. "We are not part of the Guard. We need a ship raised."

"I'm afraid you're out of luck. The Guild is closed. Evidently you haven't heard, but the Guild Master has been murdered."

"What happened to him?" asked James.

"No one knows, exactly. There was some sort of struggle, apparently. He was found dead in his room, with his possessions scattered about. He put up a good fight, but it seems his heart gave out."

James asked, "Why is the Guild closing down?"

"The Guild Master and Journeyman Kendaric were the only members of our guild capable of leading the ritual necessary to raise a large ship."

"Well, we need to speak to the Journeyman right away."

"Quite impossible, I'm afraid. Kendaric is the prime suspect in the Guild Master's murder, and he seems to have gone into hiding. With both him and the Guild Master gone, we're out of business." He let out a soft sigh. "Which is probably not so bad, all things considered."

"What do you mean, 'all things considered'?" asked James.

Jorath put down parchment he had been consulting. "Confidentially, the Guild has been losing money for several years now. The Guilds of other cities, Durbin and Ylith, for example, have developed new techniques that enable them to work more efficiently. They've been winning all the contracts."

James was silent for a long moment. Then he said, "How do you know it was this Kendaric who killed the Guild Master?"

Jorath picked up another scroll and glanced at it. "They fought constantly. At times they seemed near to blows. Abigail, the woman who cleans the Guild House, heard Kendaric and the Guild Master arguing the night of the murder."

"That's not proof," said Jazhara.

"No, but he's been missing ever since the body was found, so it's a good bet he's guilty."

Jazhara was about to say something, but James shook his head slightly. To Jorath he said, "May we look at the Guild Master's and Kendaric's rooms?"

Jorath shrugged. "Help yourself. The Guard have already been up there, but if you think you can do some good, be my guest." He turned back to his scrolls and left James and Jazhara to show themselves upstairs.

Jazhara waited until they had climbed the stairs. When they were alone, she asked James, "What?"

"What, what?"

"What didn't you want me to say to Jorath?"

"What you were thinking," said James, heading for the first of three closed doors.

"What was I thinking?" asked Jazhara.

Looking over his shoulder as he opened the door, James said, "That Kendaric might also be dead. And that someone doesn't want anyone raising a certain ship off Widow's Point." He glanced down, and said softly, "Someone's forced this lock."

He cocked his head, as if listening, motioned for silence, then held up his hand. "There's someone inside," he whispered.

Jazhara took up a position beside James and nodded. James stepped back then kicked hard against the door, shattering the lock plate as the door swung open.

The old woman inside jumped back and let out a shriek.

"Heavens!" she exclaimed. "Are you trying to shock an old woman to her grave?"

"Sorry," James said with an embarrassed smile. "I heard someone inside and saw the lock had been forced – " He shrugged.

"When I couldn't raise the master," said the old woman, "I had two of the apprentices bring a bar and force the door. I found the master, there, lying on the floor." She sniffled, and brushed at a tear with the back of her hand.

"What can you tell us?" asked James. "We're here on behalf of the Prince."

"The master was a wonderful man, but he had a bad heart. I used to fix hawthorn tea for him for his chest pain. It did him no good to be constantly arguing with Journeyman Kendaric."

"What was Kendaric like?" asked Jazhara.

"He was a poor boy from the streets, without family or friend. The Guild Master paid his admission fee to the Guild, because Kendaric was so poor. But the old master knew the boy was brilliant, and it would have been a crime to deny him because of poverty. The master was right, as the boy grew to be first among the journeymen. He would have been the logical choice to be the next Guild Master, except . . ." Her voice trailed off as more tears welled up in her eyes.

"He was brilliant, you say?" Jazhara prodded.

"Oh, he was always coming up with new ways to do things. He was working on a spell that would allow a single guildsman to raise large ships by himself. He thought the Guild would be more prosperous with his new spell, but the Guild Master wanted to preserve the traditional way, and they fought about it. He used to say that he argued with Kendaric to train him, to make his mind sharp, to make him tough enough to take over the Guild when he passed on. That's what makes it a bit odd."

"What's a bit odd?" asked Jazhara.

"Well, I just think it's odd that Kendaric killed him. Despite all their arguing, I would have sworn that Kendaric truly loved the old master."

Jazhara mused, "Everyone seems convinced that Kendaric is the killer, but isn't it just speculation?"

The old woman sighed. "Perhaps. But I heard Kendaric and the Guild Master arguing on the night of the murder. They always fought, but this time was the loudest I'd ever heard. I found the old master dead the next morning when I came to bring him breakfast. As I said, it took two apprentices to force open the door. Kendaric must have hit him and when the master's heart gave out, Kendaric must have escaped through the window. I said as much to the guards when I called them. They told me I was awfully clever to have figured it out the way I did."

James could hardly keep from rolling his eyes, but simply said, "We'll look around a bit, if you don't mind."

They realized quickly that anything of importance had been taken from the room by the Guards. "What are the other two rooms?" asked Jazhara.

Abigail said, "Those are the journeymen's quarters."

"And Kendaric's room is which one?" asked James.

"The next over," replied the old woman.

James returned to the hallway and opened the neighboring door. Instantly he dropped to the floor, narrowly avoiding a searing blast of heat that shot through the doorway. Behind him, Jazhara did likewise, although James couldn't tell if she had managed to evade the flames. He didn't have time to check, as the magician who had thrown the blast of fire at him stepped aside to allow a warrior in black to charge at the spot where James lay.

The Izmali lifted his sword and sent it plunging down toward James's head.

SEVEN

Conspiracy

James rolled to his right.

The Izmali's sword came crashing down where James's head had been a moment earlier, and the assassin raised it to strike again, with incredible speed.

James had no time to draw his own sword, so he kicked out with as much strength as he could muster. His action was rewarded by the sound of a kneecap breaking and a muffled cry of pain from the black-clad murderer. The Izmali stumbled, but did not fall.

James rolled again as the warrior fell, and came to his feet with his sword drawn in a single fluid motion.

Jazhara unleashed a spell, but the scintillating ball of red energy shot off to one side and struck the floor near the enemy magician. Despite being missed, the magician appeared alarmed to discover he faced another magic-user. He turned and fled, jumping through the open window to the street below.

Jazhara turned her attention to the assassin as James closed on the man. She raised her staff above her shoulder, the butt end aimed at the man, ready to attack high if James retreated. James lashed out with his blade, a move designed to force his opponent to retreat and put weight on his injured leg. The man was an experienced swordsman, and he shifted his weight to risk a dangerous near-miss by James's blade rather than strain the injured knee. He quickly returned with a quick inside thrust that almost removed James's head.

As James retreated, Jazhara thrust her staff forward and forced the assassin further into the room. Wisely, he took up a stance just inside the door, so that James and Jazhara would be forced to attack him one at a time. Without taking his eyes from the assassin, James said, "Jazhara! Get downstairs and see if you can find any hint of his magician friend. I'll take care of this murderous swine."

Jazhara didn't debate the order, but turned and hurried down the stairs. From below came shouts of inquiry about the sounds of struggle that could be heard.

James appraised the situation. Neither he nor the assassin was going through that door willingly. Whoever advanced was certain to be attacked the instant he stood in the portal, the frame of the door jamb limiting his choices of response. The attack was almost certain to require moving sideways. They were locked in a stalemate.

Then James stepped back, lowering his sword point, as if inviting attack.

The Izmali stood ready, his blade point circling warily, refusing to take the invitation.

James said, "Help will soon be on the way. I doubt you'll try jumping through the window with that broken kneecap." He glanced down at the injured leg. "I admire your strength. Most men would be lying on the floor, screaming in pain."

The assassin took a tiny step – not more than two inches – closer.

James continued to speak. "I've met a great many of you Nighthawks over the years. The first one I killed was trying to assassinate the Prince, many years ago. I was but a lad, then. Threw him from the rooftop."

Another inch forward.

James let his sword point touch the floor and took a deep breath, as if relaxing. "Nothing compared to that bunch down in the desert. I doubt you've heard, since you were probably up here. I mean, had you been down there, you'd be dead like the rest of them, correct?"

And another inch.

"I still don't see why your brotherhood has allowed itself to be manipulated by a bunch of religious zealots. All it's done is get most of your clan killed. The Crawler can't have that much control over the Nighthawks, can he?"

The assassin tensed.

James paused, and let his weight fall a little toward his sword, as if he were leaning on it. "Funny to find you here, really. I thought I'd left the last of your kind rotting in the sun, waiting for the buzzards."

The Izmali tensed as the shouts from outside heralded the arrival of some city guards. Then he raised his sword and lashed out at James; but James was moving the instant he saw the assassin's sword come up.

As James had hoped, the assassin had been so distracted by James's banter, he had failed to notice James's slight movement toward the door. The tip of his scimitar struck the lintel overhead and was deflected, just as James fell toward the swordsman while bringing his own blade upward. The man's weakened knee betrayed him and he stumbled, half-falling onto James's outstretched sword point.

James threw his weight behind the lunge and the assassin stiffened as the rapier rammed home. James recovered and pulled back his blade as the Izmali slumped to the ground.

Jazhara and a pair of city guardsmen reached the hallway a moment later. "The magician escaped," said the Keshian noblewoman. "These guardsmen were at the gate and I called them to come help."

Looking down at the dead assassin, one of the guardsmen said, "Looks like you weren't needin' much help there, Squire."

James knelt and examined the dead assassin. "Hello, what have we here?" he said, withdrawing a small parchment from the man's tunic. "Usually these lads carry nothing." He glanced at it, then handed it to Jazhara. "Can you read this script?"

She scrutinized it. "Yes, it's similar to the desert script used in the message to Yusuf. *Retrieve the scroll, eliminate the witness in the alley, then return to the dog.* There is no signature, nor is there a seal."

"Witness in the alley?" asked the senior guard. "That'd have to be Old Thom. He's an old sailor without a home."

"He's got a couple of crates in the alley back of this building he calls home," added the other guardsman.

James said, "Jazhara, let's see what these lads were looking for." Then he addressed the guards. "One of you stand by." He motioned to Jazhara to follow him into the room.

They looked around and nothing appeared out of the ordinary. James shrugged. "I was a little too busy to notice where those cutthroats were standing when we opened the door."

"They were in front of this desk, James," Jazhara said.

James inspected the desk, which at first glance seemed ordinary enough.

"What do you think 'return to the dog' means?" Jazhara asked.

James continued his inspection. "Probably some sort of code for a person or place." Something caught his eye and he pulled out a drawer. With a practiced eye he measured the depth of the drawer, then said, "There's a compartment behind this drawer or my name wasn't Jimmy the Hand." He knelt down and reached back. There was a click of a small latch, and a tiny door fell open, revealing a small red velvet pouch that he extracted.

He weighed it in his hand. "It's heavy. Feels like stone." Deftly, he untied the silk cord that secured the pouch and turned it over, allowing the object to fall into his other hand.

A stone of shimmering green and white, carved to look like a nautilus shell, rested in his palm.

"This is a Shell of Eortis!" Jazhara exclaimed.

"What is that?" asked James. "I met some adherents of that god when I visited Silden a while back, but I know little of their beliefs."

"I've seen one such artifact at Stardock." Jazhara held her hand over the object and closed her eyes, muttering a brief enchantment. Then she opened her eyes wide. "It is genuine! It is an old and rare item that aids water-magic. You'd have to know someone like the Masters of Stardock or the High Priest of the Temple of Eortis the Sea God to even hear of one. To possess one . . . this must be part of the secret of the Wreckers' Guild."

"But why wasn't this in the possession of the Guild Master?" James mused aloud. "Is this more proof that Kendaric had a hand in the death of the Guild Master, or did the master give it to his favorite student for safekeeping?"

"And why were the Nighthawks looking for it?" pondered Jazhara.

"Could you use this to raise a ship?" asked James.

"No, but you could use it to make the weather favorable for such an undertaking, had you the right spells to employ."

"Do you think this is what they sought?"

Jazhara thought for a moment, then said, "As it will not raise a ship, probably not."

"Then let us continue to look." He examined the other side of the desk and found another false drawer, this time one that was discovered by reaching up inside the desk from underneath.

"Very clever," James said, as he removed what appeared to be a box. "But not clever enough."

The box was roughly a foot wide, half as deep, and three inches thick. There was no apparent lock or latch, and the top was inlaid with a mosaic of stones. James tried the simple approach and thumbed back the lid. It lifted without difficulty, but the box was empty. "Nothing," he said.

Jazhara said, "No, there is something. Close the lid and open it again."

James complied and Jazhara said, "It's a Scathian Puzzle. It's a lock."

"To what? The box is empty. And the sides are too thin to contain another secret compartment."

"It's an enchantment. Its nature is to camouflage whatever is inside until it is unlocked."

"Can you unlock it?"

"I can try." Jazhara took the box and closed the lid, then set it down upon the desk.

She studied the mosaic on top of the box, then put her finger upon a tile. Its color changed from red to green to blue, and for a brief instant James thought he saw a blurred image wavering upon the tile's surface. Jazhara repeated the gesture quickly, touching a neighboring tile; again, the tile's colors mutated, and another image appeared on the tile.

Working deftly she moved the tiles around, for they slid where she directed. James was fascinated, for disarming traps and locks had been a career necessity in his days as a thief, but he had never encountered one quite like this. After a while, his eyes widened, for he realized that the tiles would fade back to their original pattern if she hesitated too long in moving one. And the closer she got to the end of the puzzle, the quicker they faded.

Jazhara's fingers were flying now, rapidly moving the tiles until at last a picture of a ship at sea was formed. Then there was an almost inaudible click, and up came the lid.

The box was no longer empty. Lying flat within the box was a single parchment. James reached in and retrieved the document. He glanced at it, and said, "Nothing I can read."

Jazhara took the parchment and studied it. "I believe *this* is the spell they use to raise the ships."

"How does it work?"

Jazhara scrutinized it even more closely. Then she whispered, "Incredible." In her normal speaking voice she added, "With this scroll and some other components, a single guildsman can raise a ship on a mystic fog!"

"What's so amazing about that?"

"Guilds like the Wreckers, who practice limited magic, usually possess only a few minor spells that are passed from generation to generation, and it usually requires several guildsmen to accomplish anything. Whoever wrote this knows a lot more about magic than the rest of the Guild." She paused, then added, "I'll wager this Kendaric never realized he was a Lesser Path Magician!"

"Then this spell must be worth a fortune to the Guild."

"Undoubtedly," said Jazhara. "Any Lesser Path Magician with an affinity for water-magic could eventually utilize it. I suspect Kendaric is the only one who can use it as written."

"Then we must find Kendaric." Pointing to the scroll, he said, "Hide that." He turned and left the room. Jazhara secreted the parchment within a compartment in the pouch at her waist, and followed James a moment later.

Glancing down at the dead Nighthawk, James said to the guard, "Keep an eye on this corpse, and if it starts to move, call me." To Jazhara he said, "Let's investigate the alley."

As they sped down the stairs, Jazhara said, "If it starts to *move?*"

With a rueful smile James glanced back over his shoulder and said, "The Nighthawks used to have an irritating habit of not staying dead."

He led her outside the building and around to the back, where, behind the building, they found a long, dark, twisting alley. While still early in the day, the gloom of the place provided a dozen shadows in which anything could hide. Reflexively, James drew his rapier. Jazhara clutched her staff and made herself ready as well.

They moved through the alley until they reached a position below the open window through which the magician had leapt. James pointed. "He must have landed here, and then run" – he glanced in both directions – "that way." He indicated the way they had just come. "I'm almost certain the other end is blocked."

"If he reached the street and simply started walking he

would just be another citizen out on his morning's business."

James nodded. "It's why I love cities and hate being alone in the wilderness. So many more places to hide in a city."

Glancing into the darkness as they continued, Jazhara said, "I know many of my countrymen would disagree; they find hiding in the desert easy."

"You may have noticed I'm not a desert man," James observed.

They came to a pile of boxes, and James pushed one aside. The stench that arose from it caused Jazhara to step back. Inside were a dirty blanket, some rotting food and a few personal items – a woolen cap, a broken comb, and a dirty tunic. "Nobody home," said James. He glanced around. "Old Thom must be out begging or thieving. We won't find anybody here until after dark."

"I find it hard to believe that people actually sleep like that."

"It's not hard once you get used to it. The trick is to use the trash to keep the guards away." He looked around the alley once more. "Let's go."

"Where?"

"Back to the palace. Let's get some rest, then after sundown we'll come back and have a chat with Thom. I think he's seen something that someone else doesn't want him talking about, and if we can find out what that is, we might make some sense out of all this."

"It's obvious someone doesn't want us raising that ship."

"Yes," said James. "And while William is chasing Bear around the wilderness, there's someone else arranging for the murder of Guild Masters and beggars."

"The Crawler?" asked Jazhara.

James said, "That's my guess. Come on, let's return to the palace and get some rest." They walked quickly out of the darkness into the daylight of the busy street.

William signaled for his patrol to halt, while a lone rider hurried down the trail toward him. They were less than an hour out of the city and following marks left by a pair of Royal Pathfinders. The rider reined in and saluted. It was Maric, one of the Pathfinders. "Lieutenant."

"What have you found?" William asked.

"A half-dozen men left the city on foot through the fields to the northeast of the North Gate. They took no pains to hide their passage. One of them was a big man, a heavy man, probably the one called Bear. His prints are wide and deep. At the edge of the fields they had horses waiting for them and rode hard up that trail. Jackson is following them. He'll leave signs."

William signaled for the men to ride on. Maric fell in beside the lieutenant. The Pathfinders were legendary, men who were descended from the first foresters and wardens of the earliest Princes of Krondor. They knew the surrounding wilderness as a mother knows the features of her children and they tended to be an insular lot who only grudgingly took command from officers outside their company. Their own captain was rarely seen in the palace, save by the Prince's orders, and they didn't socialize with the garrison's regulars. But they were among the finest trackers in the West and no man in the Armies of the West doubted their skills.

After a few moments of silence, William asked, "What else?"

"What do you mean, Lieutenant?" replied the Pathfinder.

"What is it you're not telling me?"

The Pathfinder glanced at the young officer and gave him a small smile and a nod. "These men take no pains to hide their passage. They are not afraid of being found. They hurry for another reason."

"They need to get somewhere fast," William observed.

"Or need to meet someone," suggested Maric.

"Ambush?" asked William.

"Possibly," replied the Pathfinder. "If they appear to be anxious to get down the trail, then suddenly turn . . ." He shrugged.

"Jackson would warn us."

Without emotion, Maric said, "If he's alive."

They rode on in silence.

If the alley had been gloomy in the daytime, it was inky at night. James uncovered a lantern he had secured at the palace.

After sleeping through the late morning and early afternoon, James and Jazhara had dined with the Prince and his family. It had been Jazhara's first dinner with the royal family, a privilege of her new position, and she had enjoyed the opportunity to meet and chat with Princess Anita, the Princess Elena, and the twin princes, Borric and Erland. James had apprised the Prince of their progress thus far, and Arutha had approved of James's investigation of the missing journeyman, Kendaric.

Once again dressed in her practical travel garb, Jazhara walked a step behind James as they traversed the dark alley. As they neared the crates, James signaled for silence and Jazhara touched him on the shoulder to indicate that she understood.

As they approached the crates, they heard a voice shout out, "No! No! Old Thom didn't tell a soul!"

"Thom, I'm not going to hurt you," James called out. He turned the lantern on the crate and the light revealed an old man, dressed in rags, huddling inside. His nose was misshapen and red, from repeated breaks in his youth and hard drinking in his later years. His front teeth were missing, and what little hair remained was almost white, spreading around his head like a faint nimbus.

Red-shot, watery blue eyes regarded them as he said, "You're not here to hurt old Thom?"

"No," said James, kneeling and putting up the light so that his own face would be revealed. "I'm not here to hurt you. Just to ask some questions . . ."

"Ah, a Prince's man, are you?" said the old beggar. "Fate is kind. I thought it was them murderers come back to finish Old Thom."

"Why would they want to finish you?" asked Jazhara, coming up behind James.

Thom glanced at Jazhara, then answered. "I 'spect it's 'cause I was here the other night when they broke into the Guild House."

"When was that?" asked James.

"The night the Guild Master died. A pair of 'em, all in dark cloaks, climbed right up the wall and into his room, they did."

"Nighthawks," James said. "They were going to come back, Thom, but we got to them before they could find you."

"You're a good lad, then. My thanks to ya."

"You're welcome," said James with a smile. "Did you see anything else?"

"Well, before them dark cloaks went inside, they was talkin' to somebody down the street a ways."

"Did you see who?" asked Jazhara.

"Old Thom couldn't rightly see, 'cept he was wearing Guild colors."

James said, "He had a torque?"

"Yes, that colored thing some of 'em wear around their neck."

"Could it have been Kendaric?" asked Jazhara.

Old Thom said, "Aye, the fella what was always arguin' with the old Guild Master? I seen him the night of the killin', I did. He left the Guild House early that night; never did come back."

"Could it have been Kendaric who was with the Night-hawks?" asked James.

"Coulda been," replied Old Thom. "Or maybe not. He wasn't wearin' colors when he left."

James sat back on his heels. "There are only two other men who would wear colors: the master and Jorath. The Guild is closed for the night, but tomorrow we will return to visit Journeyman Jorath."

James fished in his pouch and came up with two gold coins. He handed them to Old Thom and said, "Get yourself a decent meal and a warm blanket, my old friend."

"Thanks, son," said the old fisherman. "Old Thom thanks you."

James and Jazhara left the old man in his crate and returned to the city streets.

Morning found James and Jazhara once again at the Wreckers' Guild office, but this time they entered to a much quieter scene than they had the previous day. When they came in they found Jorath in the main office, reading documents. Looking up, he said, "Again?"

"We have a few more questions, Journeyman," said James.

"Very well."

"We have uncovered a few things, but obviously this case will not be put to rest until we've located Journeyman Kendaric. What can you tell us about him?"

Jorath said, "He was the oldest journeyman in the Guild, the only one senior to myself. There are two others, both out of the city at present. Kendaric was a man of unusual talents, and had the potential to be prime among us, perhaps even the next Guild Master. Unfortunately he was also greedy and arrogant, probably because of his half-Keshian ancestry."

Jazhara kept a straight face, but James saw her knuckles turn white as she tightened the grip on her staff.

James asked calmly, "Do you really think his ancestry matters?"

"Without a doubt," replied Jorath. "He's always been arrogant, but ever since he had to give up his engagement to a Kingdom girl, he's had it in for us. Her parents didn't want a Keshian marrying their daughter, and who can blame them?"

Jazhara said, "I take offense at your obvious prejudice toward Keshians, Guildsman."

Jorath inclined his head slightly. "Lady, I am no bigot, but as a scholar of some skill, I can tell you that Keshians, and half-breeds in particular, are generally unable to control their emotions."

Jazhara leaned forward and with an icy smile said, "As the newly-appointed court magician of Krondor, and as a great-niece of Abdur Rachman Memo Hazara-Khan, Ambassador of Great Kesh to the Prince's court, I can tell you that you are gravely mistaken. Were I not able to control my emotions, you would now be a slithering worm."

The blood drained from Jorath's face and he stammered, "I apologize most sincerely, milady. Please forgive me."

Hiding his amusement, James said, "Tell us about this woman Kendaric was engaged to."

Jorath appeared glad to change the subject. "A local shopkeeper, if I remember. I don't know the girl's name."

James looked hard at the journeyman, and said, "Thank you. If we have more questions, we'll return."

As they left the office, James glanced up the stairs. He motioned for Jazhara to be quiet and they crept up the stairway. At the top of the stairs, James indicated the third door: Jorath's room.

"What are you doing?" Jazhara asked.

"Our friend downstairs is a little too sanguine about all that's gone on. He's hiding something."

"I agree. Given that his world seems to have been turned upside down, he seems almost . . . relieved."

James deftly picked the lock of the room and they entered. The chamber was neat, with nothing obviously misplaced. "Tidy fellow, our Journeyman Jorath, isn't he?" James observed.

"Indeed."

James went to the desk while Jazhara investigated the contents of a chest at the foot of the journeyman's bed. In the desk, James found some documents and a ledger. He took them out and had started reading them when Jazhara exclaimed, "Look!"

James glanced over. Jazhara was holding up a ledger identical to the one James had in his lap. "This was hidden under some clothing."

James took the second ledger and put it beside the first. After a few moments, he said, "Well, there it is. Our friend Jorath has been embezzling funds from the Guild. With the Guild Master dead, no one would inspect the records."

"And if he could find Kendaric's spell-scroll, he could restart the Guild with himself installed as master, with a clean record," said the magician.

James nodded. He continued his reading, tossing aside scroll after scroll, then he stopped. "Look at what we have here," he whispered. He handed the parchment to Jazhara.

She read aloud. "Guildsman. You've made the right decision in coming to us with your plans. We've received the gold you promised. Show the bartender this letter and you'll find him very cooperative. My people, who will be waiting for you at the dog, will deal with final details and future payments. Orin."

"At the dog." James said.

"A place?"

James put the other scrolls away. "Yes, Ye Bitten Dog."

Jazhara said, "Ah, of course. The bartender. Lucky Pete."

"Things are now starting to come together," said James, taking the two ledgers and the scrolls. "I think we need to have another chat with Journeyman Jorath." He wrapped the ledgers and scroll in a tunic he pulled from the chest.

They hurried down the stairs and entered the office, where Jorath was still reviewing documents. "Yes?" he said looking up. "Again?"

James said, "You know who killed the Guild Master."

Jorath stood up slowly, and arranged the scrolls on the desk in an orderly fashion. "Amazing. I would have credited the Prince's servants with far more intelligence than you're currently evidencing."

Jazhara said, "We know you've been dealing with the Nighthawks."

Jorath seemed untroubled by the accusation. "Even had I the inclination to consort with criminals, who I meet with outside the Guild is my own business, unless you can prove I conspired in a crime.

"Besides, my entire life is wrapped up in this Guild. Why would I choose to jeopardize it all by killing the Guild Master?"

James unwrapped the ledgers and the scroll and said, "To prevent being caught out as an embezzler."

Jazhara added, "And there was Kendaric's new spell. With him out of the way, you could claim it as your own."

"If you could have found it," James went on. "Obviously, you needed the Nighthawks for both tasks."

"An interesting theory," said Jorath, slowly backing away. "Well thought out and complete. Tell me, if you had not interfered, do you think I could have gotten away with it?"

Before James or Jazhara could answer, the Guildsman pulled an item from the sleeve of his robe and cast it into the air. A brilliant light erupted and James found himself momentarily blinded. Reflexes took over and he instantly stepped back, knowing that he was likely to be attacked while he couldn't see.

He felt the blade just miss him as he blinked furiously, while drawing his own sword. Again he stepped back, and without hesitation lashed out, a move designed to keep Jorath back or, with luck, land a blow.

He heard the journeyman retreat and James knew he had almost succeeded in hitting him. James had fought in the darkness more times than he cared to remember, and he closed his eyes, knowing that darkness would be less distracting than the blurred images and lights that danced before his eyes.

He sensed that Jazhara had moved away from him, her own protective reflexes taking her away from possible danger. James threw a wild high blow and felt the shock run up his arm as Jorath's sword blocked his.

Without hesitation, James slid his blade down Jorath's, moving forward rather than retreating. James hoped that the guildsman was not a practiced swordsman, for if he was, James was almost certain to be wounded.

As he had hoped, James heard a startled exclamation from the guildsman as James threw his weight forward, reaching out with his free left hand to grip Jorath's right wrist. He slammed upward with his own sword, and with a satisfying crack felt the hilt of his sword smack into the man's chin.

Jorath slumped to the floor as James blinked away tears. His vision was slowly returning, enough to see that the journeyman was now lying unconscious on the floor. Jazhara was also blinking furiously, trying to clear her own eyesight.

"It's all right," said James. "He's out."

"What'll happen to him?" asked Jazhara.

"Arutha will almost certainly hang him, but he'll be questioned first."

"Do you think he's involved in the search for the Tear?"

James shook his head slowly. A Guild apprentice appeared at the door and looked down at the fallen journeyman. His eyes widened in alarm. James shouted, "Get the city watch, boy!"

The youngster hurried off.

James looked at Jazhara and said, "I think he was merely a convenience for the Nighthawks and the Crawler." Shaking his head at how little he knew, James added, "Or whoever else is behind all this madness." He sighed. "I think the Nighthawks and whoever is employing them wanted to ensure no one could raise that ship but themselves. If I'm to guess, there's someone up in Ylith who's arranging for a team from their Wreckers' Guild to head down to Widow's Point – or there will be soon." Pointing to the belt pouch in which Jazhara had Kendaric's scroll, James added, "Finding that scroll would simply have made things easier for the Nighthawks. They would have promised Jorath whatever he wanted, gotten him to raise the ship, then killed him." Glancing down at the unconscious journeyman, James shook his head in disgust. "Either way, he ends up a dead man. What a waste."

"So what now?" asked Jazhara.

"We visit Lucky Pete and see if we can uncover this last nest of the Nighthawks and stamp them out. Then we find Kendaric. I think it's safe to say he's no longer a suspect."

"How do we find him?"

"We look for the woman he was engaged to; perhaps she will know somewhere to start the search."

"Jorath said he didn't recall who she was."

James grinned. "Maybe the journeyman didn't, but I bet someone around here remembers. Probably old Abigail knows. Gossip like that doesn't say hidden long."

Jazhara said, "I'll go ask her."

James nodded. "I'll wait for the city watch."

A few minutes later Jazhara returned just as two city watchmen arrived with the apprentice. James instructed them to take Jorath to the palace and told them what to say to Duke Gardan. The watchmen saluted and carried off the still-unconscious guildsman.

After they left, James asked, "Did you get a name?"

Jazhara nodded. "Her name is Morraine. She runs a shop called The Golden Grimoire."

James nodded. "Just your kind of place. An apothecary shop with a bit of magic for sale, according to rumor. It's in the nicer part of town." He glanced around and said, "We're finished here."

"Where to first?" asked Jazhara as they strode toward the door.

"First, to the palace to collect a half-dozen or so of the duke's best swordsmen. Then back to Ye Bitten Dog."

"You expect trouble?" asked Jazhara.

James laughed. "Always."

EIGHT

Kendaric

J ames signaled.

The squire and Jazhara surveyed their surroundings as they walked toward Ye Bitten Dog. Six of the Prince's Royal Household Guard waited at the intersection of the two streets nearest the entrance of the inn, hiding in the shadows as night fell upon the city. In addition, a young constable, Jonathan Means, was positioned across the street. He was the son of the former sheriff, Wilfred Means, and despite no direct order from the Prince, he was acting in his father's stead. James had also recruited him as one of his first confidential agents in what he hoped one day would be the Kingdom's intelligence corps. Young Means would wait fifteen minutes, then enter the inn. Alternately, at any sign of trouble, he would signal to the squad of soldiers and they would rush the building.

James and Jazhara wanted to see what sort of information they might weasel out of Lucky Pete before resorting to threats. And if there were Nighthawks in residence, it would be useful to have a riot squad close at hand.

James pushed open the door. Inside, the night's revelries were starting to pick up, as whores and dockworkers on their way home from a day's labor lined up three deep at the tables to carouse.

Glancing around, James realized they had caught the attention of a worker near the door who was looking at James and Jazhara's fine clothing. "What have we here?" he said loudly.

His companion turned. "Looks like a court boot-lick and his Keshian pet, to me."

Without bothering to look at the man, Jazhara said, "Careful, my friend. This pet has claws."

The man so addressed blinked in confusion, but his friend exploded into laughter.

"That's enough," James said. "We seek no trouble." He took Jazhara's elbow and guided her through to the bar at the rear of the room, where the owner was filling tankards and handing them to a bar-boy to carry to the tables.

As they approached, Lucky Pete looked up. "What do you want now?"

James said, "Just some information, Pete."

The boy took the flagons and hurried off, and Pete wiped up a puddle of spilled ale with a filthy bar rag. "It'll cost ya. Like always."

"Did you hear about the troubles at the Wreckers' Guild?"
Pete shrugged. "Maybe."

James slid a coin across the rough-hewn planks of the bar.
"Okay, I heard something."

James slid another coin, and Pete remained silent. After a moment, James slid a third coin across the bar, and Pete said, "Seems some journeyman couldn't wait for the old master to die so he could replace him and hurried the old fellow off to Lims-Kragma's Hall. Fellow named Kendaric."

"So we've heard," replied James. "Any idea where we might find this Kendaric?"

Pete said, "This answer's for free: No."

James considered for a moment whether Pete might be lying, but rejected the notion, given Pete's appetite for gold. If he were to lie, it would be to get more gold, not less. James glanced at Jazhara and she gave him a slight nod, indicating that she, too, thought this avenue of questioning was a dead end.

James lowered his voice. "I could also use some information on obtaining some 'special' services." He slid another coin across the bar.

"What sort of 'special' services?" asked Pete, sweeping it up.

"I need the skills of some men with . . . muscle."

Pete shrugged. "Bashers are a copper a dozen in Krondor. Find 'em at the docks, the markets . . ." He narrowed his gaze. "Of course you know that already, don't you?"

James slid yet another coin across the bar. "I had heard this was the place to get in touch with a special breed of nocturnal birds."

Pete didn't touch the coin. "Why would you want to talk to these 'birds'?"

"We want to offer them a well-paying job."

Pete was silent for a moment, then picked up the coin. "You've got balls, boy, but have you the cash to back 'em up?"

James nodded. "More gold than you've ever seen, if you've got what I want." He placed another coin on the bar, then quickly put four more carefully atop it, to make a small, neat stack.

Pete swept up the coins. "First payment, only, Squire." He grinned, displaying discolored teeth. "Aye, lad, you've come to the right place. Go 'round back, if you would. There's some gentlemen in the rear room you ought to speak to." He tossed

James a key, then gestured with his hand toward a door behind the bar. "You'll be needin' this, lad."

James caught the key and started toward the indicated door. He unlocked the door and glanced over his shoulder at Jazhara, who looked ready for trouble. James estimated they now had about ten minutes before Jonathan Means entered the inn. James's instructions had been clear; if he and Jazhara were not in sight, Jonathan was to bring the squad.

James and Jazhara entered a corridor as the door to the barroom clicked shut behind them. Three more doors lined the hallway before them. A door on the immediate left revealed a pantry, and James spared it only a cursory glance. The first door on the right, once opened, revealed a miserable-looking bedroom, filthy and strewn with clothing and remnants of food. James whispered, "Must be Pete's room." He looked back over his shoulder at the door that led back into the common room and added, "Can you do something dramatic with that door, something loud enough to bring young Means and the guards in a hurry?"

With a slight smile, Jazhara nodded. "I have just the thing if I'm not otherwise distracted."

"Good," James said, opening the last door. They entered a small room, furnished only with a single table, behind which sat two men. The one closest to James, on the right, was a bearded man with dark hair and eyes. The other was clean-shaven and blond, with his hair falling to the collar of his jacket. Both wore black tunics and trousers. Each had a blade at his hip, and wore a heavy black gauntlet.

Both men looked up at James and one said, "Yes?"

"Pete said we could find someone here who might provide us with a solution for a particularly bothersome problem."

Both men moved back in their chairs, a seemingly casual move, but one that James knew gave each of them a better chance to stand and draw his sword. "What do you want?" the second man asked.

James produced the letter he had found in Jorath's room. "We know about your arrangement with the Wreckers' Guild. For a small price, we'll make sure no one else does."

The two men glanced at each other, then the blond man spoke. "If you're looking to line your pockets with gold, you should be warned that you are dealing with the Guild of Death. Those who try to blackmail us tend not to live as long and comfortably as they otherwise might. Unless, that is, you're offering some other sort of arrangement?"

James smiled. "That's exactly what I was thinking. Here's my idea – " Leaping forward, James suddenly overturned the table onto the blond-haired man, at the same time kicking out with his boot to shove the chair out from under the bearded man. "Jazhara! Now!"

Jazhara turned and pointed her staff toward the far door and uttered a few syllables. A bolt of white energy exploded from the staff, fired down the short hallway, and blew the door off its hinges with a deafening sound.

James had his sword in hand. He grinned. "That should bring them running." The first swordsman was scrambling backward, away from James's blade, while awkwardly trying to draw his own. The blond man used the overturned table as a barrier, so that he could retreat an extra couple of feet to the wall, gaining space to pull out his sword.

James had to leap away to avoid a lunge from the blond man, aimed at James's left side. Jazhara struck down with her staff at the swordsman's arm, striking his wrist with a numbing blow.

The blond man yowled in pain as he dropped his sword. As he attempted to pull his dagger out with his other hand, Jazhara struck him on the temple with the iron-shod butt of her staff. The man dropped to the floor.

James heard shouts and confusion from the front of the building, and knew that Jonathan Means and the guards were now in the common room. Unless there were other Nighthawks there, the dockworkers and other laborers would be unlikely to challenge armed guardsmen.

James lashed out with his sword, slicing the hand of the bearded man on the floor, who was still struggling to pull out his sword. It had the desired effect, for the man let go of the hilt. James touched the tip of his sword to the man's throat. "I advise you not to move if you want to keep breathing."

Jazhara turned toward the door, readying herself in case whoever came through it first wasn't friendly.

The bearded man shifted his weight slightly and James pressed the blade into the man's skin until he cried, "Ah ah!" Deftly, James flipped the man's collar aside with the sword's point, and slipped it under a chain around the man's neck. Then, with a flick, he drew the chain over the man's head. An amulet slid down the blade.

As the point rose in the air, the bearded man made a frantic grab for his own sword. Without taking his eyes off the amulet, James kicked with his left boot, taking the man on the chin and knocking him unconscious.

At this point, Jonathan Means broke through the door at the end of the hall, followed by two of the Prince's Household Guard. They were frog-marching Lucky Pete between them, his peg leg slamming against the floor in a most comic fashion.

Jonathan said, "Most of the lads in there started clearing out when Jazhara blew the door off the hinges." He smiled at her and said, "I assume it was you and not some other magician, milady?"

She nodded and returned the young man's smile.

The acting sheriff continued. "Most of the rest of them fled when they saw the seven of us rush in. That one" – he pointed at Pete – "and a couple of others tried to fight, but we had them under control in a few minutes." He glanced at the two unconscious figures on the floor. "What have we here?"

James turned his sword to Means and let the amulet slip off the blade. "False Nighthawks. Part of that band sent into the sewers to cast blame on the true Guild of Death a few months back if I don't miss my guess."

"How do you know them to be false?" asked Jazhara.

"No poison rings, and they didn't try to take their own lives," answered James. "The Nighthawks are fanatics about not being taken alive." He sheathed his sword.

"What is the significance of these being false?" asked Jonathan.

James said, "That remains to be discovered when we question these two. I suggest you get them to the palace dungeon and hold them for questioning. With the Old Market Jail gone, it's either the palace or the jail at the docks."

Means nodded. "The palace it is, Squire."

Means called for help and another four guards came in to carry the unconscious "Nighthawks" away. James turned to Lucky Pete and said, "Now, it's time for us to have a talk."

Pete tried to smile, but his face was an exercise in panic. "Now, Squire, I don't know nothin', really. I just rented some rooms and the basement to these lads."

James's gaze narrowed. "The basement?"

"Yes, through that trapdoor there and down the stairs," he said, pointing to a spot on the hallway floor.

"Damn," said James, pulling his sword out once more. To Means he said, "Leave a man here with Pete and follow me."

James pulled up the trapdoor and scrambled through it without waiting to see who was behind him. He ran down the stone stairs, which led down to a small landing halfway down, then doubled back to the basement floor below. From above, Jazhara said, "James! There is something very wrong here!"

Turning to look up at her, James said, "I feel it, too."

Energy crackled in the air which indicated that magic was being gathered nearby, and James's experience told him it wasn't anything good. The hair on his arms and neck rose as he reached the bottom steps and confronted a door. He waited until he knew that Jazhara, Means, and another guard were behind him, then said, "Ready!"

He kicked open the door and found himself in a large room carved out of the soil beneath the tavern. Near the middle of the room stood three men, two dressed in the same way as the two men upstairs, in black tunics and trousers, black gloves and with swords at their side. The third man wore robes and James recognized him as the magician they had seen at the Wreckers' Guild.

But what drew James up short and made him gasp was the figure forming in the center of the room, inside a complex design drawn on the floor in a white substance. "A demon!" he shouted. The creature was coalescing into solid form, substantial from head to waist. Its head was misshapen, with two curving horns that arched down and forward from its brow. Glowing red eyes regarded the intruders and it bellowed like a bull, its massive shoulders flexing as it attempted to reach out to them.

The enemy magician cried out, "Hold them! We are almost done!"

The two black-clad swordsmen drew their weapons and charged the short distance that separated James from the demon. Jazhara attempted to cast a spell, but had to break her concentration in order to avoid being struck by one of the two men.

James parried the other attacker as Jonathan Means and a guardsman burst into the room.

"Gods!" shouted Means. "What is that thing?"

"Kill the magician!" James cried.

The guardsman didn't hesitate. Rather than risk approaching the magician and coming within reach of a demon that was almost completely solid, the soldier pulled a dagger from his belt and with a powerful throw sent the blade spinning toward the magician.

The dagger struck the magician in the heart, knocking him backward as the demon gained solid form. The demon bellowed in rage and tried to attack, but the lines upon the floor seemed to form a mystic barrier, preventing him from reaching James and the others.

James saw Means rush to Jazhara's side, and concentrated upon his own foe. The man was an expert swordsman and James was conscious of the enraged demon he could see over the man's shoulder. The assassin was also aware of the demon behind him, for he took a moment to glance back before focusing on James. James sought to press his advantage, but the swordsman anticipated it.

James moved to one side, shouting, "Jazhara! Can you do something about that thing?"

Jazhara was attempting to disentangle herself from the

second swordsman, in order to allow the guardsman or Jonathan Means to engage with him, but the room was too crowded to allow an easy transition. "I'm occupied at the moment, James," she called.

Means cried, "Let me past!" and Jazhara instantly drew her staff toward her, holding it upright as she turned and suddenly Means was past her, lunging at the swordsman, who was forced to back away.

Jazhara looked at the demon and said, "I know almost nothing of such creatures, James!"

James beat back a high attack by the assassin he faced and attempted to back him into the demon's reach. "I'm turning into something of a expert, I'm sorry to say," he retorted. "This is the third of these creatures I've run into in my life."

"One thing I do know," Jazhara shouted. "Don't cross into that diagram and don't break the lines."

"Thank you," said James. He thrust out with his blade, managing to nick the assassin in the leg. "I'll keep that in mind," he added as he pulled back.

Jazhara saw the stalemate between her companions and the two assassins, and stopped to catch her breath. She closed her eyes, recalling an incantation, then when she had it firmly in mind, she slowly began to cast her spell. When she was finished, a crimson bolt of energy flew from her outstretched hand and struck the face of the assassin attacking James. The man cried out and dropped his sword. Clawing at his eyes, he screamed in pain and staggered backward.

Too late, he suddenly realized he had backed inside the inscribed design on the floor. He tried to retreat, but the demon seized him. Picking the assassin up from behind like a father might pick up a baby, the twelve-foot-tall demon tossed the man high into the air, literally bouncing him off the dirt and stone ceiling. Then as the assassin fell, the creature slashed with its bull-like horns, impaling him on the points. The man screamed once and died.

James ignored the gore and turned his attention to the second swordsman, reaching over Means's shoulder to slash at the man's throat. A liquid gurgle sounded as the assassin dropped his blade, a stunned look in his eyes as the blood began to flow from his mouth and nose. He made a daubing motion with his left hand at his throat, as if trying to staunch the wound, then he fell forward and expired.

James turned to confront the demon, which had finished tearing apart the assassin who had lain upon its horns. Body parts littered the room and the creature bellowed in rage as it confronted James and his companions.

"What do we do?" asked Jonathan Means, shaking now that he realized the nature of the monster they faced.

"It cannot cross out of that space," said Jazhara, "unless he who summoned it gives leave. But it will remain there for a long time unless we banish it or kill it."

"Those things are hard to kill," said James. "I know."

Jazhara turned to the guardsman. "Send word to the palace. Summon Father Belson and tell him we have a demon to banish."

The guardsman glanced at James, who nodded.

James said, "Let us back out of here and wait for the good father to show up."

Time seemed to drag as they waited for the arrival of Prince Arutha's religious advisor. James stood just the other side of the door, watching the evil creature as it raged and glared at him, full of malevolence. Several times it feigned an attack, but always it pulled up at the mystic barrier.

"What's this nonsense about a demon?" shouted a voice from above.

James turned to see Father Belson appear. The slender, black-bearded cleric arrived in a hurry, minus his usual purple and scarlet robes. Instead he wore a woolen nightshirt over which a heavy cloak had been thrown. "This idiot," he said, pointing back at the guard, "wouldn't even grant me leave to dress – " Then he glanced past James and caught sight of the demon. "Oh, my," he said softly.

"I'll get out of the way and let you go to work, Father," James said.

"Go to work?" Father Belson replied, blinking in confusion. "Work doing what?"

"Getting rid of the demon. That's why we summoned you."

"Get rid of the demon? I can't do that," said the priest of Prandur in horror.

James blinked like an owl caught in a sudden light. "You can't?"

"Demons are creatures of the lower realms, and as such often consume fire energy. My service to the Lord of the Flames prevents me from having any skills with the sorts of magic that can possibly harm the creature." Looking again at the demon, the priest added softly, "Best I can do is irritate him, and at worst make him stronger."

"What about exorcism?" asked Jazhara.

Glancing at the Keshian magician, the priest said, "That's not something my temple does. You'd have to find a priest of Sung, and a powerful one at that, or an Ishapian."

James sighed. He turned to the guard who had originally brought Father Belson and said, "Hurry to the Temple of Ishap and tell the High Priest we request the services of one who can banish a demon – and quickly. Use the Prince's name. Go."

The guardsman saluted. "Squire." He turned and hurried off.

To Father Belson, James said, "Sorry to have awakened you."

Not taking his eyes off the creature, the priest said, "Oh, I wouldn't have missed this for anything."

"Good," said James. "Then keep an eye on the thing just in case, while I go interview a prisoner."

James returned to the upper room. Pete was sitting in a chair with a guard at his side. James said, "Now, before we were so rudely interrupted . . ."

Pete looked close to panic. "I tell you, Squire, I don't know nothin'. Just some lads throwin' gold around for me to know nothin'. So I looks the other way when they want to use the down-below, and the pass-me-through to the sewers. You know how it is."

James nodded. He knew all too well how it was. To the guardsman he said, "Take him to the palace. Lock him in the dungeon, and we'll see what else he knows at our leisure."

The guard grabbed Pete roughly under the arm and said, "Come with me, little man."

The peg-legged former sailor squawked at being man-handled, but went along peacefully.

It took almost an hour for the Ishapians to arrive, a gray-haired priest of some significant rank and two armed warrior monks. Once James acquainted them with the situation below they agreed it had been a wise move to summon them.

They hurried down the steps to the basement and the Ishapian priest said to Father Belson, "You may depart now, Servant of Prandur."

Belson bowed slightly. "As you wish."

As he passed, James said, "You're leaving?"

With a wry smile, the priest said, "I know when I'm not wanted."

James was puzzled. There was a great deal about the politics of the Kingdom that James had come to understand during his tenure at Arutha's court, but the relationships among the temples was a complex knot of intrigues he had scarcely been aware of before then, and one he had had little reason to investigate.

The priest of Ishap turned to James and said, "How did this come to be?"

"That man," James said, pointing at the dead magician lying on the floor near the far wall. "He summoned the creature."

The priest looked across the room, then observed, "If he were alive it would be easier to return the creature to the plane of hell from which it was summoned."

Dryly, Jazhara said, "Unless, of course, he ordered it to attack first."

The priest glanced at the magician, but did not respond to her observation. Turning to James, he said, "So be it. Let us begin."

The two monks came to stand on either side of the Ishapian priest and began a low chant. After a moment, James felt a distinct cooling in the air, and heard the priest's voice rising above the others. The language was tantalizingly familiar, but one he could not understand.

The demon glared from behind the barrier erected by the

mystic symbols on the floor, helpless. From time to time its bovine features would contort and it would bellow a challenge, but finally it was done. James blinked in astonishment as one moment the creature stood there, then an instant later it was gone, the only evidence of its passing a subtle shift in the pressure of the air around them and a slight sound, as if a door closed somewhere nearby.

The priest turned to James. "The Temple is pleased to help the Crown but it would be better for all of us if you returned to the critical task set before you, Squire."

"We were going to leave this morning, sir, but things have proved less convenient that I would have liked. We'll go as soon as possible."

The priest nodded impassively. "Brother Solon will be waiting for you at the gate at dawn tomorrow." He turned and left the room, followed by the two monks.

James sighed. "Arutha won't be pleased if we have to wait much longer."

Jazhara said, "We have but one task left before we can go."

"Find Kendaric," James said. "And I think I know where to start."

The Golden Grimoire was a modest but well-appointed shop. It was an apothecary store of sorts, but Jazhara recognized at once the contents of many jars and boxes to be ingredients a magician might employ. A sleepy looking young woman had let them in only upon James's insistence they were on the Prince's business. "What do you wish?" she asked once they were inside, suspicion in her voice.

James regarded her. This must be Morraine, he thought, the woman to whom Kendaric was engaged. She was slight in build, with a slender face, but pretty in a way. He thought that when fully dressed and awake, she probably looked a great deal more attractive.

James produced the shell and said, "Can you tell us what this is?"

Morraine raised her eyebrows. "Place it there, please." She indicated a green felt cloth upon the counter next to which a lantern burned. James did so and she studied it closely for a bit. "This is a Shell of Eortis, I'm certain. It has powerful magic properties. There are only a few reputed to exist. It is an artifact of incalculable value to a sea captain or anyone else who must voyage across the ocean." She looked at James. "Where did you get it?"

James admired the woman's ability to maintain a calm demeanor. She would be no mean gambler, he thought. "I'm certain you know where we found it, Morraine," he said.

Morraine held his gaze for a moment, then lowered her eyes. She betrayed no surprise at hearing her name. "Kendaric. We were lovers for a while, but my family forbade us to wed. I gave it to him as a gift. It was my dearest possession." Then, almost defiantly, she added, "I haven't seen him for a long time."

James smiled. "You can stop lying. You don't do it well. Kendaric is innocent and we have proof. It was Journeyman Jorath who had the Guild Master killed to mask his embezzlement of Guild funds."

The woman said nothing, but her eyes flickered from face to face. Jazhara said, "You can believe us. I am Jazhara, the Prince's court magician, and this is his personal squire, James. We require Kendaric's presence for a most critical undertaking on behalf of the Crown."

Morraine said softly, "Come with me." She picked up the

lantern from the counter and led them to a far wall, where several volumes rested upon shelves.

Jazhara glanced at the titles and saw that many of them were herbalist guides and primers on making remedies and potions, but that a few dealt with magical issues. "I shall have to return here when time permits," she muttered.

Morraine removed one large volume, and the shelf slid aside, revealing a stairway going up. "This goes to a secret room in the attic," she said.

She led them up the stairs and into a small room, barely able to hold a single bed and table. Upon the bed sat a man in a green tunic. He wore a goatee and mustache and had a golden ring in his left ear. "Who are these people?" he asked Morraine in a concerned tone, staring at James and Jazhara.

"They are from the Prince," said Morraine.

"I didn't do it!" exclaimed Kendaric.

"Calm yourself," said James. "We have proof it was Jorath who had the Guild Master killed."

"What about those men in black?" asked the journeyman of the Wreckers' Guild. "They were trying to kill me! I barely escaped them."

Jazhara noticed a slight hint of a Keshian accent in his speech, from one of the northern cities. "They've been dealt with, as well," she said.

Kendaric sprang to his feet and hugged Morraine. "This is wonderful! I can return to the Guild. Thank you for this news."

Jazhara held her hands up. "A moment, Guildsman," she said. "We have need of your services."

Kendaric said, "Certainly, but perhaps it can wait for a day or so? I have much to do. If Jorath is guilty of murder, I must return to take charge of the apprentices. It will take a while before order is restored to the Wreckers."

James said, "Ah, unfortunately we need your help now. The Prince needs your help. And considering it might have been the Nighthawks that found you first, but didn't because of our efforts, you owe us."

"I didn't ask for your help, did I? I'm must get back to the Guild! All those debts to pay!"

"Kendaric!" Morraine said, sharply.

"Yes, Morraine?" he answered, meekly.

"You are being ungrateful and rude to people who have saved your life."

"But the expenses, my love – "

"We'll work something out. We always have." She turned to James. "He'll help you, Squire. He's a good man at heart, but sometimes he lets his personal desires lead him astray."

"Morraine!"

"I'm sorry, dear, but it's true. That's why you have me to set you straight."

Jazhara said, "You plan to defy your parents, then?"

With a tilt of her chin and a brave smile, Morraine said, "We shall have a wedding as soon as Kendaric has returned from whatever mission you have for him."

Looking defeated, the guildsman said, "Very well."

"Please watch out for him. Kendaric sometimes overreaches himself."

Jazhara smiled. "We'll take care of him."

"Thank you for restoring his good name."

They walked down the steps to the door. James and Jazhara went out into the street and waited as Kendaric bid Morraine good-bye. When the journeyman emerged from the shop,

Jazhara said, "You should count yourself lucky to be so well loved."

Kendaric said, "Luckier than you know. I shudder to remember the bastard I was before I met Morraine. Her kindness saved my life, but her love saved my soul."

James glanced at the starlit sky. "We have three hours to first light. Time enough to get back to the palace, report to the Prince, and meet Brother Solon at the gate."

As they walked toward the palace, James said, "Do you ride?"

"Badly, I fear," said the journeyman.

Laughing, James said, "By the time we reach our destination, you'll be an expert."

NINE

Diversion

William waited patiently.

His horse pawed the ground, anxious to be moving again, or to find something to graze on. Either way William had to keep a firm leg and short reins on the animal.

The day had turned cold and he could see his own breath before him as night fell. The patrol had halted in a small clearing in the woods, large enough for a camp. The men behind him were silent, avoiding the casual small talk and muttering that was common during a standstill in the ranks. They knew the enemy was close.

As evening approached and the gloom of the woods deepened, everyone was on edge. They could almost feel a fight approaching. Swords were loose in their scabbards and bows near to hand as the men kept their eyes moving, watching for any sign of trouble.

Then from ahead two figures appeared on the trail, emerging from the murk. Maric and Jackson rode at a slow canter, and instantly William relaxed. If the enemy were near, they would more likely be coming back at a gallop.

Without waiting for their report, William spun his horse around and said, "We'll camp here."

The sergeant in charge of the patrol, an old veteran named Hartag, nodded and said, "I'll post the sentries first, Lieutenant."

As the sergeant barked his orders, the two Pathfinders reined in. Maric said, "We lost them."

"What?" William swore.

The other Pathfinder, Jackson, an older man with almost no hair remaining above his ears, but with a long flow of gray hair down to his shoulders from what fringe remained, nodded. "They suddenly turned among some rocks and we lost the trail. We'll find it again in the morning, but not in this light."

William could barely hide his frustration. "So they know we are following."

"They know someone follows," said Maric. "But we can't be certain they know who and how many."

"How far ahead?"

"Two, maybe three hours. If they press on later today than we do, it'll be half a day before we find their trail."

William nodded. "Get something to eat and go to sleep early. I'll want you out as soon as you think it's light enough to pick up that trail again."

The two Pathfinders nodded and dismounted.

William rode down the trail for a few yards, as if he might just see something in the distance. The horse demanded fodder, and using his empathic talent for mental communication with animals, William sent him a reassuring message: *Soon.*

He dismounted and rubbed the horse's nose, causing its lip to quiver. He knew the animal liked the touch. All the while, he kept looking into the darkening woodlands, thinking that somewhere out there Bear was waiting. But at last he turned the horse around and headed back to the clearing. He could see fires were already being started and the men had their bedrolls out.

He found a spot close to where his sergeant stood and nodded greeting. William undid his own bedroll and tossed it to the ground, then led his horse to where the picket had been staked out. He unsaddled and removed the bridle, then haltered the beast and tied it to the picket line. Finally, he gave it a nose-bag of oats, then sent a reassuring *Grazing soon* to all the horses. Several snorted and sent back mental images that William could only equate to human sarcasm, as if they were saying: *We've heard* that *before.*

That brought a smile to William's face. A moment later he realized it had been his first smile since Talia's death. He glanced heavenward and silently told her, *Soon you'll be revenged.* As he returned his attention to his men, William wondered how James and the others were faring with their quest.

James was leading his horse. They had dismounted a few minutes earlier to rest the animals, but had kept moving. The journey from Krondor had been uneventful thus far, and James wished to keep it that way. They should reach the village of Miller's Rest in one more day, and Haldon Head another day after.

James had decided to slip out of the city with a small caravan, mixing in with the guards and merchants. At a small fork in the road, he and the others had slipped away onto a path that led to a lesser-used road headed north. They had traveled for a week, avoiding detection as far as they could tell, and James was praying that they would reach a small inn before nightfall.

The inn would be where, if all went according to plan, they'd make contact with one of Prince Arutha's agents in the field, and James hoped to incorporate that man into the network he was establishing. Presently, the man, who went by the name of Alan, was simply a minor court official whose office was that of estate manager for several of the Prince's personal holdings to the north of the Principality. Unofficially, he was a snoop and gossip who often sent important information south to his ruler.

Kendaric and Brother Solon had been silent for most of the journey. James judged the monk of Ishap a quiet man by nature, who rarely volunteered information, preferring to answer questions with simple yes-or-no answers. James had tried to engage the monk in conversation a couple of times, simply to relieve the boredom, and also out of curiosity. Solon had a slightly strange accent, which James found vaguely familiar, but the monk spoke so rarely that James couldn't place it.

Kendaric had just been sullen for most of the way. He had claimed confidence in his ability to raise the ship with the spell Jazhara had found in Kendaric's room, but he objected to the necessity for travel by horseback. He was an unskilled rider and the first few days had caused him a great deal of soreness and discomfort, although by now he was, at last, starting to sit his mount with some grace and his complaints about his aching back and legs had diminished.

Jazhara had been James's most voluble companion, though even she often lapsed into deep, thoughtful silences, occasionally punctuated by a question about their whereabouts; she found the terrain north of Krondor fascinating, the cool woodlands being new and alien territory to a desert-born noblewoman. James continued to be impressed by her intelligence and her interest in everything around her. He had decided that not only did he like her, but that she was a great addition to Arutha's court. And he now understood why she had held such a powerful attraction for William when he had lived at Stardock. James shared little of those feelings, apart from a man's appreciation of a striking woman, but he recognized how another man might easily be smitten.

Finally, Brother Solon said, "Doesn't the road ahead look ripe for surprise?" His obvious concern caused him to utter the longest single sentence James had heard from him since the day they met.

The warrior monk rolled his "r's" and said "fer" in place of "for." James halted and looked over his shoulder. "Now I recognize that speech!" he said. "I've spent enough time with dwarves to know that accent." Glancing upward, above Solon's head, in exaggeration of the man's height, he said, "You're the tallest damn dwarf I've ever encountered, Solon!"

"And you're the dimmest lad ever to serve a prince, if you think I'm a dwarf," responded the monk. "I grew up on a farm near Dorgin, with naught but dwarven lads with whom to play. So, that's the reason for my manner of speech. Now, don't change the subject." He pointed. "Do you ken what I'm sayin' about the road ahead?"

Kendaric said, "A few bushes and a wide spot in the road worry you?"

James shook his head. "He's right. There's someone hiding in the trees ahead."

"And doin' a right poor job of it, too," added Solon.

Jazhara said, "Should we double back?"

The monk handed the reins of his horse to Kendaric and said, "I think not, milady. I'll not skulk along this path like a coward!" He called out. "You who are hidden are now revealed, by my faith. Stand and face the might of Ishap or flee like the craven dogs you are!"

After a moment of silence, a small band of men emerged from concealment. They were dressed in clothes only slightly better than rags, with an oddly mismatching assortment of armor and weapons. Two bowmen stayed behind, while two other men hung to the flanks. The small band moved onto the road, and approached, stopping a few feet away from Solon.

The leader took a step forward, a gawky man of middle height with an impossibly large nose and Adam's apple. James was struck that he looked as much like a turkey as any human he had seen. He half-expected the man to gobble.

Instead, the man smiled, revealing teeth so decayed they were mostly black. "Your pardon, sirs," he began, with a clumsy half-bow, "but if you'd see the day safely to your destination, you'd be wise not to begrudge us some silver for safe passage. After all, these are rough hills indeed."

Solon shook his fist at the man. "You'd dare to rob a priest?"

The leader glanced back at his friends, who seemed uncertain as to what to do. Then he turned back to Solon. "Your pardon, sir. We wish no trouble with the gods. You are free from our demands and may go as you will. But they must pay." He pointed at the rest of the group from Krondor.

"They are under my protection!"

The bandit stared up at the towering monk and then looked again to his companions. Attempting to look resolute, he said, "They don't wear any holy vestments. They're under no one's protection but their own."

Solon stepped up close to him and said, "If you'd tempt the wrath of my god, you'd better have a very good reason!"

James said, "Let's just kill them and get on with it."

Solon said, "No bloodshed if we can help it, James." Then with astonishing speed for a man of his size, the warrior monk swung one mighty fist upward, catching the bandit leader squarely under the chin. The slight man was lifted right off his feet and flung backward. His ragtag band of companions scrambled to catch him as he fell. Solon glared out from under his gold-colored helm and said, "Any other of you daft twits think you can extort silver from us?"

The men glanced at one another, then as two of them carried their unconscious leader, they hurried off, while those on the side of the road vanished into the brush.

When the road appeared empty once more, Solon returned to his horse. "I thought not," he said.

James and Jazhara exchanged glances, then both started to chuckle. James mounted his horse and declared, "Let's go."

The others followed suit and soon they were again riding cautiously through the darkening woodlands.

As night fell, they turned a bend in the trail and spied light ahead. James signaled for caution and they slowed to a walk.

As they approached the light they discovered they had chanced upon an inn, nestled close to the road in a small clearing. A single two-story wooden building with a large shed behind for horses, the inn was marked with a cheery glow from within, smoke rising from the chimney, and a sign depicting a man with a rucksack and walking stick.

"This must be the Wayfarer," said James.

"Then the Prince's agent should be waiting for us?" asked Kendaric. "This man Alan?"

James nodded. "Before we go inside," he said to Kendaric,

"remember, don't be too free with who we are or where we're going. Bear may have agents here as well."

Kendaric said, "Look, I don't care about any of this intrigue. I just want a bed and a hot meal. Is that too much to ask?"

James looked at the guildsman. Dryly, he answered, "Unfortunately, it often is too much to ask."

They dismounted and James shouted for the hostler.

Quickly a lackey arrived from the shed behind the building and took the horses. James spent a few moments instructing the boy on the care he required for the mounts. When he was satisfied that the horses would be well-tended, he motioned to the others to follow him into the inn.

James pushed open the door and they entered a tidy, though crowded, taproom. A merry fire burned in the hearth, and travelers and locals mixed easily as they ate and drank.

James led his companions through the taproom to the bar. A stout-looking man behind the counter looked up and with a broad smile said, "Sir!" Then spying Jazhara and the other two men, added, "Lady, and gentlemen, I'm Goodman Royos, the innkeeper. How may I be of service?"

"For a start, a round of ale for weary travelers."

"Certainly!" With practiced efficiency Royos quickly produced four large pewter jacks of ale. As he placed them on the bar, he asked, "Where are you heading?"

"North," James answered. "So, what's the news in these parts?"

"Oh, everything's been pretty quiet of late, although Farmer Toth's wife just rode through for Krondor. She seemed quite upset."

"Any idea why?" asked Jazhara.

Royos shrugged. "Can't say. She and her husband have a

farm ten miles or so this side of Haldon Head. They usually stop here for a bite on their way to the city or coming back, sometimes spend the night under their wagon out back where I keep the horses. Nice folks."

Kendaric said, "You said something about Haldon Head. We're heading there. Is it far?"

Jazhara rolled her eyes. "Kendaric . . ."

Royos said, "Haldon Head? No, just another couple of days. I don't want to scare you folks, but rumor has it that Haldon Head is cursed with witchcraft!"

Jazhara said, "What do you mean by 'witchcraft'?"

Royos said, "Now don't get me wrong. I'm not superstitious myself, but ships have sunk off Widow's Point ever since men began sailing these waters. Some say it's a curse, but I figure it's just the reefs and shoals when the tide is tricky."

Brother Solon said, "You say lots of ships go down there?"

"For hundreds of years. Some fall prey to their captains' ignorance of the reefs and the tides, others are taken by pirates. There are pirates who know this shoreline like the backs of their hands. They'll run ships aground, then board them while they're helpless."

James said, "You sound like you know what you're talking about."

Royos laughed. "I wasn't always an innkeeper . . ."

James nodded. "I'll not ask what you were before."

"Wise choice," said Royos.

Solon said, "So what's up at Haldon Head to be superstitious about?"

Royos chucked. "Well, some say the area is haunted by the ghosts of all the dead sailors." He shook his head. "It's probably just the fog that lingers offshore."

"That's all?" asked Solon.

Royos frowned as his demeanor turned a little more serious. "Well, lately I've heard tales about some folks gone missing up there, and cattle getting sick and the like." Then, returning to his cheery mood, he said, "Still, cattle are always getting sick, seems to me, and people do wander off from time to time."

Kendaric said, "We're also looking for a fellow named Alan."

Royos said, "That's Alan over there in the corner to your right. He regularly stops by when passing through." Lowering his voice, the innkeeper said, "I think he does some business for the Crown, though he's not much of a talker." Leaning back, he added, "But he's a wonderful listener. Never once saw him walk away from a yarn or tale."

James threw Kendaric a black look, then turned and crossed through the crowd to the opposite corner. A solitary man occupied a small table there, watching the room with his back to the wall. James said, "Alan?"

"I'm sorry. Do I know you?"

"I don't think you do. We're from the 'Citadel.'"

Alan waved James closer. "Glad to hear it. 'Uncle Arthur' sent word you'd be coming by."

James sat at the only other chair at the table, with Kendaric and Jazhara standing behind. Solon looked around the room to ensure they weren't overheard.

"What's the word on William's quest?"

"He's doing fine. He and his friends are hunting up in the mountains. Word was sent back they've found 'bear tracks.'"

Lowering his voice, James asked, "What have you heard from Haldon Head?"

"I haven't been up there for a while. That town seems to

be under some sort of curse. I've heard about sick people, sick farm animals, missing children, and there are rumors of dark creatures roaming the night. I don't know what's true, but I've met a lot of people on the road who are getting away from there in a hurry. They say it's witchcraft."

Jazhara said, "I hate that word! What do you mean?"

Alan glanced up at Jazhara, and while he had never seen her before he must have deduced she was the Prince's new magician, for he said, "Begging your pardon, milady. There's an old woman living at Widow's Point who the local villagers in Haldon Head go to with their common ailments. They've always tolerated her, even welcomed her when they were ill, but with the strange goings-on of late, they've taken to calling her a witch."

Jazhara said, "Perhaps we can be of some assistance when we reach Haldon Head."

James said, "Where are you off to next?"

"I'm hurrying down to the garrison at Sarth. Word is we've got goblins raiding to the east of here. Likely there's a camp nearby."

"They going to be a problem to us in reaching Haldon Head?" asked James.

"I don't think so, but it's best to stay on the road during daylight. So far, I've only heard of them hitting farms for food animals." Looking around the crowded room, he said, "I'd best slip out now. I've got a small patrol camped down the road. Thought it best not to call attention to myself. I should rejoin them and start out for the south at first light." He rose. "One last thing, the patrol sent to aid you hasn't reached Miller's Rest yet. They could be there by the time you pass through, or show up later. Best to stay out of trouble at Haldon Head until you know they're in place."

James thanked Alan and the agent departed.

Kendaric asked, "Can we get something to eat?"

James nodded. "And some rooms." He stood up and returned to the bar to arrange it with Goodman Royos.

William waited patiently for the return of the Pathfinders. He had stopped his patrol at a small clearing near a brook. A tree had been blazed with the agreed-upon cut, a symbol that meant "wait here."

He could feel the tension in the pit of his stomach. The only reason for making such a mark was that they were closing in on their quarry. Time dragged as he waited for the return of the scouts. He considered his options. He had been trailing Bear for over a week now. Several times he had waited while the Pathfinders had lost the trail only to pick it up again a few hours later. On two occasions, it was clear that Bear had met with other men. The Pathfinders deduced that he was recruiting mercenaries. Twice, other riders had left Bear's group to ride off on errands of one sort or another. Three times they had come across signs of goblins in the area, and William had even dispatched one of his riders back to Krondor to carry word of their possible incursion into the Principality. William prayed this was just some tribal migration to better hunting grounds, and not a gang of raiders. He wanted to concentrate his energy on Bear and his men, not a group of nonhuman troublemakers looking to steal cows and children. He knew that if he did encounter a raiding band, he'd be honor-bound to attempt to drive them back up into the mountains and that to do so would risk losing track of Bear. As much as he wanted to avenge Talia's murder, he couldn't abide the thought of a human child being sacrificed in one of the goblins' magic rites.

Finally, one of the two Pathfinders appeared. It was Jackson who came into the clearing, leading his horse. "We've spotted a band of mercenaries, Lieutenant."

"Bear's men?"

"Maric thinks so, but we saw no sign of the man himself. From the description, he'd be a hard one to miss. Maric's staying close. They're camped in a little clearing about a mile up the road. Best if we slip half the company around them, then hit them from both sides."

William considered the plan. He disliked the idea of splitting his forces while on the march, yet he knew that if he came at the mercenaries from one side only, they might break and flee into the woods. He needed intelligence more than dead bodies. At last he nodded. "How long?"

"We can be in place in an hour."

William glanced at the late afternoon sky. They would attack the mercenaries as it was getting dark. "Good. Be ready at sunset. Don't attack until you hear us coming, then hit them hard."

"Lieutenant?"

"Yes, Jackson?"

"I recognize this company. They're the Grey Talon, up from Landreth."

"Landreth?" asked William. "Valemen."

Jackson nodded. "Tough bastards. Last I heard they were fighting down in the Vale for a trading concern against Keshian raiders. They sometimes come up to Krondor to spend their gold, but usually we don't see them this far north."

William pondered the significance of this. "They must have been in Krondor when Bear was there, and Bear's agent must have gotten word to them to head north."

"Something like that," agreed Jackson.

"Which means Bear doesn't have many of his original crew left."

"Fair guess," agreed Jackson. "But these lads will not cry quarter unless they're seriously beaten. I know that from their reputation."

"Still, it means they won't have any personal loyalty to that monster. If we can capture ..." He turned and signaled for Sergeant Hartag. "What's the lie of the land? On foot or horse?"

"Foot, I think, Lieutenant. Too noisy getting the horses in place in the evening, and if we get close before we spring the attack, we have a better chance of taking charge of the fray."

"On foot, then," agreed William. "Take half the men and go with Jackson. Picket the horses and get as close to the other side of their camp as you can. Deploy your archers to one side. They'll signal when they're ready. We'll need their covering fire to make sure that none of these ruffians escape. If you get into trouble, lead them toward the trees, then disengage and let the archers cut them down.

"Wait until you hear us attack from this side of the trail and then go in fast and hard. But remember – I want at least one of them taken alive." To Jackson he added, "Go now, tell Maric to meet me at the trail, then get these men into place."

The Pathfinder nodded, mounted his horse, and rode off. In moments the sergeant had all the men mounted, and the company divided into two squads, and he led the first up the trail to rendezvous with the Pathfinders. William waited until

Raymond E. Feist

they were well along the trail, then gave the order for his own squad to follow.

Riding into the gloom of the woodlands, William could feel his anticipation mounting. Soon he would know where Bear was hiding, and then he would face him.

The men waited for the signal. William had inspected the enemy camp and was forced to admit that the men he faced were seasoned professionals. There were about thirty of them, and while they had elected to sleep on the ground, they had still picked the most defensible site in the clearing, atop a small hillock, with clear lines of sight in all directions. The good news was that they hadn't bothered making any sort of defenses. Even a rude earthen berm fortified with cut stakes would have proven a hindrance for William's men. These men were obviously in a hurry, making camp just before nightfall, probably planning on breaking camp at first light. They would set sentries, and those would be vigilant.

William waited until the sun had set low enough past the distant hills to throw the entire landscape into a chiaroscuro of dark gray and black. He devised a plan and relayed his orders to his archers. Five of the dozen men with him would hang back.

William motioned with his sword, and walked out into the clearing, seven men walking easily alongside him. He had covered a dozen yards when a voice called out from the camp. "Who goes there?"

"Hello, the camp!" William shouted, continuing to walk casually. "I seek the Grey Talon company."

"Well, you've found them," came the response. "Come no closer!"

William stopped. "I bring a message for Bear." The agreed-upon signal to the archers was the word "Bear."

As the sentry was about to answer, five arrows shot overhead and William shouted, "Now!"

The archers had picked their targets well, and before they realized they were under siege, five of the mercenaries were down. More arrows flew from the other side, and William realized Sergeant Hartag had his own bowmen ready.

From both sides of the camp, soldiers of the Kingdom appeared, while the Grey Talon mercenaries grabbed their weapons and made ready to answer the attack. William charged the nearest sentry, who raised his shield to take the blow from William's large hand-and-a-half sword. William started to swing downward, then turned the blade in an elliptical swing that brought the huge blade crashing into the side of the shield, knocking it aside, and turning the soldier so he couldn't return the blow, since his sword-arm was now away from William. As the sentry turned to strike, William swept his blade downward from the shield, slashing the back of the man's leg, hamstringing him. The man went down with a cry and William kicked him over with his left leg. The mercenary wasn't dead, but he wouldn't be fighting. William wanted prisoners. William wanted to know where he could find Bear.

William's men had the advantage of surprise, but the Grey Talon mercenaries were a hard and experienced bunch. The struggle was bloody and only the fact that a half-dozen mercenaries had gone down early enabled William's men to carry the day. After William's third kill, he glanced around, expecting to see mercenaries asking for quarter, but he was surprised to find they were still fighting, even though there were now two of the Prince's soldiers facing each mercenary.

"Keep at least one alive!" William shouted, even as he remembered the man he had hamstrung, lying somewhere on the ground in the midst of the carnage. He turned to see how his own command was doing. The archers had put up their bows, drawn their swords, and were now entering the fray. The mercenaries continued to resist and several of William's men were down, either dead or seriously wounded. "End this!" William shouted to a retreating mercenary who was desperately attempting to keep two Krondorian soldiers at bay.

The man ignored William and kept looking for an opening. William swore in disgust as another mercenary was killed. He circled around behind one of the last remaining mercenaries, and struck him from behind across the helmet with the flat of his blade. "Don't kill him!" he shouted to the two men who were about to run him through. The man staggered, and one of William's soldiers leapt forward, grappling with the mercenary's sword-arm. The other stepped inside and struck the mercenary hard across the face with the hilt of his sword, stunning the man.

Then it was over. William looked around and shouted, "Sergeant!"

Hartag hurried over and said, "Sir!"

"What's the damage?"

"Six men down, sir. Three dead, two more likely to join them, one who might survive if we get him to a healer quickly. Several others wounded, but nothing to brag about."

"Damn," muttered William. That left him with eighteen men, not all of them fully able. "What about the mercenaries?"

"Damnable thing, sir. They wouldn't ask for quarter. Fought

to the death. Never knew mercenaries to do that. Usually they're smart enough to know when they're whipped."

"How many alive?"

"Two," answered Hartag. "One's bleeding to death from a deep leg wound and won't be with us much longer." William nodded, realizing this must be the man he'd hamstrung. Hartag continued. "The other's that fellow you banged across the head. He should be rousing soon."

The mercenary came around after a few minutes and William had him dragged over. "Who are you? Are you one of Bear's men?"

"Not anymore. Name's Shane McKinzey. Currently – " He glanced around. "Used to be with the Grey Talons. We was contacted by Bear's agent so we came to join up. We met with this Bear, and he told us what to do."

"Why the fight to the death?" asked Hartag.

"Orders." He rubbed the back of his head. "Seems our captain" – he motioned toward a corpse being dragged to a makeshift funeral pyre – "he got the word that Bear had some sort of magical powers. Said he'd hunt down and eat the soul of any man who betrayed him." He blinked, as if trying to clear his vision. "Man, I've been hit before, but nothing like that." He shook his head. "Anyway, Capt'n, he says a clean death and fast ride to Lims-Kragma's Hall is better than bein' sucked dry of blood and havin' your soul captured by some hell's spawn."

"Why were you camped here?"

"We was left to kill anyone following him. This was our first job for him. Looks like it'll be our last."

"Where's Bear now?"

"Don't know. We were supposed to camp here and kill

anyone coming this way, then meet him on the morning of the new Small Moon, at Two Fangs Pass."

Hartag said, "You're lying."

"Maybe, but since you'll have to kill me anyway to keep me from warning Bear . . . why should I be honest?"

"Since we'll kill you anyway," said William, "maybe you ought to come clean and help us get the man who set you up."

Shane looked at William, and said, "I've been a mercenary for more years than you've carried a sword, boy. I don't fear dying, but I can see you're afraid of killin' in cold blood."

William pointed to where his men piled the dead. "Take a look at the rest of your men and tell me again that I'm afraid. Still, you could live if you're honest. You've never worked for Bear before, right?"

"What of it?"

"Then you don't need to share in Bear's punishment. Tell us what we want to know and my men will escort you back to Krondor. From there you can take a ship to wherever you like. I suggest back down to the Vale."

The mercenary rubbed the back of his head as he weighed his options. "Well, I guess I've not much of a company left. All right, you've got a deal. I was lying about the killing-anyone-who-followed part. We were supposed to make it look easy to attack us – damn we did make it too easy – bleed a little, then run like hell. Bear's setting a trap for you at Two Fangs Pass. We were supposed to lead you to it. If you hurry, you can beat him there."

"You made the smart choice. Thanks." William beckoned to a nearby soldier. "You and Blake take Mr. McKinzey here back to Krondor with anyone else who's too badly wounded to go any further."

"Yes, sir!" came the answer.

Hartag spoke softly. "You think he's telling the truth this time, Will?"

"Yes. He's got no reason to lie, and getting as far from Bear as he can is obviously his best choice." William's eyes seemed to light up as he continued, "We have him. Get the men ready to ride. We're pushing through this night, and the next if need be, and we'll get to Two Fang Pass before Bear."

"Sir!" said Hartag, and he turned to carry out his orders.

TEN

Goblins

J ames awoke.

Something was wrong. He leapt to his feet and kicked at the foot of Kendaric's bed. The guildsman sat up with a sleepy expression and mumbled, "What?"

"I smell smoke."

James hurried to the next room, where Jazhara and the monk were sleeping, and pounded on the door. The hall was already blue with smoky haze and the acrid smell of burning wood stung his eyes. "Get up!" he shouted. "The inn's on fire!"

Doors up and down the hall flew open as the handful of other guests looked out to see what the fuss was about. James repeated his warning as he buckled on his sword and grabbed his travel pack. Jazhara and Solon appeared a moment later and hurried after him and the others down the stairs.

In the common room, it was obvious that the fire had been started near the front door, for now the entire wall around the exit was engulfed in flames. "The kitchen!" James shouted. He hurried through the door behind the taproom bar and saw Goodman Royos and a young woman drawing buckets of water. "Stay calm!" shouted the innkeeper.

James grabbed the man by his shirt. "Don't even try. You'll

never put that fire out with buckets of water. Get out while you can!"

The man hesitated for a moment, then nodded. He ushered the girl out of the kitchen into the backyard as the last of the guests fled through the rear door.

Screams alerted James to the fact that something even direr than a fire was at hand.

He and Solon had their weapons at the ready when they emerged from the rear of the building, only to discover a band of goblins trying to untie the horses from their picket line beneath the run-in shed.

James counted quickly: there were a dozen of the creatures nearby. The goblins stood shorter than men, and were smaller across the shoulders, but not by much. Sloping foreheads terminated in heavy brows of thick black hair. The black irises of their yellow eyes caught the firelight, seeming to glow in the darkness. James had fought goblins before and realized at once that this must be an experienced raiding party. Three of the warriors wore tribal topknots complete with feathers or bones in their hair, signifying that they were chieftains or priests. They all carried bucklers and swords, and James was only thankful that they didn't appear to have archers with them.

There were three other armed men emerging from the inn, so including Solon, himself, and a few of the guests, James counted eleven warriors. Jazhara could handle herself, he knew, so he shouted to Royos, "Get the girl behind us!"

The goblins charged, and Jazhara unleashed a ball of fire at the center of the group. It struck square on. Flames immediately consumed three goblins, while another three off to one side were badly burned.

The remaining six goblins came forward at a howling run, swinging furiously. Out of the corner of his eye, James saw Solon wield his heavy warhammer deftly, caving in the skull of one goblin before the creature could dodge away.

One more down, five to go, thought James.

Kendaric came into James's view awkwardly waving a short blade, and suddenly James realized that the journeyman had no skills whatsoever to defend himself. James leapt to one side and kicked at the goblin who had overrun his position, sending the creature sprawling. He then leapt to his right, and with a spinning blow, cut at the goblin who menaced Kendaric, slashing him across the back of the neck.

The panic-stricken wrecker stared at James with wide-eyed terror. James yelled, "Get over there by Royos!"

Kendaric seemed unable to move, and James barely avoided being struck by a sword-blow from behind. He only sensed the attack at the last second and ducked to his left. Had he ducked to his right, he thought, he'd have been a head shorter.

James spun and saw that he had been attacked by one of the burned goblins. This one's entire right side was still smoking, his eye swollen shut, so James immediately moved to his own left, attacking the goblin's blind side.

Jazhara unleashed another spell, a searing red beam that struck the face of one of the goblins approaching Kendaric. The creature screamed, dropped his sword and clawed at his eyes. The other turned toward the source of the attack, and hesitated.

Kendaric used the distraction to turn and flee, leaving the goblin isolated. Brother Solon and another man from the inn appeared in Kendaric's place and both attacked the goblin at the same instant. The goblin saw Solon's huge warhammer coming at him and dodged, while the other man attempted to strike out with his sword. The two attacks confounded each other, and the goblin turned and fled.

Suddenly the remaining goblins were all running for their lives. James gave a half-hearted lunge at one who managed to elude his sword-point, then stood up and surveyed the damage.

The inn was now completely in flames, and Royos and the young woman were watching it, holding onto one another. The stable-boy stood near the horses, his eyes wide with fear.

A half-dozen goblins lay on the ground.

James shook his head. "What brings goblins so close to the coast?" he wondered aloud.

Brother Solon came to stand beside James. "Goblins tend to be a stupid lot, but not stupid enough to raid for horses unless they've a camp nearby."

The young girl approached and said, "Farmer Toth's wife rode through on her way to Krondor, sir, looking for soldiers to come save her baby girl."

"Maria!" exclaimed Goodman Royos. "You weren't supposed to hear of such things."

"Father," the girl replied, "do you think you can shield me from every trouble in the world?" She turned to look at the burning inn. "Is my home not destroyed before my eyes?"

The innkeeper put his arms around her shoulders. "I forget that you are growing up, daughter."

The other guests, two men with swords, and another with a large hunting knife, as well as two women gathered around. Royos said, "My thanks for all that you did in driving off the goblins."

James nodded. "I wish we could have done more."

"You saved lives," said Royos. "Inns can be rebuilt. Customers are much harder to come by." He kissed the top of Maria's head. "As are daughters." Royos and Maria turned back toward the inn, to arrange a bucket brigade to douse the remaining flames.

"Aye," said Solon. "They were a'waitin' for us to come out so they could butcher us."

James scratched at his ear. "Why such a blatant raid? They have to know there'll be a patrol up in the hills after them soon . . ."

Jazhara said, "To draw a patrol away from somewhere else?"

James looked at the young magician and motioned for her to walk with him. When they were out of earshot of the others, he asked, "Bear?"

"Perhaps. It would certainly suit his cause if soldiers were not near Widow's Point and Haldon Head when he attempted to claim the Tear of the Gods."

James said, "If we knew how he planned on getting to the Tear, then we'd have a better notion of where he is likely to be."

"Were I this Bear, and failing to gain Kendaric's spell, I would wait for Kendaric to appear and capture him."

"Or wait for us to do the work, then take the Tear from us once we're back on dry ground."

"Either way, I would allow Kendaric to reach Widow's Point," finished Jazhara.

James said, "I don't wish to wait, but I'm reluctant to attempt this without the reserves down in Miller's Rest." He glanced over to where the others waited, and called out, "Brother Solon! You seem to have some knowledge of goblins. How large a camp do you judge they'd have nearby?"

The warrior monk paused to consider, then said, "'Tis hard to judge. The daft creatures do not think as you and I think. Perhaps three companies such as this one. One to hold the camp while the other two raid. They numbered chieftains and priests in this party, which is somewhat unusual."

"To what end?" asked Kendaric, now sufficiently recovered from his fright to follow the conversation.

"Ah, that is as plain as can be," said Solon. "They've taken a baby." He glanced at the sky, where Small Moon was waning. "They'll sacrifice the wee one in two days when the moon is dark, an offering to their god. So, these aren't bandits out lookin' for plunder. This is an all-out ghost-appeasement raid. Their ancestors are tellin' them to come down and spill human blood, take human slaves and horses, then come back. 'Tis a very bad business."

Jazhara said, "We must do something. If they're going to kill the child in two nights, the soldiers will not be here in time."

James said, "As loath as I am to think of a child dying in such a fashion, we have more pressing business elsewhere."

Jazhara grabbed James by the upper arm and in a low, angry tone, growled, "You'd leave a baby to be butchered like a food animal?"

James rolled his eyes and shook his head. "I'm not going to win this one, am I?"

"No. I'll go alone if I have to."

James pulled his arm free of her grip. "You have your duty."

"And you've already said this may have been done to draw away our soldiers. We will have to wait anyway, James, if you won't move to Haldon Head before the patrol gets here. If we can rescue the child and return her to her family, we lose only a couple of days, and when the soldiers following us arrive here, they can move straight on to Miller's Rest."

Sighing in resignation, James motioned for Solon and Kendaric to approach. "Solon, could these goblins be working for Bear?"

"I think not," said the monk. "Though he could be influencin' them. A few weapons or a bit of magic, as gifts, some intelligence on safe places to raid, some jars of wine or ale, they might think plunderin' down here was their own brilliant idea."

Kendaric said, "Is this Bear everywhere?"

James answered, "No, I don't think so. I don't think Bear is behind this. I think he's working for another."

"Why?" asked Jazhara.

"I'll tell you as we travel." He glanced up at the sky. "Dawn will be here in a couple of hours and we have to be ready to ride."

"Where are we going?" asked Kendaric.

With a wry smile, James said, "We're hunting goblins."

Kendaric was complaining, again. "This is not at all wise!"

James shook his head, ignoring him. To Solon he said, "They're not taking pains to hide their tracks, are they?"

The warrior monk was leading his horse as he followed the goblins' trail. "No, they're a wee bit damaged, and in a hurry to get back to their healers, I'm thinkin'."

James pointed ahead. In the distance the hills rose and behind them the peaks of the Calastius Mountains. "You think they'll be up in the rocks?"

"Almost certainly," answered the monk. "They'll have found a defensible position, maybe a box canyon or small meadow, but it'll be hell to pay to dig them out of it."

"And the four of us are going to 'dig them out?'" demanded Kendaric.

Running out of patience, James said, "No, we're not going to dig them out. We're going to hold the horses and send you in to destroy them."

Kendaric stopped his horse, looked down with a stunned expression. "Me?"

Jazhara couldn't contain herself and started to laugh. Even the taciturn Solon allowed himself a chuckle.

James shook his head. "Don't worry. I have a plan."

He turned away from Kendaric, who was now falling farther behind, allowing Jazhara to lean over and say, "You have a plan?"

James whispered back. "No, but I will have by the time we get there and I look around. And maybe he'll shut up until then."

Jazhara smiled and nodded. They rode on.

At last, Solon signaled a halt. "I'm not a proper tracker, it's true, but you'd have to be a blind man to not see this." He dismounted and pointed at the ground where James could see heavy boot-prints in the dirt.

"He's in a bit of a hurry, apparently," said the monk.

"Who is it?" asked Kendaric.

"Unless someone here has the gift of future sight," said Solon, "it's only guessing, but I suspect we're lookin' at the tracks of that farmer, come to fetch home his bonny girl."

"Good guess," said James, pointing ahead. In the distance they saw a solitary figure cresting a hill. He had been hidden from sight by a closer rise, but now they could see him marching purposefully down the trail. "We'd best catch up with him before he gets himself killed."

Solon mounted and they urged their horses into a fast canter. They overtook the farmer quickly. The man turned and regarded the riders with suspicion. He held a scythe like a weapon, across his chest, ready to block or swing.

"Hold," said James with his right hand held up palm outward. "We're on the Prince's business."

"Finally! I was beginning to think help would never come. How is my wife?"

James said, "I believe you've mistaken us for others."

The farmer asked, "What?! You mean Becky didn't send you from Krondor? I thought you had come to rescue my daughter!"

Solon said, "Be calm, Farmer Toth. You are in Ishap's grace now. We know something about your child. Please, tell us what happened to your daughter."

The man seemed to relax. "It's been almost a week, now, since my friend Lane and I were out hunting. We were in the foothills east of here, when at night we heard flutes and drums.

"We went to see what it was, and in a canyon not too far from here we came upon a band of goblins. They had a little boy, and then they . . . oh, gods . . . they cut the child in two. Sacrificed him! I cried out . . . I couldn't help myself, and they came after us. We managed to escape, but then the day before yesterday they fell upon us back at my farm. Lane and I tried to hold them back, but there were just too many. They got into the house . . . and they took my daughter! Lane's a tracker and went after them, and I sent my wife Becky to Krondor for help, and then followed after Lane. Now you've shown up."

James asked, "Which way did Lane go?"

"Back to the canyon, I'm almost certain. He left small signs for me to follow. I was going to wait for the soldiers . . . but I couldn't bear the thought of them sacrificing my little girl."

"She's safe until the dark of the next moon," said Solon.

"It was the dark of the Middle Moon the night we saw the boy killed," agreed Toth. Then he became concerned. "Tomorrow night is the dark of the Small Moon!"

"We must act quickly," said Jazhara.

"It's all that witch's doing," said Toth.

"Witch?" asked Jazhara.

"There are rumors of witchcraft up at Haldon Head – that accursed witch must have had my daughter stolen for her foul spells!"

Jazhara's eyes narrowed. "Did you see the 'witch' when the goblins killed the little boy?"

"Well, no, but . . ."

"It is of no matter now," injected Solon. "If we are to help, we must move quickly."

"I beg you do!" said Toth. "Please help me find my daughter."

Solon glanced around. "Camp here, good farmer. We shall have to strike this night, else the bonny child is lost."

James nodded. "Let's get moving."

They led their horses along the road while the farmer looked around for a place to wait. James glanced back and saw the man's face. Clearly all his hopes rode with them.

"Looks like Toth's friend Lane ran into some trouble," said James. A short way down the trail they had followed for the last hour lay a small mound of corpses. Beyond that another pair of goblins lay across a still, human form.

"He made the bastards pay," growled Solon.

Kendaric said, "But at what price? The man is dead!"

"Calm yourself," said Jazhara.

"Calm, she says," Kendaric muttered, shaking his head.

"I think that body just moved," said James, jumping from his horse and hurrying over. He pulled the two goblins off the pile and examined the man. "Bring water!" he instructed.

Jazhara hurried over with a waterskin while James cradled the man's head, watching as the magician poured a little water onto the man's face, reviving him.

Blinking, Lane said, "Goblins . . . they took my friend's daughter. I found their camp, but . . . there were too many . . ."

"Don't worry, we'll find them," said Jazhara.

"They're close. The box canyon, north of here. Please. Don't let them kill that little girl."

James started to ask a question, but Lane's eyes rolled up into his head. James put his ear near the man's mouth and after a minute, said, "He's gone."

Solon said, "He'll not die in vain. We'll see justice done."

James gently rested the man's head on the rocks, and stood. Glancing upward, he said, "It's going to be dark in less than two hours. Let's see if we can find that box canyon." He motioned for Solon and Kendaric to dismount. "We'll walk the horses and leave them at the mouth of the canyon. When we return, we'll give Lane a proper burial."

It took them less than an hour to reach the entrance to the canyon. A small stream emptied out of the rocks there, cutting across the trail, before splashing down the hillside. Turning to Kendaric, James said, "Water the horses and keep them from wandering off. We'll be back as soon as we can."

"You're leaving me here alone?" he asked, alarmed.

"Well, if you'd rather go to the goblin camp . . . ?"

"No! It's just, well, alone . . ."

James said, "As much as it pains me to say this, right now you are more important than either Jazhara or myself." He thought about it, then added, "Solon, you stay here as well. If we don't come back, go to Miller's Rest and pick up the patrol. Then go to Haldon Head, raise the ship and get the Tear."

Solon seemed to be on the verge of objecting, then saw the wisdom of the plan. "Aye, I'll wait."

James and Jazhara moved up the canyon. After carefully picking their way through the narrow opening, they came to a quarter turn, bending to the left. James peeked around the corner. Then he turned and held up two fingers to Jazhara, and mouthed, "Two guards." She nodded. He glanced up at the rim of the canyon and pointed to a spot slightly behind Jazhara.

Following his gaze, she saw a handhold, and nodded quick agreement. Shouldering her staff across her back, she climbed nimbly up onto the ridge. James followed. At the top he whispered in her ear, "I'm going to move up the draw a bit and see what's there. If there's a way to get past the guards, I'll find it. If not, we'll try the other side."

"What if there is no way on the other side?" she whispered back.

"Then we have to kill the guards and move quickly before we're discovered."

Jazhara's face revealed her reaction to that possibility. "Please find another way," she asked.

James crept along the rim of the canyon, keeping low to reduce the chance of being seen against the still-light sky. He passed the bend and glanced down to make sure he wasn't likely to be spotted by the guard stationed at the opposite side of the canyon, but to his relief the guard was nowhere to be seen.

James continued his slow approach. The rise increased in height as he reached the lip of the box canyon. Below he could see a dozen tents, dominated by a huge one capable of housing at least a dozen warriors. He sat back on his haunches for a moment and weighed his concerns. The tents were of human origin. Goblins built huts from sticks and branches in their own villages, or stayed in caves or under lean-tos when out foraging or hunting.

Then James saw a human. So: human renegades were behind the goblin raids! He half-expected the man to be wearing the black of the Nighthawks, and was almost disappointed when he approached the fire and revealed himself to be a simple mercenary. James gave that some thought: mercenaries and goblins. It seemed that Bear must be involved in the goblin raids – or whoever was behind Bear . . .

Which left James with a problem to consider at some other time, since right now he needed to focus on rescuing the child.

The mercenary kicked a goblin who grudgingly moved aside so that the human could take out a knife and cut a hunk of meat off a quarter bullock that was roasting on a spit. The man deftly impaled the meat with his dagger, tore off a piece, and turned away from the circle of goblins around the fire. James watched him chew the savory beef.

Then he heard the baby crying. An influx of emotion he hadn't expected accompanied the realization that the child still lived, filling him with relief and a redoubled sense of urgency. James's eyes glanced here and there, his gaze traveling around the camp. The old thief in him spied a course along the canyon rim that would put him above the big tent in which the child lay.

James glanced at the camp below. A couple of goblins sported wounds, obviously from their aborted raid on the Wayfarer the night before. *How to get in and out without being detected?* James wondered.

He looked up at the sky and judged it about three hours before the waning Small Moon rose. Middle Moon was a quarter full, and was now high in the sky. It would set as Small Moon rose. Large Moon was also waning, and would rise an hour after Small Moon.

James calculated. That gave him roughly an hour of relatively deep darkness in which to infiltrate the camp, steal the baby, and return to where Solon and Kendaric waited. As loath as he was to risk passing by the guards three more times, he knew he had to return to Jazhara and discuss his plan with her; he would need her help.

Moving slowly he passed the bend and reached the point above Jazhara. Softly, he whispered her name and from below heard her answer, "Here."

He jumped down.

"What did you find?" Jazhara asked.

"The baby lives and I think I can get to her, but I need to know if you have anything that we can use to keep her quiet. I will almost certainly be discovered if she cries out."

Jazhara said, "I can make something; how much time do we have?"

"I must be back above the tent within the hour."

"Then I have little time. I'll need a small fire and my things are on my horse."

James motioned her to follow. "Quietly," he said. He led her back down the canyon to where Solon and Kendaric waited. At once, Kendaric started to ask questions, but James waved them away. "The child lives and I'll fetch her out, but right now I need a fire."

Solon didn't hesitate. Instantly he started casting around for small branches and twigs. Jazhara took her pack down from her horse, and sat down on the ground, swinging the pack around before her as she did so. She quickly removed several vials, a small copper vessel, and a pair of thin cloth gloves. While she worked, she said, "Getting the child to drink anything could be difficult and she might cry out in the attempt. I can make a potion that will cause the baby to sleep deeply for a few hours if you can get her to breathe it in. A bit on a cloth, held over her nose and mouth for a few moments, will suffice. Be careful, though, not to breathe the fumes yourself, even at a distance. While it might not put you to sleep, it can disorient you and make it difficult for you to return."

"Get you killed, is what she means," said Kendaric.

Solon said, "Laddie, has anyone ever previously mentioned that at times you possess the charm of a canker on the buttock?"

James chuckled, but Jazhara was all concentration as she poured tiny amounts of liquid and powders from the five vials she had chosen. She added a few drops of water and then with an incantation placed the vessel close to the tiny fire Solon had started.

Pulling an empty vial from her bag, she removed the stopper and deftly picked up the copper vessel, holding it gingerly with two gloved fingers. Quickly she poured the contents into the vial, then replaced the stopper.

She handed the vial to James, saying, "Carefully." Then she

rummaged around in her pack. At last she held something out
to him. "Here is a clean cloth. Just before you attempt to touch
the child, pour a little of the liquid on the cloth, and hold it
above the baby's face. A few moments is all it should take. She
will not rouse, even if you jostle her or there are loud noises."

"Thank you," James said. "If there's loud noises, it doesn't
matter if she wakes or not." He glanced at the sky. "I must
hurry. Wait here and have the horses ready for a very fast retreat
if I come running." Then he thought a bit more and said, "Have
the horses ready for a very fast retreat no matter what."

"At last a wise suggestion," Kendaric said as he grinned.

James unbuckled his sword-belt, knowing that should he
have need of his blade he and the child would most likely
be facing death, anyway. He checked his dagger and placed
it firmly in its sheath. Tucking the vial and cloth inside his
shirt, he turned and hurried back toward the entrance of the
canyon.

He made his way quickly along the ridge and this time
continued until he was above the tent. Middle Moon had
sunk in the west, and Small Moon and Large Moon were
going to rise soon. The fire had burned low in the center of
the camp and several goblins lay sleeping on the ground near
it. From within several tents, the sound of snoring told James
the entire camp had turned in for the night, save for whatever
guards were on patrol. He prayed quickly to Ruthia, Goddess
of Luck and of thieves, that the goblins and renegades weren't
smart enough to have set someone to patrolling the rim. He
positioned himself above the largest tent and looked around.
Then he began his careful descent.

When he reached the ground he put his ear next to the
tent and listened, but could hear nothing through the heavy

canvas. The bottom of the tent was tightly staked, so lifting the canvas and crawling under it was not an option. He pulled out his dagger.

Quietly, he pushed the point into the heavy canvas, and cut downward in a steady, firm motion, so as not to make too much noise. He made a slit that was big enough to peer through and looked inside. The stench that struck him almost made him vomit. He knew that stink: dead bodies. He choked down his gag reflex and looked around.

Three goblins slept on bedrolls on the ground, while another lay upon a raised dais before an altar of some sort. James looked for the baby and saw a small object behind the altar, about the size of a cradle. Slipping through the cut in the canvas, he crept toward the object.

It was indeed a rude cradle and in it the baby lay sleeping. He glanced around and suppressed a shudder. There were body parts lying upon the altar, arranged in a grotesque parody of a human form. An upper torso from a woman lay above the pelvis of a man. A child's arm had been placed to the left, while the arm of an older child or a small woman lay on the right. Equally mismatched legs and feet were positioned below the pelvis. James glanced into the cradle. It seemed likely that this child was to provide the head. He had no idea of what black sorcery was being practiced, and he had no intention of lingering to find out. His recent experience in the Nighthawks' desert stronghold, where he had almost been the guest-of-honor at a demon-summoning, had left him with a strong aversion to such goings-on.

James adroitly removed the vial and cloth from his shirt and, holding his breath, dabbed some liquid on the cloth. When it felt damp, he held out the cloth, and hung it above the child's face. After a moment, he put the cloth down on the edge of the cradle, and returned the stopper to the vial. He put the vial back in his shirt and bent over to pick up the baby.

A startled grunt caused him to look across the altar. The goblin priest who had been sleeping on the other side was standing there, staring at James in wide-eyed amazement. James grabbed the cloth and flipped it, sending it spinning across the altar to cover the goblin's nose and mouth. The priest blinked in surprise then started to reach up, but as his black-clawed fingers touched the cloth, his eyes rolled back up into his head and he slumped to the floor. Silently, James said, "Thank you, Jazhara," and scooped up the baby.

Taking the child's blanket, he rigged a shoulder sling, and fled the terrible place, carrying the baby as he had often carried treasure after burglarizing houses as a boy. He climbed the rock face and quickly made his way back around the rim, expecting a cry of alarm every step of the way. When he reached a place where it was safe to descend, he jumped down and started running.

It seemed to take forever to get back to the others; but they had the horses ready and were in the saddle by the time he reached them.

"I have her," James said, and Jazhara held out her arms. James handed the child to the magician, then mounted his own horse.

The four of them urged their horses forward and soon were trotting down the trail.

An hour later they found Farmer Toth, sitting beside a small fire waiting anxiously. When they rode into view, he leapt to his feet and hurried toward them.

Seeing the bundle in Jazhara's arms, he cried, "Is that her?"

Jazhara handed the baby down and said, "She will sleep until morning, then she will be a little listless for the next few hours. After that, she will be fine."

"Thank you! Praise the gods! She's still alive and well. Thank you so very much."

James glanced around. "We'll ride with you back toward your farm. The goblins may not realize she's gone until dawn, but it's better to be cautious."

"I'm grateful to you," said the farmer, turning to walk beside them along the trail.

Jazhara said, "We have other – ill – news, I'm sorry to say. Your friend Lane is dead."

Toth said, "I suspected as much when you returned without him."

"He gave the bastards a fight of it," said Solon. He glanced at Kendaric, who was wise enough to stay silent. "He was a hero, of that there is no doubt."

Toth was silent for a moment, then said, "We had yet to name our baby, but I think from now on I shall call her 'Lane' in his memory."

"'Tis a fine honor," agreed Solon.

As dawn broke, they were miles down the road. They had taken a couple of short breaks and James and Solon had let Toth ride for periods while they carried the baby, Lane.

A little after sunrise the baby stirred and fussed. "She's hungry and her mother's nowhere nearby," said the farmer. "She'll have to wait until we reach my farm and I can milk the goat."

"How far?" asked Kendaric, who was getting a stiff neck from looking back over his shoulder every few minutes.

"Not far," answered Toth. "And with luck, if my missus got any help in Krondor, she might be back at the farm by the time we get there."

James and Jazhara let their horses fall back a little and Jazhara said, "You've been very quiet about what you saw in the camp."

"Yes," agreed James.

"Something disturbed you," she said.

"Yes."

"Something you don't wish to talk about?"

"Yes," James replied, then after a moment, he said, "No, perhaps I should talk about it, to you at any rate. You're the Prince's advisor on things magical." He described the altar and the body parts.

"Some black necromancy, certainly," said Jazhara. "It's a very bad business, but it fits in with that monster we found in the sewers of Krondor. Someone is creating agents of chaos to unleash upon the Kingdom, but toward what end . . . ?"

"Could it be a coincidence? Maybe the goblins just happened to be interested in the same . . ." The questions petered out under her disapproving look.

"You know better," she replied. "There is an agency behind this, some force that's orchestrating it all."

"The Crawler?" asked James.

Jazhara shrugged. "Perhaps, or perhaps it is someone in league with the Crawler, or someone using the Crawler, or perhaps the coincidence is that there are *two* malevolent forces loose in the West of the Kingdom."

"Wonderful," James muttered. "My old bump of trouble tells me that none of this is unrelated. It's just that we can't see the pattern."

"What if there is no pattern?" mused Jazhara.

"What do you mean?"

"What if everything we see is the product of some set of random choices? What if there is no single plan in place but, rather, a series of events designed to destabilize the region?"

"To whose benefit?" asked James.

Jazhara smiled. "Do you have an hour to run through the entire list, James?"

James nodded, yawning. "I must be getting tired," he confessed. "Kesh, Queg, some of the Eastern Kingdoms even, then a half-dozen minor nobles who would find opportunity in an unstable period to become major nobles, etc."

"Those are just the political realities," said Jazhara. "There are dark forces who have no political aims, but who have social ambitions, or worse."

"What do you mean?"

"I mean forces who are in league with dark powers who would cherish chaos as a kind of smokescreen behind which they may move to preeminence."

Solon turned. "I heard that. She's right, you know. There are forces in the universe whose only aim is to bring misery and darkness upon us all."

James said, "I have always had trouble with that as an idea, but then again I've never been a mad priest of a dark power."

Jazhara laughed, and even Solon was forced to chuckle. "Well, then, at least you're wise enough to admit something you can't imagine exists," said the monk, letting his horse fall back a little so he could ride abreast of James and the magician.

James said, "I can imagine a lot. And what you just said about forces whose only aim is to misery and chaos is certainly in character with our current mission."

"Aye," agreed the monk. "There is that."

They continued on in silence until they reached Farmer Toth's farm. A dozen horses were tied to a fence a short distance from the farm. There was a company of militia in the yard and James was surprised to see a familiar face leading them.

"Jonathan!" he called out. "What brings you this far from the city?"

The son of the former Sheriff of Krondor turned and held up his hand in greeting. "Things are still being sorted out, Squire, so His Highness thought it best if I was out of the way for a little while."

James dismounted and handed his reins to a nearby soldier, while Farmer Toth and his wife had a joyous reunion. James motioned for Jonathan Means to step away and said, "What's that mean?"

"It means Captain Garruth is trying to convince His Highness to do away with the office of sheriff and consolidate all enforcement of municipal order in the city guard's office."

"And thereby elevate his own power and authority," said James.

"And importance," said Jonathan. "I don't seek the office for myself, but there's always been a Sheriff of Krondor."

James shook his head. "Sometimes . . ." He let out his breath slowly. "It's never been wise to turn the city into a private estate of the Crown. The founding princes of the city learned that the hard way. A court of magistrates and a sheriff's office that is outside the court has always been the wisest way to deal with petty crimes and civil disputes." He looked directly at Jonathan. "I'll speak to Arutha about it when I get back. I doubt he'll agree to Garruth's proposal." Almost to himself he added, "So then what is the reason he got you out of town?"

Means had never struck James as someone with an abundance of humor, but he did smile as he replied, "Perhaps to return with some word from you regarding things in the north?"

James said, "Too iffy, unless you had other instructions after coming to the relief of the farmer and his wife."

Jonathan nodded and they moved farther away from the others. "Arutha says there are reports of some fairly horrific things going on in this vicinity. Alan, his factor, has sent along several such reports in the last two weeks – livestock sickening, monsters in the woods, children vanishing, and similar tales. You're to concentrate upon your mission, but you should be cautious. I am to rendezvous with the patrol heading up to Miller's Rest, and be ready to render aid."

James said, "So Arutha thinks a dozen Krondorian regulars might not be enough?"

"Apparently," said Jonathan. "Be wary once you're past the cut-off road to Miller's Rest. From there to Haldon Head you are on your own until we get word to come fetch you out."

"Thank you," said James. With an inclination of his head he indicated that Jonathan should return to his men.

Left alone with his thoughts for a moment, James again wondered at the scope of the attempt to seize the Tear. How did that fit into the seemingly patternless mess made up of Nighthawks, dead thieves, monsters, sorcerers, mad priests, and all the rest they had encountered since the betrayal at Krondor engineered by Makala and the other Tsurani magicians? There had always been a third player in the mix, he knew. Not the Crawler, and certainly not the Brotherhood of the Dark

Path, nor even the mad priests who had seized control of the Nighthawks.

He sensed that Jazhara was right; there was an overriding presence behind all that had occurred in the last year, and he was determined before all was said and done to unmask that presence and rid the West of it for good.

ELEVEN
Haldon Head

For two days they traveled.

James and his companions found no patrol waiting at Miller's Rest. They had little reason to linger, so they purchased some provisions at a small store near the mill that gave the town its name, and headed north toward the village of Haldon Head.

South of the village a small road branched off to the west, and led down through coastal cliffs to a broad beach. James dismounted and said, "We're only a short walk from the Point." He indicated a promontory of land jutting out into the sea. "If the maps back at the palace are correct, we should find a headland below those cliffs just around the bend."

They watered and tied up the horses, then started walking. "We have a few hours of daylight left," said James as they trudged through the sand. "Kendaric, how long does the spell take?"

"Minutes," said the wrecker. "I can raise the ship and hold it above the waves long enough to gain entrance and retrieve whatever it is you're looking for."

"We'll need a boat, then," observed Solon.

Kendaric laughed. "Not so, monk. For the genius of my spell is that not only can one man cast it, has he the talent, but it also

228

solidifies the water around the ship. You can walk over to it and retrieve your bauble."

James grinned. "Perhaps we'll get lucky and retrieve this 'bauble' easily."

They rounded the promontory and discovered that the prince's map was indeed accurate. A long finger of rock and soil extended out into the sea. The afternoon weather was moderate, and lazy combers rose and fell off the Point. They could see a few masts poking above the water, remnants of old wrecks not yet completely consumed by the sea. They made their way along the natural breakwater, until they reached the end.

Kendaric surveyed the wrecks revealed by the relatively low tide, the dozens of tilting masts like so many cemetery markers. He frowned. "Which one am I supposed to raise?" he asked.

James replied, "I have no idea."

Solon came over to them. "This is a place of death," he said portentously. "A graveyard of ships and men."

Solon gazed at the wreckage and was about to speak again when Kendaric said, "What's that smell? Like before a storm . . . sharp . . ."

Jazhara was the last to reach the point and she shouted, "It's magic!"

Gusts of wind seemed to arise out of nowhere, buffeting them and tearing at their clothes. Around them the sea began to roil, while a short distance away all was calm.

A sudden blow sent Solon reeling and he fell hard onto the rocks. James had his sword out, yet he could not see anything to strike. Kendaric dropped down, keeping as low as possible, while Jazhara raised her staff above her head and shouted, "Let the truth be revealed!"

A brilliant white light erupted from her staff, blinding enough to cause James to avert his eyes and blink away tears.

Then James heard Jazhara shout, "Look!"

He cleared his vision and, looking ahead, saw two creatures floating in the air above one of the ships' masts. Both appeared to be roughly reptilian, with long, sinuous necks and tails. Large bat-like wings beat furiously, causing the buffeting winds. The heads were almost devoid of features, save for two ruby-colored eyes and a slit for a mouth that opened and closed, like a fish gulping water.

Jazhara kept her feet and had to shout an incantation in order to be heard. A crimson ball of energy appeared in her hand and she cast the spell at the creatures. The ball of red light struck the creature on the right and it opened its mouth as if shrieking in pain. But all they could hear was a renewed howling of the winds. The monster on the left dove straight at the party, and James leapt to his feet, sword poised, as Solon also rose, flourishing his warhammer.

The creature was heading straight for Jazhara, and James cut at it. As his blade touched it white-hot sparks exploded from it as the creature opened its mouth in apparent shock. The sound of shrieking wind rang in their ears. The monster faltered, and Solon stepped forward, striking downward with his huge warhammer. Stunned by the blow, the creature fell to the rocks.

The tip of one wing struck the ground, and instantly a green flame erupted there and traveled quickly up the wing, engulfing the monster. It writhed for a moment on the rocks, flopping around helplessly, as James and his companions stepped back. Then it was gone, the faint smoke of its passing swept away by the wind, which blew only half as strongly as before.

The second creature had thrown off the effects of Jazhara's spell and was circling. It hooted, making a noise that sounded like wind gusting through a hollow tree.

Jazhara pointed, "Look!"

Another creature appeared out of the air, circled once, then joined the first. Again the wind that buffeted them redoubled in intensity and they had to struggle to stay upright.

Once more Jazhara cast a spell, this one a single piercing line of crimson energy that struck the first monster in the face. It writhed in agony, losing its orientation, and rolled over, as if trying to lie upon its side in midair, then started a slow tumble into the sea below. As soon as it touched the water, it vanished in a flare of green flames, as the first one had done.

James glanced around and found himself a rock that was large enough to have some heft, but small enough to hold. He reared back and threw it as hard as he could at the remaining creature. It too had started to make the hooting noise, which James took to be a summoning call. The rock smashed the monster in the face, interrupting the summoning.

"Jazhara!" James shouted. "If you've got anything left to deal with that thing, use it now before it calls yet another of its kind."

Jazhara said, "I have one trick left to try!"

She pointed her staff and a ball of flames erupted from the tip. James and Solon both turned aside as it flew between them, for they could feel its blistering heat. The fire went unerringly to the creature and surrounded it. The flames suddenly turned bright green, and the creature vanished from sight.

Instantly the winds ceased.

Slowly, Kendaric stood up. Looking around as if expecting another attack, he said, "What were those things?"

Jazhara said, "Air elementals, I believe, though I've never seen them before. My mentors claimed things like that once attacked Stardock."

James nodded. "I've heard that story from Gardan. If they touch fire, water, or earth they're consumed."

Kendaric nodded vigorously. "I hope to the gods that's the last we see of them!"

Solon said, "Someone doesn't wish us to raise that ship."

"All the more reason to raise it before whoever set those guardians over the ship returns," observed Jazhara.

"But which ship?" asked Kendaric.

Solon said, "You're a slab-headed fool. That one!" He pointed.

"How do you know?" asked Kendaric.

James laughed. "Because that's the one those elementals were guarding!"

Solon closed his eyes for a moment. "And I sense something down there, as well."

"What?" asked the wrecker.

"What we've come here to recover," replied the monk.

"Very well," said Kendaric. "Let me have the scroll."

Jazhara set down her backpack, and opened it. She reached in and withdrew the scroll she had been carrying since finding it in Kendaric's room and handed it to him. He took it, read it, then nodded. "I could do it alone, but with your help, magician, we should be able to do this quickly." He pointed at two places in the spell and said, "Make this incantation with me, then this other passage here. For a spell-caster of your power, this should be easy."

"I've examined your spell," Jazhara said judiciously. "I will do what I can to help."

Turning to face the sea, Kendaric pointed one hand at the mast of the ship in question and began to chant. Jazhara joined in at the passage Kendaric had indicated, and their voices filled the air with mystic words.

A fog appeared where Kendaric had pointed. It coalesced above the water, and the sea began to roil with mystic energies. A keening sound filled the air and James saw the top of the mast start to vibrate.

Abruptly, everything ceased. The fog vanished, the water calmed, and the ship stopped moving.

"I think your spell needs work," said James.

"No," contradicted Jazhara. "It wasn't his spell. As we cast it, I felt something fighting against us. Someone else did this to us."

Kendaric glanced back up at the cliffs as if seeking sight of someone. "She's right. I felt it, too."

Solon's gaze also went to the cliffs behind them. "Then we'll have to locate the source of the interference. For if we do not, the entire Order of Ishap may be in jeopardy and one of its deepest mysteries may fall into the hands of the enemy!"

Kendaric looked at James as if questioning whether this was an exaggeration. James returned a grim expression.

Kendaric nodded, and Jazhara led the way back toward the horses.

Haldon Head was a small village, comprised of only a dozen or so buildings around a crossroads. The north–south route of the King's Road ran from Miller's Rest to Questor's View. The east–west route led from Widow's Point out to farms scattered between the village and the forested foothills.

At the center of the village sat an inn, the Sailor's Rest. As the travelers rode in, they saw two men standing in front of the inn, arguing loudly.

One of them – a farmer, judging by his rough dress – was shouting. "This has gone on long enough! She must be stopped! You should have had those soldiers execute her when they were here!"

The other man wore a well-made tunic with a sleeveless over-jacket. He was of middle years and rather portly. He shouted back, "You've no proof, Alton. With all the pain we've gone through, you want to cause more?"

"You keep this up, Toddy, and you won't be mayor much longer. Hell, you keep this up and there won't be a village much longer. Lyle told me that – "

As James and his companions reined in, the man named Toddy interrupted, "Lyle is a drunk! If he thinks we are going to . . ." The arrival of strangers finally caught his attention.

The farmer said, "Looks like we've got visitors."

"Welcome to Haldon Head, strangers. Will you be staying long?" the mayor asked.

The farmer interjected, "Not if they know what's good for them."

"Alton! There's other business you'd best be attending."

The man named Alton replied, "We'll talk about this later, Toddy. By the heavens, we will!"

Farmer Alton turned and walked quickly away. The other man said, "I apologize for Farmer Alton's rudeness. He's a bit upset about some recent troubles."

"What was he saying about soldiers?" Jazhara asked.

"A squad of Krondorian guardsmen came through here a few days ago, chasing a fugitive, I think."

Jazhara glanced at James. "William's company?"

James nodded. "Could be."

Solon dismounted. "What were the troubles the farmer was referring to?" he asked.

Toddy glanced down at the ground, then looked up again. "We . . . uh . . . We've had some problems with wolves lately. What with the long winter and all . . . Now, if you'll excuse me, I must be getting back to the inn. You'd do well to join me, as I only keep the doors open for an hour or two after sunset, and I'd hate to see you trapped outside . . ." He hurried inside the inn and closed the door.

"That was odd," observed Kendaric.

James indicated that they should ride to the rear of the inn, and by the time they had reached the stabling yard, a boy was hurrying to take their horses. James instructed the boy on the care they required, then they walked back to the front of the inn and entered through the main door.

The inn was pleasant enough, if small. The lower floor was occupied by a taproom and kitchen, with a single flight of stairs running up the rear wall leading to the second floor. A fireplace off to the left contained a roaring blaze. A savory-smelling broth simmered in a huge copper kettle that hung before the fire. To one side a large spit stood ready for whatever meat was to be that evening's fare.

Toddy appeared a moment later carrying a large, spitted haunch of beef, which he put into the spit cradle. "Maureen!" he bellowed. "Come turn the beef!"

An older woman hurried out of the kitchen and nodded as she passed the innkeeper. Toddy turned to James and his companions. "I'm glad you decided to spend the night here. It may not be as fancy as you're used to, but I'd like you to consider it a home away from home. I can serve you an ale, if you like."

"That would be a start," said Kendaric.

"Well, then," said the innkeeper. "Seat yourselves and I'll fetch the ale."

He was back in a few minutes with four ceramic mugs full of frothy ale. "My name is Aganathos Toddhunter. Folks around here call me 'Toddy.' I'm both innkeeper and mayor of this small village. Hold the Prince's writ to act as justice in misdemeanor and justice of the peace in civil issues," he noted with some pride.

"Quite a bit of responsibility," said James, dryly.

"Not really," Toddy said, looking a bit deflated. "Truth is, the worst is usually a pig who wanders onto a neighbor's property and having to decide who pays damages or who keeps the pig." The attempt at humor was forced.

Jazhara said, "Why don't you join us for a drink?"

"Ah, you're being kind to spread so much cheer on this cheerless night," Toddy said. He retreated to the bar and poured himself a mug of ale, then returned and remained standing next to the table. "My thanks." He took a long pull on his ale.

Jazhara asked, "Why so cheerless?"

"Well, with the . . . wolves and all . . . we've lost several villagers already."

Solon looked hard at Toddy and said, "Wolves this near the coast are unusual. They tend to stay away from populated areas. Is there no one who will hunt them?"

Toddy took another drink of his ale. Then he said, "Please, I'm sorry I mentioned it. It's not your concern. Simply enjoy yourselves tonight. But I beg you not to go outside tonight."

James studied the innkeeper and saw a man trying his mightiest to hide a deep fear. Changing the subject, James asked, "You mentioned some guardsmen earlier. Do you know anything else about them?"

"They stayed here a single night, two days ago, and then moved on."

Jazhara asked, "Do you recall who led them?"

"A rather young officer. William, I think his name was. One of his trackers found the trail of their fugitive somewhere east of here." He drained the last of his ale and said, "Now, please excuse me while I take care of my duties. When you're ready to turn in, I'll show you to your rooms."

The only other customer in the inn was a man sitting by himself in the corner, staring deeply into his cup.

James leaned forward, so as not to be overheard by the lone drinker, and said, "Well, does anyone have any bright notions of what we should do next?"

Kendaric said, "I can't understand why my spell failed. It should have worked, but some other force . . . balked me. There is something in this area that is working against us."

Jazhara said, "It is possible that some other enchantment is in place keeping the ship under the waves until such time as Bear or whoever is employing him is ready to raise the ship himself. If that's the case, when *that* spell is removed, *your* spell will work."

James was silent for a moment. Then he said, "So what we have to do is find the source of this blocking magic and remove it?"

Solon nodded. "Easier said than done, laddie. While my knowledge of the mystic arts is far different than Jazhara's, I know such a spell is not fashioned by a dabbler. Whoever put the charm on that ship to keep it below the waves is no mean practitioner of the magician's arts."

Kendaric nodded in agreement. "This must be true. For no known force should have kept my spell from working."

James sighed. "Just once I'd like a plan to go as originally designed." With only slightly feigned frustration he added, "Wouldn't it be lovely to be back in Krondor tomorrow and say, 'Why, no, Highness, no troubles at all. We just strolled up to Widow's Point, raised the ship, got the Tear, wandered back down the coast, and here we are.' Wouldn't that be fine?" He sighed again. They fell silent.

After a few minutes of quiet drinking, the party was approached by the innkeeper. "Will you be eating?"

Noting the dearth of customers at the tables, James said, "Anywhere else around here to eat?"

"No," said Toddy with a pained smile. "It's just that some travelers are trying to keep expenses down and bring their own, that's all."

"We'll be eating," said James, nodding to where the woman was turning the side of beef.

"Food should be ready in an hour," said the innkeeper.

As he was about to depart, Jazhara asked, "Sir, a moment."

The innkeeper paused. "Milady?"

Jazhara said, "There seems to be some trouble here, or am I mistaken?"

Solon added, "We couldn't help but notice that the town seems almost deserted. What vexes this place?"

Toddy looked concerned, but he forced a smile and said, "Oh . . . well . . . just a little slow this time of year. No harvests in yet, no grain caravans . . . you know how small villages can be."

James looked directly at the mayor. "Frankly, sir, we've heard some strange things about this area. What truth is there to these rumors?"

The mayor glanced around, as if someone might be listening. "Well . . . some folks say that Widow's Point is haunted by the souls of the drowned, kept from Lims-Kragma's Hall by an ancient and horrible evil . . ." He lowered his voice. "Others claim that witchcraft has cursed our town, but I think it's all superstitious nonsense."

"This 'witchcraft' has been mentioned several times," said Jazhara.

James studied the man's face and said, "Sir, I am on the Prince's business. You are not free to repeat that to anyone, but I am on a mission of some urgency and the situation around here may prove difficult for the completion of my mission. Now, I urge you to be forthright with me or Haldon Head will have a new mayor as soon as I return to Krondor. What is going on around here? Why are the streets deserted during the day?"

The man looked defeated. At last, he nodded. "People are frightened, sir. They hurry from one place to another, and dare spend as little time outdoors as they can, even during the day. At night they bar their doors and cling close to their hearths. There is evil afoot."

"What sort of evil?" asked Solon.

Letting out his breath slowly, Toddy said, "Well, I guess I need to tell someone. This town is beset by some creature – or creatures – that stalk the night, killing good townsfolk, and stealing their souls. Even Father Rowland has been powerless to stop them."

"Who is Father Rowland?" Solon asked.

"The good father is a devotee of Sung. He's been in the area for a number of years, but he's recently decided that the witch is responsible for our troubles." At the mention of the word "witch" Jazhara stiffened her posture, but kept silent. Toddy continued.

"Now, I'd expect that kind of thinking from someone like Farmer Alton, but not a priest of Sung the Merciful and Pure."

Jazhara nodded. "'Witchcraft' does not exist. Either someone is a natural healer, and uses true magic, or simply knows the medicinal value of certain herbs and roots. 'Witchcraft' is an ignorant belief."

"You're right, of course," agreed Toddy. "The old woman has helped some of the townsfolk with poultices and brews in the past, and has been kind to most people who ask for help, but you know how people are: with the troubles now, they've come to fear what they don't understand. She lives up near the promontory above Widow's Point, if you'd care to speak with her yourself." He scratched his head, and dropped his voice to a conspiratorial whisper. "I know she's not involved with these horrors, but she may know something that will help you decide if our troubles are a danger to your mission for the Prince."

"Have you reported these troubles to the Prince?" asked James.

"Only to that patrol that went through here a few days ago, and they seemed intent upon another mission. Alan, the Prince's factor in the area, was due here last week, but he never showed up. That happens from time to time if he's on special business for the Crown. I was thinking of sending a boy with a message south, but no parent is willing to risk a child on the road . . . given the horrors we've seen."

"How did they begin?" asked James.

"I wish I knew," answered the mayor. "One day things were as they always were, the next . . . It began over a month ago. A woodcutter and his family who live a few miles to the east of the village disappeared. We don't know when exactly, but the woodcutter missed his usual delivery of wood for the village, so we began to worry. Six men went to his shack the next day, but only two returned."

"What did the two who returned tell you?" asked an alarmed Kendaric.

"Nathan and Malcolm? Malcolm, Lims-Kragma guide him, was killed last night by . . . whatever creature is responsible for this terrible situation. Nathan boarded himself up in his house and hasn't come out since. He has my stable-boy bring him food every day."

"Will he speak with us?" asked James.

"You can try. His house is less than a ten-minute walk from here. I would wait until the morning, though, sir, as he will almost certainly refuse to speak to anyone after dark." Pointing to the solitary drinker in the corner, Toddy said, "Lyle over there was a close friend of Malcolm." Leaning toward them, he added, "But I'd weigh his words carefully; his love of the spirits" – he made a drinking motion – "often clouds his judgment."

James stood up and Jazhara followed. Kendaric started to rise, but Solon reached out with one of his massive hands, firmly gripped the guildsman's arm, and pushed him back into his seat, shaking his head gently. Then the cleric rose and followed James and Jazhara. Kendaric opened his mouth to object, but Solon silenced him merely by pointing at the man's ale, indicating that he should continue to drink.

James, Jazhara, and Solon crossed to where the solitary figure sat staring into an empty mug. "Buy you a drink?" asked James.

The man looked up and said, "Never one to say no to that, stranger."

James motioned for Toddy to bring over a fresh tankard of ale, and when it was placed before the man, James pulled out a chair and sat down. "Your name is Lyle?"

"That's me," the man agreed.

"I understand you're friends with one of the men who survived some sort of attack here."

"Malcolm, he was my friend," agreed the man. "Died last night." He hoisted the ale flagon and said, "To Malcolm!" Then he drained it.

James waved for another and when it was placed before him, Lyle asked, "What do you want?"

"We want information," James replied.

"Tell us about this 'witch,'" added Jazhara.

Lyle said, "Everyone thinks she's in league with dark powers, but I don't believe it! She's a kind old woman. You can go see for yourself. Take the trail to the point and when it cuts down to the beach, stay on the small path up to the point. You'll find her in her hut most times when she's not out gathering herbs." He sighed deeply. "No, the real source of this evil is something else."

"What?" asked James.

Lowering his voice, Lyle said, "Blood-drinkers."

James's gaze narrowed and he looked at Jazhara before returning his attention to Lyle and repeating, "Blood-drinkers?"

"Night creatures. The dead returned to life."

Jazhara gasped. "Vampires!"

James looked at her. "Vampires?"

"Creatures of legend. Created by the foulest necromancy," she replied.

Remembering the dead bodies being arrayed by the goblins and the creatures in the sewers of Krondor, James said, "We've encountered a lot of that lately."

Jazhara said, "They drink the blood of the living to slake their unholy thirst, and those whose blood they take rise to join their number."

James closed his eyes for a moment, then said, "And I suppose because they're already dead, they're very difficult to kill again?"

Jazhara nodded. "They can be destroyed by magic or fire, or by cutting them up."

"Which they usually object to, I'll wager," said James dryly.

"They came from the woodcutter's shack!" said Lyle. "The woodcutter and his wife had lived there just a few months before they vanished. Six good men went to look in on that poor family. Whatever was up there killed four of 'em, and scared Nathan and poor Malcolm out of their wits."

"What happened to Malcolm?" asked James.

"Dead. Dead at the hands of those monsters. Malcolm always knew they'd come for him once he and Nathan got away, so he tried to get them first. He thought he could hide and watch for them, the old fool. He knew they came from the woodcutter's shack, but once he told me they'd desecrated our graveyard, too. He got a couple of them, first, though. Poor old sod."

"How'd he get them?" asked James.

"He found one in a grave, asleep during the daylight. He doused it with some oil we use to clear the fields, and set fire to it. Went up like a torch, he said. The other was just waking up at sundown; he cut its head off with his old sword from his duty during the Riftwar. Threw the head in the river and watched it wash away. Went back to the grave the next day and said the body had turned to dust. But there were just too many of them. They caught him out last night, old fool."

Solon, who had remained silent so far, could contain himself no longer. "Vampires, you say? Man, are you sure? They're the stuff of legend, things to scare small children on dark nights."

Jazhara nodded agreement. "I always thought they were mythical."

"But after what we've seen so far . . . ?" James asked.

Lyle said, "Nay, good sir and lady, they're real. Nathan says they come for him every night! That's why he locks himself in. He's got no fear of dying, but if those creatures get him, he says they'll keep his soul and he'll never take his turn on Lims-Kragma's Wheel of Life again!"

"'Tis a foul blasphemy, indeed, if true," agreed Solon.

James stood up. "Well, it seems this Nathan is the only one here in Haldon Head who has seen these creatures. I suspect we'd best go talk to him."

"I'd be cautious," Lyle said. "It's almost sundown and once the sun sets, Toddy locks the door and nothing you say will get you back inside."

"How far is it to Nathan's place?" asked Solon.

"Open the door," replied Lyle, "and you're looking straight at the road leading to it. Can't miss it. You'll pass two shops, and the first house on the left is Nathan's shack."

"We have time," James said, "if we hurry."

They collected Kendaric and hurried to the door. As they made to leave, Mayor Toddhunter shouted out, "Be back before the sun sets, or you'll spend the night outside!"

After they left the inn, Kendaric said, "Why are we doing this? I heard every word. Blood-drinkers! Are you mad?"

James said, "Do you think there might be another reason why your spell didn't work?"

"I have no idea why it didn't work," admitted Kendaric. "But vampires? They can't be real!"

"I hope you're right," said Solon. "Holy writ is clear on the living dead. Specifically, they are an abomination to Lims-Kragma, and to Ishap, for they defy the natural order of the world."

"Not to mention they'll almost certainly try to kill us," added James.

Kendaric glanced at the setting sun and said, "We have maybe a half-hour, Squire."

"Then we'd better hurry," said James.

They reached Nathan's house in five minutes, and even if Lyle hadn't told them where to look, it would have been easy to find. The small house, little more than a shack, was boarded up. All the windows had stout planks nailed across them; the door, obviously the only point of entry, was shut tight; nail points protruding from its perimeter indicated that it was similarly covered from within. In the red light of sunset, it looked almost deserted, though James saw a glint of flame escaping through a crack in the boards, no doubt coming from a lantern or fire pot.

"Hello, the house!" Kendaric shouted from the front stoop, a wooden platform in need of some repair. "We'd like to speak with you!"

From inside the house came a reply. "Go away, foul beasts! You'll never get me to quit my house!"

"Hello," said James. "I'm Squire James, from the Prince's court in Krondor."

"Leave me in peace, you bloody demons! I can see through your evil tricks."

James looked at Jazhara and shrugged.

Jazhara said, "Sir, I am the court magician to the Prince. We need some information about these creatures that trouble you. We may be able to help!"

"Ah, very clever, very clever indeed," came the reply. "Go away, you soul-sucking fiends!"

James shook his head in defeat. "What's it going to take to convince you, friend?"

"Go away!"

James turned to Jazhara. "Maybe you can do better?"

Solon said, "Let me try." He stepped up to the boarded door and shouted, "In the name of Mighty Ishap, the One Above All, I bid you let us enter!"

There was a long moment of silence and then Nathan said, "That's good. I didn't know you blood-stealers could invoke the name of the gods! Almost had me for a moment there, with that bad dwarven accent!"

Solon's face flushed with anger. "'Tis not a bad dwarven accent, ya gibbering loon. I grew up near Dorgin!"

James turned to Jazhara and said, "It does get more pronounced when he gets upset, did you notice?"

Jazhara said, "Let me try again." Speaking up, she said, "Sir, I am a magician and could enter your house at will, but would not violate the sanctity of your home. If you won't let us enter, at least tell us what you know about the evil that besets this town. Perhaps we can help. We have our own reasons for wanting to see it banished."

There was another long silence, then Nathan said through the boards, "Almost got me with that one, you monster!" He laughed madly. "Trying to find out how much I know so you can plot against me! Well, I'm not falling for it."

Kendaric said, "James – "

James waved him to silence. "Look, Nathan, if you don't want to come out, you don't have to, but we need to find the cause of all this trouble in the area. We have, as my friend said, our own reasons for wanting to see it come to an end. If these 'vampires,' as you call them, are real, they may be causing us our problem and we'll deal with them."

"You'll get your chance soon enough!" shouted Nathan.

"James – " Kendaric repeated.

James again waved his hand and said, "Just a minute!"

As he was about to speak again, James felt his arm gripped by Kendaric, who swung him around to face down the path to the house. "James!" shouted the wrecker. "It looks like we get our chance now."

As the sun was dropping below the horizon, dark shadows seemed to coalesce in the air at the edge of the nearby woods. In the darkness other shapes could be seen moving, and suddenly human forms appeared where there had been empty air a moment before.

James slowly drew his sword and said, "Solon, Jazhara, any advice would be greatly appreciated."

A half-dozen figures advanced from the nearby woods. They appeared human, save for their deathly pale white skin color, and eyes that seemed to glow with a reddish light. Several of them showed gaping wounds on their necks and they shambled with an awkward gait.

The one in the front spoke. "Nathan . . . Come to us . . . We miss you so . . ."

From behind it others called, "You should have stayed with us, Nathan. There's no need to fear us, Nathan."

With rising revulsion, James saw that one of the figures was a child, a little girl of no more than seven years of age.

Solon said, "There's but one piece of advice I can give, laddie. Destroy them all." He raised his warhammer and advanced on the first figure.

TWELVE

Dark Magic

J ames charged after Solon.

Jazhara shouted, "Be wary, you must destroy them by fire or cut their heads from their bodies!"

Kendaric hung behind the magician, holding his short sword, but appearing ready to bolt if the opportunity presented itself. Jazhara began an incantation and lowered her staff, pointing it toward the group of oncoming creatures. A ball of green flame erupted from the tip of her staff and shot across the space between them, engulfing four of the creatures in mystic flame. They howled and writhed, and stumbled forward, staggering for a few paces before falling face-down onto the ground.

Solon reached out with a gauntlet-covered hand and seized the child-creature, hurling the small form backward, into the green flame. The tiny creature shrieked and thrashed, then lay still.

"May Ishap bring you peace, child," shouted the monk. He swung his huge warhammer at an adult-sized creature, smashing the thing's shoulder, but still it lunged at him, its one remaining arm outstretched, the fingers bent like talons trying to rend and tear.

Solon lashed back the other way, and his hammer caved

in the creature's skull. It fell to the ground and lay writhing, but despite having half its head pulped, it still tried to rise. Jazhara ran up to the monk and shouted, "Stand back!" He retreated and she lowered her staff. In a moment, the creature was aflame.

James was having difficulty with a particularly powerful man – *or creature, rather*, he corrected himself. The thing had obviously been the woodcutter Lyle had first told them of. He had been a big, broad-shouldered man, and his arms were long and meaty. He tried to grapple with James, who dodged aside. But the damage inflicted on the creature by James's rapier did little to slow it.

"Kendaric!" James shouted. "I could use some help!"

The wrecker stood with his back to Nathan's doorway, his sword clutched in his hand. "Doing what?" he shouted back.

"My blade isn't exactly a meat cleaver."

Kendaric waved his short sword and said, "And this is?"

James ducked under a huge hand swinging through the air, and shouted, "It's a better blade for hacking than what I've got!"

"I'm not going to loan it to you!" cried Kendaric, watching as other creatures came into sight. "I've got problems of my own."

Suddenly Jazhara was at Kendaric's side and she wrenched the blade from his hand. "Yes, a decided attack of cowardice," she said with contempt. Throwing the sword so that it sailed through the air, she shouted, "James, catch!"

With a speed bordering on the supernatural, James lashed out with his rapier, cutting the shambling creature across the back of the leg. Then he leapt into the air, catching the short sword with his left hand. He tossed his rapier and the short sword in a juggle, ending up with the rapier in his left hand and the short sword in his right. The thing that had been a woodcutter stumbled onto one knee, and James lashed down with the sword, cleanly severing the creature's neck, so that the head came rolling free.

James threw the short sword back to Kendaric, and shouted, "Better lend a hand here, unless you're anxious to end up like them!"

More creatures were emerging from the woods and Jazhara unleashed several bolts of her mystic flame. She shouted, "James, I can't keep this up! I'm almost exhausted."

"We have to get to someplace defensible!" said Brother Solon, as he slammed his hammer into yet another creature, knocking it backward a half-dozen feet.

James hurried to the door of Nathan's house and pounded on it as he cried, "By the gods, man, let us in!"

"No, it's a trick and I won't be fooled!" came a shout from inside.

"Let us in, or I'll burn this place down around your ears," said James. "Jazhara, do you have one shot of that fire left?"

"I can manage," said the magician.

Loudly, but in measured, calm tones, James said, "Open this door or you're going to get very warm. Which will it be?"

After a moment of silence, they heard the creak of nails being pulled and a series of thumps as heavy boards hit the floor. Finally the door-bolt slid free, and the door cracked open a bit. A pinched-faced man peered out at James and said, "You don't *look* like a vampire."

James nodded. "I'm glad you finally recognize the obvious. Clear the way while I go help my friends. We'll be right back. We'll hammer the boards back into place once we're all inside."

James didn't wait to see the man's nod, but turned and hurried to intercept a particularly nasty-looking creature heading straight for Kendaric. The wrecker waved his sword ineffectually in the direction of the creature, which paused to consider the potential for injury.

That pause gave James just the opening he needed to circle behind the creature and hamstring it with his rapier. "It won't kill him," shouted the squire, "but it'll slow him down! Try to cut his head off."

Kendaric's expression left no room for doubt as to how he felt about that suggestion. He backed away, putting distance between himself and the creature.

"Kendaric, you useless bag of pig-swill," shouted Solon. He ran over and used his warhammer to break the creature's spine.

Kendaric proffered his sword. "*You* cut its head off!"

"Ya gibbering jackass! Holy orders prevent me from cutting flesh with a blade. If I do, I lose my sanctity and must be cleansed for a year by holy rite, fasting, and meditation! I donna ha' a year to waste on such foolishness! We ha' work to do."

Jazhara said to James, "You're right, the accent does get thicker when he's upset."

James shouted, "Open the door!" More creatures were coming into sight, and James had no doubt they would soon be overwhelmed.

Kendaric was at the door, and pounded on the planks. Nathan swung the door wide with one hand, as he brandished a hunting knife in the other. "Get inside!" shouted the villager. Kendaric entered the cottage as the others began to rush toward the house. Suddenly James wheeled at the sound of a footstep behind him, slashing out with his blade, and slicing through the throat of what had once been a young woman. She didn't fall, but faltered long enough for him to turn and run. Solon smashed another in the face and also ran.

Jazhara hurried through the door, Solon and James on her heels.

Nathan slammed the door shut behind them and threw the bolt. He then picked up one of planks he had just removed and cried, "Start boarding this up!"

Solon picked up another piece of wood and used his warhammer to drive heavy nails back into the doorframe. "This will not hold if they get determined," said the monk.

"It'll hold," said the townsman. "They're persistent but stupid and don't work well as a group. If they did, I'd have been dead four nights back."

James sheathed his rapier and sat down on a small trunk next to the fireplace. He glanced around. The building was a single room with a small kitchen off to one side. A feather bed, a table, a chest of drawers and the trunk upon which he sat were the sole contents of the room.

Their host was a wiry man of middle years, his dark hair and beard shot through with gray. He had the weather-beaten look of a farmer: once-broken fingers and heavy calluses betrayed the hands of a man who had worked all his life.

Letting out a slow breath, James said, "Just what is going on?"

"So, then we started hearing about others vanishing, from farms outlying the village. There's the odd homestead up in the hills, and some nice meadows that folks use to graze herds or grow summer wheat. Some of those creatures that attacked earlier tonight were the poor souls who lived up there. Not townspeople, but folks we knew from when they'd come in to buy provisions or sell their wares." He shook his head as if he still had trouble believing what he was describing.

James and the others had been listening to the farmer for over an hour. The narrative had been rambling and disjointed at times, but a pattern had emerged.

"Let me sum up," said James. "Someone or something has come to the area. It has infected your community with a horrible curse that is turning ordinary people into blood-drinkers. Is that right?"

The farmer nodded. "Yes."

James continued. "These creatures are feeding on others, thereby turning them into blood-drinkers, too."

"Vampires," said Jazhara. "The stories about them are full of superstition."

"But these are real enough," said Kendaric.

"Yes," agreed Solon. "But Jazhara is right. There are legends about these creatures that have nothing to do with truth, flights of fancy and tales told to frighten naughty children."

"I must be a naughty child, then," said Kendaric with an angry edge to his voice, "because I for one am very frightened."

James said, "So the woodcutter and his family were the first around here to be turned into these creatures?"

Nathan said, "Yes. Six of us went to investigate. Only two of us survived. We found a dozen or so of those creatures waiting there. A few of them were the folks from the nearby farms I spoke of; a couple were unknown to me."

"Then who was the first?" asked James.

Nathan looked around blankly. "I don't know," he said in a weary voice.

"Is that important?" asked Kendaric.

"Yes," said Jazhara, "because as James said, someone or something had to bring this plague here."

Solon said, "This sort of magic is evil beyond description."

James sat on the floor with his back against the wall. "But to what end? Why plague *this* little village of all places?"

Kendaric said, "Because they can?"

James looked at the wrecker and said, "What do you mean?"

Kendaric shrugged and said, "They have to start somewhere. If they get enough people around here to . . . become like them, they can send some of their number to other locations and . . . well, it's like you said, a plague."

"Which means we'll have to stamp out this infection here," said Solon.

James could hear the shuffle of feet outside.

Nathan shouted, "Keep away, you murderous blood-suckers!"

From outside, voices called, "Come with us. Join us."

Jazhara shivered. "I know little of these creatures, save for legends. But already I can see the legends are only partially correct."

James looked at Nathan and said, "Got anything to drink?"

"Water," said the farmer, pointing to a large crock near the table.

As James fetched a cup and went to the crock, he said to Jazhara, "What do you mean 'only partially correct?'"

Jazhara said, "The legends of the vampires tell us of great and powerful magic-users, able to alter their shapes and commune with animals, such as rats and wolves. The pitiful creatures we face here, while far from harmless, could have all been put to rest tonight, had we a trained squad of soldiers with us."

James quietly reflected on this as he remembered a time in Krondor when, as a boy, he and Prince Arutha had faced the undying minions of the false moredhel prophet, Murmandamus. "My experience tells me that things that hard to kill are far more dangerous than they seem."

Nathan added, "Besides, lady, you miss the obvious. These aren't great and powerful magic-users. These were farmers and laborers."

James said, "So that would mean the great and powerful magic-using vampire is out there somewhere. And he – it – is behind all this."

Solon said, "Aye. The Temple teaches what it knows about the forces of darkness. The blood-drinkers are an old and powerful line of evil, said to have descended from a single, cursed magician who lived ages ago in some distant and unknown land. No one knows if the tale is true, but it has been told in the chronicles that from time to time such a cursed one appears, and woe betide those who chance upon him."

"Why?" asked Kendaric.

All eyes turned to him.

Solon asked, "Why does 'woe betide' those who chance across him?"

"No, I mean why do such creatures exist?"

Solon replied, "No one knows. What the Temple teaches is that the forces of darkness often benefit when chaos reigns, so much of what they do is merely to cause problems for order and good."

Kendaric nodded. "All right, I can accept that. But why here?"

James said, "It should be obvious. Someone doesn't want us to reach the Tear."

"The Tear?" Farmer Nathan asked, bewildered.

James waved away the question with a gesture. "You don't

really wish to know, trust me. Just suffice it to say that magic around here is not what it should be."

"That is the truth, " agreed Jazhara.

"It must be that witch," said Nathan. "She's the only user of magic in these parts."

Jazhara said, "Has she been a problem before?"

"No," admitted the farmer. "But . . . well, who else could it be?"

"That is what we must find out," said James. Listening to the voices from outside, he added, "How long will they keep this up?"

Nathan said, "Until first light. They perish from its touch, it is said."

James said, "Said by whom?"

Nathan blinked. "Sir?"

"Never mind," said James, as he lay down on the floor. "I'm dubious as to the origin of many beliefs. It's a character flaw. Wake me when they go away."

Jazhara nodded and said, "Then what do we do?"

"Find this magic-using vampire and put him out of his misery."

"Aye," said Solon. "If we can do that, the rest will fade away, it is said."

James resisted the urge to ask again "by whom" and merely said, "There can't be many places around here for such a one to hide."

"Oh, I can tell you where one such place is," said Nathan.

James sat upright. "Where?"

"In the graveyard, south of the village. There's a crypt there that has been broken into. There's something in there, I'm certain."

"Why didn't you tell anyone?"

"I did," said Nathan. "But Toddy and the others wanted to hear no part of it. Father Rowland said something about the forces of the gods would protect the properly buried, or something like that, and ignored me."

"That's odd," said Solon. "A priest of Sung the Pure would be among those most interested in investigating such a desecration. Their order is in the forefront of the battle against just these kinds of dark forces."

"Maybe others are," said Nathan. "But he just holds his prayer meetings and rails against the witch. Maybe he's right."

"Again, 'the witch!'" said Jazhara with open contempt. "What has this woman done?"

"Well, Farmer Alton claims she's poisoned his cows, and Farmer Merrick's little girl lies abed with some cursed sickness the witch sent her way."

"But why?" asked Solon. "If this woman has been kind to you before, why'd she turn her hand on you now?"

Nathan shrugged. "You tell me. You're a priest – "

"Monk," corrected Solon.

" – monk, so you must know why these things happen."

Shaking his head, Solon said, "Ah, if only it were so. No, the ways of evil are a mystery."

James said, "Hold the theological debate down, will you? I'm going to get some sleep."

Listening to the low voices from outside and the shuffling of footsteps around the house, Kendaric said, "How can you sleep with that going on?"

James opened one eye and said, "Practice." He closed it and within minutes was asleep.

*   *   *

Just before sunrise the voices ceased. James woke up to find Solon sound asleep on the floor, while a fatigued Jazhara sat with her arms around her knees, her staff at hand, watching the door. Nathan sat silently nearby. Kendaric had succumbed to sleep and lay on the wooden floor, snoring.

James rolled over, his joints protesting a night spent on such an unyielding surface, and got to his feet. He gently nudged Kendaric with his boot. The wrecker sat up with an alarmed expression on his face, shouting, "What!"

Solon was instantly awake, then realizing it was only Kendaric making the noise, sat back again. "Sunrise?"

James nodded.

Nathan stood as well and asked, "What will you do this day?"

Jazhara said, "Find the source of this evil."

"Then look to the witch up on Widow's Point," said Nathan. "I still think she must be behind all this. Someone has to destroy her!"

Solon said, "Have faith, friend. We will crush her evil just as we destroyed the evil that has plagued you."

"If she is, indeed, the source of this evil," said Jazhara pointedly.

Nathan said, "Are you mad? You did nothing last night. Don't you think I've fought those things before? Except for one or two you burned with magic fire or beheaded, the rest will return. In the darkness they can't be destroyed!"

"Well, we'll see what we can do," said a tired James. "But first we need to get something to eat."

"Toddy will open the door for you once the sun is up," said Nathan. "Tell him to send my food over, would you, please?"

"What will you do?" asked Kendaric.

"Barricade my door again." Then his voice took on a frantic quality. "But you know they'll get me in the end, turn me into one of them. It's just a matter of time."

"Easy," said Solon. "We'll have none of that, laddie. With Ishap's divine guidance, we'll see an end to the troubles that plague this poor village."

James and Solon removed the boards that were nailed across the door and went outside. Before they were off the porch, they could hear Nathan again nailing them into place. Kendaric looked at the sky.

"What is it?" asked James. "Rain?"

"No, something . . . odd," said the wrecker. "For nearly twenty years I've worked the sea and I've never seen a sky like that."

"Like what?" asked Jazhara. "I don't see anything odd."

"Look toward the sunrise."

They did so and after a moment, Solon said, "Ishap's mercy! What has happened to the sun?"

In the distance the sun rose, but despite the air being clear and there being no clouds in sight, the light seemed muted, and although the sun glowed, its brilliance was dimmed.

"Magic," said Jazhara. She paused, as if listening to something. "There is something in the air which drinks the light. We didn't notice it yesterday, because we arrived near sundown, but some dark agency is lessening the sun's radiance here."

"What could do that?" asked James.

Jazhara shrugged. "A relic of great power, or a spell forged by a magician of great arts. It would have to cover a very large area indeed to dull the sun's brilliance."

"I thought it a little overcast when we arrived," said James. "But I didn't note if there were clouds over the cliffs or not."

"There is nothing natural in this," affirmed Kendaric. "But to what purpose has this been done?"

"So that things that walk the night can walk the day?" mused Solon.

James said, "Forget breaking our fast. We must go to confront this witch now."

Without further comment, James turned toward the peak at Widow's Point on the other side of Haldon Head and started walking.

As they walked through the village, they saw Toddy hurrying from his inn. "You!" he said with a broad grin as he spied James and his companions. "You survived the night!"

James smiled. "Surviving is something we do well. You seem to be in a hurry."

The mayor of the village lost his smile. "Farmer Merrick's daughter is ill, and he's gathered some of the village folk at his home. I think they mean some mischief."

James glanced at Jazhara, who returned a slight nod. They fell into step behind the portly innkeeper, who was hurrying along as best as his girth permitted.

When they arrived at Farmer Merrick's house, they found a half-dozen of the village's men, and an equal number of women, gathered before the farmer's door. The farmer and his wife stood in the doorway. A florid-faced, stocky man was saying, "We must do something. This has gone on too long!"

Toddy pushed through the small crowd. "What is this, then?"

The florid-faced man shouted, "We're going to do something about that witch, Toddy!"

"Now, now," said the mayor, holding up his hands. "Let's

not do anything rash. This lad here" – he indicated James – "is a representative of the Crown and will take care of things."

Instantly all speaking stopped and eyes turned to James. James threw a dark look Toddy's way, then said, "Very well. Now, we're here on a matter of interest to the Crown and what has been going on around here is of importance to His Highness. So, who can tell me what has occurred?"

Instantly everyone started speaking at once. James held up his hand and said, "Wait a minute. One at a time." He pointed to the florid-faced man who had been railing when they arrived and said, "You. Speak your piece."

"My cows come down sick!" the man shouted. Then he realized he didn't need to be shouting over others, and he lowered his voice. "My cows come down sick, and it's that witch. She's sent a curse to make them die slowly."

A woman in the crowd spoke up. "And we're losing our daylight, little by little. Sunrise has been coming later every morning; sundown earlier every evening. And what sunlight we do have is, I don't know how to explain it, but look around, it's different. Pretty soon we won't have any daylight at all. And you know what that means!" she sobbed.

Muttering broke out among the small crowd. James held up his hand for silence.

From the doorway, the farmer named Merrick spoke. "It's not only our cows that're sick. Our little girl, she's gravely ill."

James looked at Merrick and said, "What ails the girl?"

"She's cursed," shouted a woman from the edge of the group gathered in the yard.

Jazhara said, "May I see her?"

"Who are you?" asked the frantic-looking woman by Merrick's side, her face pinched and pale.

"I am Prince Arutha's personal advisor on magic," Jazhara answered.

Brother Solon added, "And I am a monk of Ishap's Temple. If there's evil magic afoot, we'll root it out."

The woman nodded and motioned them into the small house.

Inside they found a single room, with a small hearth on the wall opposite the door. A pair of beds stood there, one obviously big enough for the farmer and his wife and the other a child's bed. A small girl, her features wan, occupied this bed. Jazhara knelt by the side of the bed and put her hand upon the girl's forehead. "She has no fever," said the magician. "What can you tell me?"

The farmer said, "Nothing, save she's become too weak to walk or stay awake for more than a few minutes at a time. When she is awake, she seems unable to recognize us."

The farmer's wife added, "Sometimes she'll shake."

Brother Solon knelt beside Jazhara and examined the girl. "What is this?" he asked, fingering a small amulet. "This looks to be the sign of Sung."

"Father Rowland gave it to us," said the woman. Then she blurted, "I went to the old woman on Widow's Point, and she gave me a charm to heal my child. She told me a great darkness was trying to take the children. She was trying to protect them."

"Larissa!" scolded the man. "I told you not to speak of this."

"Go on," said James to the woman.

Defiantly, she looked at her husband. "She was trying to protect our daughter."

"Like she 'protected' Remy's son?"

"Yes, exactly like that!" She turned to James. "She was too late to save Remy's boy, but when I got home and put the charm under the bed, my girl stopped shaking. She wasn't getting better, but she wasn't getting any worse! Then Father Rowland returned from a journey and came here. He prayed all last night, and my daughter began shaking again. When the sun rose, I swear he seemed irritated she was still alive!" The woman's look was one of desperation.

"Larissa, that's blasphemy!" said Merrick. "The good father was trying to save her soul. It's the witch's fault. He said as much before he left."

"But what if it's not?" asked the woman.

"May I see the charm the 'witch' gave you?" Jazhara asked.

The woman drew it out from under the bed and handed it to Jazhara. She looked at the small wooden box, within which she found several herbs and some crystals. She closed her eyes and held the box for a long minute, then said, "There is nothing malicious in this. This is a simple ward to help the child's natural energy heal herself." Then she looked at the child. "But there is something . . ."

She reached out and took the small amulet from the girl's throat, then suddenly withdrew her hand as if it had been burned. "Brother Solon. You know more of clerical arts than I; will you please examine that ward?"

Solon gently touched the amulet. He closed his eyes and made a short incantation, and then his eyes snapped open. "This is no ward of Sung!" The amulet began to change and he withdrew his fingers from it. The metal seemed to ripple and warp and darken, until suddenly what had appeared to be a simple metal icon of Sung became something resembling a tiny maw, a mouth of black lips and ebony teeth. It opened wide, as if to bite, then the girl coughed. A plume of green gas erupted from her nostrils and mouth, to be sucked into the tiny black orifice. Solon grabbed the trinket and ripped it from the unconscious child's neck. The girl gasped slightly, and her tiny body convulsed once, then settled down into the bed. With a sigh she took a deep breath, then seemed to breathe more easily.

Jazhara examined the child and declared, "Already she seems a little stronger."

Solon held out the trinket, which was now revealed to be a claw holding a black pearl. "I would venture that this is the cause of the child's illness."

Merrick looked confounded. "But it was given to her by Father Rowland!"

James looked at Jazhara and the others and said, "Before we go rushing off to burn out an old woman, I think we need to have a serious 'talk' with this Father Rowland."

He didn't wait for an answer, but walked out of the tiny farmhouse.

THIRTEEN

Misdirection

J ames halted.

Looking skyward for a moment, he then turned to Jazhara and the others hurrying to keep up with him and said, "Is it me, or is it getting darker?"

Kendaric glanced to the west. "There is no weather front approaching, and I see no clouds."

Solon looked at the sky and after a few seconds said, "No, it isn't you. It *is* getting darker."

Jazhara looked to the east, and pointed. "Look at the sun!"

They all turned to face the sunrise, and as they watched with a fascination that turned quickly to dread, the sun dimmed. The brilliant white had now darkened to a dull yellow.

Jazhara said, "I can feel the heat upon my face, but the light is fading!"

Solon said, "Yes, you have the right of it. Something is stealing the light from the very air!"

"What does this mean?" Kendaric asked anxiously.

"I don't know," Jazhara said. "I know of no magic that should be able to do this."

Kendaric repeated doggedly, "But what does it mean?"

James moved to stand before the now-terrified wrecker. "Pull yourself together! What it means should be obvious."

"So what does it mean?" demanded Kendaric.

"It means that soon our friends from last night will be able to walk abroad at any time."

People were hurrying past and James overheard someone say, "Father Rowland will know what to do!"

The florid-faced man who had been inciting the others in front of Merrick's house approached and said, "If you're a servant of the Prince as you claim, you'll go burn that witch out right now!"

"And who are you?" James asked.

"My name's Alton. After I spoke against the woman at a town meeting, she fixed my cows with the evil eye, and put the wasting curse on them. Ask any of my neighbors. They've seen my animals dying. And she's done worse."

"Such as?" said James, impatiently.

"Well, take the woodcutter and his family. They were nice, normal folks, then suddenly they vanished. Then the blood-drinkers showed up. And Remi's little boy; he took ill after spying her one day up at Widow's Point. Died a fortnight later."

James said, "Your mayor doesn't seem to think she's the cause of these ills."

"Toddy's a wonderful, kind man, but he can be a bit of a fool."

James shook his head as other townspeople hurried by. "Where's Father Rowland?" he asked Alton.

"Just follow everyone else to the church across the square. That's where we're going." Suddenly, he gasped. "Look!" He pointed to the east and they could see how the sun was now darkening to an orange color as if heavy smoke were obscuring the orb.

As the farmer pointed, James noticed a glint of metal around his neck, a chain that moved as his tunic shifted. At the base he caught a glimpse of something black.

James had not been called "Jimmy the Hand" as a boy for nothing. With startling swiftness, he reached out and pulled the chain high enough to reveal a black pearl in a metal hand hanging from the chain. "Who gave this to you?"

The farmer's eyes grew round and he stepped back as James released the chain. "I . . . I found it."

"Where?"

"Ah . . ."

"We found a similar charm – around Merrick's daughter's neck," said Jazhara.

"It's just a simple bauble," said Farmer Alton.

Solon moved suddenly, far quicker than one would expect of a man his size, and came to stand just behind Alton. "Don't be thinking of leaving any time soon, my friend."

James drew his sword slowly for dramatic purpose. He didn't think this blustering farmer was particularly dangerous. But he also felt time was running short and he needed answers. "Again: Who gave you that charm?"

Alton attempted to move away, but Solon grabbed his arm and held him fast. "I think you'd best answer the lad; he doesn't appear to be in a mood for foolishness."

Alton glanced at Jazhara, whose expression was cold, then to Kendaric, who also looked as if he were running out of patience. Suddenly the farmer blurted, "I'll tell you everything! It wasn't my idea. I was just an honest farmer, minding my own business when he came to me. I trusted him; everyone does. He offered me gold, lots of gold, to poison my own cows and blame the witch, so I agreed. She's just one old lady, and she's going to die soon, anyway. But I didn't know what he really was. I thought he was human when I agreed to work for him. I didn't know – " Suddenly the man's tumbling words were cut off by a strangled, gurgling sound as the chain around his neck abruptly tightened. Alton staggered backward, his eyes bulging and his face turning crimson as he clawed at his neck. Solon found himself holding the man upright as his knees buckled, and he let the farmer slowly sink to the ground. Blood began to flow from the wound in Alton's neck. As the farmer's eyes rolled up into his head, the sounds of muscles snapping and bones breaking could be heard. A moment later, the farmer's head rolled free from his body and dropped to the ground. Solon released the man's arm and the body crumpled to the dust.

James stared at the corpse and then at the darkening sun. He motioned for the others to follow and hurried toward a small building on the edge of the village common. Upon reaching it, they saw it was a simple church with a large, open entrance. No benches or pews were provided, so the congregation stood, listening to a man in white robes, who must surely be Father Rowland.

"Again, I say, if we wait much longer, we will be swept away by a tide of evil. And where, must I ask, is the justice in this? I will tell you where justice lies. It lies in the strength of our arms, the purity of our souls, and the burning that will rid the world of the witch's evil!"

Several of the townspeople shouted agreement.

"He sounds a wee bit harsh for a priest of Sung," Solon observed.

James nodded. "He does seem to be in an awful hurry to get rid of the 'witch.'"

"And to have others do the deed for him," Jazhara added.

The priest's voice rose. "Some say this witch has summoned wolves who walk like men at night, blood-drinkers who devour the souls of the innocent, turning them into monsters like themselves! I say she has summoned darkness incarnate – spirits so foul they drain the life from good people like you and me. Either way, the blame for this lies on her doorstep. This darkness approaching signals the final attack! *We must move now!*"

Some of the men cheered and shouted threats, but James could discern their fear for many of the responses were half-hearted and weak. He pushed through the villagers to stand before the priest.

"Welcome, stranger," said Father Rowland. He was a man of middle height, with dark hair and a small, pointed beard. Around his neck hung a simple ward of the Order of Sung. His white robes showed faint stains and dirt, as if old and oft-washed. "Have you come to help rid us of this blight?"

James regarded him steadily. "I have, but I doubt the blight is what you say."

The priest looked at James, his eyes narrowing. "What do you mean?"

"Alton is dead," James said.

The priest looked shocked. "Farmer Alton is dead? Another victim of that wicked woman!" Looking past James, the priest shouted, "Is this not enough? Isn't it time for us to act?"

More voices were raised in agreement, but James heard Jazhara shout, "James, be wary! There is something not right here!"

James looked and saw that several of those who were shouting had a vacant expression, their staring eyes fixed and lifeless. James turned toward the priest, then with unexpected swiftness, reached out and grabbed at the amulet around the man's neck. With a single yank, he tore it away and held it up. Before his eyes it shifted and changed, from the benign icon of Sung to a hand holding a black pearl.

"These are servants of the Dark One! They must die!" shouted the priest, his hands reaching for James's throat, fingers bent like talons.

James tried to jump backward, but suddenly was seized by hands, holding him in place. He could hear Jazhara shouting, "The people are innocents! They are possessed! Try not to harm them!"

James felt the priest's fingers at his throat and shouted, "I'll try to keep that in mind!" He let his body go limp and dropped away, the priest's fingers slipping over his head for a moment. From the floor, James could not draw his sword, but he could reach the dagger that was tucked in the top of his right boot. He drew it and slashed upward, striking the priest in the leg.

Father Rowland shouted in pain and fell backward, and James rolled his legs under him in a crouch as strong hands tried to hold him in place. Then he leapt forward with all his strength and, as he had hoped, the hands lost their grip upon him.

Several townspeople stumbled forward, and he barely avoided being pulled down from behind. The priest was retreating. James glanced quickly from one side to the other. Jazhara was wheeling her staff, keeping the villagers at bay. Kendaric was being borne down, pinned to the floor by a pair of strong farmers, while another was attempting to kick him in the head. Brother Solon was using his warhammer to shove people away as much as strike them, in his attempt to reach the wrecker's side and render aid.

James tossed his dagger from his right hand to his left, and drew his sword in one fluid motion. He shifted his blade and struck the closest man across the head with the flat; even so, the rapier's thin blade still cut the man, but it wasn't a deep wound.

The blow sent the man staggering back a step, blocking those behind him for an instant. An instant was all James needed. He lunged forward, as Father Rowland began to weave a magic spell. Before the priest had finished, James had skewered him through the stomach.

The man looked down in stunned amazement, then his eyes widened in pain as James yanked free his blade. Then the priest's eyes rolled back into his head. But rather than fall, he continued to stand. His head lolled back and his mouth hung open, but from within a deep, alien voice declared, "Though our servant lies dead, our power remains undimmed. Taste the bitter draught of evil . . . and despair."

The priest crumpled to the floor and James wheeled, ready for the next attack, but rather than being assaulted, James was met with the sight of the townspeople standing around, blinking in confusion. Several looked at one another, or at Kendaric and Solon, or Jazhara, and then the babble of voices began.

"What happened?"

"How did we get here?"

"Why are you bleeding?"

James held up his hand and cried, "Silence!"

Voices stilled. James continued, "This man was no priest of

Sung. He was an agent of the very darkness he claimed to be fighting. He kept you distracted from the true source of the evil."

One of the women in the group screamed. "The sun!" she shouted, pointing at the morning sun.

James turned. It was even darker. "It'll be night soon," he said, not trying to explain what he couldn't. "Get to your homes and bar the doors. We'll see to the cause of this."

The villagers fled. Some had to be helped by friends, because of the battering they had taken from Jazhara's staff and Solon's warhammer, but James was relieved to see that the only corpse in the room was Rowland's.

Kendaric looked frightened, but he also seemed to have kept his composure. He brushed himself off as they all gathered around James.

"Did the rest of you hear what he said?" James asked.

"No," answered Kendaric. "I was too busy being attacked."

Jazhara said, "I heard him speak, but not what he said."

"I heard it," said Brother Solon. "He was an agent of darkness, there's no doubt of that. That he could take the guise of a servant of the Pure One is troubling. Even a false icon such as he wore should be difficult to endure by a servant of evil."

"These are very powerful enemies," said James. "I've heard that voice before."

"When?" asked Jazhara.

"Years ago, from the mouth of a Black Slayer. The servants of Murmandamus."

"But Murmandamus was destroyed," said Jazhara. Then she glanced at Solon and Kendaric, unsure of what more she should say. As Arutha's court mage, James had told her some of the truth behind Arutha's slaying of the false moredhel prophet, and the recent troubles in the Dimwood, for there were rumors that he was still alive.

James nodded. "I know he was, but while we may not be dealing with that black heart, we are certainly facing someone who is nearly his equal in power. And that means we're up against something far more dangerous than we thought."

"You knew it was dangerous when we told you about our ship being taken," said Solon. "You're not backing out now, are you?"

"No," said James, glancing at the darkening sun. "Especially not now. I can feel things rushing forward and if we hesitate, I think we are lost." He realized he was still holding his weapons and he put them up. "We don't have time to send for reinforcements, and we don't know how effective William will continue to be at keeping Bear away from here. I think this will end before more than two days pass, one way or the other."

"What now?" asked Kendaric, crossing his arms as if cold.

James let out a long breath. "When darkness finally comes, those blood-drinkers will be back, and I think they are here for no other reason than to keep us busy. So whatever we do, we have to do it quickly." He looked at Jazhara. "One thing strikes me. Rowland and Alton were too anxious to get rid of that witch for it to have only been about finding a scapegoat. There's something about her they feared."

Jazhara said, "Then we should go talk to her." Glancing at the sun, she added, "And quickly. I think we have less than two hours before night falls again."

James nodded. Walking past Jazhara he said, "Let us go visit the witch at Widow's Point."

*   *   *

As they climbed the hillside toward Widow's Point, the woods turned ominously dark. The fading sun created darker shadows on the trail than usual. "It's like traveling at twilight," whispered Solon.

James laughed. "I feel the need to speak softly, too."

Jazhara said, "Stealth may be prudent, but time is fleeting."

As they rounded a bend in the trail, James held up his hand. "Someone's ahead," he whispered.

They moved forward and James soon clearly saw a figure crouched in the gloom. It was a boy of no more than nine years of age. James walked up behind him, making no effort to be silent, yet the child's attention remained fixed upon a small hut near the cliffs. When James put his hand on the child's shoulder, the boy shouted in alarm and nearly fell down in surprise.

"Don't be afraid," said Jazhara. "We mean you no harm."

The boy's eyes were large with terror. "Who are you?" he asked.

"I am Jazhara, and this is Squire James of Krondor. That's Brother Solon, and Kendaric. Who are you?"

The boy's voice lost its quaver, but he still looked frightened. "I'm Alaric. I'm here to watch the witch. Pa says they're going to burn her real soon, so I wanted to see her do some black magic stuff before they get her."

"I think you should hurry home before it gets much darker," said James.

Jazhara asked, "Is she in the hut now?"

"I haven't seen her. Sometimes she wanders the beach below Widow's Point. I'd be careful; she's really dangerous."

James said, "Thank you. Now, get on home. Your family will be worried about you."

The boy didn't need any more urging and turned and ran down the trail.

They walked on toward the dwelling and James shouted, "Hello, in the hut!"

There was no answer.

James approached and climbed the single step to a wooden porch.

The small stoop had an overhang from which hung a variety of gourds. Jazhara inspected the corpses of a couple of small animals hung there to dry and then an assortment of herbs. "This 'witch' is either a practitioner of magic or simply an old woman well-versed in the arts of remedy. I recognize several of these plants. They are used for poultices and herbal teas."

The hut had been constructed on a wooden platform, the porch extended out a few feet from the front wall. Looking down, Solon said, "At least she's dry when it rains."

"And it rains a lot along this part of the coast," Kendaric added. He wrapped his arms around himself as if he were cold and said, "Not only is it getting darker, but it feels like rain is coming."

"Just what we need," said James. He pushed aside a piece of hide strung across the lintel, serving as a door. Inside the hut were a crude table and a single stool. A cauldron simmered before a fire.

Kendaric looked at the brown mixture. "Not a witch? Then what's that?"

James walked over and inspected the bubbling liquid. He took a ladle from a hook over the fireplace and dipped it into the cauldron. Raising it he sniffed, then sipped it. Turning to Kendaric he said, "Soup. And very good, too."

He replaced the ladle when a voice at the door said, "Come to burn me?"

James turned to see a frail-looking old woman standing in the entrance, holding a bundle of sticks.

"Well, don't just stand there, staring. You expect an old woman to gather all the wood for her own burning?"

The old woman looked barely larger than the child they had just sent home. Her skin was almost translucent with age, and her hair was completely white. Her tiny fingers looked like skin over bones, but she had all her teeth and her eyes were bright and alive.

James smiled. "We're not here to burn you, woman."

"Oh, that's what they all say," she said, pushing past Kendaric and throwing the bundle of sticks down next to the hearth.

Jazhara said, "You practice magic?"

The old woman sat down on her small stool and shrugged. "I know a thing or two. But mostly I mix up remedies for people, or tell fortunes." Her eyes got a faraway look. "Sometimes I see things, but that's . . . difficult. It's rarely pleasant."

Kendaric said, "I'm from the Wreckers' Guild in Krondor and I've tried to raise a ship recently sunk off the Point. Something is blocking my magic. It's powerful and I need to know what it is."

The old woman studied Kendaric for a moment, then turned to face Jazhara. "You practice the craft?"

Jazhara said, "I am the court magician to Prince Arutha."

"Ah," said the old woman, a bemused smile on her face. "A woman magician. Time was you'd have been put to death for even claiming to know the arts in Krondor."

"Times change," said James.

"In some ways, maybe," said the old woman. "Others, not at all."

James said, "Well, perhaps someday we can sit in more comfortable surroundings and discuss it. But right now we have other worries." He gestured outside at the fading sun.

"I saw," said the woman. "That's why I thought you might be from the village, come to burn me."

Jazhara said, "That was 'Father' Rowland. He was rallying the villagers to come here and do just that."

"How did you stop him?" asked the woman.

James said, "With my rapier. He was no priest of Sung."

"I could have told you that," said the old woman. "His pores just oozed evil. I think that's one of the reasons he wanted me gone; he realized I knew him to be a charlatan."

"There had to be another reason," said Solon. "You would hardly have been a compelling witness against him just because you sensed the evil in him."

The woman nodded. "It is because I know the secret of Haldon Head and Widow's Point."

James said, "Will the secret explain what is going on around here, and why we cannot raise that ship?"

"Undoubtedly," said the old woman.

Jazhara asked, "What is your name?"

The old crone paused and then laughed. "It's been so long since anyone has called me anything but 'witch' or 'old woman' I can scarcely remember." She sighed. "Call me Hilda."

"Hilda," asked James. "What is the secret you spoke of?"

The old woman looked around, as if fearful of being overheard. "Below the cliffs, in a deep cavern, lies an ancient place.

It is a temple of evil, older than the memory of the oldest living human."

"What sort of temple?" asked Solon, his hand reflexively going to the hilt of his warhammer.

Hilda stood slowly and crossed to an old wooden chest. She threw back the lid and reached inside. From within she removed a small cloth pouch. Handing it to Solon, she said, "Open it."

The monk did so, and when he saw what was inside, he seemed loath to touch it. "This is like those others," he whispered. He shook the thing into his hand and held it out. Upon his palm was a carved metal hand of either pewter or iron, within which rested a black orb, fashioned from a stone like obsidian. But unlike obsidian, however, it did not reflect the light of the fire.

The old woman said, "I do not know who first built the Black Pearl Temple, but they were not human."

Solon put the artifact back into its pouch. "My order has a catalogue of every cult and faith known to man in the Kingdom, the East, and down through Kesh. As a Defender of the Faithful, I have studied those documents. I have never heard of such an order as the Black Pearl."

The old woman sighed. "And yet it exists." She took the pouch from Solon. "What lies below the cliffs is a festering evil. It is partially to blame for why so many ships are drawn to their demise on the rocks below. It is why few try to farm the good land that lies between the village and my hut. Those who do try grow restless or fearful and leave after a season or two. Even the hunters avoid the woods around here."

"How is it you can abide?" asked Kendaric.

"This," said the old woman, holding up the pouch. "It is a

talisman and protects me from their evil, as if I were already one of their own. I'd like you to have it, for you face a grave challenge." She looked into the eyes of each of her guests before handing the pouch to Solon, who accepted the gift with a nod of thanks. She sat down again, and said, "And it is more."

"What?" asked James.

"It's a key. If you go down the pathway to the rocks below, turn into what appears to be a small alcove fashioned by the sea in the rocks. There you will see a small, faint pattern in the rocks, at my eye level. With this key, a door in the rocks will open."

"You've seen this done?" asked Jazhara.

"Yes," said Hilda. "Many times I have spied upon those who come and go below. One of my talents is concealment. I was standing but a few feet from the porch when you passed, yet you had no inkling, right?"

Jazhara smiled and nodded. "True."

"Have you tried to use this to get in?" asked James.

"Yes," admitted Hilda. "I've tried. But I did not get in."

"Why not?" asked Kendaric.

"Because only those who are sworn in the service of those black powers in the temple can use it. I tried, but the door would not open."

James said, "Then how can we use the key?"

"I believe you have one choice," said the woman. "In the village a creature hides. I do not know who he is or what his name is, but that he is there is certain. He is the one who first infected those who became blood-drinkers. He is a servant of those dark powers below. I don't understand his purpose, for it's only a matter of time before the Prince comes to Haldon Head with his army to set things right."

"We know why he's here," said James. "To keep us busy and away from the Point."

"So his master can raise the ship," added Kendaric.

"How do we use this knowledge to get inside the temple?" James probed.

"Find the monster who has killed so many. Kill him and remove his hand at his wrist. Bind the talisman to the hand. Then the door should open."

"Where do we find this monster?" asked James.

The old woman said, "There is an ancient crypt in the graveyard. The oldest family in this area, the Haldons, built it. None live today, but it is kept up out of respect for the town's founder. Inside is where I think you'll find the monster. And if you find him, you'll find the cause of this darkness. And when you do, please return, so that I may know that I have not sent you to your death."

James said, "We must be going. For by the time we reach the graveyard, those things will be wakening, and I would rather put paid to this before they're upon us."

They hurried from the hut and the old woman crossed to the door and stood there, watching them flee down the path toward the town. Softly she said, "May the gods watch over you, children." Then she slowly hobbled back to her stool, to wait.

FOURTEEN

Vampire

The sky darkened.

As James and the others approached the south edge of town, where Hilda had indicated they'd find the burial crypt, the light faded.

"It's getting darker," said Kendaric, his voice almost quavering with fear.

"Expect the worst," said Solon. "Assume the bleeders know we're coming for them."

Kendaric asked, "Doesn't your order have some sort of magic prayer-thing that makes these types of creatures just . . . vanish?"

"Ha!" replied the monk. "Wish it were so, laddie. The only order with the power to do so are those who worship Lims-Kragma."

Kendaric glanced around. "I thought they'd be in league with these creatures."

"Nay, boy," said Solon, the tension of the moment thickening his accent again. "They're servants of the right order of things, and despise any creature that thwarts their mistress's will. The creatures we're facing are more of an abomination to her servants than they are to us. That's why our mission is to send them along to her so she can sort the buggers out."

"Well, here comes your chance," said James as a half-dozen creatures appeared to rise up out of the gloom, from among a field of headstones. He drew his sword and dagger, but kept moving. "Don't let them delay you too long. If Hilda is correct, once we locate their master and deal with him, these will fall."

Kendaric said, "So, you're telling us to fight through these creatures, but be efficient about it?"

"That's wha' the man said, laddie," replied Solon, pulling out his warhammer, and swinging it before him in a lazy circle. "Just crack a head or cut off a leg or some such, and keep goin'."

Kendaric's face was pale, but he attempted to look resolute. "Sure. No problem."

Jazhara said, "I'll deal with this first batch." She lowered her staff and the air crackled with energy. A brilliant flash of actinic light shot out, as if lightning had been released from a bottle. It bounced across the ground like a ball. As it landed before the first of the undead creatures, it split into smaller balls, each lashing out in electric fury to encapsulate the vampires. They stiffened and howled in agony as the crackling energy seared their flesh and rendered them motionless.

James started to run. "We need to move fast!" he shouted. "There's the crypt!"

In the center of the small graveyard, a stone building rose, a small mausoleum with a peaked roof, its doors open. Within, they could see at least a half-dozen marble catafalques, upon which stone coffins rested. "Why couldn't they burn their dead properly," Kendaric muttered, "like the rest of the Kingdom?"

"We're close to Yabon," said Solon. "Burial is still popular up here."

"For once," said Jazhara, lowering her staff and pointing it toward the door, "I agree with Kendaric."

Inside the crypt, an eerie red glow illuminated figures moving behind the stone coffins. "We've got to fight our way in," said James.

Jazhara unleashed another bolt of energy and several of the creatures in the first row stiffened. James raced past them, only to be confronted by a burly-looking man, his skin pale and his eyes seeming to glow with a reddish light. Behind him, James spied another figure, not as bulky, but radiating immense power, and he knew he was looking at the master vampire.

"Kill that one!" James shouted.

The master vampire laughed. "Child of woe, I was dead before you were born!"

The burly vampire lashed out at James, and his fingers were curled like talons. James didn't attempt to parry the blow. Instead, he ducked below the swing, then rose and kicked out with his right leg, planting his boot in the vampire's chest. He shoved and the burly man was thrown backward into the path of the Vampire Lord. Then James lunged and attempted to hamstring the approaching master vampire, but the creature leapt aside with astonishing speed. James suddenly felt afraid. Nothing living should move that quickly. James's previous experience with the supernatural had been entirely unpleasant, and his one advantage in those cases had been his combination of instinct and speed. His plan had been to render the master vampire helpless by cutting his legs from under him, or otherwise injuring him, then leaving it to Jazhara to burn him with her mystical fire.

He now saw that his plan was not going to work.

"Get back!" James shouted. "We have to burn them in here!"

Solon crushed the skull of one vampire, and Kendaric managed to inflict enough damage on another that it was keeping its distance from him.

Jazhara used her staff to good advantage, tripping two of the creatures and causing a third to fall over them. She now busied herself with breaking heads with her staff; but, as they had been warned, the damage merely slowed the creatures down rather than causing permanent damage.

They started to retreat, Jazhara and Solon attempting to clear a path for James. James fought down panic. He had to back away from the pair of advancing vampires, and the burly man was shrewd enough not to let James trip him again.

James risked a glance backward and almost had his head taken from his shoulders for his trouble. Only by lashing out with his rapier did he manage to drive the Vampire Lord back.

Suddenly Solon charged forward, swinging his warhammer with both hands. He smashed it into the burly vampire's chest, sending the creature flying backward thorough the air, into its master.

The Vampire Lord was knocked off his feet, but again he sprang up with supernatural ease and speed, throwing the other vampire aside like a doll. The burly vampire, however, lay upon the stone floor, writhing in agony.

The unexpected counterattack gave James the time he needed to leap away, through the doorway of the small mausoleum.

"Close the doors!" James shouted. "Jazhara, burn them!"

Jazhara lowered her staff and a gout of green flame exploded from its tip. Kendaric struggled with one door, while Solon easily moved the other.

As James watched, his eyes widening in disbelief, the master vampire walked through the flames, unburned.

At last the doors slammed shut. Solon threw his weight against them.

"We need to block them!" shouted James.

Jazhara grabbed Kendaric by the collar of his tunic and pulled him around. "Stones!" she shouted as the wrecker almost fell over, only regaining his balance at the last moment.

They hurried to a small headstone that rose from a grave and together managed to pull it out of the ground. "Thank you, whoever you were," Jazhara directed toward the now-unmarked grave as she and Kendaric dragged the stone over to the mausoleum doors.

James and Solon had thrown their shoulders against the doors that bulged outward as the master vampire threw his unnatural strength against them. First one, then another stone was piled in place, until the door refused to give.

"I don't know how much time we've bought," said James, out of breath. "But I saw that thing walk through your fire, Jazhara. It didn't faze him."

"Then I don't know what to do." she replied.

"Maybe it has to be natural fire," said Kendaric. "We could build a fire, then light a bundle of rags in oil. Toss it in."

"I doubt it would make a difference," said the magician. She pondered. "Perhaps Hilda can tell us what to do."

Solon said, "You two run back to Hilda, while Kendaric and I endeavor to keep these doors shut." As if to punctuate this statement, there came a dull thud from within the crypt and the doors shook and rattled against the headstones. "Hurry!" Solon urged. "He may not be able to move those stone doors, but he can certainly reduce them to rubble in time."

James nodded, turned to look at Jazhara, who nodded. They set off at a jog back north through the town and toward Widow's Peak.

Nearly breathless, they reached the hut overlooking the cliffs. Hilda heard them approaching and came to stand out on the porch.

"Naught goes well," she observed.

James nodded, attempting to catch his wind. He took a deep breath then said, "The master vampire won't die."

"The Vampire Lord will be difficult to destroy," said Hilda. "But he is no god."

"He will not burn," said Jazhara.

"Ah!" the old woman responded, looking thoughtful. "Then he has placed his essence somewhere else."

James looked at Jazhara who returned a blank expression. "I do not understand," she said to Hilda.

Hilda shrugged. "I am no expert. Necromancy is the foulest of the arts and to be shunned." She paused, then added, "But over time one hears things."

"Such as?" asked James.

"It is said that some of the servants of the dark powers are not truly living; even those poor souls captured by this vampire master have a thread of life within; cut it and they fade," Hilda explained. "But a few of the more powerful servants of evil have conspired to rid their bodies of mortality completely."

"Then how do we destroy those?" asked Jazhara.

"Find the soul vessel. To attain such power, sacrifices are made, and what one gains on one hand" – she held out one hand – "one loses on the other." She extended her other hand. "To make the body immortal, the spirit essence is placed somewhere close by. It is often protected by wards or hidden in such a way it is unlikely to be found."

"We don't have time for this," said James. "That Vampire Lord is strong. Even now he may be out of the crypt and have overcome Solon and Kendaric."

Jazhara said, "And if we lose Kendaric – "

James nodded grimly. "We had no choice but to leave him with Solon. But we must hurry."

Jazhara said, "Where should we look? Will it be in the crypt with the master vampire?"

Hilda shook her head. "Unlikely. He will have brought it with him, but placed it someplace safe, as soon as he arrived."

"Where was the first place he was seen?" asked James.

"The woodcutter's cabin," Hilda replied.

"Then that's where we'll look," said James. "Which way do we go?"

"Run to Farmer Alton's farm, and follow the road that passes east before his house. A mile beyond the last fence you'll see a path into the woods and another mile beyond that is the woodcutter's home. Tread lightly, for the Vampire Lord will have other allies."

James glanced around. "It's almost as dark as night now. Have you a lantern or torches?"

The old woman nodded. "Torches. I'll get them." She went inside and a moment later reappeared with three torches – one was burning; the remaining two were held in the crook of her arm. "These are all I have."

James took the burning one and Jazhara took the two others. James said, "They will have to do. Thank you, Hilda, for all your help."

"No thanks are needed."

Jazhara said, "When all is done, I shall return and tell you of Stardock."

"I will listen," said the old woman.

James took a last look at the old woman's face. "Good-bye," he called. Then he turned, and hurried back toward the village. Jazhara followed him.

The old woman watched until they were out of sight, then turned and slowly walked back into her hut.

James and Jazhara ran most of the way, stopping only when feeling at risk. Through the town they went and onto the eastern road, until they left the road when they found the indicated trail.

The forest was plunged into darkness, as if noon and mid-night had exchanged places. Moreover, no moon illuminated the way, and the murk was both unnatural and ominous. The trail was well-traveled, but narrow, and James had to fight the urge to jump at every single noise.

The daybirds had ceased singing, but the soft hooting of their nocturnal counterparts was also missing. The air was unnaturally still, as if the magic dampening the sun was also silencing the wind.

Suddenly the night air was rent by the sound of a distant howl. It was quickly answered by others.

"Wolves!" said James.

"Hurry," Jazhara cried, and James started to go at such a pace that they risked injury on the narrow trail.

Dodging between the boles of trees and along rocky footing, they at last came to a small hut in a clearing. From within the hut came a red glow, which seeped through the cracks around the door and the tiny window next to it.

"Someone's inside," James cautioned.

"Someone's outside," said Jazhara, pointing.

Four figures emerged from behind the hut, all walking purposefully toward James and Jazhara.

Jazhara lowered her staff and again blinding lightning spilled forth from the tip. The leaves on the ground smoked as the lightning bounced along to strike the four creatures. The vampires struggled to keep moving but their bodies just twitched and shivered uncontrollably.

"Get inside!" Jazhara shouted. "I'll deal with these."

James ran past the quivering figures, two having fallen to the ground where they flopped like landed fish. He hardly slowed, but lifted his right leg and kicked hard against the door, smashing it inward.

A woman sat on a stool, appearing to care for a baby in a bassinet, but as soon as she turned at James's intrusion it was clear that she was a vampire. She rose, snarling, from her stool and launched herself at James, her fingers clawed talons and her fangs bared.

James dodged to one side and cut at the back of her leg, hamstringing her. She fell with a shriek of pain and outrage and James slashed her across the neck. His light blade struck bone and was turned aside, and at that moment he wished for a heavier blade.

He pulled the rapier free of the woman's neck and hacked away at her outstretched arms. She recoiled in pain, scrambled backward, then tried to rise.

As she stood, James leapt forward, put his foot to her stomach and pushed her outside. Her wounded leg betrayed her: as she fell backward, James lashed out with his torch, catching the hem of her skirt with the flame and igniting it.

In moments the woman was rolling on the ground, trying to extinguish the blaze. James turned his attention to the interior of the hut. There was nothing in it except for a small table, the bassinet, and a bucket near the fireplace. There was no obvious hiding place, no chest or likely receptacle for an important item such as the vampire's soul vessel.

James stepped forward and looked into the bassinet. He grimaced at what he saw: the body of a baby lay in it. It had obviously been dead for some time. Its tiny body was shrunken, the skin stretched over the fragile bones. But what was most repulsive was the red light which emanated from its body.

James hesitated, reluctant to touch the little corpse. Then, he put aside his revulsion and touched the child's stomach. Something hard resisted his finger. He pulled out his dagger, swallowed hard and cut into the infant's flesh. Inside the baby's rib-cage a large ruby-colored stone glowed with an evil brilliance.

James was forced to break two ribs to remove the object. By the time he had done so, Jazhara had reached the door. "They're all dead – " She stopped, aghast. "What is that?"

James said, "I'm not sure, but I think the baby is the vessel."

Jazhara stared at the red jewel. "Then that would be the Soul Stone," she mused. She closed her eyes and made an incantation, then opened them and said, "There is a great deal of magic locked within that gem. And it reeks of evil."

"What do we do with it?" asked James.

"Take it outside," said Jazhara.

The howling of wolves could be heard, getting closer by the moment.

"Hurry," she insisted.

James complied with alacrity.

Once they were both outside, Jazhara looked around. There!" she said, pointing to the woodcutter's work-shed. In the corner was a small bellows and forge, where tools could be repaired and sharpened. She located at once what she was looking for.

"Put the gem on this anvil," she instructed.

James did so. Jazhara reached over and took a small iron hammer and lifted it. "Avert your eyes!" she commanded, and James looked away.

He heard the smash of the hammer on the gem, then felt his skin crawl. A wash of energy made him physically ill and he had to fight to keep from retching. Next came a sense of loss and haplessness, a futility that seeped into his bones; that was followed by a blast of anger and rage that caused his heart to race and his eyes to tear.

He gasped and heard Jazhara also gasping. When he opened his eyes, he saw she had been unsuccessful in controlling her nausea.

Despite feeling light-headed and disoriented, the howl of the approaching wolves made him focus; he forced himself to become alert.

Then the sky shattered. Like a latticework of faint lines, the darkness was shot through with light. As if shards of a broken window fell from above, the black night disappeared. It looked as though pieces of the dark sky were falling down, only to dissolve and fade to insubstantial mist before striking the tops of the nearby trees. From behind each shard the brilliance of the day's light shone.

Then, abruptly, there was daylight again – total daylight.

The howling of the wolf pack ceased, and the daybirds started singing.

"I didn't expect that," said Jazhara.

"Well, expected or not, I'm glad to see the sun again," James replied. He glanced in the direction of the fiery orb and remarked, "It's barely midday."

"A lot has happened," she said. "Come, we must return to the graveyard and see what has transpired there."

They hurried back through the town and down the road to the graveyard. Along the way they saw the townspeople looking out of their doors and windows, astonished and delighted at the return of daylight. A few hardier souls had ventured outside, and were now looking at one another as if seeking reassurance that something approaching normalcy was returning.

They were out of breath and sweating from the returned heat of the sun by the time they reached the vault. Solon and Kendaric were still blocking the crypt door.

"Where have you been?!" cried Kendaric.

"You did something," said the monk. "All manner of madness erupted inside here and then the sky above shattered. I assume the two were related?"

"We found and smashed the soul-gem," said Jazhara.

James said, "I thought he would . . . die or something when we smashed the stone."

"I'm no expert in this sort of thing," Jazhara mused. "Hilda might know more. But I'm wagering now that since the gem has been destroyed, we can find a way to destroy him, too."

Kendaric asked, "Can't we just leave them locked up until they wither away?"

"Not if he's the source of whatever is blocking your spell."

Kendaric stood with a resigned expression on this face. Then he started to haul away the first of the headstones blocking the crypt door. "Care to give me some help?"

"Not really," answered James, but he set to picking up another headstone.

"Do we have a plan?" asked Solon.

"We must cut off one of the Vampire Lord's hands," Jazhara reminded him.

James said, "We let them open the doors. They don't like the light, so maybe that will weaken them. I encountered a demon not too long ago whose flesh burned in the sunlight. Perhaps it's the same with these."

"With the lesser vampires, perhaps," said Solon, heaving away another stone. "But I suspect the master vampire will find it only somewhat irritating."

"Maybe we can kill them one at a time as they come through," suggested Kendaric as he dropped a stone a few yards away, and returned to pick up another.

The door started to move, as the vampires inside threw their weight against it. "We can't burn them," said Jazhara, "or at least we can't burn the leader; we need his hand."

"Maybe we can get him to stick it out," suggested Kendaric, "then lop it off and run like hell."

Solon chuckled. "We break heads and cut throats. It's simple."

James stepped back from the doors as they began to push outward. "Yes, it's simple." Then the door swung suddenly outward and two figures leapt at him. "But that doesn't mean easy!"

James slashed the closest vampire across the throat as it staggered in the unexpected daylight. As soon as the sun touched the creature, its flesh started to blacken and it began to howl in pain.

The second vampire turned and tried to reenter the crypt, but was pushed back by two more coming after it. Solon laid about him with his warhammer and knocked them first to one side, then the other.

Jazhara struck downward with the iron end of her staff, and soon three corpses lay smoking in the sunlight. James peered into the gloom of the crypt. The bright sun made the interior dark and indistinct. Nothing appeared to move.

"I think we're going to have to go in and get him," James said softly. Turning to Kendaric, he nodded toward the wrecker's sword. "You've got the only blade that could cut that thing's head off. If we get him down, try not to chop either Solon or me while you're at it."

Kendaric went pale, but nodded.

James looked then at Jazhara and raised an eyebrow. Then he spoke again to Kendaric. "Should she be forced to set him alight, I want you to be ready to run in and chop off a hand."

Kendaric wiped perspiration from his upper lip with the back of his sleeve. "Which hand?"

"Either should do, I think," said James. He nodded once to Solon and they both charged into the crypt. They raced inside, one on either side of a central catafalque, their eyes darting to left and right.

Three sets of three catafalques dominated the floor of the crypt and both men knew that crouched behind one of them was the Vampire Lord. As James reached the second set, he had a premonition. "Solon, look up!" he shouted.

As the monk obeyed, a figure dropped from the peak of the roof, and only James's warning saved him. Reacting swiftly, he spun and swung his warhammer, smashing the Vampire Lord's ribs.

The master vampire flew across the room, slamming into the stone wall before James, who swung his rapier and lunged, attempting to skewer the creature on the floor, but with super-natural speed the creature was up and on his feet, slipping right past James's sword.

Then a second vampire dropped from above, and suddenly James was borne down to the floor. The stink of carrion assaulted his sense of smell as he struggled against the power and weight of the two vampires. "Solon!" he shouted.

The powerful monk closed upon the three figures on the floor in two strides. He gripped one by the collar of his tunic and threw him toward the door. The creature slid into the light of day and started to shriek in agony.

Kendaric stepped forward and with as powerful a blow as he could muster he chopped off the creature's head.

Jazhara cried, "Duck!"

At once, Solon crouched. Jazhara pointed her staff upward and unleashed a blast of green fire. The flames danced along the stone ceiling and two more vampires fell, writhing in burning agony.

James found himself struggling against the strongest foe he had ever grappled with. The Vampire Lord was only the size of a tall man, but his hands gripped James's chin and turned his head as easily as James might have turned a child's head. As hard as he tried, James could not resist. His neck muscles felt as if they were being ripped apart, and he tried desperately to keep his head turned toward his foe. Out of the corner of his eye he could see the creature's fangs, and realized with horror that he was about to have his throat ripped out.

Frantically, he tried to convulse his body to buy himself a moment of freedom, but the Vampire Lord had the strength of three men. Then he saw Solon appear behind the vampire. The powerful monk gripped the monster by his long flowing hair and yanked his head back. James heard Jazhara shout, "Close your eyes!"

Jabbing with the end of her staff, Jazhara smashed the Vampire Lord right in the mouth. His eyes opened wide with surprise and he froze for a moment as if appalled by this unexpected attack.

Then Jazhara uttered a quick phrase and energy exploded from the tip of her staff. The creature's head erupted in a gout of white flame, and the room filled with the stench of burning flesh.

The Vampire Lord rose howling and Jazhara pulled her staff free. James scrambled backward the instant he felt the weight lift from his body.

Kendaric hurried over and with careful aim threw his weight behind his blade, and in a single circular motion sheared the creature's head from its body. The Vampire Lord's body fell like a stone.

Kendaric looked as if he was going to be sick.

James said, "Thank you; all of you." Looking at Kendaric, he added, "Cut off the hand."

Kendaric shook his head and reversed the blade, holding it out to James. "If you don't mind, you do it. I don't think I have it in me anymore." Then his eyes rolled up into his skull and he fell to the floor in a faint.

Later that afternoon, they took their ease at the inn. James savored a bitter, refreshing draught of ale, while trying to ignore the pain in his wrenched neck.

"What now?" asked Kendaric, still embarrassed at having fainted.

"We wait until morning," said James. "We are all tired and

in need of rest. Then at first light we'll try to raise the ship. If it fails, we'll know Hilda was right and it's not just the Vampire Lord but whatever's down there in that temple."

"What about help?" asked Kendaric.

"I'll send for the garrison down in Miller's Rest in the morning. They'll be here in two days."

"Do we wait?" asked Solon.

"No, we'll explore the old temple. I've done that sort of thing a few times before. It's unlikely there's anyone down there. If there were, someone from the village would have seen something before this recent outbreak of trouble."

Jazhara sipped her ale, then said, "I am still disturbed by two things."

James nodded. "Who's behind all this?"

"Yes," said the magician. "It's clear that someone wants to keep this area isolated and allow his minions to seize the prize." She glanced around to see if any of the locals in the inn could overhear her. "The Tear," she said softly.

"What's the other thing that troubles you, lady?" asked Solon.

"Where are William and the Krondorian Guard?" Jazhara said.

James understood the double reference at once, for while Solon and Kendaric would assume she was concerned only about Bear's whereabouts, he knew she also was worried about William's safety.

James sipped his ale. He thought about those two issues and realized he was just as troubled as Jazhara by them.

FIFTEEN

Two Fangs

William watched.

Just above the top of distant trees, he could see Two Fangs Pass, silhouetted in black relief by the rising sun. Two large rocks, one to each side of the trail, rose up like a viper's fangs, giving the place its name. On either side of the fangs two clearings could be seen. As he faced north, William could see that a stand of thick forest bordered the right-hand clearing and rose up the hillside. On the left, a clearing topped a cliff overlooking a deep river gorge.

"Are they here already, do you think?" asked Sergeant Hartag.

"I can feel it in my bones," replied William. "Tonight's the new Small Moon and this is the morning the Grey Talons were supposed to lead us to the slaughter."

"We did the best we could getting here, Will," said Hartag. "If we'd pushed any more the horses would be dead and the men couldn't fight."

"Well, at least we know we're in for a fight and they're out there somewhere."

"How do we play it?" asked the sergeant.

"You're an old campaigner, Sergeant. What's your thought?"

298

The sergeant was quiet as he considered, then he said, "They're certain to be in those trees. But I'll wager Bear's got a dozen or so lying low in that meadow on the left, by the cliff. It rises then falls off behind, and I think he's got some archers crouched down over there, where we can't see them. I think his plan is to bait us to charge the pass, so the lads flee over the summit. Then we come hard right after them, and as we get to the Fangs, he hits us from the right, and as we wheel to charge, his archers take us from behind."

"That's my thinking, too," said William. "So if we see him put riders up there on the crest, watching for the mercenaries' arrival, we know you're right."

Less than an hour later, a pair of riders appeared from out of the line of the woods and took up position at the bottom of the rise. "Well," said William. "Looks like we've found the Bear."

"Shall I send the Pathfinders?"

"Send them up through the trees and have them get up as far as they can, and report back on numbers. I want them back here by midday at the latest."

Time passed slowly while they waited, and William gave orders for the men to ready themselves for a fight. He suspected Bear had a larger body of men hidden in the woods. William was counting on the absence of the Grey Talon mercenaries to tip the balance in his favor.

A little before midday the two Pathfinders, Maric and Jackson, returned. "There's about fifty of them scattered through the woods, sir."

"Horse or foot?"

"Both. Looks like they plan on tempting us by showing us foot, then riding horse over us once we take the bait."

William considered and said, "We can't play his game." He knew he was outnumbered: his thirty-six men against Bear's fifty or more. "Take a half-dozen men into the trees," he ordered the Pathfinders. "No matter what you hear, wait, then when you hear Bear's men given the order to leave the woods, strike from behind. Don't linger, but draw off as many of the horsemen as you can." He pointed to the left side of the pass. "That's where we hit first."

"How do we proceed?" asked Hartag.

"Thirty of us ride calmly to there" – he pointed to a large boulder near the bottom of the rise – "and then we charge the archers. We take them out as fast as we can, and force Bear to charge us. Either he's on foot or he's forced to retreat and mount. If Jackson, Maric, and the others can draw off some of his riders, he'll be forced to reorganize on the fly. Either he retreats and we keep following, or he charges us piecemeal and gives us the chance we need to finish him."

"If he retreats?"

"We follow and don't press until it's to our advantage. As much as I want that murderous dog, our mission is successful if we keep him from his goal."

"And that is?" asked the sergeant.

"Widow's Peak above Haldon Head."

The sergeant glanced around. "By my reckoning, sir, that's where he's leading us."

William said, "What?"

Sergeant Hartag said, "Over that rise, to the west, you'll find a trail that cuts over those peaks and leads down into a woodland just east of Haldon Head. It's less than two days' hard ride from here. If we left now, we'd be there at sundown tomorrow."

"Damn," said William. "It's not on any maps I've seen."

The sergeant smiled. "Lots of things don't get put on the royal maps, Will. Best to always ask travelers when you can, or the lads who grew up in the area."

"Thanks. I'll remember that."

"So, what then?"

"Then we don't let him get away." Will looked around. "Surprise is all we have going for us. They outnumber us, so if the fight goes badly, make for the river below."

Hartag said, "The river? Are you daft, Will? Even if we could survive the fall, those rapids below will drown a man quicker than – "

"No. If we start taking a beating, rally the men and head south. If he's bound for Haldon Head, he will not follow. We'll retreat to the portage we passed yesterday, and build rafts. We can get to Haldon Head before Bear if we use the river while he's forced to rest his horses."

"Ah," said the sergeant. "So you weren't suggesting we jump from that cliff over there?"

"Well, if it's that or be killed . . ."

"Last resort, it is," said Hartag.

William shaded his eyes as he surveyed their surroundings once again. "How soon?"

"Maric and the others should be in place now."

"Pass orders. We form up and ride at a trot until I give the command, then charge the left."

"Understood."

William waited while the men formed up, and when everyone was in position, he took his place at the head of the column. Glancing at Sergeant Hartag, he half-whispered, "First time in my life I'm wishing Captain Treggar was here."

Hartag laughed. While Treggar was an above-average officer, he had been a thorn in the side of every other bachelor officer at the garrison since before William's arrival, and while he and William had come to a sort of understanding based on mutual respect, he was still a tough man to be around socially. The sergeant said, "Yes, despite his crust, he's a man for a tight spot."

"Well, as he's not here, it's my neck on the chopping block. Ride!"

The column moved forward at a trot. William felt his stomach tighten and forced himself to breathe slowly. As soon as he heard the twang of a bowstring or sharp clatter of metal upon metal, he knew he would lose his edginess and achieve a state of mental clarity that never failed to surprise him despite the many battles in which he had fought. In the course of a fight, chaos was the rule, and whatever plans he had made always evaporated during the first moment of contact with the enemy. Early on, William had discovered that in battle he could somehow sense how things were going and what needed to be done.

Despite his falling-out with his father over his choice to leave the community of magicians at Stardock and join the army, William knew this was his true calling, the craft for which he was particularly gifted. His horse snorted in excitement, and William sent the animal calming, reassuring thoughts. There were times when his singular ability to speak mentally to animals had its uses, he thought.

When William's column reached the lowest portion of the road, the two decoy riders appeared above the crest. They made a show of riding a few yards over the crest, being "surprised," and turning to flee.

William raised his arm and shouted, "Charge!"

But rather than follow the decoy riders up the hillside, the men turned and charged across the meadow. The meadow rose to a small flat area before quickly dropping off. As William had anticipated, about a dozen archers crouched on the grass, ready to rise up and fire at William's men from behind.

Suddenly they had cavalry upon them and while a few got shots off, most were ridden down and killed before they could rally. William ordered his men to form a line, then reined in his horse.

The orders were simple. Stand until the enemy showed himself. As expected, Bear's reaction didn't deviate much from what William had predicted. A band of footmen raced from the trees and stood as if ready to charge. William did a quick head-count and saw that eighteen had been placed as bait. That meant over thirty men on horses were waiting just inside the woods. "Steady!" he commanded.

Bear's men stood in line and when it was apparent they weren't going to be charged, they started pounding their shields and taunting the Krondorians.

"Steady!" repeated William.

The two sides stood facing one another for long, tense minutes, and Hartag asked, "Should we raise the stakes, Will?"

"Do so," instructed the young officer.

"Archers!" shouted Hartag, and a half-dozen Krondorians switched weapons. "Draw and fire at will; fire!" he commanded and the Krondorian archers let loose their arrows.

Six of Bear's men fell. By the time the bowmen had nocked and drawn their second set of arrows, the remaining twelve mercenaries had turned and were in full flight. They reached the trees and vanished into the gloom. The bowmen let loose, but there were no targets on the other side by the time the arrows struck.

"Shoulder those bows!" commanded Hartag.

The bowmen did as ordered, then drew swords and hefted their shields.

Silence fell. Bear and his men waited for the Krondorians to charge; but William was determined they would fight in the open.

"What now?" asked one soldier nearby as they waited.

Hartag said, "We see who scratches their ass first, my boy."

William sat and wondered how long they'd have to wait.

Kendaric stood on the reef at Widow's Point, looking at the mast of the ship Solon had previously identified. He said, "Keep an eye out for any more of those creatures who tried to stop us last time."

James pulled his sword and said, "Get on with it."

Kendaric tried his spell again, and again it failed. He turned and said in frustration, "Nothing. Something still blocks it."

Jazhara shrugged. "As we suspected it would. Hilda told us that the Vampire Lord was not the ultimate evil."

"Time is short. We need to find that cave," suggested Solon.

They returned to the beach behind the reef and found the cave with surprising ease. It was shallow, only a dozen yards deep, and the morning light from outside cut through the gloom. At the rear of the cave they found a pattern of stones. James pressed on one, experimentally, and it moved. He listened. There was no sound.

"It's not mechanical," said James.

"Which means it's magic," said Jazhara.

"And that means I don't know how to pick this lock."

"What next?" asked Kendaric.

"We have the hand and the artifact," said Solon.

James unshouldered his backpack and took out the talisman and the vampire hand. He wrapped the fingers of the dead hand around the charm and raised it to the portal. He tried a half-dozen combinations of pressure and patterns, and finally put it down.

"Hilda didn't tell us everything," James observed as he replaced the items in his backpack.

"But she did tell us to return," Jazhara reminded him.

"Let's go ask her," said James. He reshouldered his pack and stood up.

The walk up to the top of the point took less than a half-hour. Hilda was waiting for them when they reached the hut. "Got the vampire, did you?" she asked.

"Yes," said James. "How did you know?"

"It didn't take magic, boy. If you hadn't gotten him, he'd have gotten you and you wouldn't be standing here." She turned and said, "Come in and listen."

They followed, and once inside the old woman said, "Give me the hand."

James opened his backpack and gave her the creature's hand. She took a large iron skillet from a hook above the fire and placed the vampire's hand in it. Thrusting it into the flames, she said, "This is the unpleasant part."

The flesh of the creature's hand shriveled and blackened, then a putrid blue flame sprang up around it. In a few moments, only blackened bones remained.

She pulled the pan out and set it on the stone hearth. "Let it cool for a moment."

"Can you tell us something of what we face?" asked Jazhara.

Hilda looked grim. "That is why I didn't tell you about the need to reduce the creature's hand to ash. That is why I didn't give you the pattern of the lock." She looked from face to face. "You are about to face a great evil and I had to know you are worthy. Your defeat of the Vampire Lord shows that you have the necessary determination and bravery. But you face a far worse foe.

"For many years I've known the Black Pearl Temple was under the cliffs. I have never been able to see inside, except by my arts. And what little of that I can see is evil beyond imagining."

"What 'great evil' do you speak of?" asked Solon.

"Where to start?" asked Hilda rhetorically. "The sailors who've died offshore, and there have been many, have never known true rest. Instead, their souls are enslaved to whatever dark power rules in the temple. I can feel its presence, like a great eye. It was closed for years, but now it is open and it is watching this area."

James thought about the battle at Sethanon, when the false prophet of the moredhel, Murmandamus, captured the dying energy of his servants to fuel his attempt to seize the Lifestone under Sethanon. "So we can assume that this plan – whatever it is," he added quickly, so as not to inadvertently mention the recovery of the Tear to Hilda, "has been underway for a great deal of time."

"Assuredly," said Hilda. She stood and moved over to her chest, opened it and retrieved an artifact. "But the eye didn't know that it was being watched." She held out a long, slender object, a wand or stick seemingly fashioned from frosty crystal. "I dared used this but once, and I have put it away since in anticipation of this moment. I caution you, what you see may be disturbing."

She waved the object in the air and intoned a spell, and suddenly a rift appeared in the air before them, black, but somehow with the suggestion of color within. Then an image sprang to life, and they could see the interior of a cavern. An ornate mirror hung on a stone wall. They could see a figure approaching, reflected in the mirror before them, and Jazhara and Solon both muttered quiet oaths. The figure was one James had seen before, or rather its like, a long-dead priest or magician, animated by the black arts. He had faced such a one as this under the ancient abandoned Keshian fortress in the south of the Kingdom months before, and knew that there was a link between what had been discovered there and what was occurring now.

The figure waved a bony hand and the image of a man appeared in the mirror. The man was hawk-beaked, with eyes that seemed to possess a burning black fire. His pate was bald, and he let his long gray hair flow down around his shoulders. He wore clothing of nondescript fashion, looking as much like a merchant as anything else. Then they heard the voice of the undead magician.

"They come," he said.

The man in the mirror asked, "Is the guildsman with them?"

"As planned. They will be sacrificed at dawn. Do you have the amulet?"

"No," answered the man. "My pawn still has it."

The undead creature said, "You held it, but it was the voice of our god that filled it with power. It has chosen another, just as it chose you over me."

The man in the mirror evidenced irritation at that comment. "But he is not worthy of the power."

"Nevertheless, without the amulet, we cannot proceed."

"I will find him. And when I do . . ."

Suddenly the image shifted and there upon the rocks of Widow's Point a gathering of creatures from the lowest depths of hell stood arrayed. James could barely resist the urge to speak, for he recognized some of these creatures, but others were even more fearsome and powerful. Finally, he whispered, "Who is that?"

Hilda said, "A mage of most puissant and dark powers, boy. I know not his name, but I know his handiwork, and he is allied with forces even darker than those you see in the image. Watch and learn."

The man turned to face the assembled creatures, and James's eyes widened as he saw his own body lying on the rocks, his chest torn open as if by a great hand. Nearby lay Solon and Jazhara. Still alive but bound like a calf to the slaughter, Kendaric struggled against his ropes. A massive amulet with a blood-red ruby hung from a chain around the man's neck. And in one hand he held a long blade of black. In the other he held a huge stone of ice blue. Solon whispered, "The Tear!"

With a single motion, the magician knelt and cut into Kendaric's chest, then plunged his hand into the cavity and ripped out Kendaric's heart. Holding the still-beating organ, he dripped blood over the Tear as the magician turned to show it to the demons. The Tear's color changed from ice blue to blood red and the throng shouted in triumph. Suddenly, the picture vanished.

Hilda said, "Don't let these visions overwhelm you."

Kendaric sounded on the edge of hysteria. "But they're going to kill me! Us!"

Hilda said, "They're going to try, boy. But the future is not set in stone. And evil is most adept at seeing what it wants to see. That's its weakness. It doesn't anticipate the possibility of failure. And now you do; and more, you know the price of your failure."

"Then these visions . . . ?" asked Jazhara.

"Serve as a warning. You now know more about your enemy, and what he plans, than he does about you. He knows you seek to recover the Tear of the Gods – "

Solon's hand dropped to his warhammer. "How do you know this, woman?"

Hilda waved her hand dismissively. "You are not the only ones who know how the universe plays, Ishapian. I was old before your grandmother was born and if the gods are kind, I'll live until your grandchildren die. But if I do not, I will have been a servant of good in my own way, and that contents me. Perhaps it is my fate only to be here to teach you, and after you succeed or fail, I will end my days. I do not know. But I do know that should you fail, I will not be alone in meeting a terrible ending.

"Always remember, visions are potent magic, but even the best of visions is only an illusion, a reflection of possibilities. You still can change your future. And you must!" She rose. "Now go, for time is short and there is much you must do. That creature you saw is called a liche in the old tongue. He is alive by the most powerful and blackest arts. He will lead you to whatever it is that prevents you from raising the ship. You must find him, destroy him, and end the plague that causes sailors to be entombed in their drowned vessels, servants of darkness

309

to walk the night, and old women to have bad dreams. And you must do so before the other appears, for he is even more dangerous, I judge, and for him to have that amulet . . . well, you saw what he plans."

Hilda stood and walked over to the now-cool skillet. "Brother Solon, the talisman, if you please."

Solon took the pouch from inside his tunic. At Hilda's instruction, he held open the sack as the old woman positioned a small silver funnel over the pouch's mouth and poured the ashen remains of the vampire hand into the bag. Taking the pouch from Solon, Hilda retied the strings, murmured a brief incantation, and shook the bag before handing it back to the monk.

"Now," she said, "you have the key to the temple. To use it, you must make the following pattern at the rock-face door." She traced a pattern in the air, a simple weaving of four movements. "Then the door should open."

Jazhara said, "Please show us again."

Hilda repeated the pattern and James and Jazhara both nodded.

Jazhara took the old woman's hand. "You are truly amazing. You are a storehouse of wisdom." She glanced around. "When I first entered this place, I was astonished by your knowledge of medicinal and magical herbs and plants. Now I see you have much more to offer. I will return when we are done and tell you of Stardock. It would profit the world for you to join the community there and share your wisdom."

The old woman smiled, but there was a shadow of doubt in her eyes. "First return, girl. Then we'll talk."

Jazhara nodded and then followed the others outside.

The old woman watched them retreat. When they had at

last vanished into the trees, she moved back to the fire, for she felt a chill, in spite of the warmth of the sun.

"Now!" William shouted, pointing to the tree-line. As one, his men spurred on their horses and charged the riders who were thundering out of the woods. It had taken nearly an hour for Bear to run out of patience and now William felt he had a chance, since they were fighting on open ground. He might be outnumbered, but he knew his men were better armed and trained. As the Krondorians charged across the road, William prayed silently that his eight raiders at the rear of Bear's men were distracting them enough to divide their forces.

"Keep the line! Watch your flanks!" shouted Sergeant Hartag, and the Krondorians pointed their swords, keeping their bucklers ready to block, their reins lashing the necks of their mounts, as they urged their horses on.

William's world turned to a blur of images. As it always did in combat, he found his attention focused on one thing and one thing only: the man before him. A rider came in, rising up in his stirrups, his sword high to come down hard at William's head or shoulders.

In a fluid motion, William leaned to the right, raised his left arm above his head, and let his buckler deflect the blow, while his own short-sword slashed at the rider's right leg. The man cried out and then William was past him.

William didn't know if the man had kept his seat or fallen, and he didn't look to see. For in front of him another rider was charging toward him, and in an instant the first rider was forgotten. This man came in from William's left side, giving the young officer an easy block, but making a counter-strike with the short-sword difficult. For an instant, William appreciated the Keshian's use of the scimitar, with its long curved blade, or even the Eastern Kingdoms' saber for fighting on horseback. A longer, lighter blade would serve better now.

William let the thought slip away as he timed his response. At the last instant, he ducked under the blow, instead of blocking it, and wheeled his horse about, then spurred it on after the rider who had just passed. The man was bearing down on a dismounted Krondorian soldier when William overtook him. A single blow from behind and the man was unseated, tumbling hard to the ground and rolling to his death at the hands of the soldier he had been attempting to ride down just seconds before.

Suddenly William's luck took a turn for the worse. His horse screamed and he felt it going out from under him. Without thinking, he kicked loose of his stirrups and let the horse's momentum throw him from the saddle. He let go of his short-sword, but gripped his buckler tightly. He tucked in his chin and tried to roll on his left shoulder, using the buckler as a point of leverage, unable to use his shoulders because of the long-sword in the sheath across his back.

The roll brought him to his feet behind a mercenary who was fighting one of William's men. William bashed the man with his buckler, letting the other soldier kill him. In a flash he secured his buckler to his belt, then reached over his shoulder and drew his long-sword, ignoring the sting from his protesting, bruised muscles.

William laid about him with two-handed efficiency. As always, the world contracted around him as he concentrated on staying alive. But through it all he still had a sense of the flow of battle and he knew things were not going well.

A squad of Bear's horsemen emerged from the woods,

bloodied and looking over their shoulders. The eight raiders at the rear of the struggle had obviously done some damage, but now the battle was about to swing Bear's way.

William cut down a mercenary before him, and then stood still for a second. He sent one image with all his strength at the charging horses: *Lion!*

He attempted to mimic the loud roar of the great lions of the northern forest and suggested the scent of the hunter on the wind.

The horses went crazy, bucking and snorting, several throwing their riders.

William turned and started hacking at another opponent. Moments later, he realized that the mercenaries were fleeing.

William spun full circle and saw his men either chasing those who were running or converging on the single knot of Bear's men who held fast and continued to fight. William felt a rush of exultation. The battle was on the verge of being won. And he now knew where his enemy stood. He ran forward, eager to engage Talia's murderer, to dispense vengeance.

As he closed on him, something caused his hair to stand on end, and he recognized that magic was in play. He recalled his experience as a boy at Stardock and instantly knew that his anticipation of victory had been premature.

A Krondorian staggered toward William, blood running down his face. "William!" the man cried as he fell to his knees. "He's immune to our weapons!" Then he collapsed.

William saw other men falling away. Bear's companions had no such immunity, and by the time William reached the conflict, Bear stood alone. Like his namesake creature brought to bay, Bear stood defiantly, surrounded by a circle of six Krondorian soldiers. "You call that an attack!" he shouted in defiance.

Chills ran down William's spine when he saw one of his men strike Bear from behind, only to see the blade of the sword glance off his back as if he wore invisible armor. Bear deftly reversed his sword, and stabbed backward, gutting the soldier. His one good eye was wide with madness. He laughed as if it were all a child's game. "Who's the next to die?" he shouted.

While Bear's sword was reversed, one Krondorian took the opportunity to lunge at him, but the blade glanced off his arm without leaving a mark. Bear didn't even bother to pull his sword from the dying man behind him; he simply kicked the man in front of him in the face, sending him sprawling. "You puny excuse for a soldier! You wouldn't last a day in my company!"

William spied the amulet around Bear's neck. He saw the red stone in the center aglow with a bloody light and knew that was where Bear's power came from. William grabbed the shoulder of one of his men. "Get to his right side and distract him!" he ordered.

William's plan was desperate, but he could see it was his only choice; somehow he had to get that amulet off Bear's neck.

William looked as if he was hesitating, and at that moment the other soldier struck at Bear. Despite being invulnerable, Bear had human reflexes and he turned toward the blow. At once, William thrust with his long-sword rather than cutting, but instead of trying to skewer the man he attempted to get the point of his sword under the heavy chain around Bear's neck. The links of the chain were large enough that William hoped he could flip the amulet like this, and then take great pleasure in killing him.

Instead, Bear reacted with unnatural speed, reaching out and grabbing the heavy blade. Shock ran up William's arms as the blade froze as if stuck in a vise. With an evil smile and a mocking laugh, Bear looked at William. "Smart one, are you?"

Ignoring the frantic attacks by William's men on his back and side, Bear moved toward William, forcing him to retreat or let go of his sword.

William released the hilt of his sword and dove for Bear's legs. He tackled the man at mid-thigh, and lifted. Bear's own momentum added to William's lift and sent the huge pirate flying over William's shoulders. "Pile on him!" William commanded.

Instantly a half-dozen soldiers obeyed, leaping atop Bear and attempting to pin him to the ground.

"Get that amulet off his neck!" William shouted.

Men clawed frantically at the chain as William ran around to try and seize the amulet. The pile of men heaved, but with unbelievable power Bear rose up, shaking the men from his back as a father might his playful children. He slapped William's hand away and shouted, "Enough!"

With evil glee, Bear reached out with his right hand and crushed the throat of one man near him, while smashing the skull of another with a backhanded blow from his left. William stepped back, his eyes wide with shock as Bear systematically killed every man within reach.

The remaining two men backed away from behind Bear, and William shouted, "Run!"

They needed no second command and turned to flee. Now Bear faced William. He took one step toward the young officer. William feigned a move to his left, but then leapt to his right; Bear countered the move, staying between William and the road.

Suddenly William knew he had no other choice. Bear had been playing with his men the entire time. They had routed his mercenaries, but he himself was invulnerable, and he had lured them close enough to kill as many as possible with his bare hands.

William turned and ran straight for the cliffs. Bear hesitated, then gave chase. William didn't look behind him, for he knew even a half-step could be the difference between escape and death. A leap off the cliffs would give him a chance, albeit a very slim one.

Reaching the edge of the cliffs William resisted the urge to slow and look down. Trusting to blind chance, he ran off the cliffs, kicking out as far out as possible, hoping he could hit the deepest part of the river below, a fall of nearly one hundred feet, for otherwise the rocks would surely kill him.

The fall seemed to last forever, with Bear's curses ringing in his ears. Then William struck the water and crashed into darkness.

SIXTEEN

Temple

J ames hesitated.

He closed his eyes for a moment, then nodded to himself. The pattern he had discovered in the rock face matched with what he remembered Hilda telling him. He took the ash-covered artifact and touched each plate in sequence, then waited.

They felt a low rumbling through the soles of their feet, then a section of the wall moved back, and slid to the left. James took out a torch and lit it.

They moved slowly into a dark entrance hall. It appeared to be carved out of the stones of the cliff, a rough tunnel somewhat resembling an abandoned mineshaft.

"Wait," James said as they went through. He watched the door, silently counting. After a little more than one minute, it slid shut. He examined the wall around the door and found the release mechanism. He tripped it and the door slid open. Then he motioned for them to continue to wait and counted again. At approximately the same interval as before, it shut. James knelt and put the artifact back into his pack. "Just in case there's another lock down the passage."

Kendaric said, "Well, it's good to know we can get through there in a hurry without it, if need be."

"Agreed," said Solon.

They started to walk slowly down the corridor, two abreast. James and Jazhara were in the lead, Solon and Kendaric close behind them. After traveling a hundred yards, Solon said, "Hold a moment." He pointed to a spot on the wall and said to James, "Hold your torch there."

James did so and Solon inspected the wall.

"This tunnel is ancient," he said. "Centuries old. It was carved out of the rock long before the Kingdom came to these shores."

"How do you know?" asked Kendaric.

"You spend your boyhood with dwarven lads, you pick up a thing or two about mining."

"But these tracks aren't old," James said as he turned his attention to the ground beneath them.

Kendaric looked down. "What tracks?"

James pointed to odd bits of sand and mud at various intervals. "There's no dust, but these bits are fresh, no doubt from boots that have been past here recently." He peered into the darkness ahead. "Keep alert."

Kendaric said, "As if you need to tell us, Squire."

They proceeded slowly, and moved deeper into the cliffs below Widow's Point.

They walked in tense silence for ten minutes until they reached a portal that opened into a large chamber that they entered with caution. The firelight from James's torch cast eerie shadows on the rough-hewn rock walls. Solon's hand flew reflexively to the hilt of his warhammer when he spied the first skeleton. Nine niches had been carved into the walls at intervals around the chamber. In each stood a skeleton wearing an ornate suit of armor; all had weapons and shields at their sides. A complex set of symbols had been carved into the stone floor, just deep enough to be seen in the flickering torchlight, without fully revealing their pattern.

As best as James could judge, the chamber was nearly thirty feet in height, a vast half-circle dominated by the far wall. As they approached the wall, its bas-relief design was revealed.

"Gods!" Kendaric whispered.

Creatures of nightmare were depicted in myriad ways, many of them involved with humans, frequently being sacrificed. The depravity of the scenes was abundantly clear.

Solon said, "Hike yer torch up, laddie!" in the thickest brogue they'd heard so far.

James lifted his torch to throw more illumination as they neared the wall.

"Abide!" instructed Solon, as he reached out toward Jazhara. "Lass, another brand! Hurry!" Jazhara unwrapped a torch and handed it to the monk, who lit it from the one James held. He handed it to Kendaric and said, "Stand ye over there!" pointing to the left.

"What?"

"Ah said, stand over there, y' stone-crowned loon."

Solon took another pair of torches from Jazhara and lit them. He gave a torch to Jazhara, and instructed her to stand over to the right. He raised a torch himself and walked forward. As he did so, the entire panorama of the carvings was revealed.

"By the Holy Saints and Heroes of Ishap," he whispered.

"What is it?" asked James.

"Ya see the center, lad?" Solon pointed to a blank area that looked like a round window, around which the most horrible of the creatures knelt in worship.

"Yes," James said, "it's empty."

"Nay, 'tis not empty, m'friend. It's occupied by somethin' ye canna see."

Solon paced back and forth along the wall, stopping occasionally to study closely one detail or another. Finally, he wedged his torch into a pile of rocks, and motioned to the others that they could lower their arms.

"What is this all about?" asked Kendaric.

Solon fixed each of his companions in turn with an unsmiling stare. "You must all remember what I say now. Engrave it upon your memories as you have nothing else in your lives." He turned and pointed to the wall. "This wall tells the history of a very cruel time." He stopped, and took a deep breath. "It is taught in the Temple that after the Chaos Wars, a period of great darkness descended upon parts of the world, as the forces of good and evil fought for a balance. Places like this have been found before, homes to demons and other ill-natured creatures, beings not of this world which must be banished whenever they are encountered.

"This wall tells a story. The details are not important. What *is* important, and what must be conveyed to my temple, is the news of this place, the very fact of its existence. No matter what else occurs, there are two things that we absolutely must do.

"First, we must return to tell my order so that they can cleanse it and seal it for all time. And, whatever else you may forget, you must remember to describe what you call the 'empty window,' and to tell the High Priest that I was certain it was the work of those who follow the Nameless."

"The Nameless?" asked Kendaric. "Who is that?"

"If fate is kind to you, lad," said Solon, "you will never know."
He glanced around. "Though I fear that fate is being anything
but kind to us now."

"You said there were two things," observed James. "What's
the other?"

"That we must not fail in fetching home the Tear of the
Gods. For not only would its loss prove crippling to us, I now
know why it is being sought and by whom."

"Why?" asked Jazhara.

Pointing to the blank space on the wall, Solon said, "To
open a portal much like that one, and should that portal ever
be opened, woe beyond imagining will fall upon us. No human,
elf, or dwarf – not even the Dark Brothers, goblins, or trolls –
nothing mortal will be able to withstand it. The mightiest of
priests and magicians will be swept away like chaff before the
wind. Even the lesser gods will tremble." He pointed to the
carvings showing inhuman creatures eating or raping humans
and added, "And such would be the fate of the survivors. We
would be as cattle, raised for their appetites."

Kendaric's face drained of color.

James said, "You faint again and I'll leave you here."

Kendaric took a deep breath and said, "I'll be all right.
Let's just get on with this and find whatever is blocking my
magic."

They moved to a large pair of closed doors to their left.
"They're locked," James said as he inspected them, and pointed
to a pattern of jewels set in the door.

"Can you open it?" asked Kendaric.

"I can try," said James. He inspected the device then said,
"It's a . . . magical lock, I think." He swore. "Those are always
the worst."

"Why?" asked Kendaric.

"Because," said James, "mechanical locks only stick poison needles in your thumb or blow up with a fireball if you make a mistake. I once had to open one that shot a nasty blade out that would cut your hand off if you didn't move it in time, but magic locks can do . . . anything."

Kendaric stepped back. "Are you sure you want to be . . . fiddling with this?"

"I'm open to other suggestions," said James impatiently. He studied the lock closely. "There are six gems. And six holes with a faint color around them. Something that looks like a ruby, and a red hole. A green gem and a green hole." He leaned in toward the doors, almost putting his nose to the lock. "There are tiny mirrors around the edge." He sat back on his heels. He touched a small white gem in the middle. Suddenly light shot out in six spokes. "Oh, damn!" he said. He began frantically to move the tiny mirrors around the edge of the circular lock.

"What is it?" asked Kendaric.

Jazhara said, "I think James has to move each gem and mirror so that the light moves through the gem, changes color, and is reflected into the right hole."

James said nothing, as he desperately tried to do just that.

"What's the problem?"

Jazhara said, "Given James's concentration on the problem, I suspect there may be a limit on how much time one can spend on it."

James was about to move the sixth mirror-gem combination when suddenly the light went out.

Nothing happened.

Then from behind them came a sound.

Solon had his warhammer raised and James his sword out by the time they turned.

Within all nine niches, the skeletal warriors were picking up their weapons and shields and stepping down to the floor.

"This is bad," Kendaric whispered.

William lay in darkness.

His last memory had been of striking the water and being swept along by the raging currents, then hitting his head against a rock.

He stood up and found himself dry. He looked at his hands and down at his body and saw no wound. He tentatively touched his face and head and felt no injury. No soreness or ache, not even a cut or bruise.

For a moment he wondered if he was dead and was somewhere inside Lims-Kragma's Hall.

"William!"

He spun and found that he was standing inside the Rainbow Parrot. Before him, Bear held Talia by the throat, shaking her as a terrier shakes a rat. The huge man tossed her aside and she slammed hard against the wall. Her attacker hurried off through the door leading to the rear of the inn.

William attempted to move toward the girl, but something held his feet in place. *I'm dreaming*, he thought.

A pillar of flame erupted around Talia and she rose up from the floor screaming in agony. Creatures of flame, demons with animal heads, appeared and surrounded Talia's flame-prison. "William!" she screamed.

Suddenly he found he could move. He was wearing armor and carrying a sword of blinding light. He struck the first demon from behind and it shrieked in pain.

All the creatures turned as one and began to move in concert against William, who stood resolute, refusing to concede a foot to them, and laid about with his sword. But for each one he cut, another took its place. Hot talons struck at his shield and armor. He felt pain and heat, yet the armor remained intact. He found that his arm was tiring and his legs were growing shaky, but he continued to stand fast and deal out injury with every thrust.

After a seemingly endless time, his lungs were fit to burst and he had to will each blow as if commanding an unwilling servant; his arms and legs were so reluctant to obey him. Yet the demons continued to press him, and an increasing number of their blows were getting through.

Still he could see no damage to his armor and no wounds were visible on his body, though he could still feel each talon and fang, feel the searing heat of their touch on his flesh. They bore him back and he felt despair engulf him, but each time he thought it impossible to continue, Talia's pleading voice would reach him: "William! Save me! William, help me!"

He raised his arm again, the pain threatening to overwhelm him, and unleashed another blow.

Slowly the tide turned. A demon fell, and no other appeared. He turned his pain-racked body to attack the next creature about its head and shoulders till it was gone.

As each creature fell, renewed hope rose up within William and he drove himself onward. Depths of strength he did not realize existed within him were plumbed, and he struck, again and again.

Then suddenly the last demon was gone. He stumbled, barely able to put one foot before the other. Somehow, he reached the tower of flame trapping Talia. She stood there calmly, smiling at him.

His parched lips parted and in a voice as dry as sand he said, "Talia?"

When he reached out to touch the flames, they vanished. The girl he loved hung suspended in the air and her smile was radiant.

Softly, William said, "We did it, Talia. It's over."

A rumble arose around them and the Rainbow Parrot's taproom shattered like a mirror, the shards falling away into nothing. They stood facing one another in a featureless black void.

William reached out to touch Talia, but before his hand could reach her cheek, a voice boomed out: "No, son of conDoin. Though you have freed Talia's soul from being consumed, your part in this has only begun."

Talia looked at William and her lips were motionless, but he could still hear her dying declaration in his mind.

"I swear by Kahooli I will have my vengeance!"

The deep voice came again: "I am Kahooli, God of Vengeance, and your dedication calls to me. Because of your dedication I will answer this woman's dying prayer. You will not be alone in what lies ahead of you."

Talia began to fade before his eyes. William reached for her, but his fingers passed through her image, as if through smoke.

Weeping, he cried, "Talia, please stay!"

Talia's eyes also shed tears as she spoke in a voice like a whispering breeze. "Say goodbye to me, please . . ."

At the last instant before she became insubstantial, William whispered, "Goodbye, my love."

Suddenly, his body was racked with agony and his lungs burned as if on fire. He rolled over, retching as water spilled from his lungs. Coughing, he felt strong hands help him to sit upright.

He blinked and cleared his vision. He was drenched in water, wearing the armor he had worn when facing Bear, not the mystical plate he had worn when facing the demons.

A face swam before him, slowly coming into focus. A hawk-beaked man with intense eyes regarded him.

After a moment, William said, "I know you!"

"Yes, my young friend," said the man, sitting back on his heels upon the riverbank, watching William. "You are that young officer I met some weeks ago, escorting some dignitary from a foreign land on a hunt, if I recall. My name is Sidi.

"I saw you floating in the river, and since it is unusual to see a lad swimming in armor, I deduced you were in some need of aid. It appears that I was correct."

Glancing around, William asked, "Where am I?"

"On the banks of the river, obviously." Pointing downstream, Sidi added, "That ways lies a town called Haldon Head and beyond it, the sea."

William looked around again. They were in a stretch of woodlands, and there was little to be seen nearby save trees. "What were you doing here?"

"I was looking for someone."

"Who?"

"A murderous butcher, one who goes by the name of Bear."

William felt the fuzziness in his head start to clear. "It's good you didn't find him, then. I came upon him with thirty Krondorian regulars and he routed us all by himself."

"The amulet," said Sidi. He nodded to himself. At last, he said, "Come, we'll talk as we walk."

"You know of the amulet?" asked William.

"As I told you when last we met, I am a trader, a trafficker in rare and valuable objects as well as more mundane goods. That amulet is a particularly ancient and valuable artifact. Unfortunately, besides offering the wearer significant power, it also has a tendency to drive him mad. It was intended to be kept in the possession of a magician of great art and intelligence, not a brute like Bear."

"How did he come by it?"

Sidi glanced sidelong at William. "How he got it is immaterial. How we're going to get it back is the question."

"We?"

"As you observed, if thirty-one young soldiers could not best Bear, how could I, a lone old man, hope to do so?" Then he smiled. "But you and I together . . ." He let the sentence trail off.

"'You will not be alone in what lies ahead of you,' he said," William muttered.

"What?"

William looked at him. "I think I was told that you would help me." William glanced down at himself, then over at his companion. "Given I'm without weapons – "

"That amulet is just as impervious to weapons as it is to magic, so any attack upon Bear must be by misdirection and stealth. But I have resources, my young friend. Just get me close to Bear and I'll help you retrieve the amulet. You take him away to justice and I'll return the bauble to its rightful owner."

"I don't know if I can promise that, sir," William said.

"Everything we recover will have to be sent to Krondor for the Prince's examination. If you have a claim on the item, and the Prince judges it not to be a threat to his domain, then you may petition for its return."

Sidi smiled. "That's a matter for later consideration. Our first objective is to get it from Bear. Once we have removed him from the picture, then we can discuss the final disposition of the amulet. Come, we must hurry. Time grows short and Bear will almost certainly reach Haldon Head before we do."

William shook his head to clear it. There was something he felt he must ask this man, but he couldn't quite put his finger on what it was. But whatever else, he was right about one thing: Bear must be stopped and to do so would require removing the amulet from him.

Jazhara lowered her staff and held up her hand. A ball of crimson light sprang from her palm and played on the closest skeleton-warrior as if from a lantern. The creature hesitated, then began to tremble.

Solon held up his warhammer high with one hand, and with the other inscribed a pattern in the air while he cast an incantation. Two of the warriors hesitated, then turned as if to put as much distance as possible between them and the monk.

There were still six figures approaching.

Solon charged, lashing out with his warhammer. The first warrior he attacked deftly blocked with his shield. His blow rang out and the cavern echoed with the sound. The battle was joined.

The skeleton Jazhara had cast a spell upon lay on the floor twitching and shivering. She turned her attention to the rest coming closer. Shifting her staff, she lashed out, but with unexpected speed the skeletal warrior blocked the blow with his shield and slashed at her with a long curved sword. She barely had time to dodge backward. Suddenly she realized that the wall was only a few feet behind her. Getting pinned there would be a trap. So she began to slip to her right, attempting to gain herself as much room in which to maneuver as possible.

Kendaric tried to be resolute, but as soon as the skeleton-warrior facing him struck out, he fell to the floor and rolled. His foot caught the warrior's ankle and the creature lost its balance, toppling over. Kendaric lashed out with his boot and it felt as if he had struck iron, but he was rewarded with a cracking sound.

He rolled to his feet as another warrior slashed down and he barely avoided being decapitated. Trying to run, he slammed into another warrior, knocking it backward. He rebounded off it and again fell to the floor. This time he fell across the back of the legs of the creature facing Solon.

The skeleton-warrior fell forward and Solon smashed down with his hammer, shattering its skull. The skeleton twitched and was still; then its bones fell apart.

Kendaric turned and scrambled forward on his knees, over the now-loose bones. Solon looked on in amusement. He said, "You're an ambulatory disaster disguised as a man, but at least this time you're causin' them more annoyance than us." He bashed another skeleton-warrior with his warhammer, sending it backward, then reached down and hauled Kendaric to his feet by the collar. "Now, go see if you can trip up another one without getting yourself killed. That's a good lad." He gave Kendaric a push and smashed at the shield of the nearest warrior.

James dueled with another spectral creature and found it no match for his swordsmanship. But the problem was inflicting damage. His rapier would slide off the bones and occasionally nick them, but there was nothing to hit. He was bound to tire eventually, and then the creature would surely injure him.

James glanced over and saw that Jazhara had successfully gotten herself some distance from the foe she faced, while another creature crept up on her from behind.

"Look out behind you!" he called to her.

She turned and ducked as a sword slashed through the air, and, with a deft blow, got her staff between the warrior's feet. The thing went to the floor literally with a bone-rattling crash.

James had an idea. "Get them on the floor!" he shouted. "Trip them!"

Jazhara reversed her staff one more time and tangled the feet of the creature that had first been stalking her, sending it clattering to the floor. James feigned high, then went low. He dove between the creature's legs, grabbing them one in each hand, then stood up, toppling the creature behind him. Instantly, he turned and leapt into the air, landing on the creature's skull with all his weight. A shock ran up his legs as if he had jumped upon hard rock, but he heard a satisfying crunch and felt the bones break beneath his boots.

Kendaric scrambled like a crab, ducking under blows and rolling from side to side. Jazhara followed James's example and crushed the skull of one warrior with her staff while the second sought to regain its feet.

James hurried to where Jazhara stood and kicked at the rear of the creature's legs, and she brought her staff down with a savage blow. James looked around the chamber. "Three down."

"Four," she said, as Solon crushed the skull of another warrior.

"Let's work together!" James shouted.

"How?" Kendaric cried as he ducked under another savage sword-blow, blindly waving his own weapon above his head as if it would somehow dissuade the creature's attack. He scrambled away from the warrior that was pressing him, right into the path of another. With a terrified squeak of alarm he jumped to his feet, and fell backward into a third, knocking it down before Solon.

Jazhara tripped another, enabling James to smash its skull, while Solon finished the one that Kendaric had tripped.

Soon it was quiet, and the only skeletal warriors left were the two still trying to escape from Solon's magic. Jazhara dispatched them with her crimson flames, and at last they had a chance to catch their breath.

"My gods!" Kendaric said. "That was too much. What more is there to expect?"

"Worse," said James, turning his attention back to the lock. "Almost certainly, there will be worse." He studied the arrangement of gems, mirrors, and holes, and said, "A moment of quiet, please."

He pressed the center of the lock and the light erupted. With deft precision, he moved the gems and mirrors swiftly into place. When the last, a topaz-like gem, threw a yellow light into a yellow hole, they heard a click followed by deep rumbling, and the doors swung wide.

The area before them was vast, and they could smell sea salt as the scent of water reached them. Moving forward, they saw two immense pools, providing narrow walkways on either side or between the two.

"We have to go there?" asked Kendaric.

"You see another route, laddie?" asked Solon.

James hesitated, then said, "Wait."

He took off his pack and unbuckled it, removing the artifact that had got them through the outside door.

"I think it might be wise to have this handy."

They set off down the center walkway and when they reached a point halfway between the doors and a distant wall, two pairs of enormous tentacles rose up from the water on either side of them. Kendaric let out a yelp of terror, but James merely held the artifact high above his head.

The tentacles stood poised, as if ready to strike. They quivered in anticipation, but they didn't attack.

Jazhara whispered, "How did you know?"

"I didn't," James replied. "I guessed."

Solon looked over his shoulder as they moved out of striking range of the tentacles, which then slipped back down into the brine. "Good thing, lad. Those would crush us like bugs."

James said nothing, leading them deeper into the darkness.

SEVENTEEN

Black Pearl

K endaric pointed.

"What is that?"

Solon whispered, "It looks like a temple, albeit more of a pit of black madness, and unless I'm mistaken these are archives."

They were entering another vast chamber, full of floor-to-ceiling shelves stacked with rolled parchments and ancient leather-bound tomes. Above them, a series of suspended walkways vanished into the gloom. Light from an occasional torch broke the darkness of the room, while sconces in the wall and torch-brackets on the shelves themselves remained empty. James observed, "If they used it, it would be better lit. Those torches are placed only to help people navigate through this vault."

They were warned of someone's approach by the sound of boots upon stone, and James led them away from the lights, behind some shelves. Peeking between scrolls piled upon the shelves, they saw a small company of goblins hurry by.

After the goblins had vanished, James said, "Well, now we know those raiders were not just coming down from the mountains."

"What are goblins doing here?" asked Kendaric.

"Establishing a base, I'll wager," said Solon. "This temple is huge and must have barracks. The goblins must be there."

James waited for a moment, and said, "What I don't understand is how all the recent troubles in Krondor fit in with this, now?"

"Maybe they don't," observed Jazhara. "From what you told me, there is a connection between this Crawler and his plans to take over the underground in Krondor, and whoever is behind this attempt to steal the Tear of the Gods, but it may be they are partial allies, nothing more."

James said, "I wonder if I'll ever plumb the depths of this mystery." He looked ahead into the gloom. "Come along," he whispered.

They moved cautiously and at one point paused for James to get his bearings. Two lights showed in opposition to one another, at right angles to the path of their march, and James tried to establish his bearings, knowing that what they sought was almost certain to be in the deepest part of the temple, far below the surface of the earth and sea.

Jazhara read the spine of a text and whispered, "Merciful gods above!"

"What?" asked Solon.

Pointing to a tome, she said, "That text is Keshian, but ancient. If I read it correctly, this is a most powerful, black volume on necromancy."

James said, "That fits with everything else we've seen so far."

Kendaric said, "I'm just a poor wrecker. What is it about necromancy that so disturbs the rest of you priests and magicians?"

It was Solon who answered. "There is a basic order to the universe, and there are limits to power, or at least there should be. Those who deal in the essences of life and who flout death violate the most fundamental tenets of that order. Or are you too thick ta' understand that?"

"I was just asking," said Kendaric, his voice approaching a whine. He touched the binding and said, "Nice cover."

Jazhara said, "It's human skin."

Kendaric pulled his hand away as if he had touched a hot iron.

"Come on," said James. They moved deeper into the temple.

Time passed and they continued to wend their way through the stone halls. Several times they paused while James scouted ahead. They heard others in the vast temple, and at times were forced to hide, but they managed to avoid contact and kept moving.

An hour after entering the temple, they reached a vast, long hall with a gigantic statue at the far end, a heroic figure seated upon a throne. When they reached the base of the statue, they stared up. It rose two stories into the air above them.

The figure was apparently human, with broad shoulders and powerful arms as it sat there in a position of repose. Sandaled feet of carved stone poked out from under the hem of a floor-length robe.

"Look," said Kendaric. "Look at the face." The entire face of the statue had been chipped away.

"Why has it been defaced like that?"

Jazhara spoke softly. "As a ward against the evil that it represents."

"Who is it?" asked Kendaric. "Which god?"

Solon put a hand gently upon Kendaric's shoulder. "You will never know, and for that give thanks."

James motioned for them to continue.

James stopped and smelled the air. He held up his hand.

"What?" whispered Kendaric.

Solon moved forward and whispered, "Can't you smell it?"

"I can smell something," said Kendaric. "What is it?"

"Goblins," said James.

He held up his hand to indicate that they should stay put, then he knelt and duckwalked toward an open door. He moved smoothly onto his stomach for the final four feet and wriggled forward to peer into the room.

Then he turned, crawling backward, and leapt to his feet in a single fluid motion. As he came toward them, he drew his sword. "That patrol we saw had most of them; there are two sleeping on the beds and two eating something out of a pot at the far end," he said softly.

"I can take care of the ones who are eating without a sound," said Jazhara.

"Good," replied James. "I'll silence the other two."

Jazhara closed her eyes and James felt the hair on his arms rising again, in response to her magic. She remained motionless for a good two minutes, then opened her eyes. "I'm ready."

Kendaric said, "What was that?"

"A slow cast. The spell is almost done. I need only to make a final incantation and it goes off. Very useful for accuracy. Not very useful if you're in a hurry."

"Ah," he said as if he understood. But it was clear that he didn't.

James motioned her forward. They reached the door and she stepped through. She spoke her phrase aloud.

One goblin heard the first words and his head came up. He started to rise, but Jazhara's spell discharged and he was paralyzed, trapped like an insect in amber. His companion sat back on his haunches, his bowl in his lap and his hand halfway to his mouth.

They both remained motionless, caught in a sheer energy field of scintillating white, a field like gauze flecked with diamond dust.

James moved purposefully to the bunks where the two sleeping goblins lay, and quickly cut their throats. He then did the same to the two frozen goblins. To his companions he said,

"We must hurry. That patrol will almost certainly be back before the end of the day."

They hurried to the far end of the barracks room and James opened a door. Beyond it, a kitchen stood empty, with a bubbling cauldron before a fire.

Kendaric went pale and had to clutch the doorjamb while Jazhara's face also drained of color. On the butcher's block rested the remains of what had once been a human torso. A head lay cast aside in the corner, along with a hand and foot.

"Mother of gods!" whispered Solon.

James was speechless. He merely motioned for them to follow him. Leaving the kitchen, they moved down a short, dark passage, and again James halted.

"Smell that?"

"Goblins?" asked Kendaric.

"Sweat and filth," answered Jazhara.

They turned into a long hallway, carved into the rock. They

could see light at the other end. They crept down the passage until they could clearly identify what lay ahead of them, then James held up his hand and moved forward alone. He reached an open doorway, and glanced around the room beyond it, then motioned the others forward. The room was square, with two passages crossing in the middle between four huge cages. A few dozen humans were packed in each cage. Most appeared to be sailors, though a few looked to be farmers or townspeople.

One of the prisoners looked up and elbowed the man next to him as James's party moved into sight. They both leapt forward and gripped the bars.

One man whispered, "Thank Dala that you've come!"

James looked around the cages. Other prisoners started to spread the word and soon the bars were packed with eager people.

James held up his hands for silence. He knelt and inspected the locks, then asked, "Who has the key?"

"We don't know his name," said the man closest to the cage door. "He's the leader of the goblins. We call him Jailer."

"Probably out leading that patrol we saw earlier," said Solon.

James took off his backpack. He rummaged around and pulled out a small pouch in which he had several picks. He selected one and tested the lock with it.

"Interesting," observed Jazhara.

James didn't take his eyes off the lock as he said, "Old habits."

There was a click and the door opened. "Wait," commanded James, "until I get the others."

After a few more minutes, all four cages were open.

"Do you know the way out?" asked Jazhara.

"Yes, ma'am," said a sailor. "We're laborers here and when they don't slaughter one of us for food, they have us cleaning up this place. It looks like they're getting it ready for the arrival of more goblins."

"Can you find weapons?"

"There's a barracks nearby, with a weapons room, but there are goblins in there," said a thin man.

"Only four," answered James, "and they're dead."

The men muttered excitedly.

James was silent for a minute, then said, "Would you do us a service?"

The thin man said, "They were going to eat us if you didn't come. They killed one of us each day. Of course we will. What would you have us do?"

"Wait here – I'll leave the doors unlocked, but keep them closed – in case someone comes by before we've finished our mission. If you hear any sounds of fighting, run to the barracks room and get weapons, then fight your way out. If you don't hear anything in, say, an hour's time, you're free to go. Is that agreeable?"

The man looked around and saw several others nod. "It is," he said.

"Good," said James. The men returned to their cages. The doors were shut and one man sat down and began a slow rhythmic count, to track the time till the hour was up.

As they left the slave pens, James said, "See you in Haldon Head. There should be a Kingdom garrison there by now. If there is and we're not back, tell them what you've seen here."

"I will." The thin man looked at James and asked, "Where do you go now?"

"To the heart of this black place," answered Solon.

"Then be wary of the leader," replied the prisoner.

"You've seen him?"

"Yes," the thin man whispered.

"What did he look like?"

"I suppose he was a man, once, but now ... he is an undead ... thing! He's all rotten and decayed, wearing tattered robes that stink to heaven, and he's guarded by creatures I can't even name. We didn't see him often; he stays in the lower levels and few of us are taken there, and only infrequently."

"May the gods be with you," said James.

The man nodded.

James led his companions off down another dark hallway.

They went down a stairway they had passed a few minutes earlier that led to a series of tunnels. Several times James had paused and decided that the best course of action was to continue along the main passageway that ran from the base of the stairs, on the assumption that the shortest course would take them to the heart of the temple, and all other passages led off to other areas. At least he hoped that would prove to be true.

Before long they came to an opening in a stone wall and they passed through it. On the other side they discovered what could only be called a gallery – a huge room, all four walls of which contained niches every few feet. Instead of containing skeletal warriors, these niches held statues. Some depicted humans, but many did not, and James didn't recognize all the races memorialized in stone.

Heroic statues – of figures garbed in warrior dress or robes – stood atop pedestals placed at regular intervals around the floor. There was a consistent look of evil to all of them.

At the far side of the hall was a pair of doors. James tested the latch and it clicked open. He pushed slightly and peeked through the crack. "This is it," he whispered.

He pushed aside the door to reveal yet another square room. Three walls were lined with human skulls and the fourth was tiled with a huge mosaic depicting the same tableaux as the bas-reliefs they had seen at the entrance to the temple. The "empty window" dominated the center of the images as it had before.

Four huge columns supported the ceiling, carved stone showing human skulls entangled by tentacles. The floor was inscribed with arcane runes.

In the middle of the floor rested a giant altar, caked with blood so ancient it was black, and inches thick. Above this sacrificial surface rested a giant clawed hand, apparently made of silver or platinum. Clutched in its fingers was a giant black pearl, twice the size of a man's head. Its surface shimmered with mystical energy. Faint colors radiated across the surface, like the dark rainbow of oil on water.

Jazhara said, "Yes, this is indeed 'it.'"

She hurried to the object. "This is the source of the mystic energy that blocks your spell, Kendaric. I am certain of it."

"Let's destroy it and be on our way," said Solon, unlimbering his warhammer.

"That would be imprudent," said a dry voice emanating from the shadows.

A figure emerged from a dark alcove. It was clothed in tattered robes, and James instantly recognized the figure from the vision. Jazhara reacted instantly, lowering her staff and unleashing a bolt of crimson energy.

The creature waved his hand and the energy deflected away

from him, so that it struck the wall, where it crackled and spread before diffusing. It left smoking char where it had hit.

"Foolish woman," he whispered, his voice an ancient wind that sang with evil. "Leave me the guildsman and you may leave with your pitiful lives. I have need of his talents. Resist and you die."

Kendaric stepped behind Solon without a thought. "Me?"

James said, "No."

The creature then pointed at them and ordered, "Kill them!"

From doors at each end of the room two giant figures appeared. Each was a skeleton-warrior similar in appearance to the others they had fought earlier, but these were taller again by half. Nearly nine feet tall from foot to helm, each of the giant creatures also possessed four arms and held a long, curved blades. Their heads were covered with wide flaring helms of crimson trimmed with gold.

"This isn't good," said Kendaric. "No, not at all."

Solon reached behind him and grabbed Kendaric by the sleeve, pulling him aside. "Try not to get in the way, that's a good lad."

With an unexpected burst of speed, the monk charged, his warhammer held high above his head and cried, "Ishap give me strength!"

The skeletal warrior closest to Solon hesitated for only an instant before its swords became a blur of motion. With surprising deftness, Solon's hammer took blow after blow as he blocked the warrior's attack. Then he knelt and delivered a crushing blow to the skeleton-warrior's left foot. An audible crack filled the room as the bones of the creature's big toe shattered.

Blades flashed as the silent creature registered no pain or reaction to the damage, and Solon barely escaped with his head. His arms and shoulders bore several cuts and he was forced to retreat and concentrate on defending himself.

James said to Jazhara, "Help him out. I'll see if I can distract the other one."

James hurried to face the creature approaching from the far door while Jazhara lowered her staff and unleashed a spell against the warrior attacking Solon. The spell that had proved effective in the first chamber simply bathed the creature in scintillating pale blue light for a moment before winking out. Solon used the creature's momentary pause as an opportunity to dart in, smash at the same foot as before, then retreat quickly.

The creature teetered slightly when it advanced.

James charged the second creature and tried to gauge the pattern of its blade strokes. If there was one, it wasn't apparent, so he was reluctant to get too close. Still, he had to keep the thing distracted if they were to have any chance of survival. Together, the creatures would overwhelm them in a matter of minutes.

James started counting silently, and as the first blow from the creature's sword descended upon his head, he recognized the pattern. Up went James's blade, deflecting the first blow, then he blocked to the right, then down to the right, then across to the left side of his body, turning slightly. The hall rang with the sound of steel on steel, and James knew that he could only block this creature's attacks for a minute or two at the most. He tried not to think about what would happen if the creature changed the pattern of its blows.

Jazhara attempted another spell and it also failed. So she

leapt forward with her staff above her head, as if trying to block the multiple sword-blows. At the last second, she let her right hand slide across to her left, leaving her holding the staff like a long club. She smashed down with all her strength on the same foot Solon had damaged, and was rewarded by the sound of cracking bone.

She barely escaped with her head, and took a long nasty cut to her left shoulder. Blood flowed as she dodged to the side and then Solon was back, attacking the same foot.

The creature slashed and Solon took the point of a blade on his breastplate. The armor held, but the force of the blow sent him sprawling. The creature advanced and it was clear the monk would not regain his feet in time to survive.

Kendaric watched in mute horror as the creature advanced on the fallen monk. Jazhara tried to flank the skeleton and was rebuffed with a sidelong thrust of a blade, then the creature bore down on Solon.

Kendaric threw himself away from the wall where he was crouching. He leapt in front of Solon, frantically slashing in all directions with his blade.

"No!" shouted the liche. "Don't kill him!"

The creature hesitated, and Solon rolled over, got to his knees, and rose up, warhammer held with both hands above his head. He smashed down with as much might as he could muster and shattered the creature's left foot.

As Kendaric and Solon backed away, the creature attempted to advance. It teetered and then fell forward, crashing into the floor at Solon's feet. Kendaric hesitated only for a second, then he reached down and grabbed the base of the creature's ornate helm. He ripped the helm away just as Solon's hammer again smashed down with a force driven by desperation.

A dry crack filled the hall, and the creature's skull shattered. The skeleton went limp and rattled against the stone floor.

Jazhara was already approaching the creature with which James was engaged. The former thief declared, "I could use some help over here." He was drenched in perspiration and his arms were heavy with fatigue, but he was successfully blocking the warrior's blows.

Solon turned to the liche. "We don't have time to try to take down the other warrior," he said to Kendaric.

Kendaric nodded, gripping his sword.

They advanced upon the dead magician, who held up his hand. A blast of white energy shot toward Solon, who barely had time to dodge aside. Kendaric ran forward and impaled the creature on his sword point.

The liche looked down contemptuously. "You can't destroy me, boy," it said as its bony hand shot out and grabbed Kendaric's arm. "And now I have you!"

"Solon!" shouted the wrecker despairingly. "He won't die!"

Jazhara was trying to distract the second skeletal warrior in order to give James a reprieve. She turned and shouted, "He must have placed his soul in a vessel!"

Solon hesitated, then shouted, "Where?"

Jazhara looked wildly around the room. "It could be anywhere. It could be in another room or even . . . the pearl!"

Solon moved with purpose toward the pearl on the altar.

"No!" shouted the liche.

Solon raised his hammer and struck down, landing a powerful blow on the pearl. The black surface swam with angry energies, tiny lines of hot white fire spreading out in a latticework pattern across its skin. He struck again, and the pearl emitted a dark fog. A third blow shattered the pearl, and it exploded with enough force to throw the monk of Ishap back across the room.

The liche looked upon the scene with wide-eyed horror. "What have you done?" it asked softly.

Kendaric felt the grip on his arm release, and the liche turned and said, "You still have not succeeded, guildsman."

The second skeleton-warrior began to tremble and his attack slowed. James staggered backward, barely able to lift his arms, and Jazhara offered him a supporting hand. The creature took two drunken steps, then went crashing to the stones.

The liche groped toward Kendaric. "I am not done with you, my friend."

Kendaric's hand reached out and he grabbed the hilt of his sword, which was still protruding from the liche's stomach. He gave the blade a twist and the liche contorted in pain.

"But *I* am done with *you!*" Kendaric declared. "Now, it's time for you to die." He yanked the blade free and the undead magician shuddered in pain and fell to his knees. Kendaric turned with unhesitating precision and cut through the dead man's neck. The skin parted like dry paper and the bones snapped like brittle wood. The liche's head rolled free and bounced across the floor.

James stood with his arm draped across Jazhara's shoulder and said, "Well, that was interesting."

Solon pulled himself to his feet, his face covered in tiny cuts from the shattering pearl. "That's not the word I'd choose, laddie, but your point is taken."

"What now?" asked Kendaric.

"We need to look around," said James. "There may be others down here who will cause us trouble."

Jazhara said, "I think as we go, we should scourge this place with fire."

"Yes," said Solon. "Evil is so entrenched here that this place must be purified. And if we wait for my temple to send others to purge it, much of the evil here may flee to another location."

They went to where the liche's body lay. Behind the alcove where he had appeared stood a door. Passing through it, they came into a large room, obviously the liche's private quarters. Large and small jars were amassed on tables, and in the far corner a cage had been fastened to the stone walls.

Inside the cage a creature rested, somewhat resembling the thing they had encountered in the sewers of Krondor. It looked at them with pain-filled eyes and beckoned with a clawed hand. They approached slowly and when they were close, the creature's mouth opened. A child's voice said, "Please . . ."

Jazhara's eyes grew bright with tears and she whispered, "Is there no end to this evil?"

"Apparently not," said Solon.

James moved behind the creature as it spoke. "Pain . . . please."

With a quick thrust of his sword, James cut the back of the child-turned-monster's neck and it slumped to the floor without a sound. His face was set in a mask of fury.

Jazhara looked at James and said nothing.

Finally, Solon said, "It was a mercy."

"What now?" asked Kendaric.

Softly, James said, "Burn it. Burn everything." He hurried to a wall where tomes and scrolls were arrayed. He grabbed the shelf and toppled it. A small brazier rested on the worktable nearest the shelf and he grabbed it. Hurling it, he sent flames and coals into the paper on the floor and the fire spread rapidly.

"Look over here!" Kendaric said.

They turned and saw that the wrecker had found another pearl. Unlike the other orb, this one appeared to be translucent, and within it they could see an image of Haldon Head.

Jazhara said, "This is a powerful scrying device."

The image shifted and they could see Widow's Point and the hut of the old woman, Hilda.

"Could this have been what was countering my spell?" asked Kendaric.

"Yes, I think so," said Jazhara. "This creates a wide field of magic in the area under observation. Not all magic is blunted, but this could have been used specifically to prevent your spell from working until they had you in their control."

The flames behind them were spreading. James asked, "What do we do with it?"

Jazhara picked up the large pearl and threw it into the fire. "That should take care of it."

"Good," said James. "We should leave now. Get torches and set fire to anything that burns as we leave."

"What if the goblins object?" asked Kendaric.

Solon, looking resolute despite his wounds, said, "Well, if the escaping prisoners haven't sorted them out, we'll just have to do it ourselves, won't we?"

James nodded. "Come on. Let's go raise a ship."

They started their return to the surface.

EIGHTEEN

Tear of the Gods

The sun was low in the west as they left the cavern.

James asked Kendaric, "Can you raise the ship?"

"Now?" He shook his head. "I can try, but I thought that after all we've been through, we'd wait until morning."

"Actually, after all we've been through, I'm not inclined to wait. Bear is out there somewhere and the faster we can find the Tear and get it back to Krondor, the happier I'll be."

Solon nodded. He was bleeding from several small wounds all over his body. They had encountered a few servants of the dead liche during their escape – a pair of goblins who had put up a struggle, and two more of the skeleton-warriors. They had also come upon the mayhem that had been visited upon other servants of the Black Pearl Temple as they worked their way back to the surface. The escaping prisoners had clearly found weapons in the barracks armory and had been unkind to any who attempted to stop them.

Jazhara nursed a rough compress she had fashioned to staunch the bleeding in her shoulder. She said, "I fear that if we encounter trouble from here on, we may be out-matched."

James motioned to the others to walk out to the end of the rock spire. "We've been outmatched every step of the way," he said. "But we've been lucky."

"Luck is the result of hard work," Solon said, "or at least my father told me so."

"I'll still make a large votive offering to Ruthia when I get back to Krondor," James observed, mentioning the name of the Goddess of Luck, the patron goddess of thieves. He added in a mutter, "Even if she is a fickle bitch at times."

Solon overheard this remark and chuckled.

They reached the end of the rocks, and Kendaric said, "If this works, the ship will rise and a fog will form from here to the hull and it will become solid. It should last long enough for us to get to the ship, offload the Tear and return."

"Should?" asked James. "How long is 'should'?"

Kendaric smiled and shrugged. "Well, I never had a chance to test it. I am still working on duration. Eventually, the spell will hold a ship on the surface until all the cargo can be offloaded. Now, well, maybe an hour."

"*Maybe* an hour?" James shook his head in disgust. "Well, we can't start any sooner."

Kendaric closed his eyes, and held out his hand to Jazhara, who had carried the spell-scroll in her backpack. She handed it to him and he began reading.

First the sea around the ship calmed, the combers and breakers seeming to flow around the ship in an ever-widening ring of calm water. Then a fog appeared on the surface and suddenly the mast of the ship began to twitch. Then it shook, and the ship began to rise. First broken spars and tattered sails could be seen, then dripping ropes that dangled from yardarms and limp banners that hung from the flagstaffs. In minutes it was floating upon the surface, bobbing as water flowed from its decks.

Seaweed clung to the railings and crabs scuttled off the deck to fall back into the sea. The fog around the base of the ship thickened and solidified and after a few moments the ship stopped moving.

Kendaric turned to Jazhara and James, amazement lighting his face. "It worked!"

Solon said, "You had doubts?"

"Well, not really, but you never know . . ."

James regarded Kendaric with barely-concealed rage. "Try not to think what I would have done to you had we discovered the artifact in the temple had nothing to do with you failing last time. If it had just been 'the spell doesn't work' . . ." He forced himself to calmness. "Let's get to the ship."

Kendaric touched the toe of his boot to the solid fog experimentally, then put his whole weight on it. "A little soft," he observed.

Solon stepped past him. "We are wasting time!"

The others followed the monk as he hurried across the mystic fog toward the ship.

They reached the side of the ship and found several dangling ropes to climb. James and Kendaric climbed up easily, but the wounded Jazhara and Solon took some time and needed help. When they all had reached the deck they looked around.

Slime covered the decks and decaying bodies trapped by falling timbers or ropes were already beginning to fill the air with a malodorous reek. The scent of rotting flesh, brackish water, and salt was enough to make Kendaric gag.

"Where do we go?" asked James.

"This way," said Solon, indicating a rear door into the sterncastle, leading down to the lower decks. They held tight to soaking rope handrails as they climbed down slippery wooden steps in the narrow companionway.

At the bottom of the steps, Jazhara lit a torch, since the interior of the ship was as dark as night. The flickering light threw the scene into stark relief, and shadows danced upon the walls as they walked. The water was slow in draining from the lower decks and the hold, so they found themselves wading through knee-deep brine.

"That way," said Solon, pointing to a rear door.

Halfway across the deck, Kendaric let out a yelp.

"What?" asked James, drawing his sword.

"Something brushed against my leg!"

James let out a long, exasperated breath. "Fish. Fish swim in the ocean."

Kendaric looked unconvinced. "There could be a monster lurking down here."

James shook his head and said nothing.

They reached the door and found it jammed shut. James examined it. "Someone broke this lock, but the flow of water must have closed it again, and now it's totally jammed into place. Better break it off its hinges."

Solon used his hammer on the hinges, knocking them loose, and the door exploded outward with a sheet of water. Dead bodies were swept along as the water in the two compartments equalized. Solon looked down at one corpse that floated at his feet. Flesh was rotting off the bones, and signs of fish having feasted on the face were obvious. The eye sockets were empty.

"Good and faithful servant of Ishap," Solon said with respect. Then he saw something and reached down. He pulled a large warhammer from the corpse's belt and declared, "The Warhammer of Luc d'Orbain! It once belonged to an Ishapian saint from Bas-Tyra. It's a relic treasured by the Temple and awarded as a mark of service to my order's leader. It's a magic talisman of great power. Not a bad weapon, either." He looked down at the corpse again. "That was Brother Michael of Salador." He shook his head regretfully. "It would be logical that he would personally lead the group protecting the Tear."

"Well, bring it along," said James, "but let's find the Tear and get off this ship before it goes down again."

"That way," said Solon. He indicated a passageway to a rear cargo hold.

When they reached the next door, Solon said, "Wait." He reached into his tunic and pulled out a tiny chain from which hung a small blue gem. The gem glowed faintly. "The Tear of the Gods is near."

"What is that?" asked James.

"A shard from the old Tear. It was given me by the High Priest to help us locate the Tear if it had been removed from the ship."

James reached for the door-latch and again Solon said, "Wait!"

"What is it now?" asked James.

"There is a ward around the Tear. If Bear or one of his men got too close to the Tear before the ship sank, it may have been triggered."

"And this ward does what?" asked James, obviously irritated at hearing this at the last possible minute.

"The soul of a . . . dragon was captured and confined. It manifests itself and will attack whoever comes close to the Tear if certain rituals are not observed."

"You were going to tell us this sooner or later, right?" asked James, his voice dripping with sarcasm.

"Until we found the Tear there was no reason, Squire. Look, the beast is mindless and will attack any of us if it's been released."

"How can a dragon fit in that cargo hold?" asked Kendaric wonderingly. "They're really big, right?"

"It's not a dragon, but the spirit of one. A ghost, if you will."

"Nothing you're saying is making me any happier, Solon," James observed. "Why don't you tell us something good?"

"I have the ritual to banish the creature and return it to the spirit realm."

"That's good," said James.

"But it'll take time."

"And that's not good," said James. "Let me guess: the dragon will attack us while you're trying to banish it."

"Yes."

"And the ship might sink while we're fighting the dragon while you're trying to banish it."

Kendaric said, "Yes."

James said, "This has not been a good day, and it just keeps getting worse." Grabbing the door-latch, he said, "So, let's get this over with."

He flung open the door to reveal a room bare of any furnishings save a single table.

"This is the captain's cabin," said James. "He must have turned it over to the temple and slept elsewhere."

"And that's the Tear," said Solon.

A single large box, carved with the image of a dragon, sat atop the table. It glowed with a mystic blue light and even James could feel the magic emanating from it.

A flickering of light around the box was the only warning they had. Suddenly a gust of wind swept through the cabin. An invisible blow struck Kendaric, knocking him off his feet into the ankle-deep water.

An image formed in the air, a floating dragon made up of faint golden mist. Solon shouted, "Keep it away from me, else I won't be able to banish it!"

James waved his sword, attempting to distract the creature, while Jazhara kept her eye on Kendaric to make sure he didn't drown. Then she raised her staff, holding it high above her head with both hands, and started a spell.

The dragon turned its attention to James. Its spectral head darted forward. James felt the air pressure build before the creature's snout, and he rolled his head back with the blow. The punch was still significant. He let out an "oof" of pain while trying to draw the creature away from Solon.

Glancing at the monk, he saw that he brandished the Hammer of Luc d'Orbain before him, his eyes closed and lips moving furiously in ritual incantations.

Jazhara finished her casting and a sheet of crimson energy erupted into the air. It flowed across the ceiling of the cabin and then fell upon the dragon, encasing it in a ruby net. The creature thrashed and attempted to attack Jazhara, but it was bound in the netting.

"How long will that hold?" James asked.

"I don't know," said Jazhara. "I've never done this before."

"How's Kendaric?"

"Unconscious, but he'll live, I think."

The wrecker sat slumped against the bulkhead, chin on chest, as if asleep.

James said, "Glad to hear it. That thing hits like a mule kicks."

They turned toward Solon as his voice rose, obviously nearing the end of his incantation. They watched in amazement as the golden dragon expanded, seeming to stretch the ruby netting to its breaking point. As the final words of Solon's prayer rang through the cabin, the dragon began to shrink till it was a mere golden pinpoint of light that winked out before their eyes.

Suddenly the netting was empty and floated down to the water where it vanished.

"It's done," Solon pronounced.

"Good," said James. "Now let's rescue that damn box and get off this ship before things get any worse!"

Solon nodded, hung the second warhammer on his belt, and gently picked up the box containing the Tear of the Gods. James and Jazhara grabbed Kendaric by the arms and lifted him. He started to rouse as they moved him. "What?" he mumbled.

"Come on," said James. "Time to go home."

Kendaric said, "Best thing I've heard in days." He took his arms off their shoulders and said, "I can walk."

They scrambled up the slippery companionway, Solon having to hand up the box with the Tear in it to James, then reclaiming it when they were on deck. James, Jazhara, and Kendaric went down ropes into the mystic fog and then Solon tossed the box down to James, and followed.

They hurried along the fog as night fell. Just as they were nearing the rocky point, James said, "Damn."

"What?" asked Kendaric.

"Armed men, on the beach."

"The escaped prisoners?" asked Jazhara.

"I don't think so," James answered. "Look!"

Coming down a path from the hills above they could see a massive figure, a dark silhouette. But from his chest a red glow emanated.

"Bear!" said James.

"This fog is starting to weaken," said Solon, and even as he spoke, James felt his feet sinking a bit.

They hurried the last dozen yards to the rocks and walked toward the beach. "Do we have any choices?" asked James.

Solon said, "None. We must fight."

From the gloom of the rocks, Bear's voice boomed: "Your choices are few and my patience grows short. You will give me the Tear, or we will slaughter you."

"Why do you seek the Tear?" asked Jazhara. "What use can it be to you?"

They stopped where the rocks met the sand, and Bear's men approached, their weapons drawn.

"Ha!" said the huge man. "Hasn't the monk told you? The Tear allows us to talk to gods, doesn't it, Ishapian? And there are other gods besides Ishap!"

Solon shouted, "You are a fool not to fear the power of Ishap!"

"I've got all I need to take care of you . . . Ishapians!" said Bear, fingering the amulet around his neck. "You can never touch me." He drew a large sword. "But *I* can touch *you*! Now, give me the Tear!"

Suddenly from the rocks above him a figure emerged, crouched and leapt. William hurled himself into Bear, knocking the giant man over.

The surprise of the ambush shocked everyone. The mercenary closest to James turned away toward the commotion, and James took advantage of the opening to pull his sword and plunge it into the man's back. The man died before he could even turn to face James.

Solon set the box containing the Tear on the sand and pulled out the Warhammer of Luc d'Orbain, silently mouthing a prayer to Ishap. Jazhara lowered her staff, pointed the end of it at a cluster of Bear's men and let loose a bolt of energy.

Kendaric drew his sword. "I'll guard the Tear!" he cried.

William grappled for a moment with the huge pirate, trying to pull the amulet from his neck. Then Bear reached back with a thundering blow, and clubbed William aside.

William landed hard on the ground, his armor transmitting the shock through his body, but still he rolled and came to his feet.

Bear leapt up quickly, and with an evil smile said, "Bravely done, boy. For that alone I'll kill you quickly."

William looked up to the ledge above where Sidi stood watching. "Help me!"

Sidi shrugged. "I said get the amulet, lad, and I'd help you. Without it, you're on your own." He looked contrite.

Frustration overwhelmed William and he shouted, "Kahooli! You said I'd not be alone!"

Bear laughed. "Kahooli? You call upon a lesser god!" He held up his amulet, and pointed to where the Tear rested in the sand. "With this amulet I'm invincible. With the Tear in my possession, I'll have the power of the gods. I will *be* a god!"

William again threw back his head. "Kahooli, give me vengeance!"

A loud keening sound commenced, causing James, Jazhara, and several of the pirates to cover their ears in pain. Even Bear was forced to step away from the source. Only William seemed unaffected by the shrill whine. Then a form appeared between Bear and William, translucent and pale, but recognizable.

"Talia!" William breathed.

The girl smiled and said, "You are not alone, William."

She moved toward William and stepped into his body. He glowed with the light of the apparition and his armor seemed to flow and shift over him.

Before everyone's astonished eyes, William was transformed. He grew in stature so that his already-broad shoulders became even more massive. The armor darkened from the silver chain of a Krondorian officer to a blood-red plate so dark it bordered on black. A helm appeared over his head, hiding all his features, and the eye-slits glowed with a crimson light. A voice that was neither William's nor Talia's, spoke: "I am Kahooli. I am the God of Vengeance."

The figure raised its hand and a sword of flames appeared. With a blindingly quick blow, the blade cut across Bear's arm.

Bear flinched and retreated, his good eye wide with astonishment. "I'm bleeding! I can feel pain!"

He pulled out his sword and struck at the figure in red, and shock ran up his arm as the incarnation of the god took the blow. Then Kahooli's avatar slashed out and Bear looked down to see a wide bleeding cut on his chest. Staggering backward, Bear cried, "No, this cannot be!"

Bear swung again, but one more time the spirit of the God of Vengeance, manifested in William's body, took the blow and turned it. Then with a straight thrust, it ran its sword up to the hilt in Bear's stomach.

Bear sank to his knees, clutching the flaming blade. "No," he said in disbelief. "You said this couldn't happen. I can't die. You promised me! You said I'd never die!" He fell over on the sand, his one eye staring at the night sky. "You said . . . I couldn't . . . die . . ."

The figure stood above him for a moment, looking down, then it shimmered and transformed itself back into the shape of William.

The young warrior staggered, as if suddenly weak. He dropped to his knees and looked around. The shade of Talia appeared once more. Softly he said to her, "We did it, Talia. It's over."

The spirit of the young girl smiled at him. "And now I may rest. Thank you, William."

William's cheeks were wet with his tears. "Talia, no! Please stay."

As she faded from sight, Talia's spirit whispered, "No, William. Life is for the living. You have a long life ahead of you and I must take my new place upon the wheel. Say good-bye to me, please."

Just before she vanished, for the briefest instant, she seemed to shine with a bright light. She reached out and her hand touched William's cheek. Then she faded from view.

Tears running down his face, William said softly, "Good-bye, Talia."

James looked around and saw that Bear's remaining men had fled. He put up his sword and saw that Solon had safely gathered up the Tear.

James and Jazhara moved to where the still-kneeling warrior rested. James said, "Well done, Will. She is avenged."

Jazhara placed her hand gently on William's shoulder. "And the Tear is safe."

William said, "So it is true what he said about the Tear?"

"And more," said Solon. "The Tear commands great power,

and you've seen to it that its power will not be used for evil." He held tightly to the case containing the Tear. "However, this was only a minor skirmish. The war is not yet won."

Jazhara said, "What of Bear's amulet?"

"It's too powerful an artifact to leave here," said Kendaric.

James used his sword to pick it up. "I wouldn't touch this for any price," he said. "It seems to bring out the vicious side of a man's nature."

He walked back to the point of the rocks overlooking the sea and reached back. Using the sword for leverage, he hurled the amulet as far out into the water as he could. In the gloom they didn't see it strike the waves.

He walked back to where his companions waited. "If the fates are kind, there's a column of soldiers up in Haldon Head and we'll have an escort back to Krondor."

Battered and bruised, they limped up the path toward Haldon Head.

Dawn arrived with rose- and golden-tinged clouds in the eastern sky as Jazhara walked through the woods to Hilda's hut. She reached the clearing and as she caught sight of the building, she felt a stab of concern.

The hut was deserted. She could tell even at that distance, for not only did no sign of a fire or light come from within, but the door hung open. And the plants and herbs hanging from the porch roof were missing.

Slowly she climbed the step to the porch and entered the hut. Inside, the single table and stool were all that remained. The chest and other personal belongings were gone.

On the table rested a single piece of parchment.

Jazhara picked it up.

Girl, it read,

*My time is done. I was placed here to keep watch over
evil until such time as someone came to rid this place
of it. You are brave and resourceful young people.
The future is yours. Serve the forces of good.*

Hilda

"She's gone," Jazhara said to the person who had quietly
mounted the porch after her.

William stepped into the hut. "Who was she?"

"A witch, they say," replied Jazhara.

"You don't believe that," said William. Raised on Stardock,
he knew as well as she the prejudices toward women who
practiced magic in the Kingdom. "Who was she really?"

"A wise woman," answered Jazhara, folding the note and
putting it in her belt. "A servant of good. She's gone now."

"Did she say where?"

"No," said the young magician. She glanced around, then
looked at William. "Why did you follow me?"

"I wanted to talk before we were surrounded by others, on the
long trip back to Krondor."

Jazhara said, "We can talk while we return."

William stepped aside as she moved through the door, then
fell into step beside her on the path back to Haldon Head. After
a few steps, Jazhara said, "Talk. I'm listening."

William let out a deep breath. "This is awkward."

"It doesn't have to be."

"I said some things – "

She stopped and touched his arm. "We both said some things. You were young . . . we both were young. But that . . . misunderstanding, that's in the past."

"Then we are all right with each other?"

Jazhara nodded. "We are all right."

William started walking again. "Good. I've lost . . . someone I cared about, and . . . I didn't want to lose another friend."

Jazhara said, "You'll never lose me, William." She was silent for a while. "I'm sorry about your loss. I know Talia was special to you."

William glanced at Jazhara. "She was. As are you."

Jazhara smiled. "And as you are to me."

"We're going to be seeing a lot of each other in the years to come. I just didn't want it to remain difficult."

"Me neither."

They continued on in silence the rest of the way, content to have begun healing the rift between them.

The return journey to Krondor went without incident. The relief column from Miller's Rest was in Haldon Head waiting for them when they reached the summit. It escorted the four of them back to Krondor.

Without ceremony they rode through the city four days later and into the marshaling yard of the palace. Grooms and lackeys took charge of mounts and James, Jazhara, Solon, Kendaric, and William were directed straight to the Prince's private reception quarters.

A horseman had been dispatched as they had approached the city, and the Prince had alerted the High Priest of the Temple of Ishap, who now waited with the Prince for the weary party.

James led the way, with Solon at his side, holding tightly

the case containing the Tear. Kendaric, William, and Jazhara entered behind them.

James bowed. "Sire, with great pleasure I report we have achieved our goals. Brother Solon holds the Tear of the Gods."

Solon looked at the High Priest, who stepped forward and opened the box the monk held. Within the box rested a large pale blue crystal, the size of a large man's forearm. It seemed to glow with an inner light and as they beheld it, a faint tone, as if distant music filled the air, could be heard.

"Few not of our order have ever seen the Tear of the Gods, Highness," said the High Priest. "All here are more than worthy of the honor."

They stood transfixed for a while, then the High Priest closed the box. "We leave at dawn to transport the Tear to our mother temple in Rillanon," said the High Priest. "Brother Solon will personally oversee the transport."

"If you don't mind," said Prince Arutha, "I'll just happen to have a full company of lancers riding along behind."

Bowing slightly, the High Priest indicated that he had no objection.

To Solon, Arutha said, "You serve your god well."

The High Priest added, "He is our good and faithful servant. He shall be elevated to replace Michael of Salador. Solon, we entrust to you the leadership of the Brothers of Ishap's Hammer, and entrust to you the safekeeping of the Hammer of Luc d'Orbain."

"I am honored, Father," said the monk.

To the others in the room, the High Priest said, "Your bravery, and the strength of your spirit, have restored to us that which is the cornerstone of our faith. The Temple of Ishap owes you all its eternal gratitude."

Arutha said, "As does the court of Krondor to you, Brother Solon." Looking at William, he added, "You've acquitted yourself admirably, Lieutenant. You're an honor to the Household Guard."

William bowed.

"Guildsman Kendaric," said Arutha.

The wrecker stepped forward and bowed. "Highness."

"You've done the Crown a great service. We are in your debt. We understand that with the death of your master, the Guild is currently in disarray. As it is a patent guild, dependent upon the Crown's favor, it is our desire that you assume the rank of Guild Master and restore your fellowship."

"Your Highness," said Kendaric. "I am honored, but the Guild is in ruin. Jorath's embezzlement left us without a copper, the other journeymen who've left . . ."

"We shall attend to those details. The Crown is not ungenerous to those who serve us. We shall restore your treasury and ensure you recover."

"Your Highness is most generous," said the new Guild Master.

Then Arutha said, "Lady Jazhara. You have proven my choice of court magician a wise one."

Jazhara inclined her head and said, "Highness."

The Prince of Krondor rarely smiled, but this time his expression was almost expansive. With pride in his eyes, he said, "James, as always you are a good and faithful servant. You have my personal thanks." He stood, and said, "You've all done well."

James spoke on behalf of the others. "Our duty and our pleasure, sire."

"I have asked that a celebration in your honor be readied for tonight," Arutha said. "Retire to your quarters and return this evening as my guests."

He departed the throne room, motioning for James to follow him.

Jazhara turned to Solon and said, "Will you join us?"

"Nay, lass," said the large monk from Dorgin. "As head of my order I must ensure the safety of the Tear until we reach Rillanon. It will not leave my sight until then. Fare you well, all of you." He motioned for two monks who had stood silently in the corner to approach. They turned and bowed respectfully to the High Priest. The two monks fell in behind the High Priest and Brother Solon and left the room with the Tear.

William asked Kendaric, "What now?"

Kendaric said, "I will go to Morraine and bring her with me tonight. As Guild Master I will earn enough to satisfy even her family. We shall be wed as soon as we can."

Jazhara said, "I am happy to hear that."

Kendaric nodded enthusiastically. "I must hurry off. I'll see you both later."

William said, "May I escort you back to your quarters, lady?"

"No need," said Jazhara. "I have to learn to find my way around this place sooner or later. If I get lost I'll just ask a page for directions."

William knew she knew the way. He smiled. "Until tonight."

As he started to leave, she said, "William?"

"Yes, Jazhara?"

She stepped forward and lightly kissed his cheek. "It is good to be here with you again."

He looked into her dark brown eyes and for a moment he was speechless. Then he returned the kiss and said, "Yes, it is good."

They parted and went their separate ways.

*　　*　　*

366

Arutha sat behind his desk. "You can give me a full report tomorrow," he said to James. "You look like you could use some rest before this evening's festivities."

"Well, four days' riding was hardly restful, but most of the bruises and cuts are healing."

"The Tear is safe, which is the main thing. What else did you discover?"

James said, "Of the Crawler, nothing. I think the man was one of several agents of a man called Sidi."

William had told James all he knew of Sidi, both at the time of the attack on the Duke of Olasko, and during this latest encounter. James recounted what William had said to him, finishing with, "He seems to be a trader of some sort, a renegade, dealing with the goblins and those north of the mountains as well as those in more legitimate commerce. At least that's what he *appears* to be."

"You suspect more?"

"Much more. He just knew too much and . . ." James paused. "I caught but a glimpse of him on the cliffs above the beach while William fought with the pirate, Bear. He makes my skin itch, Highness. I think he's much more than a mere trader."

"A magician or a priest?"

"Possibly. Certainly he was desperate to get back the amulet that Bear wore, and I suspect he gave it to Bear in the first place."

"What dark agency do we face?" asked Arutha.

James said, "That question, Highness, plagues me as well." Arutha was silent as he rose from his desk and crossed to the window overlooking the marshaling yard below. Soldiers were at drill, and he saw young William hurrying to the bachelor officers' barracks. "William did well," said the prince.

"He'll be Knight-Marshal of Krondor some day," said James, "if you ever decide to let Gardan retire."

The prince turned and faced him with what could only be called a grin, an expression James had not seen from Arutha more than a few times in the ten years and more during which he'd served him. "He told me the next time he's just going to walk out, and take ship to Crydee. Then let me send soldiers to fetch him back."

"What are you going to do?"

"Let him serve a bit longer, then recall Locklear and give him the position."

"Locklear, Knight-Marshal?"

"You yourself have told me that as long as I run the army I should use an administrator. Locklear certainly has the knack for that job."

"Indeed," agreed James. "Never had much use for accounts, myself."

"I'm going to let him sit for one more winter with Baron Moyet, then I'll fetch him back and send Gardan home."

"For real this time?"

Arutha laughed. "Yes, I'll let him return to Crydee and sit on Martin's dock fishing, if that's what he really desires."

James stood. "I have a few things I need to do before tonight, Highness. With your leave?"

Arutha waved James from the room. "Until tonight."

James said, "Highness," and showed himself out of the room.

Arutha, Prince of Krondor and second most powerful man in the Kingdom of the Isles, stood at his window in a reflective mood. A young man when he had taken command at the Siege of Crydee during the Riftwar, he was now middle-aged.

He had many years before him, if the gods were kind, but he felt a calm reassurance knowing that the fate of his kingdom rested in the competent hands of younger men and women, men and women like James, Jazhara, and William. He allowed himself the luxury of one more peaceful moment, then returned to his desk and the reports that begged for his attention.

James hurried through the palace. He needed to send word to Jonathan Means, and two of his other agents, to let them know that he was back in Krondor. Then he needed to duck into the streets for a quick visit to one of his informants who was keeping an eye out for signs of activity by the Crawler and his gang. Now that the matter of the Tear of the Gods was settled, James was determined to turn his attention to this would-be crime lord and find out once and for all who he was. Then he would rid the city of his presence.

James counted down the things he needed to do. If he hurried, he would just have time to return for a bath and change of clothing before the Prince's celebration.

He was tired, but there would be time to sleep tomorrow. At this moment he was doing what he wanted to do more than anything: serving his Prince. And he was where he wanted to be more than anywhere in the world: Krondor.

EPILOGUE

Challenge

T he solitary figure dripped water as it slogged along the dark corridor of the long tunnel. The air reeked of smoke and dead bodies.

Sidi found that the small fire he had started that morning was still burning. He fetched a torch from a wall-sconce. Lighting it, he continued his journey.

Finally, he reached the room in which the dead liche lay, its body quickly turning to dust. "Idiot!" he shouted again at the unhearing form.

He moved behind the throne and found the secret latch. He tripped it and a section of wall moved aside. He entered a room even the liche hadn't known of, one Sidi used exclusively for himself.

As he entered, a voice said, "You've lost."

"No, I haven't, old woman!" he shouted to the voice in the air. He stripped off his dripping tunic.

"You didn't find the amulet." There was mockery in her voice.

"I'll keep looking. It's only been four days."

"Even if you find it, what will you do? You have no servants or allies."

"Talking to the air is tedious. Show yourself."

A faint figure appeared, translucent and without much color, but recognizable as a woman of middle age. Stripping off his trousers, the magician reached for a blanket and wrapped it around himself. "I tire of cold and damp places . . . what are you calling yourself these days?"

"Hilda, most recently."

"Yes, Hilda. I am tired of this place. Servants I can get with gold. That I have in abundance. Allies are almost as easy, once I discover what they desire." He looked at the pale image. "You know, I sensed you've been close by for some years now, but didn't think I needed to ferret you out."

"You can't get rid of me, and we both know it."

The man sighed. "You have no worshipers, no clerics, not one person in ten million on this world who even knows your name, yet you persist in lingering. That's very bad form for a goddess."

The shade who had once been the old woman in the hut said, "It is my nature. As long as you seek to serve your master, I must oppose him."

"My master lives!" said Sidi, pointing his finger at the image. "You don't even have the good grace to admit you're dead and go away!"

The figure vanished.

Instantly Sidi felt regret. As much as he disliked the woman and all her incarnations, she had been a part of his life for several centuries. He had been the first to discover the amulet in over a thousand years. He had succumbed to its power. For years he had felt impulses he couldn't explain and heard voices no one else had. He had grown in his power, and for a long time, in his madness. Then his mind had gained clarity beyond madness. He had learned whom he served: the Nameless One.

He had used the amulet before, to trap others in his master's service, such as the liche Savan and his brother. That had been a mistake. He sighed. Serving darkness required you to use whatever came your way.

The old woman had appeared soon after he had gained his powers. She was the opponent of the Nameless One, and she had refused to give Sidi any rest. He was forced to admit she was the only person – if one could call the ghost of a dead goddess a person – he had known for longer than a few years. Most of the others had got themselves killed in one grisly fashion or another. In a strange way, he was somewhat fond of the old goddess.

He sighed. The battle had been lost, but the war would continue, and he would seek to do his master's bidding. Eventually his master would return to this world. It might take centuries, but Sidi had time. His master demanded a high price for his service, but he rewarded as well. Sidi might look to be a man of fifty, yet he had lived nearly five times that number of years.

He lay down on the bed. "I must find a better place to live, soon," he sighed.